Merran glowered. 'What d'... it for? Nothing to do with ... ...ing with warships.'

'What are you on your high horse about?' Mr Jago said. 'What difference did a bit of war ever make to Cornwall? Farming, fishing and tinning – that all goes on, same as ever.'

Merran sighed. 'I hope you're right.'

'Course I'm right,' Pa Jago said.

Lizzie looked around her, at the sunshine, the corn, the sea and the cliffs. Of course he was right. Those things were eternal.

'Anyway, won't come to anything,' Pa Jago said. 'Sabre-rattling, that's what it is. All have blown over in a fortnight, you mark my words. Now, what about another piece of rhubarb cake? And then we'd better get this grain in. There could be a storm before the week is out.'

Pa Jago was right about that, at least. Three days later the world had gone to war.

Rosemary Aitken is a specialist in English Language and has written several bestselling textbooks. Her short stories have been published in a number of women's magazines including *Bella*, *Women's Realm* and *Chat*. She has also written two prize-winning plays and writes detective novels under a different name. Born in Cornwall, Rosemary Aitken now lives in Cheltenham.

By the same author

The Girl from Penvarris
The Tinner's Daughter

CORNISH HARVEST

Rosemary Aitken

ORION

An Orion paperback
First published in Great Britain by Orion in 1998
This paperback edition published in 1999 by Orion Books Ltd,
Orion House, 5 Upper St Martin's Lane, London WC2H 9EA

A CIP catalogue record for this book
is available from the British Library.

Printed and bound in Great Britain by
Clays Ltd, St Ives plc

To my cousins Pat and Doug,
and to my uncle Reginald Symons,
for all their help

Prelude: 1st August 1914

'Lizzie? Where are you to, my handsome?' That was Father's voice shouting up from the yard below. She could see him through the open kitchen door, smart as paint in his butcher's smock and striped apron, red bands above his elbows to keep his sleeves from the meat, and his straw hat set at a natty angle. He was slight and dark, like Lizzie herself, with the same light-blue eyes and ready smile. A man of few words, Father was, but whatever he did say was said with a twinkle.

'I'm up in the house,' Lizzie called. She put down her knife and the bucket of beans she had been stringing and went to the door. 'I'm doing these here vegetables for supper, give Mam a bit of a hand.'

Father grinned up at her. He was standing out the back of the shop, at the bottom of the flight of granite steps leading up to the house above – steep enough now, on a gloriously sunny Cornish afternoon, but outright treacherous when you wanted a pail of water on a wet winter's night, even when you had your own tap right there in the yard like the Treloweths did. 'Be long, will 'ee? Only Eddy and me promised to go out to Penvarris this afternoon, to kill one of Jago's pigs for him, and I know how you dearly love a ride in the wagon.'

Lizzie's heart lifted. At sixteen, the idea of a whole afternoon in the company of her beloved father was a rare treat. Tell you anything, Father could, about smugglers and mining – all sorts – you only had to ask him. He talked to Lizzie seriously, as though she were a boy, and wasn't forever fussing about frocks and getting the chores done as mother was apt to do. Going out to Nanzeal Farm, too, where there would be fresh splits and clotted cream and home-made jam, and perhaps – since it was August – the chance to picnic with the first harvesters in the golden glow of a Cornish afternoon.

All the same, she hesitated. 'I don't know what Mam will say. Saturday afternoon and me out gallivanting. There's things to do.'

There were always things to do. Lizzie had seven sisters and a brother, with less than two years between any of them – so there was always something wanted doing: if it wasn't washing and ironing it was potatoes to be peeled, babies to be watched. And a lot of it seemed to fall on Lizzie. Daisy was the eldest but she had been 'fragile' as a child, and even now (though Daisy looked stronger than an ox, Lizzie thought) Mam had got out of the way of asking her. Daisy did give Mam a hand with 'light work' in the shop. Mam didn't serve usually, that was left to Father and Eddy, but she helped with the accounts, made the sausages and pies and saw to the orders. No wonder she was busier than a pig in a turnip field, even when Gan – her own mother – came in every day to help.

'There's things to do,' Lizzie said again. 'Mam'll want me.'

Father winked. 'You leave your mam to me.' Lizzie grinned with relief. That was good enough. Father could charm Mam into anything. 'Have her hop barefoot to Helston if he'd a mind to,' Gan always said. And Father knew it. He gave Lizzie a conspiratorial grin. 'Where's everybody else?'

Lizzie counted them off on her fingers. 'Daisy's down with Mam in the shop. Agnes, Millie and Penny have gone down the town with twopence, see can they buy a tin whistle for Eddy's birthday . . .'

Father laughed. 'Have they now?' With so many birthdays in the household nobody got presents as a rule, especially not bought ones – except perhaps now and again a new pair of boots. But Eddy was a boy, and naturally they did make a bit more fuss of him, with an iced bun from the baker and all. 'A whistle, eh?' Father said. 'And I suppose if they find one for three-ha'pence, Agnes will spend the change on pear drops?'

Lizzie grinned. Agnes was famous for her sweet tooth. 'Perhaps! Anyway, Alice and Elsie are up here with Gramps tearing up newspapers for fire-spills. Dot's asleep in the crib. And Eddy – I don't know where he's to.'

'Gone up the stock-yard to fetch the horse,' Father said. 'He'll be back directly. You get on with your stringing, my handsome, or you won't be ready before he comes. I'll go and speak to your Mam.'

He gave her another cheerful wink, and disappeared into the back shop. Lizzie went back to her beans. It was a tedious job, pounds and pounds of the things – some for supper and some to salt down in the great earthenware 'bussa' – but her fingers moved like steam-shuttles, and by the time she heard the creak of the gate below, and knew they were getting the wagon out into the street, she was

2

already taking off her dirty apron and tying on a new one ready to go.

Eddy had been quick. It was a long way to the stock-field, and then he'd have had to catch the horse. Father didn't own the field, he hired it from Trevarnon, the big house up on the edge of town, and used it to fatten up beasts he'd bought from the Penzance cattle market. It could take days to put back the condition they'd lost being driven into town – fifty miles sometimes if the drovers had them from Bodmin. So he needed the field, but didn't need to keep the cart-horse all the way up there. There was a stall in the slaughteryard, but Father rarely used it. Beasts can smell death, he said, and he always brought Kitty round to the front instead of down the back lane where the slaughterhouse was. Not that it made much difference, Lizzie thought. You could smell the slaughterhouse a mile away.

Still, that was like Father. Walk a mile to save a man grief, and do the same for any animal, butcher though he was. So whenever he wanted the wagon out, he opened the big arched gate into the main street, manhandled the cart into the entry and hitched Kitty up to it there. She was an old horse, and didn't mind it. Knew the rounds, Father said, and could walk the two weekly routes – miles round the villages down twisting lanes – without a hand on the reins, stopping of her own accord when they reached a customer's door. There were plenty of customers. Father was the best butcher in Penwith. Still, there would be no deliveries this afternoon, just a gentle amble out to Nanzeal. Father would be hitching Kitty up now, while folk walked round them on the pavement.

Mam came up, with Daisy – who disappeared in the direction of the bedrooms. 'Well,' Mam grumbled, 'your father's been talking to you already, so it's not a bit of good my saying anything. Off out like this at a moment's notice – whoever heard the like? But I thought Daisy could go with you, since you're going. Put a bit of colour in her cheeks. And she'd like to go to Jago's, besides.'

It was obvious when you thought about it. Peter, the eldest Jago boy, had been sweet on Daisy for years, and though Daisy only tossed her head and pooh-poohed any ideas of settling down, she had recently consented to 'walk out' with him, and coloured very prettily whenever he was mentioned.

'Oh, good,' Lizzie said, though she would have preferred to have Father more to herself. She was already going to share him with Eddy.

3

'Very good for some, no doubt! How I'm to manage in the shop single-handed I'll never know. Serving customers besides, I daresay – with your father out.'

Lizzie felt an unexpected twinge of sympathy. It couldn't be easy, with a house full of children and a shop to run. No one ever suggested that Mam might like a run out to Penvarris in the wagon, or a picnic in the arrish fields. Expected to stay home and 'see after things', like all the other wives: although Father was thoughtful, and would often bring home a bunch of wild flowers for her, or some ribbons from the peddler.

'You're some good to spare us, Mam,' Lizzie said softly. 'I'll stop home if you want.' She leaned forward on an impulse and planted a kiss on Mam's cheek.

Mam reddened and scrubbed at the place with her sleeve. 'Get off, you soft thing.' But she looked pleased, and her tone was gentler as she added, 'No, you two go and enjoy it, while you can. Come to you soon enough, all this – house and husband and family. You won't have a chance then. Now you get off down, and don't keep your father waiting. And . . . Lizzie . . .'

'What?'

'You've done a good job with them beans.' That was high praise, coming from Mam – she was better at finding fault as a rule, at any rate to your face. Lizzie had heard her say, many a time, 'I don't know what I'd do without our Lizzie' – but never when she thought Lizzie was listening.

So the unexpected praise was doubly sweet. As Lizzie skedaddled down the steps the afternoon seemed even sunnier than before.

Eddy was already sitting in the wagon, holding the reins, proud as a peacock at being in charge and looking every inch of his almost-fifteen years. Father was closing the gates and talking to a ragged young tousled-haired man with a barrow. It was the Cat's-meatman (Russell Richards his name was – though no one ever called him by it) come in his hand-me-down coat and patched trousers to buy a few unwanted scraps from the slaughterhouse. He and his widowed mother scratched a living selling 'blown meat' for pets. Father was good, gave him all sorts of odds and ends for a few coppers, and sometimes let him have a pennorth or two of poor tripes, which had to be washed and washed before they were fit to sell. Mam grumbled about that, but Father said it was hardly worth the trouble cleaning tripes, without you had

4

customers waiting. So that was that.

Lizzie put her foot on the iron step and swung herself up beside Eddy. It was nice being up on the wagon. You could see over the slate roofs, towards the station where the smoke from a waiting engine chuffed up and clouded the air. Penzance was at its midsummer best, even the grey granite walls and pavements seemed to sparkle in the sun. Bright awnings over the shop-fronts. Baskets of colourful goods spilling from every doorway: shoes, crabs, saucepans, cabbages and fruit. The street was alive with business: horses and carts, the postboy on his bicycle, the baker's lad balancing his long flat basket full of a dozen kinds of bread. Housemaids in caps and striped summer dresses. Mothers in swishing skirts and feathered wide-brimmed hats. Girls with hoops and boys with marbles. Even, briefly, a clattering roar as Lord Beswetherick's coachman – turned chauffeur suddenly, in a peaked cap and goggles – thundered down the street in an automobile, no doubt transporting the young ladies from Gulveylor up to Trevarnon for tennis and tea.

Lizzie fidgeted on the seat. She was impatient to leave, before Mam thought better of it, or the shoppers came back from their mission and demanded to be taken, too. She glanced up at the house, trying to glimpse Daisy, but there was no sign.

Their home was a funny old place, when you came to think of it. Granite, like the rest of the street, and older than anyone could remember. Used to be the bake-house once, before Mam and Father took over the shop. But there was little of the bakery left now: only the old oven out the back – used as a cold room, all lined with kapok to keep it cool – and the dough-bench which Mam used as a curing-block, where the hams were covered in salt. And, though it said 'J. Treloweth – Purveyor of Fine Meats' in fancy gold letters on the shop-window, if you went down the pavement-steps a bit you could still see the old sign 'White's Family Baker' picked out in flaking paint over the windows upstairs.

The windows all faced this way, because of the smell and the flies. You couldn't help flies out the back, what with the blood and straw and the cows doing their business in the lane. But, though the flypaper that dangled in sticky loops from the ceiling might be black with corpses by the day's end, the shop itself was spotless. All smart tiles – plain white out the back, and in the front shop wonderful cream panels, edged in dark green, with pictures of a pig's head and a lopsided cow all done in the tiling. Cost a fortune,

Gan said, but Mam wanted it done and what Mam said went – when it came to practical things like decorating the shop.

But here was Daisy now, threading her way through the customers – all decked out in her Sunday best. Figured white muslin and a bonnet with ribbons, and for a picnic too! She was tall with reddish hair, like her mother, and she could look a picture when she tried – just as Mam had been a bit of a beauty once.

'Going courting, are you then?' Eddy said with a grin as their sister climbed up beside them. His own red hair stuck up like a bottle-brush.

Daisy coloured. 'You mind your tongue, Eddy Treloweth, or it'll find itself in with the orders!' And then Father came to join them and they were off at last.

It was a long way to Penvarris, a lurching journey on dusty roads, but Lizzie always enjoyed it. Away from the busy bustle of the town, out past the new 'town houses' which led down to the Promenade, and then they were into the country – narrow lanes, high stone walls, and dusty verges full of wild flowers. Chickens clucked at farm gates, dogs dozed, and a sleepy pig at Crowdie's farm raised its incurious head to gaze at them as they passed.

'We'll be out with a knife after him next,' Eddy said with a wicked leer. He loved to tease the girls about the bloodthirsty aspects of butchering 'Mind you, if we aren't going to Nanzeal, I don't suppose Daisy'll be with us, decked out like a Christmas tree.'

Father and Lizzie grinned, but Daisy turned pinker than her ribbons. 'It's all very well to snigger, Eddy Treloweth. You'll do the same yourself one of these days,' she said.

'What, in a dress and bonnet? Shouldn't need to stick the pig then, the poor thing'd die laughing,' Eddy said, and made them grin wider than ever.

Though it was true, Lizzie thought. When Father was fifteen he was courting. And when Mam was Lizzie's age, she was already Mrs Treloweth with Daisy on the way. It would be nice to be married, of course it would, but sometimes Lizzie had a crazy longing to do something – anything – before she settled down to be a wife and mother for ever. But it was no good thinking like that. What was there for a girl to do, except go into service somewhere or maybe work in a shop if you were lucky? And if you were going to do that, Lizzie thought dismally, you might as well work in the family business. Anyway, there was time enough to worry about that.

They were near Penvarris now: Lizzie could hear the thud of the

6

stamps at Penvarris mine – a thud so rhythmic and constant that once, so they said, when the engine was stopped for a fault in the boiler, folks around were kept awake by the silence, and walked around bad-tempered for a week until the familiar lullaby began again.

'Here we are then,' Father said, as they trotted past the little cluster of houses at the Terrace. 'That's Nanzeal Farm up ahead. Everyone's out in the cornfield by the look of it.' You could see them in the distance, a dozen or so people in one of the bottom fields. 'They'll get it stacked nicely, this weather. Now, Daisy and Lizzie, you want to get down and walk over stiles? Eddy and me will go and see to this pig – Mr Jago will be waiting for us. Or if he isn't you can send him on.'

Daisy was off the wagon so fast that Eddy laughed. 'You go any quicker and you'll meet yourself coming back!'

Daisy grinned, but she was defiant. 'Well, I'll be glad to see the Jago boys and no mistake. And I aren't the only one, eh Lizzie?'

Lizzie flushed. 'I don't know what you're talking about.' But she did, of course. There were four Jago boys: and they were all nice. Peter, the sportsman, always out with his dogs and his gun. Paul, quiet and thoughtful, like his mother. And then there were the twins. Merran – 'pick of the bunch' Gan always said – though he'd make your hair stand on end sometimes, the things he said. A socialist Merran was, all 'for the common man' – though there was nothing common about him: he'd won prizes at school and he sang in the choir like an angel.

But where Merran was, his twin brother would be also, and that was what brought the pink to Lizzie's cheeks and made her heart beat faster. Michael Jago, good-looking like his twin, but taller and darker, and with something in his brown eyes which could turn a girl to putty. Lizzie had secretly adored Mike Jago ever since she could remember. For him, she felt, she might almost be ready to give up her dreams of 'doing something' and settle for a wedding ring.

'I don't know what you're talking about,' she said again. But she was already down from the cart and following Daisy over the grid of granite stones which was the first stile. She was glad to walk across fields instead of going up to the farmhouse. She never did care to hear a pig squeal as it was being killed.

Daisy hastened off, her long skirt snatching at the daisies, but Lizzie didn't hurry. It was pleasant to wander across the farm in the sunshine, through fields of ripening corn dappled with poppies, or to pick your way through cabbages and turnips and watch the animals huddling up on the other side of the gate. There was a golden stillness in the air, peaceful and content, as if the afternoon was sleepy with the scents of summer – grasses, sunshine, and the warm smell of the beasts. Lazy bees buzzed in the hedges, and the day was so still that you could hear the cows tearing the grasses as they grazed, and in the distance the sounds of the reapers and the far-off surging of the sea.

She was nearing the harvest field now and she could see them clearly. Paul Jago on the binder, and Old Man Hunnicutt walking in front of it lifting the corn with a pike to stand it upright for the blade. Men and boys were already 'opening up the cut', reaping the edges of the field with scythes, to make room for the horse-drawn machine. Other reapers were waiting to pick up the bound sheaves and stack them into mows. That binder might be the latest thing, Lizzie thought, but there was a lot of hand-work even then.

But Peter had seen them, and put down his scythe to come and greet Daisy, and one by one the other reapers stopped too. Merran came and offered his hand to help Lizzie over the last stile.

'Now look, we've interrupted you,' she said.

He grinned. 'Glad of a rest, if the truth were known. Badgers've been in this field and rolled it something wicked.' He gestured to the flattened stalks. 'We've been taking turns to "rull" out the corn, but it's hard work in the heat. Any road, Pa'll be here in a minute – soon as ever they've finished with that pig – and we'll have a jug of tea and some crowst.'

'I'll give a hand with the stooking,' Lizzie said, and she did.

It was a joyous afternoon. Lizzie loved every moment of it – the warm scented prickliness of the corn and the slippery weight of the sheaves. The binder moved round, in ever-diminishing circles, and Peter stood by with a gun, shooting the rabbits which emerged from the standing corn and made a bolt for cover. Lizzie carried corn till her arms ached, and then stopped for a moment to look about her at the farm.

It was perched in the curve of the hill beyond Penvarris, a little island between the road and the sea. She could see the distant cliffs, the waters glistening, and seabirds wheeling in the cloudless sky.

'Lovely,' she said to Merran Jago, as he walked past her to sharpen his scythe. 'Never realised you could see the sea so clear.'

He nodded and said gruffly. 'Look at it for ever I could. Even got a little cove of our own, with a cave and all, though you can't get down there these days 'cause the cliff's fallen away. My pa used to go fishing there when he was a boy.'

'A smuggler's cave?'

Merran laughed, 'An old adit, more likely,' he said. 'There was a mine here, one time, but the seam ran out and it was capped years ago. There's half a ventilation shaft up on Rocky Acre, still, but that's about all.'

Lizzie nodded. Rocky Acre was one of the fields on the cliff-top. All the fields had names of their own. Some went back centuries, Father said.

'Got it all here, haven't we?' Merran said. 'Farm, tin and water. The soul of Cornwall. Anyway, here's Mother with the tea.'

So they all stopped and had some. Soft yellow saffron cake, fresh from the baking-stone, rhubarb cake, splits, sandwiches and hot sweet tea. After a minute or two Michael came and sat beside her, and Lizzie was so overcome by delight and embarrassment that she could think of nothing whatever to say to him. So she sat, warm and happy, feeling the prickle of the corn stubble through the rug Merran had spread for her, smelling the meadowsweet in the hedge and listening to the bees.

Old Hunnicutt was telling about his 'frock' – the old-fashioned smock he wore for reaping – and how it was better than 'they newfangled leathers and corduroys'. His father had worn one, he said, and his father's father. 'It'll see me out. And I aren't aiming to go in a hurry.' And indeed, he did look good for another sixty years, sitting under the shade of a blackthorn tree with the cider flagon to his lips.

Presently Father and Eddy came with Pa Jago, a broad giant of a man who always had an opinion about everything, and the men soon started talking about the Irish Question and the trouble in the Balkans.

'I hear Mr Asquith's put the Navy on a war footing,' Father said.

Mr Jago shook his head. 'Nine days' wonder, that's what.'

'Good thing if it did come to a fight,' Peter Jago said, putting down his gun and sitting in the grass beside Daisy. 'Give the Germans a good drubbing. I'd sign up, first in line, if there was a war.' Peter had been in the Officer Training Corps at school.

Daisy looked at him admiringly. 'You are brave, Peter.'

Merran glowered. 'What d'you want to drag us into it for? Nothing to do with Cornwall, all this posturing with warships.'

'What are you on your high horse about?' Mr Jago said. 'What difference did a bit of war ever make to Cornwall? Farming, fishing and tinning – that all goes on, same as ever.'

Merran sighed. 'I hope you're right.'

'Course I'm right,' Pa Jago said.

Lizzie looked around her, at the sunshine, the corn, the sea and the cliffs. Of course he was right. Those things were eternal.

'Anyway, won't come to anything,' Pa Jago said. 'Sabre-rattling, that's what it is. All have blown over in a fortnight, you mark my words. Now, what about another piece of rhubarb cake? And then we'd better get this grain in. There could be a storm before the week is out.'

Pa Jago was right about that, at least. Three days later the world had gone to war.

PART ONE: 1915

Chapter One

'My dear Lizzie! You're never going to go marching in there and make an exhibition of yourself?' Daisy fetched down a string of 'Treloweth's prize Cornish sausages' and slapped them onto the butcher's block. 'They want *ladies* up at these bandaging classes, not the likes of you.'

Lizzie looked up from the chop she was trimming and gave her sister a defiant glance. 'Well, I am going, any road. "Young ladies and respectable female persons over the age of sixteen are invited to volunteer for weekly classes in First Aid" – that's what the notice says. I'm respectable, I'm female, and I'm seventeen, near as nothing.' She wrapped the chop in a length of white paper drawn from the roll and placed it in the box with the rest of the order. 'You ought to go along yourself, come to that. You're coming on eighteen. Do something. Support the war effort.'

Daisy wiped a pair of sausage hands on her butcher's apron. 'Do something? What do you call this then? You and me and Mother running the shop, as well as chasing round town all hours delivering orders! If it wasn't for Gramps coming back to do the slaughtering, poor man, Mam would have had us out there doing that, and all.'

Lizzie laughed. 'Don't be so wet. There's no "poor man" about it. Gramps was missing the slaughteryard anyway, and he's happier'n a horse in a hayfield. Anyway, without Gramps, Father wouldn't have volunteered in the first place.' Still, there was some truth in what Daisy said. Since Christmas, when Father had answered the Army's urgent call for 'cooks and butchers', the two sisters had learned a lot about butchering. These days Lizzie could take down a carcass from one of the steel hooks on the painted iron rails, put it on the chopping block, and joint it as well as Eddy could, if not better.

Daisy looked at the coil of sausages on the hanging scales. 'Oh, dang it! Two ounces short. That'll mean going down there tomorrow, special, with the extra. Won't be time to make any more before then – especially if you insist on going to these tomfool classes of yours, instead of giving a hand here. Anyone would think you were a man, with a way to make, the way you go on. As if you didn't have enough to do as it is.'

That was true, Lizzie was busier than ever now Father was away. Not just in the shop, either. It could take a morning sometimes, just to polish the boots – ten pairs of them all lined up in graduated sizes in the yard, like an invisible parade.

'What classes are these?' It was Gan, coming into the back shop, her face as wrinkled as a winter apple, and her grey hair whipped from under her black flounced bonnet by the sharp May wind. She threw back her cape and held up her hand to show four fat chickens dangling upside down, their dead eyes glassy and their heads askew. 'Look at these beauties. Something handsome, they are. Got them from Luke Jago. They might as well go straight out the front.' She was already securing each pair of scrawny claws with a piece of string, and they saw her go out through the front shop and hang them on a hook at the street-entrance amongst the ducks and the game-birds, and the furry bodies of rabbits. Make people stop and look, that would, like the mechanical pig in the window endlessly lifting his cleaver up and down and smiling fatly over his striped apron and smart bow tie.

Presently Gan came back through, her hands empty. 'What classes are these?' she said again. Gan was like that, she always seemed to have her mind on half a dozen things at once.

Lizzie was about to explain, but Daisy was too quick for her. 'It's Lizzie. Lady Beswetherick sent down for us to display a notice in our window – something about bandaging classes Miss Tamsin is arranging – and Lizzie's gone and promised she'll go. Daft I call it.'

Gan turned a pair of mild grey eyes towards her. 'Keen on these classes, are you, my handsome?'

Lizzie nodded. 'There's a meeting about it tonight.'

'Well, you shall go then, if they'll have you. I can give your mother a hand with the sausages and hams.'

Lizzie caught Gan's eye and smiled. Gan was good to her. She seemed to keep a special eye out for Lizzie. 'You'll spoil that girl!' Mother said, but Gan only ever laughed and said, 'Same as I spoiled you!' and that was the end of it. Mam didn't mean to 'put upon' anyone, it was just that she was rushed off her feet, and worried sick about Father. He wasn't in any danger, so he said in his letters. He was at Command Base miles behind the lines, but it kept Mam awake nights, all the same.

And Mam wasn't the only one. Lizzie missed her Father sorely, though it wasn't her place to say so. Proud as punch he'd been to go, and Lizzie had managed to send him off with a smile on her face, though her heart was sinking so far through her boots that it seemed likely to make a dent in the station platform. Still, she didn't want to think about that. These classes, that was the thing. Give her a chance to amount to something, and 'do her bit' for the country as well.

'I'll just take this order up to Trevarnon House,' Lizzie said, 'and then I'm done here for the day. It's past six, so I'll have time if I hurry.'

'Mind you eat your tea, then,' Gan said. 'Agnes and I have made liver and onions, special, with a bit of plum cake to follow. And see you wear something halfway decent – your Sunday dress is washed and ironed. You can't go up to Gulveylor in your working skirt.'

Lizzie glanced down at the faded serge with its much-turned hem. 'No,' she said, 'I won't. And I won't miss my tea, neither.'

'Organ meat' like liver was finding its way onto the Treloweth table more often these days, but Gan's cake was a rare treat. Sugar was getting scarce with this war on – not many humbugs for Agnes now.

'Well, 'tisn't up at Gulveylor, is it?' Daisy said sourly. '"Workers' Educational Hall" – it said on the paper, so you needn't bother to dress yourself up like a Christmas fairy.'

'Hark at you!' Lizzie was nettled. 'Who was it was saying a minute since . . .' but she caught Gan's eye and lapsed into silence. Daisy was not herself lately. Peter Jago, too, was away in the Army. It was worse for her, really, because if anything did happen it wouldn't be Daisy they told. She'd have to wait for the news to reach her, roundaboutways, from Nanzeal. 'Anyway,' Lizzie finished lamely, 'I'll be off. Shan't be more than half an hour.'

She went out with her boxes and put them on the hand-cart. It was old, and heavy. Used to belong to the Cat's-meat-man, but poor Russell Richards had gone for a soldier long ago – the army paid better than old tripes – and would never be coming back. His mother had offered them the cart and Gramps and Eddy had painted it up. It saved hitching the wagon, but it weighed a ton and wouldn't go where you pushed it, so it seemed a long weary journey up through the lanes. It was heavily loaded as well – there was to be a Charity Supper at Trevarnon tomorrow in aid of the Red Cross. The family had offered Little Manor, the second house in their grounds, as a Home for the Wounded and this 'do' was to raise funds – though the price of the food on the cart would have equipped a bed or two all on its own, Lizzie thought.

Still, Mam would be glad of the order. People weren't buying meat like they used to. The men weren't home to eat it, Gan said, but in any case food had got so expensive recently, a lot of people couldn't afford luxuries like butcher's-meat. So it was almost a pleasure to struggle down the steps to the back-courtyard at Trevarnon with her boxes, and there was the cheerful chink of half-crowns in her pocket as she set off back down the lanes with her empty cart.

There was a hubbub down by the station. She could hear it all the way down Lescudjack Hill. Music, drums, shouting and cheering. It must be a recruiting rally. She had seen them before and they were really quite stirring: the street full of bands and banners, marching soldiers in uniform, and pictures of General Kitchener pointing – *'your country needs YOU'*. Crowds of people always turned out to see – and sometimes it was comical, the urchins strutting along in time to the band, in cloth caps too big for their cheeky faces and scuffed boots too tight for their toes. And now she had missed it.

No she hadn't! The market-house clock was striking three-quarters, there was just time before she went up to the classes! She left the cart in an entrance – she would collect it on her way back – and slipped down the Arcade steps into Market Jew Street.

The rally was nearly over. The 'brass hat', whoever he was, had finished his speech, and a woman in a spangled dress was preparing to sing, while a group of young men were filing forward to give their names to an officer at a table. It was beginning to get dark, besides.

Lizzie was about to turn away, disappointed, when a hand on her arm made her jump.

'Merran!' she said in surprise, and then seeing the look on his face added, 'Whatever's to do?'

'See for yourself. That damfool brother of mine has volunteered!'

Lizzie's heart gave a lurch of dismay. 'Not Michael?'

Merran nodded. 'As if Mother didn't have enough worry, with the other two already at the Front.'

It couldn't be. Not Michael! Lizzie swallowed hard. 'You aren't going too, are you?' she managed.

He snorted. 'Me? Not likely. Who would hold the farm then, do you suppose? Besides, I know your da is away and all, Lizzie, but it's like I said before – this isn't Cornwall's war. Archdukes and assassinations – what's that to do with us?'

'But aren't you proud of him? Signing up – like a hero.' Her own heart was breaking, but it was swelling with pride.

Merran's face softened. 'Oh Lizzie! They are heroes, these boys – but not the way you mean. It isn't knights on horseback now, you know. They are going to feed the guns – that's all. The guns and other men's ambitions.'

People were turning to look and Lizzie blushed to hear him. 'Sshh!' He'd get himself tarred and feathered if folk heard him talk like that. 'He's got two brothers gone and another going, and there's a farm to think of,' she said breathlessly to a stout woman in a fur coat who was glowering at them ferociously. The woman snorted and turned away.

Merran shook his head with a rueful smile, 'You musn't apologise for me, Lizzie. But thank you anyway. Now, there's Michael looking for me, will you come and speak to him?'

Lizzie coloured, 'No.' If she tried to talk to Michael now she'd more than likely burst out crying, and that would never do. Besides, with Michael, she could never think of anything to say. 'No, I'm late already. I've signed up myself today – for some First Aid classes got up by Miss Beswetherick. It's the first meeting tonight, and we start bandaging next week. Why don't you come? They are looking for volunteer patients. You could do that, even if you don't want to be a soldier.'

Merran was smiling down at her. 'And that would redeem my character? Well, I might, at that. Good night little Lizzie. Good luck with your classes.'

Lizzie scuttled back to rescue her cart – two urchins were giving each other rides on it – and hurried home to change. But the image of Michael Jago signing his name as a volunteer refused to leave her mind. 'Going to feed the guns.'

The image still haunted her an hour later as, full of liver and onions and wearing her Sunday dress, she set off for the Educational Hall.

Tamsin Beswetherick was standing at the door of the Hall to greet 'her' volunteers as they came in. She felt delightfully important, much older than her sixteen years, as she entered the names in a sweet little tasselled notebook with a tortoiseshell cover, which she had sent down for, specially.

The list was growing. Twenty or thirty names at least. Most of

17

them ladies from the better families round about, but there were others too: Mrs Tavy, the solicitor's wife, and even two girls from the haberdashery, still in their draper's black. And people were still arriving.

'Lizzie Treloweth, ma'am.'

Tamsin knew the face slightly. The skinny girl from that odious butcher's shop. But even she had made an effort, you could see that. The dreadful blue dress – all folds and flounces and hopelessly unfashionable – was cheap and faded, but it was pressed and clean; and the odour of suet which clung to it was partially masked by a liberal dosing of cheap violent scent.

Tamsin managed her most gracious smile, 'How good of you to come. We must find you a seat, mustn't we?' And she guided the girl into a corner beside the stage – as far as possible away from everyone else.

It was, Tamsin thought, a disagreeable place for a meeting. A draughty, dusty old hall with no furniture beyond a piano and a table, and half a hundred chairs set out in rows. But Mama was right, it would never have done to meet at Gulveylor, as she had first suggested. All those people, traipsing over the carpets – and the likes of poor Lizzie Treloweth would have been terribly out of place. She met the girl's eye and gave her a warm, encouraging smile.

Lizzie gave her a shy grin in return, blushing to her eyebrows at the attention. Tamsin felt that glow of pleasurable importance again. Yes, altogether, these classes promised to be a great success.

Papa had been quite dampening about the idea, at first. She had thought of it, quite suddenly, one evening over dinner. Mama, Papa, and her older sister Helena had been droning on as usual about the war and how difficult it was to get things and how everyone had to pull their weight – and the talk had turned to this new convalescent hospital the Trevarnons were setting up.

'Damn fine gesture,' Papa said, helping himself to the early strawberries from the greenhouse. 'I shall give something, of course – I hear quite everybody is making a contribution. Lord Chyrose has offered beds – and even Silas Farrington has promised a hundred pillows – cheap.'

There was a general laugh. Farrington was well known in the town. He had money and a couple of businesses, but he wasn't invited to the better houses. Inclined to sail a shade too close to the wind, and there was a question over his parentage, so Papa said.

'Well I shall offer my services,' Helena said. 'I hear the Red Cross

18

has a register of volunteers – Voluntary Aid Nurses they are calling them.'

That was just like Helena. Always stealing the limelight with her ideas. Tamsin said crossly, 'Whatever use would you be in a hospital?' But already her mind was conjuring pictures – arranging flowers by the bedside, soothing the fevered brow. She heartily wished she had thought of it first.

'Oh, there are examinations one can sit,' Helena said. 'And classes. I daresay one could discover where they are held.' Helena took everything so seriously! Before the War she had wanted to try for a place at university – of all things – but Mama had put a stop to that. 'Nonsense, child. Whoever would marry you then?'

Tamsin half expected her mother to say something similar now, but Mama was smiling. 'That's nice dear. I hear it's quite the thing in London – since, of course, no one is "coming out" this year, and there isn't the Season to think of.'

Papa said, 'Good for you, Helena. Just the ticket.'

That did it. Helena had 'come out' before the War, and now it looked as if Tamsin would not even have that satisfaction. She searched her brain furiously, and then said – casually, as if she had been contemplating it all along – 'I was considering that I might organise some First Aid classes myself.'

'My dear girl!' Mama was gratifyingly captivated.

That was when Papa said, 'Splendid. But remember, Tamsin, this cannot be one of your "enthusiasms", to be forgotten at the first sign of difficulty.'

Tamsin made a little moue. 'I am no longer a child, Papa. Besides the Hospital will need trained volunteers. Even if we have some professional staff.' She said 'we' as though it were a settled thing, but no one made any comment. On the contrary, they made a wonderful fuss of her.

It had not been difficult, either. Tamsin spoke to her friend, Rosa Warren, who lived at Trevarnon House. There was a 'Nightingale Trained' nurse coming down to be matron of Little Manor. 'A real Gorgon' according to Rosa – and she was Mrs Trevarnon's sister, so she ought to know. 'But wonderful with her patients. I should think she would be delighted to come and organise some bandaging classes while they are getting the Hospital ready.'

And so it had proved. Mrs Rouncewell was here now, taking up an uncomfortable amount of space on the stage. She was a big woman in her green uniform and starched apron – not fat, but big, with a

19

long face and muscular arms. She reminded Tamsin irresistibly of Bessie, the old carriage horse that Papa had given to the Army.

Tamsin put away the lists and went up to speak to her. 'I think that is everyone, Mrs Rouncewell. We could begin, if you wish.' She glanced at Lizzie Treloweth and the shop-girls, and gave Mrs Rouncewell a confidential smile. 'Not perhaps all exactly what we hoped, but I am sure everyone has a contribution to make.'

Mrs Rouncewell shot her a glance. 'Yes, it is a pity but voluntary classes always seem to attract people without the slightest notion of hard work – modern flibbertigibbets who buy a starched apron and cap and suppose it turns them into nurses, all of a sudden. But don't you worry, Miss Beswetherick – that's why I wanted this initial meeting, to make it clear that we are interested in real nursing – not flitting about in a fancy uniform.'

Tamsin felt herself pale. Her own dress had been 'run up' for the occasion by the sewing woman at Gulveylor – green taffeta with a little frilled apron in the style of Florence Nightingale.

Mrs Rouncewell smiled. 'Well, we'll make a start, shall we?'

Tamsin had intended making a little speech of welcome. She had thought of one or two rather witty things to say, but Mrs Rouncewell was already on her feet.

'Now then girls' – she pronounced it 'gels' – 'I am here tonight to dispel any illusions you may have about what First Aid nursing in a war is likely to entail . . .'

She spoke for perhaps twenty minutes. It was almost, Tamsin thought, as if she was determined to ruin the enterprise before it began, by putting off all the volunteers. Dreadful things – about boiling the blood out of bandages before you used them again. How you could use a pipette to suck the pus out of wounds before applying a dressing. It was disgusting. Tamsin felt herself blanch, and several of the ladies turned quite green.

'Really,' she said to Rosa Warren afterwards, when the 'volunteers' were filing out into the fine Cornish drizzle which had begun to fall, 'what does she suppose we are? All that horrible bandaging is bad enough, but fetching water and making beds! It may be all right for the likes of Lizzie Treloweth – I daresay she is used to that sort of thing – but me? I've never made my own bed in my life.'

'Well, Mrs Rouncewell was only telling us what First Aid was likely to consist of,' Rosa said. 'You don't have to do it if you don't want.'

'Yes I do,' Tamsin said miserably, 'or Papa will laugh. And I said so in front of everybody. And now Mrs Rouncewell wants "live" victims for us to practise on instead of a manikin – I'm sure I never imagined anything so humiliating.'

Rosa grinned. 'Perhaps we shall spend a pleasant evening binding up some good-looking man at the next class! I should have thought that would please you, Tamsin – I have never known you without some young "dasher" whose heart you were breaking.'

Tamsin made a little face, but she couldn't suppress a smile. 'Oh don't be absurd, Rosa. With this War on we shall be lucky to see a single man under the age of forty! Either that, or some spotty schoolboy. No, it will be the boy scouts and balding bank-clerks we have to deal with – you mark my words. Mrs Rouncewell wants "male casualties" – I suppose so that we don't all turn pale at the sight of a gentleman's naked arm – but everyone is away at the Front, so I don't know where she supposes she will get them from.'

'Oh Tamsin, how you do exaggerate,' said Rosa. 'Not everyone has volunteered. Someone has to stay behind and run the farms and mines. There must be dozens of young men, even on the Gulveylor estate, who would gladly come if you asked them.'

'Me?' Tamsin was horrified.

'Well, you are supposed to be arranging the classes,' Rosa said reasonably. 'Hasn't your coachman got a son?'

Tamsin shook her head, 'He's gone in the Navy. But there is the stable-boy – imagine bandaging him! – and there are those good-looking Jago boys up at Nanzeal. They rent a couple of fields from us, I suppose I could ask them.'

Rosa laughed. 'Better than balding bank-clerks?'

Tamsin felt herself flush. 'Oh, it is no use looking forward to a little gentle flirtation. Mrs Rouncewell won't stand for it. You should hear her talk about "demonstrating the tourniquet". I swear she has planned it on purpose. Our cousin, Ashton, is coming to Gulveylor for a week or two now the Cambridge term is over, and I was going to ask him – I thought we might have a jolly evening – but I can see it isn't the slightest bit of good.'

'Ashton?' Rosa said. 'Is that the young man from Fowey?'

Tamsin nodded. 'His mother has a house there – though she has shut it up for the Duration, and moved to her flat in Belgravia. The Government has been urging people to do that, and let the servants join up. I daresay Aunt Alice won't mind. She always found Fowey a bit dull. She'll be back in London presiding over dinners for the Regiment. Ashton's father died a hero in the Sudan, you know, and she still knows everyone who is anyone in the Army. No, I imagine Ashton will have better things to do than attend our bandaging classes, though I suppose I must come myself, since I said I would.'

'And there are the First Aid examinations,' Rosa said. 'You will sit those, won't you?'

Tamsin stared at her. 'Whatever for? We studied it at school.' All the Easter leavers at Mrs Tucker's Academy for young ladies had spent an hour a week with 'First Aid for Girls' during their last term.

Rosa made a face, 'Sprains, scalds and foreign bodies in the eye? Well, if anyone comes to Little Manor Home for the Wounded because he got a fly in his eye and tripped over the regimental kettle I should think we would be invaluable. Otherwise, I imagine, there is a lot to learn.'

Tamsin laughed. 'Well, I'd better do as you suggest and try to find us some "victims" to practise on. Anything is better than balding bank-clerks and smelly stable-boys!'

Tomorrow, she thought to herself, she would find an excuse to go down to Nanzeal and ask them, very charmingly, in person.

'Well,' Gan said, as soon as Lizzie got home, 'how did you get on then?' She was up in the kitchen, busy at the stove, and the air was steamy with the fragrance of fresh-boiled hams.

Lizzie grinned. 'Grand. Proper nurse they've got doing it. There's going to be examinations and all.'

'Well, don't you say to your mam about that,' Gan said. 'There'll be fees to find, and no end. What did they learn you tonight?'

'Only said what we were going to do,' Lizzie said. 'Start for real next week. Proper grisly, some of it. Made me come over queer, and I've been brought up with meat. Goodness knows how some of they ladies are going to get on.' She looked around the empty kitchen. 'Where is everybody? The place is empty as Newlyn Sands in a thunderstorm.'

Gan prodded at the hams with a fork. 'Millie's down in the shop helping your mam to scrub . . .' Lizzie nodded – the 'tree-trunk' chopping block had to be scrubbed every evening with hot water and bleach. 'Agnes is putting the aprons in the copper, Eddy and Gramps have gone out for fresh sawdust for the shop-floor, and Penny is putting the little ones to bed. Oh, and Daisy's upstairs with a letter. Came last post and I haven't seen hair nor hide of her since.'

Lizzie flashed Gan a quick look. Letters could mean trouble.

Gan smiled. 'It's Peter Jago's writing on the cover, so he was all right when he wrote it!'

'I'll go and see, anyhow,' Lizzie said.

Daisy was sitting on the bed in Mother's room – to be a bit private, Lizzie guessed. Dot and Elsie were still young enough to sleep in Eddy's room, but the other girls all shared the same big bed, three each end, head-to-tail like sardines. Alice would already be tucked up in her corner, so Daisy couldn't read her letter there.

She looked up now as Lizzie came in. 'Can't get a bit of quiet, nowhere,' she said, but her eyes were dancing.

Lizzie knew what that meant. Daisy wanted to share her news. 'What does he say then?'

Her sister broke into a grin. 'Oh, Lizzie. He wants me to think about getting wed – next time he's home on leave. Get a special licence he says.'

'And will you?' Lizzie's mind was racing. She had guessed it would happen of course, but now it came to it, the prospect seemed strange. Daisy gone, the beginning of the end of the family.

'I should be a Jago then,' Daisy said, with a sideways look at her sister. 'So you and your precious Michael would be related, near enough.'

Lizzie felt her cheeks burn scarlet, but she simply said again, 'Will you?'

'We meant to save a bit first,' Daisy said thoughtfully. 'Build ourselves a bit of a house. But I daresay we could manage – there is a spare room at Nanzeal we could have. Just until Pa Jago retires and we take over the farm.'

Lizzie tried to imagine her sister presiding over the milking shed and looking after the ducks and geese. She failed. 'Will you like farming?'

'Shan't dislike it,' Daisy said. 'Fresh air, fresh food – and Peter likes it. Nanzeal will come to him since he's the eldest, so I could do a lot worse.'

Lizzie frowned. It was hard to understand Daisy sometimes. 'Could do worse!' If she had been in Daisy's shoes and Michael Jago had asked her to marry him she would have snatched his hand off. It wasn't as if Daisy had any other dreams. 'You do love him?' she said.

Daisy gave her a little push. 'Don't be so wet! You read too many of those penny romances that Mabel Larkin gives you. No, Peter

23

Jago's a nice boy, and I shall write and tell him yes, if Mam agrees.'

She needn't have worried about that. When Mam came in, she was so delighted that she carved into one of the shop hams and gave them all a slice, for a celebration supper. Lizzie caught Gan's eye, and took the opportunity to mention the First Aid examinations, but Mam was in such good spirits that she didn't even complain about the fees.

Chapter Two

The fine drizzle of the early afternoon had ceased, and a thin spring sunshine was drying the hedges by the time Merran, with his cart-load of seaweed, lumbered up the lane to Nanzeal. But there was no sunshine in his soul.

He was wet through, for one thing. His shirt clung to his back beneath the damp corduroy of his waistcoat and trousers, and his leather boots were 'clagged' with damp and sand. He hadn't noticed it on the beach – the work of forking the smelly, slippery harvest onto the cart had kept him warm enough – but now, leading the load home in the late afternoon, he could feel the chill of it.

He had Hercules, the old shire horse, between the shafts and he was making heavy work of it. Time was, he might have taken Trojan and driven the cart 'chainers' – one horse behind the other – but the Army had taken the younger animal. Taken the cob and mare too, though they left the pony. They had taken a lot of horses. Just came into the town one afternoon and simply commandeered them. Paid the owners there and then whatever the price the army vet decided, and people had to get their carts home the best way they could. They'd taken the Treloweths' cart-horse, for instance, and made them arrange to share an animal with another shop.

And now, Merran thought savagely, they were taking Michael. Well, not so much taking – Michael had volunteered to go, and that was even worse.

It was that, he admitted to himself grudgingly, and not the weather which was responsible for the bleakness of his mood. In the ordinary way there was nothing Merran liked more than a walk home up the lane with the horses – and a spot of rain never hurt anybody.

The farmhouse was hidden from his view by the steep curve of the lane, but he could already see it in his mind's eye; the chickens, ducks and grey-barred geese clucking at the gate – always ajar, unless the goats were loose. Then the great yard and its gaggle of buildings. The house itself, grey, except where the stone around doors and windows was whitewashed against the flies, and the attendant ricks of hay and fern – half-used at this time of year. No turf and furze for the kitchen now, though. Pa had installed a spanking new Cornish range.

Everyone would have coal ranges, soon, Merran thought. And electric too, for lights.

There was no electric at Nanzeal. There were paraffin lamps, half a dozen of them, and hurricane lanterns which died on you at the first hint of a hurricane. Candles too, stored in one of the out-houses. There was a 'house' for everything, a root-house for turnips, a cart-house, a cow-house, and a stable, half empty now with the horses gone – but still with the store-house over, full of cats and drying grain, and reached by a flight of stone steps outside, which the goats kept climbing. And that was without the milking-sheds and the pig-sty.

But even the beloved farm couldn't please him today. Michael was going to the War.

Even now Merran could hardly believe it. They thought and acted as one, as a rule. All his life he had known what Michael was thinking and feeling almost before Michael knew it himself. And when Merran, as a child, broke his arm climbing trees, Michael cried out and clasped his wrist – though he was fields away.

They didn't look all that much alike – Mike was much bigger than he was – but they were close. All the brothers were close. Peter and Paul, Michael and Merran – all the saints, Mother used to say. Pa said he'd never heard tell of a saint called Merran, but Mother said yes there was, because there was a well to prove it. You couldn't argue with a well.

But not even a well could make Merran feel very saintly today. 'What does he want to go and get enlisted for?' he muttered savagely, opening the outer gate to let Hercules and the cart go trundling through. 'Bad enough Peter – though he always said he'd go. Then Paul. But now Mike. Wants locking up he does. And what's Mother to do?'

What am I to do, he meant. Michael is my twin. Part of me. But he didn't say that, not even to Hercules.

His temper was not improved by the sudden appearance of a smart little donkey-cart trotting towards him from the direction of the house. He was obliged to lead Hercules into a gateway to let it pass, and he had a fleeting glimpse of a young woman, dark curls bouncing under her bonnet, all in smart lemon from the top of her fashionable parasol-umbrella to the soles of her neat buttoned boots. She waved one gloved hand at him in salute and the donkey-cart trotted by.

Merran's scowl deepened. Half the big houses around were affecting donkey-carts as a 'patriotic gesture', though most still had horses in the stables, their carriage-animals were too spoiled to be of much use for dragging guns. But she didn't need to use that whip so much. Showing off, he guessed, for his benefit. Well, he wasn't impressed.

He led Hercules through the second gate, closing it behind him – which was more than she had done. He would have to go back later and check the top gate, or the cows would find that gap in the hedge and be off down the lane after the vicar's cabbages again.

He rode the cart into the cobbled yard. Michael was there, with an inane grin on his face, leaning on his 'eval' – the six-pronged fork – and doing nothing with it. Smitten, you didn't have to be his twin to know that. 'Whatever was that then?' Merran said, getting down from his seat. 'Tamsin Beswetherick it looked like.'

'It was too, then,' Michael's grin broadened. 'Said she'd come up to remind us that Sir Gilbert wants us to plough up his tennis field for potatoes this week. As if we'd forget. Come to something, hasn't it, when folk like that have to give up their bit of tennis to grow dinner?'

It's come to something when some folk have to give up three sons to go to the Army, Merran thought savagely, but he didn't say so. Bad enough losing Mike like this without sending him away on a quarrel. 'Don't know what Beswetherick wants us for. There must be dozens of men down Gulveylor could do it for him.'

'They haven't got a plough, have they?' Mike said reasonably.

'Why didn't he ask Trevarnon's men to do it then?' Merran demanded. 'Or those Belgian refugees? We got enough to do, and we're short-handed as it is.'

'Because he asked us, and Pa'll be glad of the money,' Mike said. 'Now, are you going to stand there grumbling all night, or are you going to help me unload this cart and put this horse out to grass?' He was already moving around to unfasten the cart-chain.

'Anyway,' he added, peering round Hercules' rump to give Merran a wicked smile, 'I don't reckon that was really what she came for at all.'

'What then?' Merran was busy with a buckle.

'Came to ask if we'd come to those First Aid classes you were on about, if you ask me. Took a long time working up to it, but that was it, all right.'

'And what did you say? We were going anyway because Lizzie asked us?'

Mike grinned. 'Don't be so daft. After she'd come all the way out here to ask us special? Course I didn't. Just said we'd be pleased to go. Won't do us any harm, keeping in with the Beswethericks. And I shan't be complaining. She's some pretty girl, that Tamsin. A smile you'd sell your socks for.'

Merran glowered. 'You're going soft in the head, Mike Jago. Girl like that, you think she'd look at you twice? You've already got Lizzie Treloweth eating her heart out after you – isn't that enough?'

'Lizzie?' Mike's face softened. 'She's only a child.'

'She's older than Tamsin Beswetherick,' Merran retorted. 'Well come on then, you go and get Pa and Mr Hunnicutt and we'll get this here fertiliser shifted. Or we shall still be standing here, Christmas. Oh, and check the top gate while you're about it. I suspect Miss Fancy Beswetherick forgot to shut it behind her.'

He led the horse away.

Lizzie enjoyed the first bandaging class. She was a bit less in awe, this time, and had more chance to take in her surroundings.

It wasn't much like a hospital, the Education Hall. Just Mrs Rouncewell behind a table, with a pinboard covered in pictures of bandaged limbs, and a few chairs set out in rows. There were fewer ladies, this time, Lizzie noticed. Perhaps Mrs Rouncewell's speech last week had put some of them off.

Tamsin Beswetherick read out the 'register' and then the volunteer patients were brought in from a back room where they had been quietly freezing to death, by the looks of them. Lizzie's heart gave a little leap. Michael Jago had come! And Merran too. They looked straight at her and Merran gave a little nod. Lizzie looked away, crimson.

But Mrs Rouncewell was on her feet, piling an array of bandages onto the table, and the class had begun.

She began with something she called a 'tour-neekay', and she demonstrated it by picking on Michael, of all people. It looked wicked, tying a bandage so tight it made his poor arm go white and his fingers blue. Even then Mrs Rouncewell was not satisfied, she took out a little piece of cane from her bag and wound the bandage tighter.

'There, gels,' she said, as Michael gritted his teeth and several of the other 'volunteer victims' turned pale, 'that's how it's done. A good tight tourniquet can save a life. Now then, let's see you do the same.'

She released Michael, and Lizzie saw him make a face as the blood coursed back through his deadened arm, and he turned away, shaking his fingers.

'You can take a rest, young man,' Mrs Rouncewell said, 'and let some of the others be patients for a while.'

'I do believe she does it on purpose,' one of the draper's girls whispered in Lizzie's ear. 'Picks on the best-looking one and makes a misery of him.'

Lizzie managed a smile, but she was disappointed. If she had been asked to bandage Michael's arm she wouldn't have known where to put herself, but she had secretly been hoping to do it, all the same. Instead, Mrs Rouncewell led over a balding bespectacled man from the county offices, who rolled up his sleeve and let Lizzie set to work. She had bandaged people before – Eddy was always slicing himself with the butcher's knife – but this was different and she was not altogether pleased with her efforts. When she looked up, however, she could not restrain a grin.

Helena Beswetherick had made a fair fist of it, but most of the others were too funny to laugh at – more like decorations than bandages. But Mrs Rouncewell insisted, and everyone managed in the end.

Then they moved on to splinting. This time Michael Jago was among the 'victims', but Tamsin Beswetherick pounced on him at once, and Lizzie found herself bandaging the clerk for the second time.

It was more difficult than the tourniquet, but Lizzie persevered and managed to produce a passable imitation of Mrs Rouncewell's picture-illustration, a strangely wooden-looking gentleman with a moustache, and an impossibly neat bandage, edge over edge like a plait.

Other people were less successful: Tamsin Beswetherick, in particular. Mrs Rouncewell was quite severe with her. 'My dear gel, you could grow runner beans up the inside of that splint. Take it off and do it again.'

Tamsin did so, blushing furiously. Serve her right, Lizzie thought. If she'd spent a bit less time chattering to Michael Jago and a bit more concentrating on her bandaging, perhaps it wouldn't all come concertinaing down like an accordion. But Michael didn't seem to mind – on the contrary he was laughing and smiling as though he and Tamsin had been friends for years.

It was almost enough to put you off the evening, but as she was collecting her coat to go home, she heard Tamsin talking to her friend Rosa Warren in the porch. Lizzie didn't mean to eavesdrop but Tamsin just went on talking as though butcher's daughters were invisible. 'I declare, Rosa! I never was so embarrassed in my life. Being bossed about by that great mare of a woman, and in public too. And then bandaging up that boy from Nanzeal . . .'

'You looked as if you were enjoying it to me,' Rosa teased, and Lizzie felt her ears turn a brilliant pink.

'Oh, he was handsome enough,' Tamsin said. 'But I have quite enough to do, just organising the evening – I don't think I shall bother with the actual bandaging another time. Though I suppose Papa will say . . .'

Lizzie jammed her hat on her head and fled.

Merran came into the farmyard next morning, fuming. He tried to hide it, but it was no use. Mike knew exactly what he was thinking, as always. Well serve him right. First that ridiculous business about signing up for the Army, and then last night, mooning about over a pair of green eyes and a bunch of dark ringlets. Merran stumped into the stable to see to the horses.

Old Man Hunnicutt was already there, readying Hercules for the ploughing down at Gulveylor. He looked up and raised an eyebrow when he saw Merran. 'What's up with you then, Master Merran? Lost a shilling and found sixpence?'

Merran scowled. 'It's nothing,' he said savagely, picking up the bucket of 'tub-meat' – a mixture of bran and oats – and sprinkling some into the manger.

'Pretty serious nothing, by the looks of you.'

Merran searched around for something to say. 'It's Michael I suppose. Does he want to go and get himself shot to pieces? Leave the War to the generals, and the financiers up London, I say.'

'Here, we'll have none of that socialist talk round here. You feel like that, you go and join they "bolly-svics" in Russia.'

Merran picked up the pike and began forking fresh hay from the barrow into the feed-baskets at the end of the stalls. 'And what about the farm? There'll only be you and me and Pa left here to see to it, and somebody's got to plant the potatoes and bring in the corn.'

'I reckon we three are worth half a dozen of some folk,' Hunnicutt said. 'And there's your ma. She's a wonder.'

She was too. A tiny slip of a woman under her great sunbonnet and smock-apron, but she did the work of a dozen men. She seemed to be everywhere at once, baking bread and curing bacon in a permanent whirlpool of energy. There were no butter-girls and laundry-maids in Nanzeal like there were on some farms. Mother did it all herself – and helped with the milking besides.

'Yes. Well,' Merran said. He put down the fork and began to rake up the used straw from the stable floor.

Hunnicutt looked at him shrewdly from under his battered cap. He wore it backwards, like all farmers did, rain or shine and it was impossible to imagine Hunnicutt without it, except for chapel on Sundays. He ran his finger round the band of it now.

'Well,' he said, 'I know one thing. You've been madder'n a randy ram ever since you came home from that First Aid class last night. What is it then, put your brains in a sling, did they?'

Merran raked at the floor savagely as if he was expecting to shift the cobbles and rake clean through to Australia. 'Not *my* brains,' he said. 'Michael's more like it. Come home all cluttery-dozy over Tamsin Beswetherick, if you ever heard the like, just 'cause she flashed her eyes at him and tied up his arm in a knot. And there's poor Lizzie Treloweth fit to break her heart for him, and he never even notices.'

'Ah, well,' Hunnicutt said. 'There's the pity on it. Just as well, though, Master Merran. Never do if the two of you were sweet on her, would it?'

Merran stared at him. 'Nothing to do with me!' he said furiously. 'I'm not sweet on anybody.'

Hunnicutt shook his head. 'Wonder then,' he said slowly, 'what it is you're getting so worked up over. C'mon Hercules, work to be done.' He caught up the rein and went out, the great animal shambling beside him.

Merran watched them go. Drat Hunnicutt. Of course he wasn't sweet on Lizzie Treloweth. Too skinny by half, and in any case she had eyes only for Mike. He was still scowling as he shovelled up the old straw from the back of the stall, and began to spread fresh straw, new and sweet-smelling from the stack.

'Penny for them?' Mike had come up behind him, making him jump.

'Thinking 'bout you making an exhibition of yourself last night, if you must know,' Merran said, spreading the straw with such vigour that he raked clear through to the floor again.

Michael laughed. 'Oh, come on, it wasn't as bad as that. Pretty girl, though, isn't she? Do you think she noticed me?'

Merran rounded on him. 'And if she did, what do you suppose she saw? A farmer's son, with his arm in a sling and a bandage round his ear! Don't be so daft Mike, she wouldn't notice you if you were bleeding to death at her feet.'

Mike looked crestfallen. 'She was very pleasant to me.'

'Well, of course she was, they were her classes. Honestly Mike, you want your head read sometimes. First that enlistment business and now this.'

'You're not still carrying on about that?' Michael said hotly. 'Not Cornwall's war. Of course it's Cornwall's war. Do you think if the Kaiser's men get over here they are going to stop short at the Tamar?'

Merran said nothing. It was the first time they had quarrelled, at least over anything that mattered.

Mike seemed to read his thoughts, as usual. 'All right, Merran. Don't let's quarrel – my papers could come any day.'

Merran managed a smile. 'Anyway, perhaps you're right. Any Germans come here threatening Nanzeal, I'll see them off personally, with a pitchfork. Thing is,' he added gruffly, 'I shall miss you.'

Michael put a hand on his shoulder. 'Yes.' That was all, but Merran felt comforted. No point in falling out over a bit of a girl. Not even Lizzie Treloweth.

Chapter Three

Life was busy. Daisy was too taken up with thoughts of her wedding to be much help in the shop or anywhere else, so, what with one thing and another it was Thursday before Lizzie thought about bandaging again. Even then it was Old Hunnicutt who put it into her mind.

It was market-day and she was up to the cattle market with Gramps and Eddy. An extra pair of hands was always useful if you were driving beasts up to the stock-field. And if you were shooing a steer down to the slaughterhouse those extra hands were essential – the poor things did seem to sense it, like Father said. As soon as they got near the tethering-ring in the wall they came over all skitterish and tried to run away.

Lizzie was always happy to go because Michael Jago might well be there – and even if it was only Merran she was sure of a smile and a friendly word.

It wasn't either of them today. It was Hunnicutt, still in his cap, but with his boots polished and with his best jacket pulled on over his 'frock'. Gramps had bought some 'beef on the hoof', and there was quite a lot of laughter, and gossip about Mr Farrington, who had apparently been up Nanzeal way several times, driving about 'looking at the crops' and saying nothing to anybody.

'Though it's my belief,' Hunnicutt said, 'that he's looking for an old stable or something, cheap, to use as a factory. Talking of going into munitions, they do say, though I don't believe Farrington would know a shell-casing from a drainpipe.'

'If the Army's got any sense,' Gramps said, 'they wouldn't buy munitions from him anyhow – you'd find he'd bought damp gunpowder on the cheap, and the bally things wouldn't go off.' He laughed. 'Well, this won't buy the baby new bootstraps, I'd better go see after those beasts.'

Gramps and Eddy went off to see the auctioneer and Lizzie found herself talking to Mr Hunnicutt alone.

'I hear you were at these classes the other night, then?' he said. 'Did a good job and all, Master Merran says.'

Lizzie flushed. 'Never knew he noticed.'

Hunnicutt twinkled. 'You'd be surprised what Master Merran notices – though other times, it's true, he can't see what's plain as a pikestaff and right under his own nose. Still, it'll come to him, one of these days if it isn't too late, and then – no doubt – you'll hear about it soon enough. But you, now. Going to go nursing as a volunteer, are you then?'

Lizzie stared at him. 'I can't go working as a volunteer,' she said. 'Whatever should we do for money, if I did that?'

Hunnicutt ran a callused finger around the band of his cap. 'Well they do call they nurses "VADs" – though that isn't the right way of it, I'm sure. Voluntary Aid Detachments that stands for – beats me how one woman can be a whole detachment. But whatever you like to call 'em, – I know "Voluntary" comes into it – I heard tell the Government was going to pay them, all the same. Twenty pounds a year, someone told me. Was all in the papers.'

'Twenty pounds a year?' Lizzie did a little mental arithmetic. 'That's eight shillings a week, near enough.' A sudden crazy hope was forming in her mind. Eight shillings a week, that was handsome. If she sent six and sixpence home she'd be worth more to Mother than in the shop. That would still leave one and six to call her own. Her mind was racing – there was a beautiful skirt in Richards' shop for only nine shillings. Lizzie had never owned a new skirt in her life.

She turned back to Hunnicutt. 'You sure about that, are you? Doesn't seem right to me, volunteers getting paid.'

'Don't take my word for it, young Lizzie, go and ask that Nightingale woman. And if you want to do it, my handsome, you go, afore the Government sends you somewhere you aren't half so keen on. Haven't set up that register for nothing, have they?'

That was true. Only a few months ago every male and female of working age had been asked to register with the authorities, and you had to carry your card with you. Nothing had come of it – yet – but Gramps was certain there'd be 'Public Works' before so very long. And conscription to the Army too, before the year was out . . .

'I will then,' Lizzie said. 'She's up at Little Manor already, supervising the alterations. I aren't wanted in the shop this afternoon, so I'll see if I can't find half an hour to go up there. Don't you say anything, mind. I want to talk it over with Gan first.'

'I won't,' Hunnicutt promised, and then the others came back and it was time to drive the animals up to the stock-field and bring a couple of steers down for slaughtering. One of them was wilful, charged down the wrong road and nearly got into someone's front garden before Lizzie turned it back. It all took a long time, and it was quite late before Lizzie managed to slip away, and go and see Mrs Rouncewell up at Little Manor.

Mrs Rouncewell was making lists. There was so much to do. Mr Trevarnon had been very generous but it would never have occurred to a man, she thought, to see that the details were properly carried out.

Still, everything was progressing nicely. Forty metal bedsteads had arrived from Lord Chyrose and were waiting to be installed.

Perhaps tomorrow, when the smell of distemper had faded. The painters had done a good job in the end, though she had to tell them several times about getting right into the corners. The rooms in the house were spacious, and with hygienic linoleum in place of carpets they would make excellent wards. There was room for seven beds here in the music room alone.

She went into the linen room with her inventory. It was almost full – towels, coverlets, blankets knitted by the Girl Guides, and – since this was to be a Home for Officers – starched sheets and pillowcases. The Ladies' League was sewing bandages, and even Mr Farrington's pillows had arrived, and were in the garden airing, since they smelt of smoke.

Yes, she thought. It was all getting along very nicely. Mr Trevarnon would be able to write and offer it 'equipped and ready to run' before he left to take up his commission at Home Establishment. There were to be two trained nurses at Little Manor, besides herself. Most convalescent homes had no idea of providing so much professional care. But of course Mr Trevarnon – Major Trevarnon, she should be calling him now – had been wounded himself in the South African War, and he understood.

He had promised some real nursing equipment, too: a respiratory pump for gas cases, an angled bed with a drip tray under, for burns victims, even a small operating theatre with an ether pump and a carbolic anti-infection spray.

She went to the dispensary and began to tick the items off the list. Iodine, fenugreek, salves . . .

She was interrupted by a timid tapping at the door. She turned in surprise. It was getting late. Surely the workmen had all gone by now? But it was not a workman, it was a girl – skinny, in a thin skirt and apron, heavy boots and a worn blouse.

'Excuse me, ma'am,' the girl said. 'You won't remember me.'

But Mrs Rouncewell did remember. Of course – the child from the First Aid classes. And the only one, apart from Helena Beswetherick, who seemed to have any idea about her.

'Yes, I remember you. Lizzie is it?' Mrs Rouncewell prided herself on her memory for names. 'Well come in, come in, don't hang about in the doorway like wet washing. What do you want, gel?'

The girl took a deep breath. 'It's only . . . you'll think me very forward, ma'am . . . but I did hear . . . The thing is, someone told me as how there might be a payment from the Government for VADs. I was wondering, ma'am – is that right?'

Mrs Rouncewell felt her face soften. Poor child, she was hoping she might be able to volunteer. But it was no use. Little Manor was a private voluntary venture 'to be run without cost to the Government'. And even if the Red Cross did eventually recognise it for VAD service there was a whole month of probation before you saw a penny. The girl could hardly afford that.

It was a pity. The child was keen, and she showed signs of being genuinely useful. For a moment Mrs Rouncewell toyed with the idea of persuading Lord Chyrose or Mr Trevarnon to find a little extra – just enough to match the VAD payment. But then she shook her head. You could hardly pay one volunteer and not the others. Especially when there were also to be *professional* nurses in the place.

She looked at Lizzie's face. It was hard to disappoint her. But it had to be done. 'I'm afraid,' she said, 'that the VAD payments might not apply here.' She saw the face fall, and added quickly, 'At least, not yet. Besides you are too young. You have to be eighteen, even for General Duties. You might join Little Manor's own volunteers, but there will still be uniforms to think of, and it's quite a little expense. The outdoor coat alone is several guineas, I believe.'

'Oh well,' Lizzie said, in a very little voice, 'I might as well not come to the lessons then, after all.'

Mrs Rouncewell made a swift calculation. A shilling or two – Lord Chyrose would probably agree to that. He had been very good in a number of ways – even allowed her to bring her parrot, Albert. It was a malevolent old creature with a startling vocabulary, but it had belonged to her husband who was a sea captain when he was alive, and Mrs Rouncewell was very attached to it. Lord Chyrose had agreed at once, and offered to pay for a proper cage for it. Perhaps a shilling for a 'hospital helper' a couple of afternoons a week? Well, she would see.

'It may be,' she said, 'that I would have an opening – just a few hours a week, for someone to give me a hand. Not straight away, you understand . . .' she added quickly, before the girl could start to hope too much. 'To begin with, I imagine we shall have simple convalescents – people with bronchitis, or rheumatism, or perhaps recovering from frostbite. But with the facilities we have here, I shouldn't be surprised if, before long, they are sending us more critical cases. And if that happens, I might need a little extra assistance, if the patrons agree. No promises, mind. But I will let you know. In the meantime, I should continue to attend the classes.'

'Thank you, ma'am.' The girl was still subdued, but there was hope in her face.

'I'm getting soft, Albert,' Mrs Rouncewell said, as she put the cloth over his cage that evening. 'But that girl would be a sight more use than most. All good intentions and high sentiments, until it comes to getting your hands dirty. Quite hopeless, some of them. And now look what I've done. Honestly, Albert, these girls are more trouble than parrots.'

Albert only looked at her maliciously from one yellow eye, and pecked her finger by way of reply, but she knew that he understood.

Mike never did go to another bandaging class. The next session was cancelled suddenly because the hall was wanted for a War Relief Concert and before the following Tuesday Mike's papers had arrived. Report to training camp in three days.

Merran had known it was coming, of course, but somehow the reality shocked him. Ma felt it too – she turned whiter than limewash when the letter came, but she said nothing, just took it out on the ironing. Even Pa was quieter than usual. Mike himself seemed positively relieved.

Time he went, he said. He had been stopped twice in Penzance. 'Some dreadful old lady with a tray of white feathers. Wanted to know why I wasn't serving my country. I told her I was only waiting my papers but she obviously didn't believe me. Gave me a look that would curdle cream.'

Merran nodded, grimly. He had been offered the white 'coward's feathers' himself once or twice. Who did these women think was going to feed the Army if somebody didn't stay home and mind the farm?

He needed to mind it too. Pa had cut his hand on an old ploughshare and it swelled up poisoned, twice the size of the other. He struggled on with it for a day or two, but it was his right hand. The fingers came up like sausages, and apart from the pain, he couldn't bend them enough to buckle the harness on the horses, let alone drive the cart. In fact, when it came to it, Merran had to go to Penzance on his own to take Michael to the train.

They didn't say much at parting. The platform was crowded with people, hugging and weeping, and trying to put a lifetime's words into five minutes. Then somebody struck up 'Trelawney' and the crowd joined in. Merran bought a cup of tea from the station stall and stood sharing it with Mike, saying nothing as the seconds ticked by.

Suddenly Mike handed the cup down out of the window. 'Look,' he said. 'See who's here.'

He nodded towards the station master's office. It was Tamsin Beswetherick and her sister. They seemed to be having difficulty over a parcel.

Merran felt an unreasonable surge of anger. Drat the girl. Why did she have to be here at a time like this? She intruded, somehow, between him and his brother. Perhaps she would not notice them.

But she had seen them already and was coming over, a playful smile on her lips.

'My dear Mr Jago, do you leave us already? It is too bad of you. I am sure I don't know what our First Aid group will do without you. Or you, Mr Merran.' She turned to each of them, offering a neat gloved hand. Michael, Merran noticed, held it for far too long.

'A sad day,' she said. 'It must be so difficult to say goodbye.'

'Very hard,' Merran said pointedly. 'These last few moments together.'

She smiled. 'Then I shall not interrupt you. I just wished to say goodbye to my bandaging partner. I just came to collect my uniform – Mother had it made, specially, by a little woman in London. And now the hatbox is missing. Such a pity.' She smiled at Michael, who was gazing at her like an idiot. 'So you will never see me in it, after all.'

Michael found his voice. 'I am sure, Miss Beswetherick, that you will look perfectly charming in uniform. As in anything else.'

She coloured prettily. Damn the woman, Merran thought, she could not really be flattered by Michael's attentions. Why couldn't she leave him alone?

But Tamsin was smiling. 'It is not at all ravishing, I assure you. A coarse green frock, and a pinafore, and a great thick coat like a British "warm", I shall look like a scullery-maid. But you are most gallant to say so, Mr Jago. A perfect knight. That's what I feel like – a medieval lady, sending her knight into battle.'

Michael had turned crimson, and said in a sudden breathless rush, 'A knight was allowed to kiss his lady's hand, before the tournament.'

Tamsin looked startled, and Mike himself turned scarlet with apology. Whatever had possessed him to say a thing like that?

Then Tamsin laughed. 'You have been reading the wrong books, Mr Jago! But it is a charming idea, and you shall have your kiss.'

And to Merran's astonishment she offered her hand. Mike bent over the glove, burying his lips in it.

'Goodbye then,' Tamsin said, and disappeared towards her boxes.

'Well,' Mike said, and Merran said, 'Well,' and then there was nothing else to say. The guard came out, looking at his watch, and raised his flag. Merran felt as if the world had suddenly stood still. The whistle. Mike put out his hand and Merran gripped it a moment, and then the train drew slowly out of the station. The steam must have got into his eyes, because they seemed quite misty, suddenly, and he had to rub them hard.

It seemed a long, lonely way home, and when he got there, Pa was worse. Mother tried everything – hot fomentations, salt and sugar poultices to draw the poison – but it wasn't a bit of good. In the end Pa turned feverish and Merran had to take him to the doctor in Penzance to have the hand lanced.

Pa was supposed to stay in bed as long as he felt shivery, and bathe the hand regularly in disinfectant, but of course he wouldn't. It got a little better, but a week later he was still as weak as water, and what with Mother fussing about over Mike's things, and knitting enough socks to kit out a centipede, it was left to Merran and Hunnicutt to see to everything – from milking the cows, to lifting the second potatoes.

'Picking 'taters' took twice as long as usual, too, because most of the itinerant pickers had gone off to the war, and they had to rely on children coming in after school for a few pennies: one to lift the haulms, one to shake and others coming behind with their buckets.

Merran had his hands so full that he couldn't have gone to the bandaging classes if he'd wanted. But in any case, he didn't want to. He wanted nothing to do with Tamsin Beswetherick, and for once, he didn't want to see Lizzie either. Bad enough missing Michael, without Lizzie doing it too, and making matters worse.

He tried to help Ma with the churning, but the weather was thundery and the butter wouldn't form. It didn't surprise Merran. The way things were at present, it would have amazed him if anything turned out right.

Chapter Four

Weeks went by, and Lizzie still hadn't heard from Mrs Rouncewell. Little Manor was officially 'opened' – a little ceremony with bunting and ribbons. But there were no patients.

'It defies belief,' Mrs Rouncewell said when Lizzie went up at last to ask for news. 'Here they are, desperate for beds, and when you offer a hospital, ready to run, all they do is tell you they will "be in touch".'

Lizzie almost gave up hope, especially when she heard that one Voluntary Hospital in Sussex had to be disbanded. She kept on with the First Aid classes though, and when it came to the exam she did better than most.

It seemed real, suddenly. Every time they learned how to apply a sling, or how to make a bed – proper hospital fashion with mitred corners and sheets so tight the poor patient couldn't breathe – Lizzie thought to herself 'This could be for Michael.' It made the War seem awfully close.

The 'Little Manor Volunteers' had their uniforms already, and they looked quite the part. The ones who had joined the Red Cross and got their certificates could wear a red cross on their apron-breast, and what a difference it made! With their white kerchiefs, and a pair of starched collars and cuffs, they looked like nurses. Even Tamsin Beswetherick looked much more efficient suddenly, practising her bedmaking, even if she did imprison Mrs Tavy – who was pretending to be a casualty – by tucking her petticoats up with the sheets.

It was the uniform, Lizzie thought. Once you were in uniform people looked up to you, and let you do things – just as if you were a man. Even if you came from one of the big houses. Look at Tamsin Beswetherick now, strolling into the Educational Hall in the company of a young gentleman – without a hat (apparently it still hadn't arrived from London) and without a chaperone!

Mind you, that did cause quite a little stir among the ladies. Everyone knew who he was, of course – it was her cousin from Fowey who was staying at Gulveylor, awaiting his call-up to the Flying Corps.

Tamsin introduced him. 'My cousin, Ashton Masters. He has come to be a patient for the evening.'

'My life!' One of the draper's girls whispered in Lizzie's ear. 'Wouldn't mind holding his hand for him!'

He was handsome. Not rugged and good-looking like the Jago twins, but handsome in an elegant sort of way. Tall and slim with a mane of blond hair and a pair of hooded brown eyes which seemed to glow when he smiled.

Tamsin had obviously brought him with the idea of bandaging

him herself, but Mrs Rouncewell was too sharp for that, and it was Lizzie who found herself practising 'burn-dressings' on his face. Tamsin was furious, anyone could see, but there wasn't anything to be done about it.

Lizzie placed the piece of gauze and lint over his eye and began to bind it into place. He winked at her with his remaining lid.

'And what,' he said, 'is the name of my enchanting nurse?'

She told him.

'Treloweth. That's a good Cornish name.' His voice was light, educated, but gentle. Not a bit 'stuck-up', as she said to Daisy afterwards. 'How do you do, Lizzie Treloweth. I'm Ashton Masters. I can't shake your hand, because it's too full of bandages.'

It made her laugh. It was the first time she had ever really talked to a gentleman from the gentry – unless you counted Lord Chyrose when he came and gave the prizes at the school-treat. But it wasn't difficult at all. He asked her about all the family, and seemed so interested and easy that she said with a sudden boldness, 'You're going in that Flying Corps, so I heard. Some brave, I call that. Flying about in the clouds with nothing to keep you up but a few struts and bits of string. Saw an aeroplane, once, I did – didn't look at all safe to me.'

He laughed delightedly. 'You wouldn't like it, then?'

She shook her head. 'I would not. How it didn't fall down then and there I'll never know. Aren't you afraid?'

'Of flying? Not really. Of fighting – yes, a little. I suppose we all are, really. Knowing you could be killed, or worse – blinded, or burnt. But I think this is the hardest thing – waiting. Knowing you have your name down, and waiting for the papers that never seem to come.'

She looked at him, suddenly understanding, but he wasn't really talking to her. To himself, more like. He looked at her from his unbandaged eye, and smiled, embarrassed, as if he'd said too much. To her, she realised, because she was a stranger, because she was Lizzie Treloweth the butcher's daughter. He would never have said so much to Tamsin.

'Well, hold still,' she said, knowing that an answer would embarrass him further, 'I can't tie this if you are wriggling like a worm.'

He smiled again. 'I'm sorry, nurse!' But afterwards, when the class was over he stopped at the door, flanked by his cousins and deliberately sought Lizzie's eye, to flash her a smile.

He was a good-looking fellow, Lizzie thought, as she hurried back up Market Jew Street. Was that how Michael had felt, that the waiting was worst? Probably. But imagine Ashton Masters confiding his thoughts to her.

'What are you grinning like a gargoyle about, then?' Daisy was sitting on the stool by the kitchen fire, peeling a bucket of potatoes, but she looked up sharply when Lizzie came in. 'Heard the news, have you?'

'What news is that?'

'Peter's got his leave coming – home in four weeks he says. And maybe Michael too. Peter knows his commander. Thinks he might be able to get Michael a weekend pass – so he'll be a witness at the wedding.' Daisy's words were all coming out in a rush. 'And you can be the other, if you've a mind. Peter won't have more than a few days, but I've been down already to see about posting the banns.'

'Had a letter, then?' Lizzie demanded, slipping off her coat and bonnet and tying on her apron.

'No. Gramps was out to Penvarris with the wagon,' Daisy said. 'Luke Jago told him. Had word this morning.'

Lizzie nodded. Gramps had kept up one weekly round since Pa went away, using a borrowed horse. The carcasses were hung from ceiling hooks under a canvas frame on the wagon, with a canvas curtain at the back – like a gypsy caravan – and Gramps would stop at the crossroads and cut 'half a pound of pasty steak' for any housewife who asked him. More hit and miss than Father's rounds, but it was something.

'You'll be married then,' Lizzie said, hardly trusting herself with the words. She concentrated very hard on scrubbing the potatoes.

'Looks like it,' Daisy said.

'You don't seem very cock-a-hoop about it. Thought you would be doing somersaults with this news.'

Daisy put down her knife. 'Trouble is, Lizzie, I can't think why he hasn't written to me too. Generally he belongs to write to me, same time.'

'It's the War,' Lizzie said, comfortingly. 'Been held up somewhere or another, that's all it is. Probably written you such a big fat letter it'll take them a week to censor it. Now, what about this wedding outfit of yours? Are you going to make up that bit of pre-war silk Gan was offering you, or what?'

'I aren't sure there's enough for a dress,' Daisy said, more cheerfully. 'But I might make it up into a blouse to go with my good costume, and use the ends of the silk for some pink roses to trim me hat. What do you think?'

The conversation turned to bonnets, and the best way of cutting a pattern. But Lizzie's mind was only half on what she was saying. Ashton Masters was all very well in his way, but Michael Jago was coming home on leave.

'Well, cousin,' Tamsin said, as the carriage bounced down the lane towards Gulveylor. 'How did you like our little First Aid session? Our Mrs Rouncewell is a regular Tartar, but it is in a good cause, don't you think?'

Ashton Masters leaned back against the dusty leather cushions and looked at the two sisters. Worth looking at too. Tamsin with her dark hair and sparkling green eyes would have sent any man's pulses racing. Deucedly pretty – so pretty in fact that Helena, with her fair hair and gentler ways, seemed quite dowdy beside her. Though Helena was a looker, too, by Jove.

But he was wary of Helena. Mater had made no secret of her intentions in sending him here. 'Nice girl, your cousin. Educated, intelligent – attractive too. And I shouldn't be surprised if Gilbert doesn't leave Gulveylor to his girls, and not to a Beswetherick. He never did get on with his brother. Now, it's no good looking like that, Ashton. You'll never want for money, it's true, but I don't have land to leave you. Your father's will provided only for my lifetime. If he'd known you were on the way, he would have done differently, no doubt, but that is the fact of the matter. So you will go to Gulveylor and make yourself agreeable to the girl. You are not obliged to marry her of course, but the prospect might not be as unpleasant as you suppose.'

Ashton sighed. It was no good arguing with Mater. But certainly, he wasn't going to marry Helena just to oblige anybody.

Fortunately, he was in no danger. Helena was all fired up with this ambition to go as a VAD – abroad, she was talking about now – and train as a doctor after the War. She was not remotely interested in Ashton Masters. Rather piquing, in fact. He favoured Helena with his most winning smile.

'Oh, I thought the class was a great success,' he said warmly. 'Tamsin has done a splendid job of organising it.'

'I am sure I did not intend you to fall into the hands of the butcher's daughter,' Tamsin put in. 'I hope it did not make you entirely regret your evening.'

She was blushing. Dammit, she was confoundedly attractive when she blushed. Strange, the last time he had seen Tamsin she was an awkward child in pigtails.

42

Helena smiled. 'Poor Ashton. You have put him under the necessity of saying something charming. Though I daresay he is equal to the task.'

That was like Helena. She had this uncomfortable way of seeing right through a fellow, as though he were made of window-glass.

He said, managing a laugh, 'I was only about to remark that, if I am shot down one day, perhaps I may be grateful for the butcher's daughter and her bandages. She was engaging enough.' That was true. Perhaps he should not have said so, however. He saw Tamsin's face fall, and added quickly, 'Although, if I were wounded, I can think of no kinder fate than to open my eyes and find one of you two charming ladies at my bedside.'

Tamsin rallied, and clapped her neat little gloved hands to her cheeks. 'Oh, pooh! Ashton! Let us not even talk of such horrid things. I refuse to think about you going away to that dreadful Flying Corps. And as for being shot down, I positively forbid you to do any such thing.'

He smiled at her, feeling suddenly very mature. For he would be going away. Soon. He should have gone before now. He had volunteered months ago, when he was first up at Cambridge. Proust and Walters had started it, coming in with tales of the new Flying Corps. 'Wouldn't that be a jape. Would they have us?' And they had all three written up at the same time. When the letter came – the interview – he had said nothing to Mater. But someone had recognised him.

'Aren't you Alice Masters' boy?'

'Yes, sir.'

'Mother know you're here?'

'No, sir.'

'Well, you've got spirit, I'll say that. How old are you?'

'Seventeen,' truthfully. His birthday was still weeks away then. Proust and Walters had been wiser and more anonymous. 'Eighteen' and they were gone. Gone for ever, now. Just two more names among the list of names, column after column of them, in the papers every day.

And he? He 'had his name down'. The RFC had been taking men at seventeen, then, but his papers had never come. 'They'll call you when they want you,' Mater had said, when he plucked up courage and told her at last. 'It doesn't pay to fuss. I know the Army.'

The age was eighteen now, and his turn would come. Any day perhaps. It was the waiting that made his throat turn dry.

'Now look,' Tamsin said. 'We have quite wiped away poor Ashton's smile. Let's turn to more pleasant matters. Shall we go riding tomorrow? There are still two or three decent horses in the stable, though the rest have gone to the Army.'

Helena smiled. 'Poor Ashton. He can hardly refuse, though I am sure there are pursuits more to his taste than bouncing down dusty lanes on a bumpy saddle. He is not accustomed to our country ways.'

Drat the girl, she was right again. There was a perfectly good Bentley in the motor-house, gathering dust; but Gilbert Beswetherick had some notion of preserving petroleum 'for the war effort'. What use it was to the Army, stacked up in petrol-tins in the loft, Ashton was at a loss to see. Still a fellow could hardly argue with his hosts.

'I should love to accompany you, ladies,' he said, gallantly, 'though I am no great horseman.'

Tamsin rewarded him with a glowing smile, and the next day, as they ambled down lanes even bumpier and dustier than Helena had suggested, she was so charming and vivacious that he half-forgot his discomfort.

And when at last he helped the ladies down from their mounts, Tamsin did not take his hand for support, as he expected, but slid down bodily into his arms and pressed herself against him for a moment before she ran lightly off.

A man would have to be made of stone, not to find his pulses racing. He followed her into the house, thoughtfully. Aunt Winifred was waiting for him.

'Tamsin is so fond of you. It is quite a delight to see you together. Shall you take tea in the drawing-room?'

Dammit, she must have seen. Ashton felt his cheeks flame. And she was virtually giving him her approval. Except, of course, that he had no intention of courting Tamsin.

Although, when you came to think of it, a fellow could do a good deal worse. Tamsin Beswetherick was a deuced attractive girl.

Mrs Rouncewell got a wire from London. Little Manor was to open at once. And not just for the simplest cases. There had been terrible casualties sustained in – a peculiar name, Gallipoli was it? – and the port hospitals needed all their beds to cope with the ship-loads of wounded.

Lord Chyrose came to see her. The first casualties were expected next morning, some of them severely injured. Could Mrs Rouncewell possibly open up the hospital within twenty-four hours? Mrs Rouncewell could, especially if the committee would agree to an additional helper – say two six-hour shifts a week, at a shilling a day?

Lord Chyrose was helpfulness itself. 'My dear lady,' he said, 'we are eternally indebted to you. Eternally. This will be noticed in high places – so anything you need, anything, you just apply to me.' And he had bowed himself out, a stout little gentleman on absurdly thin legs, like an amiable penguin on stilts.

Nurses were the first priority. The two professionals were 'wired for' and her volunteer ladies were requested to present themselves at the hospital at seven the next morning. Lord Chyrose, at her request, got onto the telephone to Devonshire House and had Little Manor recognised as an official Auxiliary Hospital. That might mean having some proper VADs one of these days.

In the short term, there was Lizzie. Mrs Rouncewell went down to tell her personally, on the pretence of buying some mutton for the kitchens. Lizzie was so thunderstruck that there was almost an extra joint – of finger – with the order.

'You mean, I can start? Soon as you open?'

'Two shifts a week, starting tomorrow morning. You will report at seven, sharp. You will need a uniform of some kind, later, but that can be waived for now. Just a navy skirt and a white apron, I daresay I can find you a cap.'

The girl was gazing at her with shining eyes. 'Thank you, ma'am . . . Matron.'

A thin, tired, tousle-haired woman looked up from slapping giblets onto a greaseproof sheet. 'That's all very well, but I ain't sure as Lizzie can be spared. It's market-day tomorrow and . . .'

'Oh, for heaven's sake, Bess.' That was the child's grandmother, clearly. 'You can see the poor girl's dying to go. We'll manage. Agnes is big enough to give a hand, and Millie and me will do grand. And you won't be sorry to see a few extra pennies in the house, I'll be bound.'

Lizzie's mother frowned. 'Where are we to get this outfit from, just like that?'

'I got a skirt she can have, and she's got that sheeting apron that she made for her First Aid classes. Now, stop your fussing Bessie, do. James would be proud of her – helping the war effort. So, Lizzie, you say thank you to the lady and tell her you're grateful for the chance.'

'Thank you,' Lizzie said, dutifully. 'You won't regret it, I promise.'

Mrs Rouncewell cleared her throat. It had never occurred to her that there might be difficulties. 'Seven o'clock then. And don't be late.'

And before that there was so much to be done. The 'professional nurses' came on the early train and had to be settled into their quarters in the stables. Just before seven the first volunteers arrived and were soon on their hands and knees with scrubbing brushes and disinfectant. Tamsin, to Mrs Rouncewell's disgust, had to be sent home to take her rings off.

But where was the Treloweth girl? Seven o'clock, Mrs Rouncewell had said, and it was now almost five minutes past. Surely her mother had not prevented her at the last minute?

No, here she was at last, fairly scampering up the path, her hair tousled and her skirts awry. An extraordinary skirt, Mrs Rouncewell noted – an immense Victorian creation, all tucks and flounces, several sizes too big, and hastily 'taken in' at the seams. And it still gave off a faint odour of cows.

'I'm that sorry, Matron,' Lizzie burst out, before Mrs Rouncewell could speak. 'We've had a problem at home – our Alice was took bad in the night. And then Gan's skirt wouldn't fit . . .'

'That's enough!' Mrs Rouncewell kept her voice carefully stern. If you let these girls know you were sympathetic, however slightly, then they took advantage. 'We will overlook it, this once. But you'll work your tea-break to make up your time. Now, let's see you look lively – there's a bucket and scrubbing brush in the scullery.'

Lizzie gave her a grateful glance and scuttled off, and a few minutes later Mrs Rouncewell saw her hard at work. Doing a good job, too – not afraid to use a bit of elbow grease. She looked around with satisfaction – the place was abuzz with industry. Even Tamsin Beswetherick had come back and was giving a hand with the beds.

By half past nine the first two wards were ready – ten beds in each. Matron gave the 'gels' a break while she herself set off to meet the train in the 'ambulance' that Lord Chyrose had provided. After a little deliberation, she took Lizzie Treloweth with her.

There were eleven men. Three were walking wounded, with sodden bandages around their ashen faces. One had lost an eye, poor fellow, and gazed at you vaguely with the empty socket. Most of the rest were amputees, but two had been caught in a blazing building, their blackened limbs swathed in bandages, and there was the sweet, suppurating, unmistakable smell of burns.

Beside her, she heard Lizzie Treloweth catch her breath in horror. Poor child, Mrs Rouncewell thought. No amount of First Aid examinations could prepare you for this. But this was no time to encourage weakness.

'Come along then, Miss Treloweth,' she said. 'Work to be done. We'll get these men into the truck, and when we get back to Little Manor I shall want you to assist me with these burn cases.'

The poor fellows were writhing and moaning and calling for water – the journey had been an unremitting foretaste of hell for them – and she attended to them herself, easing back the bindings as gently as she could and bathing and disinfecting their appalling wounds.

She kept Lizzie by her side throughout, seeing to it that the girl was useful. And she was a real help. Almost, Mrs Rouncewell thought, as though she could sense what was wanted – fetching hot water and cold water and ointment and oils. She handed crisp white bandages and pins; she carried away used, bloodied dressings, stiff with indescribable slime, and boiled them clean. She worked unremittingly and without complaint, and although the horrors beneath those bandages turned her face to chalk she still managed a smile and a cheerful word to the men.

A born nurse, Mrs Rouncewell thought.

The same could not be said of everyone. You could tell the trained women at a glance – and not just by the uniforms. On one hand rows of neat beds, and an air of quiet efficiency; on the other a confusion of dishevelled bedclothes and dropped thermometers. The professional nurses made it worse than it needed to be, too, by leaving all the worst jobs for the volunteers.

But there was no time to linger. Blanket baths, temperatures, enemas, and then the ward had to be tidied and spotless for the doctor, who came to issue orders for the necessary ointments, antiseptics and fomentations. Tamsin Beswetherick, of course, forgot herself – she knew the doctor socially, and had to be severely reprimanded for not standing up when he came in, and speaking to him without being spoken to.

Altogether, at the end of the first day's shift, some of the volunteers looked as if they ought to be in a hospital bed themselves. Only Helena Beswetherick seemed able to pull her weight and earn a grudging respect from the others, and poor little Lizzie, with her preposterous skirt and face the colour of porcelain – steadfastly bathing a shrapnel wound which had laid bare the arm to bone and sinews.

'Very well, Miss Treloweth, you may go off duty now. Report again on Friday.'

And from the way the girl said, 'Thank you, ma'am,' with a face wreathed in delight, you would think that Matron had given her something wonderful, instead of inviting her for another day of drudgery.

Chapter Five

Mike wrote home to say that he was settling in. Had his uniform at last and was getting used to bulling his belt and braces, and going out on the downs for rifle-practice. It all sounded very military. Billeted on a farm, he said, and feeling quite at home there. Had a head start over the others, too – they found it purgatory to wake at five but it was only like getting up for milking. And the dummies on the downs were better behaved than cows. Stood still while you bayoneted them, and didn't try to suck your bottom as soon as you turned your back. Pa read the letter and laughed till the tears stood in his eyes.

Ma was prouder of the last paragraph. Singled out for officer training, on account of he had two officer brothers already in the Army. Merran felt neither laughter nor pride, but he read the letter a dozen times, as if it brought Mike closer. He would never have believed how much he missed his twin.

The second letter came early one July morning. Merran had just come in from thinning the mangels up in 'Higher Daisy', slow, back-breaking work. Higher Daisy was a poor field, sour old soil on top, and nothing but granite chippings under so you couldn't plough deeper than an inch or two. It would never grow many mangels, but with the price of hay rising so, any extra feed would be a blessing – even supposing the Army didn't buy up all the hay, anyway, like last winter.

Merran came into the yard and was washing his filthy hands at the pump when he saw the postboy cycling up the lane, a letter in his hand.

Not a telegram. That was the first thing. Odd. He could remember a time when a letter at Nanzeal was a real rarity, enough to bring everyone scurrying for news – 'who's wed, who's dead, who's bred,' as Pa used to say. It was different these days. Mother got regular letters now.

It didn't stop him from dropping everything, and going inside to read it. From Peter, perhaps, about this wedding. Or from Paul even – he'd have something to say about it, even if he couldn't be home for the ceremony. It wasn't from Michael. He'd have known that, somehow, in his bones.

What was it really like out there in France, he wondered. Peter and Paul never said much – just that they were missing Nanzeal, and how much they looked forward to Mother's parcels and letters from home. Couldn't say much, probably – everyone knew that mail was censored. But the war news was good. The Ypres offensive was progressing well, and a breakthrough was expected hourly. So perhaps they would all be home for Christmas, as Mother said. Only trouble was, people had been saying the same last Christmas.

Besides, there were things in the letters which worried Merran. Little things. Peter's request for lice-powder and rat-bait, for instance. Made it into a joke – said it was just like being down the stables again – but he had wanted it all the same. Rats and lice. As if it wasn't bad enough sitting in a foreign country waiting to be shot at. Or shooting, come to that.

Neither of them ever spoke about that. Merran remembered the pictures in the paper, when those German ships shelled Hartlepool. All those twisted beams and ruined houses: over a hundred people dead. Mother had been horrified. 'Whatever's the world coming to? Attacking women and children?'

But Merran had other thoughts. If it was like that in England, after one attack, what must it be like in France?

And Mike would soon be out there. He couldn't bear to think about that. But at least there was this question of weekend leave. Perhaps that was what this letter was about – Peter had hoped to arrange it. He quickened his pace and hurried back towards the farmhouse.

He had to grin as he crossed the yard. The postboy, having delivered the envelope, had encountered the two goats on his way out. They had him now pinned up against the wall, Jessie with her front paws on his chest, trying to lick him to death, while Toots looked on with her mad yellow eyes and nibbled the buttons on his trousers. Merran whistled, and they both shambled over, looking for sugar, while the postboy beat a hasty retreat back to his bicycle and pedalled off down the lane for dear life with Lass barking at his heels.

But his grin faded when he went into the house. 'Mother?'

She was in the kitchen, standing in the window-bay with the open letter, rocking in misery. She held out the paper wordlessly.

'Mike?' he could not stop the word. It was forced from him as though someone had punched him in the stomach.

She shook her head. 'It's Peter,' she managed.

He took the paper. 'Peter?' But it was Paul's writing. Nothing was making sense. 'Not dead? Surely not dead? They'd have telegrammed.'

The world seemed to have slowed down. The fly that buzzed among the drying herbs on the ceiling-beams seemed to take an age to drone from rosemary to sage.

Ma shook her head. 'Not dead. Wounded. Caught in a shell-burst. Last week it was, while we were all sitting here, laughing and talking and planning this wedding – just as though nothing had happened.' Tears were pouring down her face as she spoke, but she made no move to brush them away. 'Touch and go for days, it's been with him. Saved his life, but not his legs. His precious legs. Both gone. Paul has seen him – they gave him special leave. Wanted to write himself before they told me, official. Here, see for yourself.'

He took the letter and began to read. It was not a long letter but the pictures which leapt from those few short lines haunted his dreams for ever.

Lizzie was weighing out kidneys for the policeman's wife, when Merran Jago and his pa arrived in the shop, and when she saw them – all dressed up like Christmas in their Sunday best – her first thought was to smile. They looked so awkward and unnatural in their high starched collars and stiff polished boots, twisting their bowler hats in their hands.

But then she saw their faces, and suddenly she did not feel like smiling any more. She paused in the act of wrapping the kidneys to give Mother a nudge.

Mam was skewering a roll of rib and she turned sharply. 'Here! What do you think you're playing at . . .' But Lizzie nodded towards the two men, and Mother's face softened. 'My lor!' she muttered. 'Something's happened to one of they boys, see if it hasn't.'

50

Lizzie had worked that out already. Her heart was pounding at her own ribs so hard, you'd think it was trying to get out. Suppose something had happened to Michael? You did hear of it. People who were accidentally shot, or killed in a training accident. Dear God, don't let it be Michael. Her eyes sought Merran's.

'Where's Daisy?' His lips framed the words soundlessly. Lizzie clutched the counter with relief. Not Michael then – only Peter.

Only Peter! She regretted the feeling instantly. Poor Daisy. How bad was the news? Lizzie's mind, which had been paralysed by shock, seemed to build up steam and get into action again. They weren't wearing armbands, either of them; so maybe Peter was not dead, after all.

Mother jerked her head towards the rooms upstairs. Daisy was there today. As often as not it was Lizzie who was left upstairs of a morning with Gan to do the washing or the baking, with one eye on the soup kettle and the other on the baby (Dot was not three yet, and too little to go to school). But today Daisy had volunteered. 'I'll have a go at this mending,' she had said. 'There's socks need darning, and Penny is half-out of that skirt. And after, if I have time, I'll make a start on this blouse for my wedding.'

'Daisy's up there sewing this blessed minute,' Mother said in an undertone, as though she too was struck by the irony of it. 'You take them up to her, directly you've finished serving that customer. Put the kettle on, I'll be up myself as soon as ever I've got a moment.' She turned back to her skewers, but she was shaking.

Lizzie felt her own hands tremble as she added the little grease-proof bundle to the parcels in the woman's basket. Poor Daisy. No wonder she hadn't had a letter. The policeman's wife gave a little cough, and Lizzie pulled herself together. 'Anything else, Mrs Owens?'

'Nice piece of suet,' Mrs Owens said, 'and that'll have to be all this week. I was going to have a bit of skirt steak for a stew, but I can't run to it. It's cost me well-nigh a shilling for a bag of flour, a twist of tea and a few vegetables. And there's no sugar to be had. Still . . .' She cast a meaningful look at the two Jagos. 'I daresay there's worse things than being short of a drop of sugar for your tea.' She dropped her voice sympathetically. 'Trouble is there?'

Lizzie was chafing with impatience – Mrs Owens was better at spreading news than the town crier – but she said courteously enough, 'Shan't know for a minute. This piece do you, Mrs

Owens? It's all I can spare you at the moment. Everybody seems to be after suet these days.'

'I'm not surprised, with butter such a price,' Mrs Owens said. And then, mercifully, she counted out her coppers and Lizzie was free to go over to the two men.

'Daisy's upstairs,' she said, breathlessly. 'Is it . . .' She hesitated, refusing the word. 'Bad?'

'Bad enough,' Luke Jago said. They followed Lizzie through the back shop and up the stone steps. 'Lost his legs, poor lad. Both of them. His mother's that shaken up, you wouldn't believe, and I don't know what your Daisy will make of it when she hears . . .'

But Daisy had heard already. She must have come down for water because there was a sudden cry behind them, and there was Daisy clinging to the iron rail for support, while the enamel bucket bounced and clanged away down the steps, spilling its contents as it rolled.

Merran was beside her in an instant, offering a supporting arm, and he and Lizzie helped Daisy up into the kitchen, while his father went down to refill the bucket. By the time Mother came up a few moments later, Gan had the kettle hissing, and Daisy was already supping Gan's medicinal 'plum brandy' which tasted like varnish, but brought a little colour back to Daisy's ashen face.

'It's all right, Mam,' Daisy said, when the story had been told again for Mother's benefit. 'It'll just have to make no difference. Didn't you read in the paper about that girl whose fiancé was killed? Volunteered to marry any blinded airman. Well, I can marry Peter – it's just, he won't have any legs, that's all. My part of the war ef . . . ef . . . effort.' Her voice broke on the last syllable and she dissolved again into tears.

Luke Jago stood, still turning the brim of his hat between his hands. 'I'm some sorry, Daisy,' he said, humbly. 'Only of course, he's our lad too, and you can imagine what his mother thinks. We should be getting back – isn't fair leaving her on her own too long, time like this. Only we thought you should know.'

Daisy blew her nose very hard in Gan's pocket handkerchief. 'Well, I'm glad you did.' She sniffed. 'You'll tell me, won't you? Soon as he gets back to England? I'll try to get and see him, if it's not too far. I'll scrape the train-fare somehow.'

Lizzie saw Merran exchange glances with his father. 'Paul says they'll be sending him back as soon as he can be moved. Pity they couldn't send him to that hospital of Lizzie's – Little Manor or whatever it's called. Be near home, then, and we could all see him. Wonder if they would. What do you think, Lizzie? Lizzie?'

But it was no good. She could not answer him. She had a sudden vision of what she had seen in the wards – the chafed stumps, legs laid open like maps by shrapnel, rivers of blood and sinew across continents of flesh. And Peter, Peter Jago whom she knew, suffering with wounds like that.

When Merran reached her, she was leaning against the wall in the backyard, sweat standing on her forehead, being quietly sick. Merran put his arm around her, and she leaned against him, grateful for his silent comfort. 'I'm sorry,' she managed, after a moment. 'I don't know how you must feel. Worse than the rest of us, even. You always said, it isn't Cornwall's war.'

His response surprised her. He took her by the elbows and gazed into her eyes. There was so much grief and anger in his face that it almost shocked her. 'I said that,' he said, 'and I meant it too. But that was before they took off Peter's legs. "One for All" – the Cornish motto. I tell you this, Lizzie. It's bloody well my war now!'

'Well, Ashton,' Aunt Winifred said to him one day over breakfast. 'What shall you do today? Have you any plans?'

Ashton looked up from his scrambled eggs. They were alone. The Beswethericks kept an old-fashioned 'buffet' breakfast with chafing-dishes, and rarely ate together. Sir Gilbert seldom came down before ten, whereas Helena and Tamsin had left for their 'Hospital' hours ago.

'I thought I might go into Penzance and see if there is a letter,' he said. 'I am expecting one from the Flying Corps, any day. But they seem to be taking an unconscionably long time about it. Unless it has missed me somehow – though Mater did promise to send it on as soon as it arrived.'

His aunt smiled. 'I should not alarm yourself on that account. I am sure your mother has thought of everything. But I am glad you have a purpose – I feared you might be finding it tedious at Gulveylor now that your cousins are so much away, and you lack young company.'

He looked at her sharply. Was she telling him he had outstayed his welcome?

It seemed not. She went on with a smile, 'We are quite hoping, you know, that you will consent to spend the rest of the summer with us, until you go back to Cambridge.'

'Oh, I shall have my papers long before that.'

Winifred looked at him shrewdly. 'You think so? Well, I am sure you are right. Whichever is the soonest, naturally. Would you care to stay? We are a little dull, I daresay, after London, but perhaps these German air-attacks are making the capital a trifle *too* exciting these days.'

'If a fellow is waiting for call-up he can hardly avoid danger by staying out of London,' he said with a laugh. 'But I confess that I should like to wait it out here, above all things.'

It was hardly surprising. The life-style here was very agreeable. This breakfast, for example, the sideboard groaning with hot dishes and a table full of fruit and preserves, all from the estate. At home Mater was making 'economies' because of the War – only one marmalade and no cream – and at Cambridge too, a chap could hardly be seen to indulge in luxuries at a time like this. But Gilbert Beswetherick kept a good table, war or no war.

'Damn Huns,' he said, 'already laid up my motor-car for the duration. Dashed if they shall keep me from my breakfast too.'

No, decidedly, there were attractions at Gulveylor.

Including Tamsin. She found him attractive, there was no denying that. The way she smiled up at him as he talked and asked his opinion on every subject. Fingers that lingered a little too long on his arm as he escorted her to dinner, eyes that met his more often and more deliberately than strict convention would allow. He would have to beware, there, but it was deuced flattering.

It was endearing besides, to see her come home from that hospital, with her poor little fingers red and sore, her neat little ankles swollen and aching, and her pretty cap and apron all awry. Helena had 'done the thing properly', signed up with a Voluntary Aid Detachment, and even registered as 'willing to serve overseas'. Tamsin though, was too young. She was only helping part-time and even then she came home white-faced and exhausted.

'Your cousins will be glad of your company to walk home,' Aunt Winifred said, reading his thoughts. 'The nights are drawing in, and it will be getting dark by then. I hear there is talk in Whitehall of changing the clocks next summer, so that we shall have an extra hour of daylight, though I do not understand how. I remember my mother telling me that when she was young, one had to alter one's watch when one travelled from one town to the next, but I do not recall that it ever delayed the sunset. But, here is Sir Gilbert arriving. No doubt he can explain it to you. Do, please, have some more plums. Fresh this morning from the kitchen-garden.'

There was no letter in Penzance, and the afternoon hung heavy on his hands. Perhaps, after all, a chap ought to go back to London. He idled through the town, and later wandered up towards Little Manor. He was still far too early, and he found a stile where he could see the sea, and sat there, dreaming of aeroplanes and heroism and the great empty vault of the sky.

A squeaking rattle interrupted his reverie. It was that girl from the bandaging classes, struggling up the lane with a cumbersome cart. One wheel had lurched up against a tree-root in the path and she was wrestling to free it.

Some stirring of chivalry made him climb down from his stile and go to her aid. 'Why, it is my little bandager. Miss Treloweth! Allow me.' And he lifted the cart with one hand – though to tell the truth it was damnably heavier than he expected.

Lizzie Treloweth was gratifyingly impressed. 'That's some good of you, sir. I got this meat to take up to Trevarnon, but I daren't be long, 'cause I'm due at the Hospital.' She looked at him with that enchanting smile, which lit up the thin face like a magic lantern. 'What are you doing here, any road?'

For some reason he didn't tell her that he was waiting for Tamsin. Instead he said, 'I was watching the water. It's a beautiful place, Mount's Bay.'

She nodded. 'Yes. Look at the sunset on the water. Like a river it is, all golden and pink. A highway to heaven, my Gan calls it.'

'She's quite a poet, your Gan,' Ashton said. 'I wish it was my highway. I'm still waiting to hear, you know. I can't understand why they are taking so long.'

'The Flying Corps?' She looked at him shrewdly. 'That'll be your Mother's doing, won't it? She knows no end of people in high places.'

He stared at her. 'Mater!' Why hadn't that occurred to him.

But Lizzie was shaking her head. 'Here, no, I shouldn't have said. It's just – well, that's what folks are saying.'

'Are they now?' Ashton felt a cold anger rising in him. Mater! Well, he would soon see about that. He would write to the Air Ministry. Tonight. And as suddenly as it came, the anger left him. 'Thank you, little Lizzie, you have done me a service. More than you know.' He felt so light-hearted that he lifted her hand and kissed it, and smiled to himself as she scurried off, blushing and flustered, as fast as her cart would permit.

He was still smiling when Tamsin came out a few minutes later. 'Oh, Ashton,' she said, falling into step beside him, 'I am too tired to wait for Helena tonight. Such things they expect you to do! I have spent the day serving soup and washing . . . receptacles.'

'Receptacles?' And then he blushed. Of course, bedpans, she meant. Poor little Tamsin. 'Oh, I see, receptacles.'

She flushed. 'Yes.' She looked up at him and her eyes were full of tears. 'And then Mrs Rouncewell told me off because I forgot to stand to attention when she came in. As for the blanket baths – well, I blush to tell you. And my shoes pinch and my feet ache. Honestly, Ashton, if those wretched classes had not been my idea, I wouldn't stay another minute.'

She looked so positively wretched that he bent forward and kissed her. He regretted it instantly, of course. It was a disgraceful liberty, and in a public place too. 'I'm sorry . . .' he began.

'No, don't apologise. I have been hoping you would do . . . something like that.' She seized his hand. 'Does that mean that you might . . . care for me?'

Dammit, he had not meant that to happen. It was brought on perhaps, by his meeting with Lizzie. He said quickly. 'Of course I care for you, you are my very dear cousin,' and saw Tamsin's face fall. He added gallantly, 'But this is not the time. You are tired, and I should be escorting you home. Besides, here is Helena, come to join us.'

All evening he was aware of Tamsin's glances, and her little special smiles. But he made no move towards her, and excused himself early.

He went upstairs and wrote a carefully worded letter to the Flying Corps.

Chapter Six

Peter Jago did come to Little Manor, though it was irregular. Possibly Major Trevarnon had wangled it somehow with the War Office. But however it was managed, there was the name, among the lists one day. Lieutenant P. Jago.

He actually arrived when Lizzie was not on duty, so the first she saw of him he was lying back in bed. He looked pale and shaken, but otherwise pretty much the Peter Jago she had always known. She went over to speak to him.

'Peter?'

His eyes were closed, but he opened them as she spoke. 'Lizzie?' His surprise was so total that she almost laughed, but she had worked with sick men long enough to know that this instant recognition was a good sign.

'You're awake then?' In your right mind, she meant. 'Is it bad?'

He grimaced. 'Bad enough. Worse now than when it happened. I was more concerned then because I'd hurt my elbow. Shock, I suppose. But now it throbs something wicked, and the stumps won't heal. The worst of it is, my legs ache most of all where they aren't there any more. The right one specially. It's only a ghost of a leg, and it's giving me murder.'

Lizzie nodded. Another good sign. Some men didn't realise the extent of their injuries – one poor fellow had begged and begged to have his foot removed, to stop the agony, when none of his leg remained below the knee.

'Family know you're here?' she said.

He shook his head. 'Nor Daisy neither.' That was a request.

Lizzie nodded. 'I'll tell her, soon as I get home. Now I'd best be working. I'll come and see you again before I leave.'

She hurried off to help Nurse Blight, one of the professional nurses, cleaning the 'conservatory ward'. There were eight patients there, what Nurse Blight called 'respitory cases' and the big windows were kept constantly open – as if, Lizzie thought, the poor fellows had not enough to bear without a September gale whistling around them.

Still, 'fresh air was the best medicine' Mrs Rouncewell said, and several had improved enough to sit out in wicker chairs in their 'blue boys' uniform, with its white collar and red tie – and others could lie propped up on pillows, and sweep under their own beds with a long-handled broom. No question now of pulling out the beds to disinfect, there was scarcely space, and three men were anyway too ill to be moved. The carbolic scrub was reserved nowadays for when a bed was vacated.

That was happening on some wards. Officers, minus an arm or leg, were being restored to their families. Others, with 'more fortunate' wounds, went home for a brief respite before going back to face another shell or bullet or gas grenade. One or two had recovered sufficiently to be passed 'fit for duty', and sent back on the first train. But it was not all success. The fellow with the phantom foot succumbed during the night, and Lizzie had seen him, mouth agape and head lolling, before he was hurried away, wrapped in a blanket. It was their first loss at Little Manor.

'Mind you,' Nurse Blight said to Lizzie, as they polished the bedsteads and dusted the radiators, 'we're lucky here. You see a lot worse at the Base hospitals and as for the Casualty Clearing Stations, well!'

'How could it possibly be worse?' Lizzie said, but one of the officers chimed in from his wicker chair nearby.

'She's right there, miss. Up to our ears in mud and blood we were when they brought us in, and verminous besides.'

The two girls turned crimson, they should not be chattering on duty, and they had forgotten that the men might overhear. They busied themselves silently with pulling out and disinfecting the empty bed vacated by poor Captain Rossiter – who, after a fortnight of staring silently at nothing, was discovered at midnight in the pouring rain, standing sentry by the duckpond and seeing off imaginary intruders with a mop-handle. 'Taken away' this morning, poor fellow, neither dead nor alive.

'Now gels.' Mrs Rouncewell swept into the room, and Lizzie scrambled upright. 'How are we doing here?' She strode down the ward, straightening a coverlet here, running a finger over a bedstead there. Matron seemed to have grown younger, over the past few weeks. Her step was firmer, her back straighter, and even her starched cap and apron seemed crisper. Sometimes even Nurse Blight looked ready to drop with fatigue, but Mrs Rouncewell seemed to have endless energy. She could stay up all night with a man in crisis and still be on duty next morning, eyes and tongue as sharp as ever.

The men adored her. And with reason. Lizzie had seen her hold, with her own hands, a lighted cigarette to the lips of poor Lieutenant Linton, who was so terribly burnt. Nothing was ever too much trouble for her 'boys' – although her 'gels' often had a very hard time of it. Here she was now, finding fault with one of Lizzie's 'envelope corners', but charming a smile out of the gas-victim under the bedclothes. Heaven knows the poor fellow had little enough to smile about.

'Very well, Miss Treloweth, when you have remade that bed you may go off duty. And Nurse Blight, you may take down a tray of tea to the library. Lady Beswetherick has arranged one of her "entertainments", and the musicians may require refreshment. Oh, and you may take Albert with you. Some of the officers find him diverting.'

Lizzie and Nurse Blight exchanged glances. Albert's antics at these 'entertainments' were a legend. The performers were mostly amateur sopranos and lady violinists, and all the men who were well enough to be out of bed, but not well enough to escape into the garden, were more or less obliged to attend. The men did their best to be grateful, especially when the musicians were young and pretty, but Albert was less predictable. He had once 'joined in' with a particularly painful lady contralto, and several times 'escaped' during a recital, so that the concert had to be abandoned while he was recaptured.

Other treats, though, were eagerly awaited, especially the motor outings and the visits of local ladies bringing flowers and cigarettes.

Visitors were arriving now. Lizzie had remade the offending bed and hurried back to see Peter Jago, but his parents were already at his side. It seemed a shame to interrupt them, so she tiptoed quietly away.

Instead, she went home and told Daisy. 'Here, your Peter is in the Hospital. Arrived yesterday, and looking forward no end to a visit. Go up there now, you could. Just got time before they do the evening dressings.'

But to her surprise Daisy did not go at once. 'Is he . . . Well . . . How is he?'

'Grand,' Lizzie said. 'Except for his legs, of course. But he's over the worst. Mrs Rouncewell had him up for an hour, in a special sort of chair they have for double amputees – like a sort of outsize wicker pram. Talking about getting some artificial legs for him, when the stumps have healed properly.'

But Daisy seemed strangely reluctant to go. It was half an hour or more before she set off to see Peter.

She came back, just as they were eating their tea – a bit of stew Gan and Millie had boiled up with scrag-ends from the shop. She looked shaken and white, and sat down without saying a word. Gan took her up some stew and Daisy sat, stirring it on her plate and eating very little.

'How was he then?' Penny said, but Daisy just shook her head. Then, after a minute or two, she got up suddenly, put on her coat and went out, slamming the door.

'What's up with her?' Penny said. 'I was only asking!'

59

Gan shook her head. 'She'll tell us in her own good time. Now then Penny, where are those children to? Time for them to do their lessons and get to bed. Millie, d'you go down and fetch up some water so we can wash these here crocks, and Lizzie, there's a couple of late orders want delivering up Heamoor . . .'

So the moment passed in a flurry of activity. Daisy did not come home for supper, and Mam was beginning to get anxious, but much later, when everyone was in bed, Lizzie heard the latch of the door. Daisy came in, slipped off her dress in the darkness, and climbed shivering into bed. Lizzie could tell that she had been crying.

'All right, are you?' she whispered, very softly so as not to wake the others.

'I'm . . . no . . . We're not . . . I don't want to talk about it.' Daisy turned away fiercely to face the wall.

Lizzie said nothing, but presently she reached out a hand under the coverlets. Daisy gripped it tightly and they lay there like that, unspeaking – as though they were little girls again – until Daisy had finally wept herself to sleep.

'Report Brooklands twenty-first.'

Ashton looked at the telegram blankly.

'Report Brooklands twenty-first.'

Comprehension dawned. Report Brooklands. It had come. Finally come. What was the date today? September 17th. If he caught the train tomorrow . . . there would be just time to call on Mater in Belgravia and then . . .

'Report Brooklands twenty-first.'

Absurd. He was ready to dance and sing. He wanted to run out, startle Beswetherick or his aunt at the breakfast table, shout for the world to hear.

'Report Brooklands twenty-first.'

Instead he took his time. Sauntered slowly in to breakfast. This morning, blessedly, they were all there – Helena and Tamsin had the morning off. Still he said nothing. Helped himself to porridge from the chafing-dishes. Honey. Cream.

'Morning, Ashton.' Beswetherick from behind his paper. 'Letter for you on the sideboard salver. From your mother, I fancy.'

Ashton found his voice. Carefully casual. 'Actually, there was a telegram too.'

Silence. Beswetherick put down *The Times*. Aunt Winifred stopped with a piece of toast halfway to her lips.

Tamsin said, 'Ashton!'

'Yes,' he said, 'it has come at last. I'm to report to Brooklands on the twenty-first. I'm in.'

Suddenly they were all speaking at once.

'My dear boy,' Gilbert Beswetherick came over and was wringing his hand as if he would shake it off. 'You have wanted this a long time, I know.'

'You're welcome here, you know, at any time.' Aunt Winifred.

Helena said, 'You must come and see us in uniform.'

'So, you are really going, at last?' Tamsin's voice was very high and strained. She pushed back her plate, and stumbled from the room.

'Women!' Beswetherick snorted. He picked up his newspaper.

'She will miss you,' Aunt Winifred said. 'Naturally.'

Ashton looked at the door. 'I think,' he said awkwardly, 'I should . . .' He followed Tamsin out of the room.

But he did not look for her. Instead he went into the garden, gazing up into the sky as if by willing it he could conjure some wandering aeroplane from the clouds. But the sky was empty. Only the birds soared, effortless and silent, over the distant sea.

At last he went in and opened his letter. It was from Mater, a hurt and angry letter, full of self-justification. 'It was for your own good, Ashton.' She was afraid for him, he realised. Afraid that he would become – like Proust and Walters – just another name among the illustrious dead.

Strange – he had never felt so alive. Every leaf, every flower seemed individual, distinct. Every colour was more vibrant.

Tamsin came to join him. She came towards him, her cheeks unnaturally pink, and held out her hands. 'I am sorry, cousin. I am a brute, I know, not to share your happiness.'

'A brute? Never!' He would have to be a brute himself, who did not take the little hands in his and press them, reassuringly. And when, with a little sob, she leaned herself against him, it would have been churlish not to gather her into his arms. She was so young, so pretty, so yielding.

It was she, besides, who lifted her face to be kissed, so he could hardly be blamed for leaning forward and pressing his lips to hers, holding the shapely head between his hands so that the dark hair cascaded between his fingers, while she pressed her soft curves against his chest.

'Farewells already?' Aunt Winifred.

Tamsin turned scarlet, disengaged herself, and hurried off. Ashton felt his own cheeks burning.

'There isn't . . . There's no . . . uh . . .' he began.

Aunt Winifred looked at him. 'No, I imagine not. It seems, Ashton, that you forget yourself.'

'An unfortunate incident,' he found himself mumbling. 'These are emotional times.' Something more was obviously expected, and stammered out, 'It will not happen again, Aunt Winifred, I assure you.'

'I should hope not, indeed.' She paused. 'Unless, of course, there was some understanding between you.'

'You mean . . . ?'

She waved a hand. 'My dear Ashton, one would have to be blind not to see that Tamsin is devoted to you. And we live in such uncertain times. Good men are becoming hard to find. Should you decide – I know that it is not your present intention and I have no wish to chivvy you – but should you decide to . . . come to some understanding, you should know, Ashton, that you would have my fullest support. And Sir Gilbert's too. He would be glad to know that one of his girls was properly settled, since Helena seems quite resolved upon these nonsensical medical studies of hers. You might find him, I think, inclined to be generous.'

He stood, gaping like a schoolboy. He had expected a wigging for his behaviour, and here he was instead being virtually proposed to by the girl's mother. He hesitated, not knowing what to say.

Aunt Winifred saved him the necessity. 'Now, here is Helena, so we will say no more about it. Shall you require the carriage tomorrow to take your trunk to the station?'

There was, in fact, a great deal to be organised. Packing to supervise, tickets to book. Tamsin, whether overcome by embarrassment or under instructions from her mother, pleaded a headache and did not come down to dinner.

First thing in the morning he was on the London train.

Merran went up to the hospital to see Peter. It was a painful business. Peter seemed to have changed overnight. Mother had said he was pale and drawn, but in good spirits, but when Merran came in Peter just glanced at him and turned away, staring at the wall.

'Peter? It's me, Merran.'

Peter did not turn his head. 'I can see that. Is me legs are missing, not me eyes.' He sounded so bitter and angry that Merran winced.

'Here, that's not like you, Peter. What's the matter, all of a sudden?'

It was a foolish question. Peter whirled his head to face his visitor, and said, in a voice trembling with fury, 'All of a sudden? I've had my legs blown off, that's what's the matter. So, that's the stone end, isn't it? Not like cutting your toenails, you know. You can't grow new. So, I'm to be stuck here like a cabbage, wheeled about like a baby in a pram, useless. That's what's the matter.'

Merran shook his head, 'I'm sorry . . .'

'*You're* sorry! Not half so sorry as I am. Stuck here like an exhibition for people to gawp at. Well, you've done your gawping now. Seen your bit of the freak show. So you can go home now, and leave me in a bit of peace.'

Some sixth sense prompted Merran to say, 'It isn't our fault, you know, Peter. I can't guess how you're feeling, but we're pretty wretched too, watching you.'

Peter met his eyes, then. 'No,' he said, in a quieter tone. ''Tisn't your fault. And doubtless it isn't what you expect, either. Supposed to be delighted, aren't I, just to be home. The war hero patiently bearing his wounds. Well, it's not like that, Merran. It isn't the pain – I can bear that, for the most part. What I can't stand is the pity. Daisy came here last night, and you know what? When she looked at me all I could see in her was pity. It isn't me here any more, it's some legless soldier. I, me, Peter Jago – I don't exist any more.'

'But Daisy'll . . .'

Peter interrupted, 'No she won't. She tried to say that she'd marry me, Merran. Tried to. But you know what? The words wouldn't come.'

'It's the shock,' Merran said. 'That's all it is.'

'So?' Peter said. 'Supposing it is? What then? Marry me out of pity, and live to regret it the rest of her life? No. Better like this. I told her, go. Not fair to any girl, to saddle her with half a man. But I aren't going to smile and nod and pretend it is all wonderful, because it's not. It's a black, miserable, diabolical, hellish mess and I wish they'd got me when they got my legs. So go away, Merran, and let a man sleep, there's a good fellow.'

'Michael is coming tomorrow,' Merran said. 'He's got twenty-four-hour leave. They are posting him to a training establishment. Isle of Wight. He's furious – writing letters to everyone to get an overseas posting.'

Peter said nothing.

'He'll want to see you.'

Peter turned his face to the wall, wearily. 'Well, I'll see him, of course. I'm sorry to be so sour – but I feel sour and that's the truth. But I'll be glad to see Michael. Lizzie Treloweth's here – you know that I'm sure – doing a bit of part-time helping, and a grand little nurse she is. She'd like to see him too.'

That was more like the old Peter and Merran was more cheerful as he set off home.

Next morning, Michael arrived. It was odd to see him. The old closeness seemed to have gone, and he was a stranger, this official-looking figure in smart uniform. Especially when a couple of private soldiers saluted him on the station.

They went to Nanzeal, almost in silence. Ma had spent hours baking and there was bread and saffron cake, and even a blackberry tart, though where she managed to find the blackberries was a mystery. People had picked the hedges dry. No buns, though, she couldn't get the sugar.

Pa had saved the last of the harvest so Michael could be there for the 'neck'. They had always 'cried the neck' at Nanzeal, and always the same way, though Hunnicutt swore they did it different up country when he was a boy. In fact, Hunnicutt's complaints were as much a part of the tradition as the ceremony itself.

Other years, of course, there had been scores of people at the 'neck', but this time there were only the twins, Mother and Pa and Hunnicutt to do it. Pa went to ask Old Man Treloweth in off the butchery-wagon for the occasion, but after that business with Daisy they wouldn't come. Embarrassed, most like. So there were just the five of them.

They went down to Corny Edge, the best of the cornfields, and stood, awkwardly among the stubbled fields. Most of the corn was in, neatly ricked and covered in the yard, but there were still a few fields 'stooked', with the stacks of freshly bound sheaves leaning together in 'corn-mows' waiting to be taken down to the last remaining rick. And there in the far corner of the arrish, the last stand of corn.

Pa's hand was still troubling him, and Michael was in uniform, which wouldn't have been 'fitty' as Hunnicutt said; so it fell to Merran himself to take the scythe and cut those last few golden stalks with a clean, swift cut. He held the little clutch of corn triumphantly above his head.

'I have 'en.'

And they chorused back, 'What 'ave 'ee?'

'A neck! A neck! A neck!'

And then he was off, helter-skelter across the fields with the rest of them in mock pursuit until he came to the house. Mother would weave the corn into a 'dolly' to be taken to 'harvest home' and blessed, and then brought back to hang over the fireplace, 'blessing the harvest' for the year to come.

Then there was cider and home-made apple wine, and Mother's blackberry tart and cream. Michael began telling funny stories about his training camp, and Hunnicutt perched on the settle and told everyone who would listen how they did it quite differently in other places.

Altogether, it was quite like old times, except for the memory of Peter, lying in Little Manor with his legs shot off. Then Pa and Michael went into Penzance to see him, and Merran went off to busy himself with wall-mending. There was a nasty gap in the stone hedge up at Windy Tops, next to the stile, and he'd been meaning to deal with it for days, because he wanted to let the pigs out in that field after the late farrowing.

He liked walling. There was something pleasing about finding the right stones for the job, and settling them so balanced and perfect that a good dry-stone wall was firmer than any bricks and mortar. The stones were piled ready, but they were heavy, and it was warm work. He almost welcomed that. It took his mind off Peter.

He was so absorbed in his work that he didn't notice the man watching him from the lane.

'Master Jago?'

It was a fat, pink, smiling man, a gold watch-chain straining across his waistcoat, and he made a little hissing sound as he spoke, like a steam kettle. He was clutching his bowler hat to his stomach with both hands, and half-bowing over it.

'Farrington,' the man said. 'Silas Farrington. Perhaps you remember me? I believe I have had the pleasure. It's Merran Jago, isn't it? Your family owns this farm, I understand?'

'What's it to you?' Merran said shortly.

It was not polite, but there was something about Farrington that Merran had never liked. It was hard to know why. But Lass was growling, and baring her teeth, and on the other side of the hedge the pigs were restless. Never trust a man who doesn't get on with pigs.

Farrington ignored the rudeness. 'Choose your own crops, though, that sort of thing?' he persisted. 'What do you grow here, as a rule?'

'The usual things,' Merran said. He put down the stone he had been heaving into place. 'Look, what is all this about?'

Farrington smiled, and tapped the side of his nose with a forefinger. 'That's just it. The usual things. Potatoes, broccoli, a bit of fruit for the town. Thought of branching out, have you? Marrow, sugar-beet – and fancies, asparagus under glass? You got glass, I suppose?'

Merran said nothing.

'Thing is,' Farrington said, 'I might have a little proposition. The Government are on the lookout to buy all the soft fruit this year. Make jam, see, for the troops. Believe me, I've got friends in high places. And what's the result? Shortages, that's what. Marrow jam, that's the ticket. For the home market, see. And sugar-beet. That's where the money is. You grow it, I'll sell it. So much an acre too, guaranteed.'

'And asparagus? Who's going to buy asparagus, with a war on?'

Farrington tapped his nose again. 'Ah, you don't read your papers, Master Jago. Government's encouraging folk to eat luxury things. Leave more ordinary food for the poor. No, there's money in it. You mark my words.'

'Well,' Merran said. 'You'll have to talk to Pa. But I can't see it myself. We haven't the hands to run the farm as it is, without starting on new crops we know nothing about.'

'Ah,' Farrington said. 'Maybe I could be of use to you there. There'll be compulsory call-up soon, you take my word for it. From that register of theirs. Now, there's plenty would be glad to give their occupation as "agricultural" – and pay a premium for the privilege.'

'That's dishonest,' Merran said.

Farrington looked shocked. 'Dishonest, Master Jago? Nothing dishonest in that. They want the farm-work, you need the workers. And the Government needs to feed the fighters. Everybody's happy. And if a little money changes hands, well – that's only an arrangement fee. An apprenticeship, you might say.'

'You'll have to talk to Pa about it,' Merran said, turning back to his walling. 'Tomorrow, perhaps. He's in Penzance today.'

'I'll do that,' Farrington said, and he did. Merran took Michael in to the station next morning, with the cart, and when he came back Farrington was closeted with Pa in the sitting-room.

That was the week, Merran realised afterwards, that the War really came to Nanzeal.

PART TWO: 1916

Chapter Seven

Christmas had come and gone. A strange Christmas. Lizzie spent the day at Little Manor.

There was a present – cigarettes or chocolates – for every man, and the Ladies' League came with handmade 'comforts', embroidered bookmarks, or warm mittens and scarves. Some were expertly made though Lizzie saw one pair of socks which would have fitted the Giant of Newlyn. But people were very good, they sent down hams and figgy pudding, and there were no end of concerts and 'entertainments'. The chapel choir sang carols in the wards and the Guise players did a show. Lots of up-country officers didn't know what the 'geese' players were, but they laughed as loud as anyone at their antics – especially the doctor and the apothecary.

But there was still nursing to be done and the beds to make, and one poor fellow even slipped away on Boxing morning. Lizzie was up at the hospital twice in Christmas week. Mam complained – too busy in the shop, she said – but Millie was home now to give a hand and in any case there wasn't the usual trade. You couldn't get the beasts. Not just the usual winter shortage, this year the Army had bought up what meat there was (boiling the life out of it, and sticking it in tins, Gramps said) and good beet was harder to find than Methodists in a brewery.

'If this goes on,' Mam grumbled, as they sat down to their own feast dinner on Twelfth Night (a nice bit of pork, a gift for slaughtering Crowdie's pig), 'we shall have a thin time of it by spring.'

Lizzie knew what was coming. Worries about money these days always fetched up with Mam wondering out loud how long it would be before one of the girls 'got their feet under someone else's table' and went into service. If Mam ever insisted on that, there would be an end to Lizzie's hopes of ever amounting to anything. A year ago Mam wouldn't have dreamed of it – they were respectable 'trade' – but times were bad. Very bad indeed if money was the subject of dinner-time conversation. Lizzie held her breath.

Gan sensed her alarm. She said, as she helped herself to potatoes, swede turnip and apple-sauce, 'You could try branching out a bit,

Bess. James was thinking of trying his hand as a dairyman one time.'

That was clever. 'James' was Father, and Mam might consider his ideas. But she shook her head. 'Eggs, cheese and butter? Same problems there – every mortal bit is taken by the Army or one of these charities for the wounded. Still, we aren't about to starve yet, I daresay. It'll just be a question of tightening our belts and being a bit careful.'

Eddy, who had been just about to help himself to a little more potato, put down his fork and tried to pretend that he hadn't.

'Oh, I aren't meaning you, Eddy my lover,' Mam said. 'It's only, if one of the girls was to . . .'

Lizzie swallowed hard.

Suddenly Daisy put down her knife and fork. 'Well, one of the girls just might.' Everyone turned to look at her and she blushed. 'I've been meaning to say something, anyhow. Since Peter's come home my heart just isn't in the shop. The up and down of it is, Silas Farrington is starting a munitions factory, out Penvarris way, and they're looking for workers. Twelve shillings a week. I've a mind to go and put my name down.'

Mam gasped. 'You, go as a munitionette? You never would, surely?'

'Twelve shillings?' Penny looked up from mopping the last morsel of gravy with a crust-end. 'Aren't you ashamed to tell such whoppers, Daisy Treloweth?'

'Well, it is then. Be a bit less starting, of course, but that's what it'll be in a month or two. Handsome, I call it.'

Lizzie's mind was racing. A factory – that was even worse than going as a maid somewhere. She glared at Daisy, willing her to stop, but her sister raced on, spelling out all the advantages. 'There's to be a canteen for cheap meals, and all sorts. War Office contract, see, so they have to pay Union rates. Two shillings a shift.'

Gan nodded. 'Trade Office made him agree, I suppose, to get the contract. I thought it didn't sound like Silas Farrington. Get a free day too, I daresay?'

Daisy nodded. 'Won't be Sunday, though, more than likely. Keep the factory running, that's the idea. Three shifts a day, six days a week, staggered.'

'Working nights?' Mam frowned. 'I aren't sure I like that.'

'Why not?' Daisy said. 'They do up the hospital. But in any case, Mam, it's no good us sitting here waiting for things to happen. Me and Lizzie are on that workers' register, and Agnes will be before so long. They're taking women for busdrivers and all sorts. I'd sooner go and work for Silas Farrington, down Penvarris where I know, than be sent to London or someplace strange to work for somebody who might be a darn sight worse.'

'It won't come to that,' Mam said. 'I can't see the Government sending people where they don't want to go. Not in England.'

Gramps looked up from his last piece of crackling. 'Well, that's where you're wrong, Bess. You haven't heard the news. Cabinet has decided, it appears. I've said it was coming for months, ever since they made that register, and now it's come. Announced in the papers this morning.'

'What's come?' Lizzie demanded.

'Why, conscription,' Gramps said. 'No more volunteer soldiers. Every man over the age of eighteen has to go in the Army. So you want to go and work for Silas Farrington, Daisy my lover, you go. Before you're sent.'

And they could send me, too, Lizzie thought. Unless I can get to be a proper VAD. The thought was so upsetting that she could not eat her helping of baked apple, and Eddy had to eat it for her.

Tamsin Beswetherick was by no means happy either. Everything seemed to be happening on purpose to vex her. The weather for one thing – day after day of relentless drizzle.

To make matters worse, there was no carriage this morning. Papa had lent it to Katie Trevarnon for the day since her own carriage horse had gone lame. And of course the stable-boy had gone with it, to act as driver, so now there was not even the prospect of taking the donkey-cart, unless she was expected to harness the creature herself!

Just like the Army, she thought crossly, depriving people of horses and menservants, just when they were needed most. So here she was facing a long dreary walk to Little Manor in the cold and wet. It wasn't fair. She might have persuaded Papa to send down for a hansom cab, but Helena was preparing for that same walk with such sunny good-humour that it was quite impossible to make a fuss.

'Do not alarm yourself, Mama,' Helena was saying. 'We have our greatcoats, cap and gaiters, and I am quite certain we should be proof against wetter days than this. It is hardly raining at all now, and it is not above a mile. I am sure Tamsin and I can very well walk it, just for once. Can't we, Tamsin?'

And Tamsin was obliged to mutter, 'Of course,' and smile over her marmalade, but she went to her room afterwards in a gloomy sulk. 'Greatcoat, cap and gaiters,' she complained to the maid, who was helping her dress. 'I am sure Captain Scott himself was never so muffled up as this. I shall never be so pleased in my life as the day I can get married and suit myself, so I can put this wretched uniform aside.'

The girl finished arranging Tamsin's hair and settled the cap at a becoming angle. It was against the rules to wear it like this, rakishly, but Tamsin made no move to straighten it.

'Well, I think you look a picture, miss, and no mistake. That green suits you something handsome, much nicer than that old Red Cross blue Miss Helena has. But don't you worry, miss, I'll have the curling-irons on, soon as ever you come back, and you'll be a treat for sore eyes this evening by the time your cousin arrives.'

'My cousin?' Tamsin whirled around on the stool to stare at the girl. 'What do you mean, my cousin?'

The girl turned scarlet. 'I'm ever so sorry, miss, if I've spoken out of turn, but it's all the talk downstairs. The master got a telegram, yesterday. Due to arrive for dinner, so Cook says. Always supposing his leave is not cancelled.'

It was Tamsin's turn to blush. She fairly stormed down the stairs and into the breakfast-room, where her parents were still sitting over the early papers. Mama looked up mildly as she came in.

'My dear Tamsin, whatever is the matter?'

'Am I to learn from the servants, in future, when we are to entertain guests? I understand Ashton is expected. The whole house is abuzz with it, but no one cares to trust me with the information.'

She saw her parents exchange a glance.

'It is quite true, Tamsin,' her father said at last. 'We have received a telegram, and he hopes to be here this evening. But it is not the first time that he has planned such a visit . . .'

'No,' Tamsin burst out, 'he was hoping to spare us a day or two before Christmas. But it was cancelled.'

'Precisely,' her father said. 'There was a sudden break in the weather, and they were able to recommence training. But you were so cast down that we thought it best, this time, to leave you in ignorance until it was quite secure. The Flying Corps is more than usually dependent upon climate. You cannot fly an aeroplane in wind and rain.'

'So I suppose if the sun comes out for five minutes together it will prevent his coming again?'

She meant to be ironic, but her father said soberly, 'I should think it quite probable. They are desperately short of young pilots at the front, and now he has completed his training, no doubt they will order him to France.' He glanced towards the window, and at the bare trees dripping dismally in the garden. 'However, if the weather here is anything to go by, I should think we might quite safely expect to see him this evening. He has already been to see his mother I understand.'

Tamsin had a hundred questions to ask, but she was interrupted by Helena, in the famous greatcoat and cap, putting her head around the door. 'My dear Tamsin, we must hurry. We are due on duty for ten o'clock and it is half past nine already.' So there was nothing for it but to brave the damp and go. At least, she consoled herself, they were on late duty this month. Walking to Little Manor in the chilly dark of six o'clock would have been beyond human endurance.

Still, the knowledge that Ashton was expected took some of the gloom from the morning, and the round of beds and bedpans did not seem quite as hateful as usual. She was acutely aware, though, of how red and swollen her fingers had become, and how her feet and ankles ached. Hardly the coquettish picture she wanted to create.

She said as much to Rosa Warren when, in a snatched half-hour, they were eating their sorry 'luncheon' of bread and cheese. 'Rosa, what am I to do? He is to come tonight, the last time before he goes abroad, and I shall look a perfect fright.'

Rosa gave her a cheerful grin, 'I daresay he will be enchanted to see you, however you look.'

Tamsin sighed. 'But I shall not be finished until six, and when I get home there is scarcely time to dress for dinner. Besides, I am so tired these evenings, I am half-yawning over the soup, and ready to drop asleep before we reach the cheeses. And this is part-time. I don't know how Helena manages.'

'Does she still talk of working abroad?'

'She has her name down,' Tamsin said crossly. She did not want to talk about Helena. 'But this does not answer my problem, Rosa. What am I to do about Ashton?'

'Why, do as you always do. Speak to him charmingly. And if you are a little tired, I am sure he will think the more of you, because you are serving your country.'

73

'Serving my country!' Tamsin retorted. 'What help is it to England to have me running around like a scullery maid? I wish I had never started, but I cannot withdraw now – Papa will say I am flighty. But I tell you this. I mean to marry Ashton if I can—' She broke off as the door burst open. Lizzie Treloweth stood there, a thermometer in her hand.

'I'm sorry Miss Beswetherick,' the girl said. 'Only Mrs Rouncewell sent me to find you. It's time to do Mr Jago's legs.'

Tamsin got to her feet with a sigh. Peter Jago was always a problem. He seemed to have no idea of taking his weight on his arms while you strapped on the harness, so even if there were two of you, it took all of your strength to lift him. And he was not like the other men, either. Most of them were stoically uncomplaining, but Peter Jago got impatient and railed at everything, the heavy harness, the chafed patches on his stumps, and his own inability to help himself. He would not *be* helped, either, so that his attempts at walking usually ended with Jago lying helplessly on the floor and the nurses struggling to hoist him up again. And he was so heavy! Sometimes Tamsin could have stamped with frustration.

This afternoon was no exception. Jago took perhaps four lumbering steps before he stumbled and fell. Lizzie Treloweth was there to help, and she was as strong as a horse, but it took ages before they had him, panting, in a chair.

Then Mrs Rouncewell came striding down the ward. 'Stout effort, Mr Jago. Keep at it, that's the ticket. Help him up, gels.' And the whole performance had to be repeated.

Mercifully, Nurse Blight came in to announce that Mr Jago had a visitor, and Tamsin was able to lower him into his wickerwork cart-chair, and take off his legs.

'There now Lieutenant Jago,' she said, tucking a blanket around him with a silent sigh of relief. 'Get your family to give you a little push around.'

'Like a baby in a pram,' Jago muttered.

'Some big baby,' said a pleasant voice. 'Miss Beswetherick. And you, Lizzie. How nice to see you both here.'

Tamsin looked up. It was that nice Jago boy from the bandaging classes. Looking very handsome too, in his uniform. Lizzie Treloweth seemed to think so. She had gone a deep, embarrassed pink with pleasure.

Tamsin did not like to be outdone, especially by a butcher's daughter. She summoned her most charming smile. 'Ah, it is my very gallant knight. Home safe, I see.'

Michael Jago laughed ruefully, but she could see that he was flattered. 'Too safe, perhaps. Stuck in a training camp, while other men fight my wars for me. I keep writing to every regiment I can think of, but it has done no good as yet.'

His brother struggled upright against his cushions. 'Don't you be so anxious, Mike my son. Want to end up like me, do you? You stay in your training camp and be thankful. It isn't the picnic it's cracked up to be, out there in France.'

Then the other brother, Merran, came to join them and Tamsin slipped gratefully away to spend the rest of the afternoon writing letters for the men. But Peter Jago's words alarmed her. Ashton – good-looking, eligible Ashton – would be in France before long. 'Want to end up like me, do you?' It could happen to him, or worse. And where would she ever find a husband then? Something, definitely, would have to be done.

Lizzie was heartily grateful for Merran's arrival. It forced Mike to tear his eyes away from Tamsin Beswetherick for one thing, and for another, conversation could get back to something like normal again. Michael's sudden appearance had left her mumbling with embarrassment as usual.

It was months since she had seen him. He had been to the hospital, once, when Peter was first admitted, and again just before Christmas, but Lizzie had not been on duty either time. She had all his news, of course, from Merran, who came in regularly. More news, perhaps, than she would have had from Michael himself, because Merran was easy to talk to. Mrs Rouncewell had spoken to her sharply once or twice for 'gossiping' on duty.

But now Michael was here himself and she was as tongue-tied as ever. It was maddening to watch Tamsin Beswetherick chatting to him, so easy-like, and to see him grin with pleasure at her attentions. For two pins, Lizzie thought, she would tell him about Tamsin's plans to 'marry Ashton'. But of course, she did nothing of the kind, only stood by silent and embarrassed until it was time for him to go, and then spent the next hour thinking of a hundred witty things she might have said.

So it was a complete surprise to her when she ended her shift, to find Michael Jago waiting for her in the hospital porch. It was still raining, and as she came into view, he came towards her and opened an umbrella.

'Lizzie? Or should I say Nurse Treloweth? You look such a woman all of a sudden.'

Lizzie felt the back of her neck turn a dull brick red, but she managed to say, 'Not really Nurse Treloweth. Though sometimes patients call me that.'

'Oh.' He seemed to hesitate. 'I wanted to ask you, about Peter. Is he . . . will he get better? It seems to be taking an unconscionably long time.'

It was disappointing, perhaps, that he only wanted her professional opinion, but secretly Lizzie was rather grateful. On this subject, at least, she could find something sensible to say. 'It will take time. The stumps have to become accustomed to the harness, and the chafing can be dreadful. But his left leg is progressing nicely.' That sounded efficient, like Mrs Rouncewell talking to the doctor.

Mike looked at her, lifting the umbrella so the rain dripped from the points of it, and ran down the brown cloth of his army coat. 'Little Lizzie. What dreadful things you have seen.' His voice was unexpectedly warm. 'Merran says you have been good to Peter. His favourite nurse, he says.'

Lizzie felt embarrassment flooding back. 'Doing my job, that's all.'

He smiled at her, that slow smile that always sent her heart spinning. 'Well, I shall be happier to know that *you* are doing it. I worry about him, you know – being so far away. Merran writes when he can, but . . .'

Some demon impulse prompted her to say, 'I could write to you, Michael, if you like.' And then, overcome with the enormity of what she had done, she rushed on, 'Just to tell you how he is doing, that's all.' Why not, she asked herself fiercely. Young women were putting advertisements in the paper, offering to write to unknown soldiers. Why shouldn't she write to Michael, whom she knew?

He grasped her hand with his own wet one. 'Would you do that? Write to me with the news? I should like that.'

She was already regretting the impulse. 'There may not be much to tell.'

'Tell me everything. All about that terrible Mrs Rouncewell and her parrot. Rouncewell, indeed! "Bounce-well" I should call her.'

Lizzie laughed, delightedly.

'And the other nurses. Tamsin Beswetherick, for instance.'

76

Lizzie felt the laugh die on her lips. She was tempted to tell him, 'Hoping to marry her cousin, she is, soon as ever she can persuade him. I heard her say so this very day.' But she didn't say it – no point in upsetting Mike when he was going away. If Tamsin succeeded he would find out soon enough.

Instead she managed a smile, and said with a pretence at lightness, 'Ah, but you must promise to tell me your news too. How are your family?'

And they talked of other things. But he told her how to direct the envelope, and the next week, very daring, she did write to him. By that time she had news to report.

Chapter Eight

It had been difficult saying goodbye to Mater, and Ashton was relieved to find himself back at Gulveylor again. Gilbert Beswetherick was flatteringly interested in his stories about flying, while Aunt Winifred exclaimed over the uniform – the double-breasted brown tunic, the Sam Browne belt and the cap with the RFC emblem. Even Helena was impressd. Altogether they made him feel quite 'the thing'.

As for Tamsin, she didn't seem able to take her eyes off him.

'How daring you are. And do you do these "loops" we are hearing so much of?'

Ashton looked at her for a moment. He had 'got his ticket' and his commission. His Majesty had appointed 'our Trusty and Well-beloved Ashton Masters' to the rank of Second Lieutenant and he sported the coveted 'wings' on his flying jacket. But he was only a beginner. Fourteen hours in the air, dual and solo. 'Looping' – that was for the real fliers.

But he didn't say that to Tamsin. 'Oh,' he said, as casually as he could, 'it is not all it is made out to be. You need a good aeroplane, like the FE2. Take her up to a hundred, cut off your engine at the top, spot of right rudder to counteract the pull, and there you are.' He knew that much, the mechanics of the loop were the constant topic of conversation in the mess.

'A hundred miles an hour?' Tamsin said. 'Why, I should think the wings would fall off!'

It was not as foolish as it sounded. There had been pilots who had dived too steeply, so the wings of the aircraft folded back and deposited them abruptly, in a twisted mass of timber and fabric. Or dipped a wing, and spun – and once you did that it was a near-certainty that you'd never get out of it. Not all casualties in the RFC were caused by enemy action.

He thought back to his first solo landing. A moment of panic, and then with a bounce and a rumble he was down. Proudly out of the cockpit.

'All right then?' nonchalantly to the mechanic as he handed the aircraft over.

And the man saying glumly, 'Yes. Amazing what they'll take, these old machines.' It had taught him humility, at least in the aircraft sheds.

But there was no need for humility here. He flashed Tamsin a warm smile. 'I'm careful.'

She frowned charmingly. 'I cannot bear to think of you going back to such danger. And so soon.'

It was soon. He had only two days' leave, and tomorrow he was obliged to go and see Mater's agent at Fowey about letting the house there. It was a tedious journey, by train, and it was late by the time he returned to Gulveylor. The family had retired for the night. That did not surprise him. The Beswethericks kept early hours now the girls were required at Little Manor in the morning.

He had hot milk and sandwiches brought up, and some extra coals, and then dismissed the maid. He would sit and read for a little – Sir Gilbert had suggested at breakfast that he might borrow a book from the library. He took his nightlight and went downstairs.

Tamsin was in the library. She was sitting in the firelight, in one of the deep leather chairs, waiting for him.

'I hoped you might come. Mama said that you were going to borrow a book.'

He looked at her with something like panic. This was comprom-ising. She should not be here. Being with a young lady in public was one thing, but this – cloistered alone in a darkened room when everyone else was abed – that was quite another. He had never, in all his life, been alone with a young woman in private. Servant girls, perhaps, though he was far too much of a gentleman to do more than flirt, even then. But not a young lady of his own class. He was aware of his heart thumping and his mouth was dry.

She had done it on purpose – that was obvious. She was still wearing the dress that she must have worn at dinner, a deep blue silk that flattered her shoulders and neck. He was uncomfortably aware of the whiteness of that perfumed skin. He dragged his eyes back to her face. 'Cousin', he stammered, ' . . . surely . . . ?' His mouth was so dry with desire that he could scarcely form the words.

She smiled up at him. 'You must not be vexed, Ashton. I sent the girl away. Only, I could not bear that you should leave tomorrow and that I should not see you even for a moment, alone.'

She was as good as inviting him to kiss her. He wanted to – God how he wanted to. He burned with the fierceness of it, but convention held him back.

'Do not be angry with me Ashton. I have waited so late to see you. In the morning I must go to that hateful hospital again. It makes me so weary. And see what it does to my hands.'

She stretched out an arm to him.

He should not have taken it. Should not have kissed the little roughened fingers. But he did, and once he had done so, he was lost. He sat down, close beside her in the flickering firelight, breathless with excitement and desire. Her next action made him moan aloud.

She took his hand and laid it against her breast. He sat there, stupidly inept, almost afraid that his tingling fingers would burst into flame.

He knew he should draw back. This was a trap, a snare, but he could no more have resisted it than he could have quenched the fire in his loins with a sip of water. He sat transfixed, feeling the warmth of her through the flimsy fabric, with the blood swelling in his veins. And then she leaned towards him, presenting her lips to be kissed, and he succumbed to the moment entirely.

He knelt over her, grasped her to him and kissed her, urgently.

'Ashton!' She sounded breathless.

He drew back then, recollecting himself. What was he doing? He was a fool.

'Oh, Ashton!' She twined herself around him again, pressing her body to his. He could feel the curve of her breasts thrusting against him. It was too much. He kissed her hungrily, his hands moving the bodice-straps aside to reveal even more of her white shoulders, his lips buried in the giddy, sweet white softness of her flesh.

'Ahem!' Sir Gilbert was in the library. 'What,' he growled, like a creature from a melodrama, 'is the meaning of this, sir?'

There was a terrible silence. Ashton glimpsed a dishonourable future – Tamsin compromised, himself sent back to London in disgrace. There was only one thing to be done. He did it.

He scrambled to his feet. 'I wonder. Would you have any objection, sir, to my offering for your daughter?'

Beswetherick coughed. 'I see. Well. That puts a different complexion on it.' He looked at Tamsin, who was readjusting her shoulders. 'It seems I had better give my consent. But be good enough to reserve your enthusiasm, in future, until *after* the marriage.' The suspicion of a smile flickered at the corner of his mouth. 'Well, my boy, I imagine this calls for a toast.'

He rang the bell, sent for Winifred and Helena and the deed was done.

Ashton could hardly sleep that night. Excitement, anticipation and doubt kept him tossing on the pillow. He had enough to think of, going overseas. He had not intended to tie himself to anyone. But Tamsin had raised such fires in him – and it was an excellent match. Mater would be delighted.

Next day he wired her with the news, and took the early train back to camp. They were forming up a squadron to go to France.

Miss Beswetherick's engagement was all the talk at Little Manor for days. When Lizzie went up on Wednesday, Nurse Blight told her all about it.

'Sent her a diamond as big as a cherry-stone, he has. His mother's ring apparently. She's coming down Friday to show us, and then she's giving up the hospital work. Going to join the Sewing League, so she says, now she's to be married, and probably get up a few stunts to raise money for the hospital. Mind, it's my belief she couldn't wait to get out of nursing. Not like that sister of hers – had her VAD inoculations yesterday and going abroad any day.'

But then Mrs Rouncewell arrived, and Lizzie was sent off to administer steam inhalations to an officer with bronchitis, so that was the end of the conversation. But secretly, Lizzie was delighted. She could hardly wait to get home and write to Michael with the news. If Tamsin was spoken for, she thought, perhaps Mike would stop dreaming and look a bit closer to home.

There was other news too. Lizzie poured it all out to him. How Daisy had put her name down for this factory of Farrington's. 'Starting in a week or two, making pieces for aeroplanes,' Lizzie wrote, 'though what Daisy knows about aeroplanes could be written on a postage stamp. Dot has gone to school. Millie is helping in the shop now, and the four of us – me, Daisy, Agnes and now Millie – seem to be for ever under one another's feet.'

She put down her pen and sighed. It was true. There simply wasn't work for them all. Meat was getting so scarce. In London they had whale-meat to fill the shortage, 'snoek' they called it, but it was whale-meat all the same. Treloweth's hadn't come to that yet, but it was really just as well that Daisy was going to her factory. It was only a matter of time before someone suggested that Lizzie went there too. She didn't want to go.

If only, only, only, she could find some way to be a VAD. But she was still months short of eighteen, and she still couldn't afford even the Little Manor uniform. Mrs Rouncewell had looked out a cap and skirt for her, but she still wore her sheeting apron, and although she had her two shillings a week there was no chance of increasing that. She was lucky to be paid at all. Unless, she thought suddenly, Tamsin Beswetherick might help. After all, she wouldn't be needing her uniform again.

She sent off the letter, but the idea stayed with her. She mentioned it to Merran a week or two later when he came to visit Peter.

'D'you think she might?'

'Give it to you? I don't know. I could speak to her father about it if you like. I've got to see him about some more ploughing he wants done. Or ask Michael to do it, next time he's home, since Tamsin's so all-fire charming whenever he's about.'

It was just how Lizzie felt herself, and she flushed guiltily.

Merran grinned at her. 'I'm sorry, Lizzie. I didn't mean to be beastly. I know how you feel about Michael. But she makes me sick, the way she carries on, and he's too foolish to see it. Still, he's writing to you now, he says.'

Lizzie nodded. Mike's reply to her letter had astounded her. It was a real letter, straight from the heart, pouring out his disappointment and misery at Tamsin's engagement, and finishing with the touching notion that Tamsin was 'doing her duty' rather bravely against her will. Lizzie had written back immediately, a warm, comforting, supportive letter – and received an equally immediate, grateful answer. It was ironic, but on paper she was closer to Mike Jago than she had ever been in person.

'Yes,' she said. 'We've written once or twice.'

Merran smiled gravely. 'He said you were quite friends these days. That's something any rate. And I don't set out to be poor-tempered, it's just . . . well, things are difficult, home. Short of hands now, of course, and with Pa's troubles . . .'

Lizzie nodded. She knew about that.

It had started at Christmas. Pa Jago had been obliged after all to submit to the doctor and the chloroform and have his fingers sawn off on the kitchen table. He had mended well afterwards, and was back to something like his old health and strength. But his personality had changed. Like as if, Merran said, when they took his hand they had removed part of his manhood with it, and he had to shout and stamp to keep up his self-esteem.

'What with Peter's legs,' Merran said. 'Pa seems to think the whole family is being whittled away, joint by joint. And it will be difficult on the farm. I don't know however we shall manage. We've got a new man, but he's useless. We'll have to get one of these land-girls, I expect. Never thought of that, I suppose, Lizzie? Might suit you – you were always good with animals. Fair pay, too, and your keep – and they are running proper courses for it now.'

She could not help grinning. 'You just want me up Nanzeal, running around after you,' she said cheerfully. 'I know what you're like, Merran Jago.'

'Well,' he said, 'it's worth a thought. Fresh air and sunshine. Better than up that factory with Daisy.'

Merran was always like that, understanding her feelings without her saying a word. She was grateful, but she kept her tone teasing. 'Sunshine!' she began, nodding past him at the damp drizzle clouding the windows. 'It's . . .'

'Miss Treloweth!' Mrs Rouncewell pounced. 'Are you to stand there gossiping all day? Albert has escaped and is making a mess in the library.'

'Yes, Mrs Rouncewell,' Lizzie said, and went to capture the parrot in a towel. But working at Nanzeal sounded oddly attractive, all the same.

Nanzeal, though, was not the place it had been.

Merran came in through the dairy and shut the kitchen door to keep out the creeping damp of February. He glanced across the hallway towards the door of the parlour. It was closed but his mother's raised voice could be distinctly heard.

'I warn you, Luke, I don't like it. I've said it before and I'll say it again. That man is a waste of the good fresh air he breathes.'

Merran paused, trying not to be heard. He hated these arguments.

'Hasn't done an honest day's turn since the day he got here – and now you're talking of taking another. Want your head read you do Luke Jago, and that's a fact!'

Merran took off his coat and jacket and hung them in front of the range to dry. They were as wet with mist and drizzle as if he had walked home in a rainstorm, though he had only been out to see to the pigs. From the parlour he heard Pa's voice, muttering something in reply.

Mother laughed, a mocking sound with no mirth in it. 'Your famous Silas Farrington. He'll be the ruin of us, see if he isn't. Couldn't tell the front end of a cow from a pile of bricks, and here he is telling you how to run the farm. Sugar-beet and asparagus! Out here! That man couldn't sprout beans in a bucket of water. What does he know? Potatoes, swede, broccoli – a few parsnips and runner-beans. That's what we want, not all these fancy crops.'

'There's money in it,' Pa said, dangerously subdued.

'There's ruination in it. Well, I won't stand silent and see it happen, Luke, and that's for certain. Silas Farrington can go to perdition if he's a mind to – and a good riddance – but he won't take Nanzeal with him, if I can help it. If Farrington's so keen to have this fellow, why doesn't he give him a job in this new factory of his, instead of sending him here where he's less use than a pig-killer in a china shop. If Farrington doesn't want him, I'm sure I don't.'

Silence. Then the sound Merran had been half waiting for. The thump of Pa's fist on the table and Pa's voice, hoarse with anger. 'You'll do as I say, woman. I say we shall take Farrington's man, and we will, so there's an end on it. I may have only half a hand, but I'm master in my own house yet, and don't you forget it.'

'But . . .'

'Don't "but" me!' There was a crash, and the sound of shattering glass. Merran could guess what that was – his parents' wedding photograph, knocked flying from its stand. Pa roared, madder than ever, 'Now look what you've made me do!' and stamped away.

This was no moment to be caught loitering. Merran took the stairs two at a time, and was on the landing before the parlour door flew open.

'We'll grow whatever I say we'll grow and no argument!'

Slam! The door thudded behind him. Merran went to his bedroom thoughtfully. It was true what he had said to Lizzie. These 'scenes' were becoming more and more common.

Mother was right. Pa could storm all he liked, but everyone could see where the real problem lay – with this man of Farrington's who had arrived shortly before the New Year.

He was called Tom Liddel, and he was well-named. Everything about him was 'Liddel' – small and pinched, from the thin anxious face to the sloping apologetic shoulders. Merran could see him now, through the window, down in the yard getting hay for the animals. The rick was almost finished, so the hay did not need cutting from the stack, but even now, prodding at the remains of it with a pitchfork, there was something helpless and ineffectual about Liddel. He was standing hunched against the damp, holding the fork as if each stalk of hay was individually conspiring to slip deliberately through the tines.

Merran sighed, took off his shirt and began to wash in the pitcher of cold water on the washstand.

It was difficult to be angry with Liddel. That was part of the trouble. The man was always working – as now – with an air of desperate application. And always, as now, he accomplished in two hours what the veriest baby could have managed in ten minutes.

Merran towelled himself dry, and glanced back towards the courtyard. A little, not much, of the hay had found its way into the wheel-barrow, and Liddel was shambling off with it towards the stable. Merran shook his head. The man was hopeless. Even Peter, with his poor useless stumps, could have sat in a chair and shifted more hay than that in half the time.

Oddly, the thought cheered him. Not many weeks now and Peter *would* be coming home, in good earnest. A few tasks would make him feel useful. He could weed, perhaps, help with the butter-making, bunch the carrots for market. Woman's work, mostly, but it would free Mother to give a hand with other things.

If only it were possible for Peter to take over. It was absurd. A year ago, when he could have enlisted, Merran had been passionately against the War. Now, when he burned with an icy fury and yearned to go, he couldn't. 'Essential work' the exemption panel would say, and as long as Pa was injured and Liddel useless, he was needed here.

Liddel! Everything came back to him. Because, somehow he was no ordinary farm-hand. It appeared impossible to get rid of him.

They hadn't wanted to, first. Everyone had been tolerant. Liddel was a townsman after all, assistant in a gentleman's outfitters, and he had to learn. It had been comic almost, watching a grown man scampering across the farmyard with the gander after him, or struggling to budge the cover from the well, which Merran could lift easily, one-handed.

'He'll learn,' Pa had said, and laughed till the tears ran at the sight of Liddel dancing around the paddock with the harness while Hercules eyed him disdainfully, always a hand's-breadth out of reach.

But Liddel didn't learn. Days lengthened to weeks, and he was more useless than ever. Pa spoke to Silas Farrington about it. And then the troubles really began.

Liddel didn't leave. Pa locked himself into the parlour with Farrington and emerged an hour later red-faced and furious.

'A contract, Mr Jago,' Merran heard Farrington say, as he left. 'And I shall hold you to that. Good day.'

Chapter Nine

Father was coming home. Wounded.

'Only a flesh wound,' Mam said. 'Shrapnel in his arm.'

Lizzie, who had some idea what a shrapnel wound could look like, was less comforted by that, but Father's letter was extremely cheerful. In his own handwriting too, which was a good sign.

They were all shocked when they heard. Mam, like Lizzie, worried about Father all the time anyway, but mostly she could console herself that he wasn't near the front line. Father was in the catering corps – naturally, if you came to think about it – and spent his time doing in uniform what he used to do in the shop, usually near Command Headquarters a long way from the fighting. But even that wasn't safe now, with the new long-range guns and aeroplanes the Germans had. It was a bomb had wounded Father, and killed three horses too.

He was to be home for a fortnight, His first 'Blighty leave' since the War began. Mam came all over skittish. Went out buying scented soap and curl-papers, and titivated up the place with bunches of snowdrops. When the day came, she was like a raindrop on a griddle-iron, all a-hop, and everyone was quite glad when she set off at last down to meet the train.

Lizzie was quite shocked at the change in Father. She remembered him that day in the arrish fields – a smiling, roundish man, with a twinkle. Now, he seemed thinner, almost wiry, and shorter too. That worried Lizzie, until she remembered that she herself had grown an inch or more in the last year. But he had lost weight, and – though he joked and said it was a pity he hadn't lost a bit more, then, so the Germans would have had less to aim at – you could see that he had changed. Some of the twinkle had gone out of him.

He spent the first few days staring into the fire, and all Mam's chatter and Gan's cooking couldn't rouse him out of it. Any loud noise though, disturbed him something terrible. Eddy dropped an empty bucket, and Father leapt out of his chair with a roar you could have heard in Mousehole. Lizzie had seen men like that before, up at Little Manor, but it was sad all the same. At least the wound in his arm was healing nicely – although Mam paled when she saw it.

Lizzie put a bandage on it – it was scarcely needed, but it seemed to please Father. 'Some good little nurse you are, Liz,' he said to her, more than once, and even told her stories about life in the Army – nothing terrible, but he shut up instantly if anyone else came in.

Gradually, as the days passed, she could see the tension draining out of him and Mam began to look happier again. Only two things upset him now: Dot (who didn't recognise him at all, and buried her head in Gan's dress every time he spoke), and 'the state of the shop' as he said. He was inclined to blame Eddy and Gramps for that, but it wasn't their fault and he knew it, really. It was just that he wasn't used to seeing the cold-room half-empty and bare hooks at the window.

Then he was passed 'fit for service' and it was time for him to go to France again.

In many ways, it was worse than the first time. Father had his wound-stripe up on his uniform, proud as punch, but the strain was back on his face before he even reached the station. No end of customers had heard he was home, and came to say goodbye and shake his hand, which was as well, because otherwise Mam would have broken down completely.

'Waste of a good butcher,' someone shouted. 'Sending him out to kill meat when he could be butchering Germans.' So Father departed on a laugh – but the place seemed doubly empty afterwards.

There was a woman ticket-collector at the station when Father went. 'Directed' from the register, she said, and Lizzie began to worry about her own position. While Father was home, nothing else had seemed important, but suddenly she realised that it was urgent. Silas Farrington had put in a request to the Trade Office for more 'war workers' and it was only a matter of time before people got 'directed' to him.

One thing Lizzie was quite determined on. Twelve shillings a week or no twelve shillings a week, she didn't want to be up at Penvarris at that factory. She needed that uniform.

But what could she do? She could hardly barge up to Miss Beswetherick and ask her, just like that, if she would consider selling it. And you could hardly expect Miss Beswetherick to think of it for herself. In the end, at Merran's suggestion, she plucked up her courage and spoke to Mrs Rouncewell about it.

To her surprise, Mrs Rouncewell was very sympathetic. She sat down and spoke to her very kindly. But what she said was hardly encouraging. 'Of course, gel, I will gladly put in a word to Miss Beswetherick, but I don't want to encourage you in false hopes. You are not yet eighteen, are you.'

'June,' Lizzie supplied. 'Three months' time. You think the War will be over by then?'

Matron smiled sadly. 'I fear that the need for nurses will be greater than ever. But, this is only an auxiliary hospital. Our sponsors are very good, they pay the wages of the professional nurses, but everything else is voluntary effort. Even the doctor gives his services free! Everyone does.'

Except me, Lizzie thought to herself. She had never realised quite how privileged she was. She shook her head slowly. 'Well, it's no good then. Mam could never afford to keep me if I was bringing nothing in, not with trade how it is. Mam's right. I'll have to go out to the factory with Daisy.'

She must have sounded forlorn, because Mrs Rouncewell frowned. 'Don't do anything in a hurry, Lizzie. If you could get a job in town, and come to us in the evenings I daresay we could keep on with the arrangement as it is. I should be sorry to lose you.'

Lizzie murmured, 'Thank you, ma'am,' but she came away wishing that she had never started the conversation. Better to have a hope, however foolish, than to be left with no hope at all.

Day after day set in with leaden skies. Flying in these conditions was impossible, and even when the weather cleared it was only for an hour or two and it was difficult for the machines to get in and out.

One squadron had already gone. Ashton watched them out, his heart lifting with the aeroplanes as they rose into the air, swaying a little as the wind took them, and growing smaller and smaller, little double-winged birds, insects, dots, until they disappeared altogether into the vastness of the sky.

Gone to what? Battle? Glory? Death? It was a stirring thought. It made him resent being stuck here, everlastingly waiting. He turned away with a sigh.

'Sounds mournful, old son, what's the trouble then?' Paddy Lowe, one of the senior pilots, fell into step beside him.

Ashton contrived the air of world-weariness which was expected of him. 'Hoped to be away with that show. Turn will come, I suppose.'

Paddy looked at him. 'How many hours have you got up? Nineteen? Twenty?'

'Near enough.' In fact the count was sixteen.

'It's murder, that's what it is, sending you fellows out there with so little flying. Well, you've got a reprieve. Get up there, every minute you can. Fly until you can fly in your sleep. When you've got fifty, sixty hours up you'll be something like useful. Until then, you're nothing but a danger to yourself, and a likely waste of good machinery.' Ashton must have looked aghast, because Paddy went on, 'Not you, particularly, Masters. You've the makings of a decent pilot, from what I've seen of you. Come on in, and I'll buy you a drink.'

They went together into the bar. Paddy pushed the whisky towards him. 'Here you are. One of the advantages of service life. If this was a civilian bar, I could be prosecuted for buying you this.'

Ashton grinned. 'And the King's turned teetotal for the length of the War.'

Paddy laughed. 'Well he can afford to, he doesn't have to fly a collection of struts and wires at an unsafe height over the buildings. Come on, down the hatch.'

Ashton lifted his glass. 'Happy landings.'

'I'll drink to that.' Paddy drained his glass. 'Tell me, Masters, Penzance, Penvarris, that's your neck of the woods isn't it?'

Ashton flushed. 'My mother has a house at Fowey – that's a fair few miles away.'

Paddy summoned another round of drinks. 'Oh come on, Masters. It's common knowledge you've got a woman hidden down there somewhere. All those scented letters.'

'My fiancée, yes.'

Paddy laughed. 'God, Masters, what an old woman you are. I don't give a damn if she's your fiancée or a pantomime horse. All I want to know is, would you fancy an opportunity to get down there for a day or two?'

Ashton frowned. 'Apply for leave, you mean?'

This time Paddy's laugh was a chuckle. 'Not exactly, old boy. All in the course of duty. That's the charm of it. Thing is, there's some new factory opening down there, making propeller bits, or some such thing. It seems the fellow wants to make a song and dance production of the opening, and the War Office agreed. Wanted the CO to go down there, shake a few hands – kiss a few babies, for all I know – and generally make himself agreeable. Represent the service, that sort of thing.'

'And?' Ashton could not see what that had to do with him.

'And the CO thinks the whole thing is a lot of rot. Couldn't refuse outright of course, with it coming from the top brass, but discovered a dozen pressing things he had to be doing on that day. But he promised someone. Asked me to sort it out.'

Ashton stared at him. 'Me?'

Paddy shrugged. 'Why not? Make a good morale story, if that's what they want. Local hero dependent on local industry – that sort of thing. And while you are about it, you can call in on your girl.'

'I'll write this evening.'

''Fraid not, old son. Frightfully hush-hush. Official photographers, and the pictures released to the press afterwards. Mustn't ruin his little surprise. Besides, think of her face if you turn up, unexpectedly.'

Ashton said nothing.

'So, you'll go?'

Ashton was wary. His few weeks in uniform had taught him not to volunteer for anything without weighing up the pitfalls. But for the life of him he couldn't see any problems with this one. Perhaps it was the whisky, but the whole thing sounded like a good idea.

'Don't want to miss my posting,' he said.

'No question of it.'

'Well,' Ashton nodded. 'I will then.'

'Good egg.' Paddy pushed another brimming glass towards him. 'Next weekend. You'll miss the bash here Saturday,' – Ashton suddenly understood why Paddy had not been keen to go himself – 'but I'm sure you can find your own amusements. Call in and collect your rail pass from the CO's office. And remember. Keep it to yourself, at least until the confounded factory is open. Cheers.'

Michael had more leave due. It was the only advantage, he wrote to Lizzie, of being in Training Command. He was managing one weekend pass after each six-week course.

Lizzie was anxious. Writing was easy. She had got into the habit, over these past weeks, of making her letters a sort of diary, and telling him all her hopes and fears. And he shared things with her, too. 'There was a time,' he wrote once, 'when Merran was the other half of me. Now I sometimes think that you are – that I can tell you anything, and you will understand.'

And he did tell her. About firing ranges, gas mask practice and dawn parades. About lumpy mattresses in the billets, and scrounging tea and scones on Sunday afternoons. About how he had begun reading poetry, and most of all, how he longed and feared to be posted abroad. 'I may get wounded, I know. But at least I shall have faced it. It makes a coward of me, when I am stuck here like a schoolmaster, sending other men to their fates.'

Lizzie read the letter with tears in her eyes. He was wrong about her understanding. She did not understand this at all.

And now he was coming home, and suddenly everything was threatened. He would be there, big and handsome in his brown uniform, and she would blush and be at a loss for words, as usual. She was closer to him, when he was away.

But there! He would be home on Saturday, and call at the Hospital to see Peter. And as it happened, she would be there, too. Two Volunteer Ladies had left suddenly – 'wanted at home' – and with the Beswethericks gone Little Manor was in danger of being understaffed. Lizzie had agreed to change her afternoon to help out. Mam had created, of course. She'd planned to go to Penvarris and see Daisy's factory opened, and she wanted Lizzie in the shop, but Gan and Agnes told her to go anyway. They'd manage.

Lizzie was worried about Mam. She wasn't herself these days. Whiter than suet some mornings, and off her food besides. Concerned about Father, probably – the trouble had only started since he came home. Lizzie mentioned it to Gan, but Gan just smiled and said, 'Well, we'll see' which didn't help anyone.

Altogether it was an anxious Lizzie Treloweth who went up to Little Manor on Saturday. She was almost late. Daisy had been fussing over her new uniform – brown with red collar and cuffs and a brown mob-cap affair pulled over her ears – and had spent so long preening herself in the speckled mirror over the washstand that Lizzie scarcely had time to rinse her face.

Mrs Rouncewell saw her scamper in. 'Miss Treloweth. Workers in this hospital do not gallop! Pull yourself together and walk with more decorum. I hope I shall not regret speaking to Miss Beswetherick about that uniform!'

Lizzie gaped.

'Well, come along, gel, don't stand there gawping like a goldfish. Nurse Blight is waiting for you to help her with the music-room ward.'

'Yes, Mrs Rouncewell.' And she hurried off, as quickly as she dared.

She was too busy, at first, to think about anything, even Michael and the uniform, but after her lunchbreak she found she could think of nothing else. Merran came in, and together they got Peter onto his feet – he could stagger across the ward now, with crutches, though he'd had a bad period when his stump got infected.

'You are doing well,' Merran said, though Peter only glowered in reply. 'I'll have to go now, Lizzie. I promised to go up and see the vet – ask him to come out to Hercules. Tell Michael if he comes up to Heamoor, I'll take him home from there in the cart. We've borrowed a horse from Crowdie.'

'How is Hercules?' Peter said, suddenly taking an interest. Lizzie could understand that. A shire was a valuable animal. Losing Hercules would be a real blow. And it must be serious, to call the vet. Cost more than doctors, they did – though some farmers would sooner call a vet to a calving than a doctor to a birth.

Merran shook his head. 'If he doesn't do better soon we'll have to think of buying another. Though what the price will be in this War, goodness knows. Anyway, if I go see the "vetinary" perhaps it won't come to that. Tell Mike for me.'

'Glad to,' Lizzie promised, and she was. She was able to tell Michael all about Hercules and the problems with the cart and before you knew it, they were chattering away quite cheerfully. It really wasn't very awkward at all.

Chapter Ten

Tamsin trotted the donkey-trap up the lane to Little Manor, feeling as sunny as the bright March afternoon. She was in a romantic mood. Everything delighted her, the shy faces of primroses among the grass, the deep green gloss of the camellias against the grey granite of the walls.

She had taken a trip to Truro yesterday with Mama, and they had seen the divinest little wedding outfit: the dress all crêpe de Chine and lace, and an elegant 'Russian' jacket trimmed with swansdown. 'Economy' cut, of course, with the new narrow skirt and higher hems, but Tamsin had no objection. The fashion flattered her figure, and afforded a tantalising glimpse of ankle, besides. She had been measured at once, for one just like it.

When the time came, she thought, she would be the envy of every bride in the duchy. Supposing that one could get enough sugar for the cake.

Not that she was in any hurry. She had a hazy notion that there was more to being married than changing your name: though she wasn't quite sure what, exactly. Helena had told her something once, but looking at her mother and father over the breakfast table – eating toast as if being married was the most reasonable thing in the world – Tamsin refused to believe it. Recently though, she had begun to have doubts. People gave you such arch looks when you spoke of your wedding-trip, and Helena was right about anatomy. Little Manor had shown her that! Helena's outrageous notion might turn out to be true after all. Tamsin enjoyed being kissed, even caressed, but she wasn't anxious to subject herself to . . . that!

Being married, then, was worrying. *Getting* married, however, was another thing. And as for being engaged, that was absolutely enchanting. Everyone was envious, and it made one feel so wonderfully important.

Like joining the Ladies' Linen League for the Hospital. That had turned out splendidly. Everyone had been perfectly charming: asked her advice, and deferred to her opinion on everything, because she had actually 'worked on the wards'. Tamsin had almost begun to feel that those hateful hours of scrubbing and fetching had been worthwhile after all.

And her uniform had caused a sensation. Most of the ladies wore uniform of sorts to the Linen League, because it was hospital work, but in the full green of the Little Manor Voluntary Helpers, with its starched collars and cuffs, Tamsin had quite eclipsed everyone. She hadn't been there a fortnight before they asked her to be liaison lady, to list what dressings the Hospital needed, and ensure that any linen for mending reached the circle in time for the weekly meeting.

It was very flattering. Just the kind of job she relished. She bought another tasselled notebook, and had been delightfully occupied with her lists and appointments ever since. All because of the uniform.

And now she had been asked to give it up. Mrs Rouncewell had asked her when she went up to deliver the dressings and collect a dozen pillow-slips for mending last week.

She had protested. 'But I need it myself!'

'Ah.' Matron had become quite deferential again now that Tamsin was no longer one of her 'gels'. 'In that case, of course . . . But if you did feel able to part with it you would be doing the girl, and the Hospital, a real service. She is willing to pay, but her notion of values is based on the sixpenny bazaar and the sum she has in mind will be quite trivial I imagine. But should you decide to sell it, or donate it, Miss Beswetherick, I for one should appreciate your beneficence.'

Beneficence. It was a fine word. It made her feel quite saintly. Some poor shop-girl, perhaps, or one of the local ladies' maids.

Beneficence.

On the other hand, the uniform did give her such an air. Well she would see. She had promised to consider it, that was all.

She bowled up to the gate, and a young officer stepped smartly aside to get out of the way of the trap. It was the young Jago boy from the bandaging classes. Handsome as ever in his officer's uniform.

He looked up and saw her. 'Miss Beswetherick.'

'Why it is my Sir Galahad!' she exclaimed. He looked quite flustered to see her. She smiled. 'Are you visiting the Hospital?'

He shook his head. 'I have just come from there. My brother . . .'

Oh dear! Bad form. She should have remembered that. 'Of course,' she said warmly. And then, to cover her awkwardness, she added, 'I'm going there myself. I am "Liaison Lady", you know, for the Linen League.'

'Yes, I heard that you'd left nursing. You are to be married I hear. I should congratulate you.'

He sounded so downcast that she had to smile. 'Thank you,' she said. And then on an impulse, 'The lane is muddy Mr . . . I should say *Lieutenant* Jago. Would you care for a lift somewhere? It is not above a step to the end of the lane and it is no trouble with the donkey.'

He was smiling himself now, gazing at her with such adoration that it gave her a little glow. 'I should be enchanted. But . . . perhaps . . . ?'

It would not be proper, he meant. He looked so forlorn there, gazing up at her. Almost – could it be? – with love. And who could blame him. She cut an attractive figure, she knew, in her neat blue costume – exactly the colour of bluebells – and the fetching little matching hat with the turned up brim. Poor boy, she felt almost sorry for him.

'Oh, pooh,' she said gaily, knowing that the little toss of her head was half coquettishness, 'Ashton would not care a fig. Besides, we are old friends are we not, you and I?' She stretched out one hand to help him aboard, aware of how delicate her fingers looked in the elegant blue kid-glove.

He seized the hand, kissed it as he had done before, and went on holding it. 'You are happy then, to be marrying this man?' He looked down at her fingers. 'He is wealthy, I suppose.'

'My cousin.' Poor boy. How unattainable she must seem to him, as far above him in life as she was in fact, looking down at him from her seat on the trap. She moved her hand, but he did not relinquish it and she did not insist. 'And you, Mr Jago, do you like the Army?'

'I do my duty.'

'And I mine.' It was prettily done. It hinted, regretfully, at the impossibility of a different world, in which Michael Jago was truly a gentleman, and not merely a wartime officer.

He seized her words as he had seized her hand. 'So, if things had been otherwise, you might perhaps . . .'

She looked into his eyes. Nice eyes. Dark, tender, burning. Burning! She remembered suddenly the things Helena had told her. Surely he wasn't thinking . . . ?

She felt the blush start at her ears and flush across her cheeks.

He had seen her colour, and misinterpreted. He was on the step of the cart in a moment, seizing both her hands, turning her towards him. 'You might?'

Tamsin fought down panic. She had not intended this. Supposing someone should come. How could she disengage?

Beneficence.

She withdrew her hands from him, slowly, and cupped them instead against his face. 'It is impossible,' she said. 'Impossible. You know it. Goodbye, sweet knight.' This was better. She was in control again. She thought for a moment of kissing his forehead in farewell, but instead she said again, 'Goodbye.' The melancholy of it misted her eyes.

There *was* somebody coming. A roar, a flurry of stones and a motor-cycle swerved to a halt. Ashton Masters, his face the colour of fury, looking from her to the man on the cart-step and back again. She dropped her hands.

There was a moment's silence. 'I intrude, I see.' Ashton lifted a hand in mock-salute and roared away down the lane again.

'Ashton!' He did not look back.

She turned to Michael Jago, furious, and pushed him with both hands from the step. 'Now see what you've done!'

She urged the donkey-cart into motion, but it was no match for a motor-bicycle. The lane was empty. Ashton had gone.

The motor-bicycle belonged to Silas Farrington. He had lent it to Ashton after the ceremony for a 'consideration', naming a sum which – together with the hire of the goggles and gloves – would probably have bought the wretched machine outright. Farrington had a sharp eye for a deal.

Take this factory for instance. It was in disused mine buildings, out towards Penvarris. The mine had been 'capped' years ago, when the tin-seam ran out: but the mine-buildings were still there, the forge and the tool-room – and in the carpenter's shop some of the old lathes and turning machines had been left rusting where they stood. Silas Farrington had turned the place into a factory. Not aircraft – they would have been expensive to transport – but little pieces for aircraft. Nuts and bolts and bearing cones for propellers, and there were plans for making tail planes soon.

Farrington had got hold of the equipment from somewhere, and it was all installed. The buildings had been swept and cleaned, windows and doors repaired. The old tin-shed had a new tarpaulin roof and, with the tin-tables removed, had become the 'canteen'. But Ashton felt, more care had been expended on repainting the gates and setting up the big notice 'Farrington Works' than on anything else. At the rear of the factory, behind a hastily constructed fence, there were rusting tramming carts, ore-kibbles and shovel handles, lying haphazard among the spoil-heaps and tumbled stones.

Still, the Home Office inspector – from the Factory Department –

seemed happy enough with what he saw. A new system, like Mr Ford had in America, he told Ashton enthusiastically. Each person doing one job and then passing it over, instead of one man doing the whole thing from start to finish.

In fact there were very few 'men' about at all. A few – to show the others what was what – but most of the workers were women. And although they looked very businesslike in their Ministry of Munitions overalls, it was clear to Ashton that most of them had never been near a drilling machine before. Farrington's boasted 'output' was not going to happen overnight.

Farrington seemed unperturbed, and so did the man from the Home Office. Ashton made a short speech and had his picture taken with two pretty young ladies each holding one of the 'pieces' which had been sent down as pattern. The man from London did not like that, for security reasons, and in the end a couple of carpenters knocked together a crate, and the young ladies and Ashton were photographed with that. At least, he thought, it was something really made in the factory that day.

Then Farrington was keen to show them the canteen, where the cook was boiling up huge quantities of fish in a cauldron for the first 'works meal'. Very cheap, Farrington explained, and stopped off the wages at the week's end. One girl, who was to act as 'tallyman' for the dinners, proudly wrote down their names as a sort of preliminary practice.

'Good show, didn't you think?' the Factory Department fellow said as they walked in a group to the gate.

'Ye-es,' Ashton said doubtfully. 'But it might be my life depending on those propellers one of these days. I hope the workmanship is up to it.'

The man looked at him oddly, as if Ashton had suggested a whole new view of things. 'Of course. Regular inspections anyway, but I'll bear that in mind. Good afternoon . . . and good flying. I won't forget.' And he shook Ashton's hand, and went off in the carriage with the Mayor.

Ashton paid Farrington the agreed sum and got onto the motor-cycle. It was a dreadful old affair, spluttering and heavy, and about as biddable as a bull in a stampede.

He got the hang of it at last and rattled his way to Gulveylor. Aunt Winifred was delighted to see him, and plied him with tea (although he had omitted to bring any sugar, as one was expected to do these days), and then pressed him to luncheon – a soufflé which made the dreadful 'works meal' seem more disgusting than ever. Tamsin, however, was not there.

'She went off this morning with the trap,' Aunt Winifred said. 'She was to lunch at Trevarnon, and call at the Hospital on her way home. I don't know, Ashton, what young ladies are coming to. I'm sure I never dreamed of driving a trap in all my life, and here Helena writes that she is learning to drive a motor-ambulance. Most unbecoming. But their father permits it, so what am I to do? I put it down to these Suffragists myself. Votes for women! They will be wanting to be Prime Minister next.'

Ashton laughed. 'It will never come to that, I'm sure! But young women are doing a good many strange things these days.' He told her about the factory.

Aunt Winifred sniffed. 'For girls of that sort, it is different. They have always worked at something. But a gently raised girl like Helena! And she is being taught by some young doctor. It all sounds exceedingly improper to me.'

Luncheon was finished and cleared, but still Tamsin did not come.

'It is a pity,' Ashton said. 'I hired the motor-cycle on purpose to see her. But I dare not miss my train. I have to be back at camp.'

'You might find her at Little Manor,' Aunt Winifred said, and the die was cast.

His first reaction when he rounded the corner, was one of disbelief. It couldn't be Tamsin. And, when he saw that indeed it was, he felt ridiculously embarrassed, as if it was he who had transgressed, by finding them together. He turned away.

He delivered the motor-bicycle, as arranged, to a motor-bus garage by the station. Mercifully he saw no one – questions about his ride would have shattered his self-control.

Anger came later, on the train. Anger and outrage. How dare she! When she had been so anxious to entrap him into marriage. Well, it could be undone. He had cause enough.

He got back to his billet very late, and went to bed composing the letter he would write to Tamsin next morning. But she was ahead of him. A telegram, special delivery.

'Not as you think stop saying farewells stop ever your own Tamsin.'

He thought for a long time, then wrote a short note to Gulveylor. It said very little beyond that he was expecting to be posted soon. He did not mention the incident in the lane. The tone was very cold, very correct. It gave him time to consider.

The next Friday a new squadron was posted to France. Ashton went with it, flying an FE2.

Lizzie of course, had no idea about the little drama in the lane. Simply, when she left the hospital she found Michael Jago sitting on the stile looking wretched.

He was so shaken, so different from when they had parted an hour before, that she quite forgot her usual embarrassment and marched straight up to him.

'Here,' she said, by way of greeting. 'You all right are you? Look like that cat that swallowed the cage instead of the canary.'

Michael seemed to drag himself back from somewhere a long way off. He smiled wanly. 'I'm all right. Thinking, that's all.'

'Not worrying about Peter, are you? He gets into a proper frazzle sometimes, I know, when there's things he can't manage, but he's doing a treat, really. Doctor's no end pleased with him.'

Michael shook his head. 'No, it's not that. It's nothing. I'm fine, really.'

'Well you don't look it,' she told him severely. 'Had a turn have you? Or a fall?'

That strange smile again. 'You could say that. A sort of fall.'

'Well, you can't stay here sat on that stile like Humpty Dumpty. Weren't you supposed to be meeting Merran up at Heamoor?'

He got to his feet shakily. 'Lord, yes. At the veterinary. I'd forgotten.'

'Well, I'll come with you. Not fit to be out, you aren't, the way you look. Come on. Lean on me if you feel funny again.'

'I'm all right, Lizzie, really,' but his smile was for her this time, and he did allow her to put a hand under his elbow and walk with him to the top of the lane. She was acutely aware of him, of the warmth of his arm through the sleeve of his uniform, though it did not burn her fingers and send her pulses racing as she half-feared it might. Still, she was embarrassed enough to keep up a constant flow of chatter all the way without waiting for an answer – as if he were really one of her patients and her prattle might cheer him.

'Dear Lizzie. You are very good,' he said, as they got to the top of the lane, for all the world as if she was his sister.

Merran was still at the surgery. He had seen the 'vetinary', and he'd promised to come out again and see Hercules. A sick shire was a serious business, especially nowadays. The assistant was making up a horse-powder, grinding something up in a granite mortar. It looked hard – more likely to grind away the marble pestle than the other way round, and the boy was frowning with the effort of it. Lizzie watched him, fascinated.

'Anyway,' Merran continued, looking at Michael. 'What's up? Hurt your ankle have you? Coming in here with a nurse at your elbow?' He didn't sound very pleased, Lizzie thought.

'I walked up with Michael,' she supplied. 'He had a sort of fall . . .'

She saw the two brothers exchange glances, one of those private looks they sometimes shared where they seemed to have a whole conversation without needing to say anything. 'I saw Tamsin in the lane,' Michael said.

Lizzie looked at him, surprised; it was the first she had heard of it.

Merran's reply surprised her more, it seemed to make no sense. 'It's like Pa's finger,' he said. 'Better off without. Told you that long ago.'

'Perhaps. I never would have believed anyone could be so horrid.' He glanced towards Lizzie. 'Don't know when I'm well off, that's my trouble. Well, today has taught me something. Had a real diamond on my doorstep all the time, and couldn't see past the paste.'

Lizzie had the uncomfortable feeling that she was being talked about in some way, and she flushed. She hated it when they talked like this, as though they lived in their private world, and no one else existed. She turned away and began to examine the bottles on the shelf. The dispensary was strangely similar in some ways to the dispensary at Little Manor. The benches here were mahogany, but there was the familiar polishy smell of beeswax and turpentine. The same glass bottles too, except that these were labelled 'Horse Drench', or 'Mixture for Mange' – and even then she recognised 'Fenugreek', 'Tincture of Gentian', 'Morphia'. She looked around her with genuine interest.

'We should be getting on,' Merran's voice interrupted her. 'Give you a lift down to Market Jew Street if you like.'

They took her home. It was awkward: Michael was still subdued and upset about something. Then, to make matters worse, they met Daisy coming in. It was the first time Daisy had met any of the Jagos since Peter came home, and Lizzie was uncomfortably aware of it. Not that you would have known to listen to Daisy. She prattled on about her day at the factory, and about Lieutenant Masters' visit until the Jagos made their excuses and left.

'My lor,' Lizzie said, 'you're some cool, you are. Never think there was a time when you were engaged to their brother and you broke it off.'

Daisy flushed. 'I never did. It was him told me not to come back. And he's never asked for me again, has he?'

Lizzie thought of Peter Jago, flushed and cursing at his useless stumps. It was true, he had never mentioned Daisy again. 'No,' she admitted, 'but . . .'

'There you are then,' Daisy said. 'No good crying over spilt milk, is it? Better off without me, more than like. Besides,' – she gave Lizzie a sideways glance – 'there's a lad up at Farrington's I got my eye on. Skilled man, he is, but he's got a gammy hand where it went in a machine years ago, so they wouldn't have him for the Army. But he's nice-looking, for all that, and I think he likes me, and all.'

Lizzie shook her head. 'How can you talk like that, and that poor Peter Jago lying up there with his legs shot off?'

Daisy looked defiant. 'Well, I aren't going to help him, sitting at home like a nunnery, am I? He told me to go away and find myself a proper man and that's what I'm doing!' She ran up the steps and by the time Lizzie got in she was already telling Gramps and Eddy all about the factory and how difficult it was to cut a screw-thread.

Only later, when she crept into bed, she leaned over and kissed Lizzie's hair. 'I'm sorry, Lizzie. I never meant to snap. Only you don't know what it's like, having your life fall apart, like that. And I hope you never do, my handsome. I'm trying to make the best of it, that's all.'

'It's all right,' Lizzie said, 'I understand.' But she didn't really, and the knowledge of it lay between them, like Penny, on the pillow.

Chapter Eleven

Michael went back to camp and life at the shop settled back to normal – or what passed for normal these days. Mam was no better, still off her food and looking pale and tired.

Lizzie plucked up her courage and spoke to Gan about it again.

'Well, we'll just have to hope it's a boy this time.' Gan saw Lizzie's face and laughed. 'And why not, my girl? Your mother's not forty yet.'

Another baby! It was a worrying thought. Not that she was concerned for Mam, her mother had had so many babies by now she knew what she was at, but it would be another mouth to feed. And that might be a problem.

Lizzie had expected that with the spring things would look up a bit, but so many farmers had turned their acreage over to potatoes that there still weren't the animals to be had.

There was less in the cold-store than Lizzie could ever remember, and what there was seemed to disappear very quickly. Even the 'block-ends' – the bits and pieces left over after a day's butchering, and which Mam had always sold to the market-women for a penny a bag, were now finding their way into respectable shopping-baskets or, increasingly, into the Treloweths' own stock-pot.

'We're all right,' Gan said one night, dolloping out a generous helping of broth for Lizzie when she came home, 'marrowbone soup is warm and nourishing. But I saw Mrs Richards in the town today – poor woman, she's been living on bread and dripping since Russell was took. "Tighten your Belts and Beat the Kaiser" so they say, but hers'll be meeting in the middle soon.'

Mam looked at Lizzie, a spoon halfway to her mouth. 'Daisy's getting a decent meal, anyway, up at the canteen,' she said, meaningfully.

Gan snorted. 'Decent enough I suppose, as long as the inspector keeps an eye on it. But it makes a sorry hole in her wages at the week's end.'

Lizzie nodded gratefully. Even Mam had to agree with that. The promised 'twelve shillings' had turned out to be calculated on piece work – you had to make so many pieces before you got the full wage – and then there were stoppages for dinner, and uniform (which had to be paid for, Farrington said, because they weren't 'shell workers' to have it issued free) and the cost of spoiled work was taken from her wages, besides. 'Never mind,' Mam said, 'she's making a fist of it now. Faster than some of the men, she says, and bringing home eight or nine shillings. Just as well. That extra money's a blessing and no mistake.'

'I'll have to go down there too,' Lizzie said, miserably, when Mam had gone. 'I aren't keen, but it will come to that.'

'Millie was saying the same,' Gan said. 'She was all for going down there and asking, only your Mam said no. Too small to work nights.'

'Farrington won't take you as young as twelve,' Lizzie said.

'No, I told her that. But she's looking out for something. She's

101

restless, here in the shop, and the money would be useful, too, no denying. Still, I daresay we shall get by without having you down Penvarris for a little while yet.'

Lizzie said nothing, but her heart was heavy. Eddy and Gramps did their best – butcher a blackbird if there was meat on it – and still going out on the wagon-round once a week. Sometimes they bought a few rabbits or hares while they were out, and came back with more meat than they set off with. Not that it made much difference. Anything extra they brought home was snapped up, quicker than you could say 'knife'.

'I see Mam has moved the poultry in from the shop-door,' Lizzie said, to change the subject from factories. 'The street front looks awfully bare.'

'Makes the place look less empty inside and besides, it might walk off while you weren't looking, left out there. It's the same all over town. You don't see shoes, or baskets or apples out on the street like you used to. Sign of the times,' Gan said. 'Everything's changing.'

Lizzie nodded. There were times things could turn quite nasty. The poor little Italian hurdy-gurdy man had been set upon with sticks last week and chased out of town for being a 'furriner', though he had come to Penzance for years, with his squeaky old barrel-organ and his skinny monkey on a string, and was as harmless as a sparrow.

Later she wrote to Michael, and poured out her worries to him. She had been expecting a doleful letter after his visit home, but his reply, when it came, was particularly warm and thoughtful. One paragraph especially made her heart sing. 'I'm sorry you are feeling down, Lizzie. I think a lot of you – I never realised how much. Next time I'm home, find an hour or two, and we'll go walking out to Marazion perhaps or up St Just and watch the sun go down. I've been thinking a lot, and there is something I want to ask, but I want to do it in person and in private, and not in a letter that the censor is going to read.'

She read the words and reread them – told herself she was a fool to hope, and reread them again. But always she came to the same conclusion. He was, wasn't he, asking her to walk out with him? Or did he just want a long heart-to-heart chat about his chances with Tamsin Beswetherick?

Merran came in to see Peter. She longed to ask him about it – she always felt better when she talked to Merran – but she didn't dare. Besides, there was enough else to talk about. Peter had been ready to leave hospital, once before – but his bad stump had flared up again. Now at last it was healing nicely, and the doctor was talking of letting him go home.

'Soon be out of here,' Merran said, after they had walked Peter painfully but proudly all the way down the garden and back again on his crutches and left him on his bed to recover.

Lizzie nodded. 'Me, and all. I shall have to give up the Hospital and go and work in that factory. I don't want to do it, but I must before they send me some place worse. I'm eighteen next week.'

Merran looked at her. 'I've told you,' he said, 'you want to try for a land-girl. You must have seen the posters. Much better than that horrible factory. People are coming round to it, too. Even Pa says if it came to a choice between a German prisoner of war or a woman, he'd have the woman every time.'

Lizzie grinned. She knew Pa Jago and his views. 'You've still got that extra man on your farm, though, haven't you?'

Merran pulled a face. 'Hopeless, he is. Worse than a dozen Germans. But he's got to go in front of the conscription tribunal soon, and Pa won't do anything to save him. Farrington won't like it, but there you are. But never mind him, Lizzie, you ought to think of it. You get free instruction – and your keep if you sign on for a year. And after a month they'll give you four bob a week on top. Pocket-money, they call it. Used to be a wage, that did, before the War.'

'Really?' Lizzie had seen the posters, of course – *To the Women of the Nation – Our Soldiers Must Have Food* – but she had never stopped to read them closely. 'Four shillings?' She might enjoy it, too. She remembered that day in the arrish field, and how she had loved the harvesting.

'If you get to be a supervisor, they'll pay you a pound a week. You got to find your keep then, of course. But it's good money, for a girl. And you never know – might come in useful.'

He was looking embarrassed.

Michael, she thought suddenly. He did mean what I thought he meant! And Merran knows. Of course, there were never any secrets between those two. 'Well,' she said, colouring. 'It might at that. I'll pick up a form from the Employment Exchange on the way home.'

She did too, but when she got home there was great excitement. Millie had gone after a job as a ladies' maid. Agnes didn't know where, quite, but somewhere in Penzance. Five shillings a week, all found, uniform provided. Live-in too, so there would be one less

103

body in the bed. It was handsome pay for a twelve-year-old, but the proper girl had left to go to Farrington's.

'So there will be just the two of us in the shop with Gan,' Agnes said. 'Mam won't be serving much longer.' She threw Lizzie a look. 'Found her today in the kitchen with a bowl of water and needle in a cork. Trying to find out if it's a boy, though she swears she doesn't believe in it.'

Lizzie laughed. But at the same time she felt unreasonably disappointed. It wouldn't be the factory, then, or the Land Army either. No chance of the Hospital, uniform or not. She was needed here. Still she could go on helping at Little Manor for a bit, as she was now. That was a blessing, at least.

She went to her drawer and put the registration form carefully away.

Tamsin was still smarting. It was so unfair of Ashton, turning up like that unannounced, and as for that wretched Jago boy and that incident in the lane! It was all his fault, insisting on leaping up on the cart-step and giving her such a fright. If it weren't for that, none of this would ever have happened.

Well, she had done her best. Sent an immediate telegram – though that had been a trial too, for Mama had heard of it and insisted upon knowing why. Tamsin had given her a 'censored' report, of course, but there was a lot of family interest in Ashton's reply.

He had sent a note, curt, formal, saying that he was going away, and after that, nothing.

Tamsin had been prepared for almost anything – anger, recriminations, tears – and she had worked out a dozen pretty ways of countering each. She had even rehearsed a scene of injured innocence and irresistible contrition if the very worst happened and Ashton had burst into Gulveylor demanding an explanation in front of Papa. But she had not been prepared for silence.

At least he had not cancelled the marriage outright and demanded that she send back the ring. For a few moments, Tamsin had wondered if he might, and that had frightened her. There were so few eligible young men about these days. Especially if scandal should ever become attached to her name!

That hadn't happened, but his silence weighed upon her worse than any reproach. All the plans and projects for the wedding – the guest list, the lacy camisoles, the fittings for the crêpe de Chine dress – which should have filled her days with delight, made her irritable instead.

Besides, that wretched Michael Jago had created trouble elsewhere. She had been so disturbed, that afternoon, by the sudden appearance of Ashton that she had driven off after him, completely forgetting her errand at the Hospital. Mrs Rouncewell had been most displeased: she had been relying on some of the dressings which Tamsin was supposed to deliver.

There was a certain coolness at the next sewing meeting. Tamsin continued to act as 'liaison lady' but the warmth had gone out of the arrangement, and not even her uniform could quite reinstate her. And, to cap it all, when she got home it was to find that her maid had left. The wretched child had given notice, and the moment Mama found a replacement, the girl upped and went – that same afternoon – with hardly a 'by your leave'. Tamsin knew nothing about it until she came in, tired and irritated, from her Linen League meeting.

She went to her room and found the maid turning down the bed. Tamsin hardly gave her a glance, but went over to sit by the mirror and let down her hair as usual for the girl to brush.

It was a little routine they had. Tamsin had got into the habit of sitting on the dressing-stool and pouring out the worries and excitements of the day while the girl brushed out her hair with long, sweeping, relaxing strokes. And Annie would murmur, 'Yes, miss,' 'No, miss,' 'Well, fancy that, miss,' while the rhythm of the brush never faltered.

That was what Tamsin wanted tonight.

'That Mrs Rouncewell!' she said, shaking her head so that her dark hair fell in agreeable rivers of waves across her shoulders, and the girl took up the silver-backed brush. 'Do you know the other day she had the impertinence to ask me to give up my uniform, for some dreadful clodhopping shop-girl I expect. Ow, Annie! You are pulling my hair.'

'I'm sorry, Miss Tamsin.' The girl modified her brushing. 'And it's Millie, miss, not Annie. I started this morning.'

Tamsin lifted her head and inspected the little freckled reflection in the mirror. No, of course it wasn't Annie. Annie had been much prettier. And this girl was so clumsy. Tamsin was put out. It was not fair. She was accustomed to Annie – Annie knew how she liked her clothes laid out, and what temperature to bring the washing water. And instead, here was this new creature who would have not the first idea about anything. She frowned. It was so difficult to keep trained staff these days. Girls seemed to be coming and going every five minutes, and Papa hadn't had a proper valet or footman since the War began.

'What happened to Annie? And don't I know you from somewhere?'

'She went to the munitions, miss. And it's my sister you are thinking of. Lizzie Treloweth. Came to your First Aid classes and used to work with you up at Little Manor.'

'I remember.' She did remember, that frightful girl who had made her look such an idiot at the bandaging classes. Whom Ashton had taken such a liking to. Who was, surely, a friend of those odious Jago boys.

'It's Lizzie, miss, who wanted to buy your uniform,' the girl went on. 'She'd like to be a VAD really, but she couldn't afford to work Voluntary. Mrs Rouncewell has been very good, finding her a shilling or two . . .'

'Has she!' Tamsin was furious. It was a travesty, paying a volunteer helper. Whatever was Mrs Rouncewell thinking of? And now trying to obtain a uniform for next to nothing! It was against the whole spirit of a charity hospital. Helena hadn't accepted a penny from anyone, and she was in France in the most awful conditions.

She said sharply, 'Well, I am afraid you will have to tell your sister that there is not the slightest chance of it. I require that uniform myself. I mean to mention it to Mrs Rouncewell tomorrow. Tell your sister I am sorry to disappoint her.'

The decision made her feel a little better, but the next evening when Lord Chyrose came to dine, the subject of the Hospital came up again.

'Damn fine supporters,' Chyrose said. 'Damn fine. Running a hospital isn't cheap, but there's enough money in the kitty for the next six months. The last concert in Penzance raised nigh on fifty pounds, and the ladies are getting up another sale of work and selling little flag affairs, on pins. Don't know what we'd do without the ladies, eh Tamsin?'

And Tamsin found herself saying, without having planned it, 'It is a pity don't you feel, Sir James, that *all* of our ladies are not voluntary? Other hospitals pride themselves on running without any additional costs. We have our professional nurses of course, but when so many are *giving* their service, a paid assistant is . . . unfortunate, don't you think? Even for a few shillings a week? It might cause . . . friction.'

Chyrose looked at her, his face turning brick-red. 'My dear Tamsin, I did not suppose you even knew of it. But why ever didn't you mention this before? I've just agreed to continue the arrangement for the next month or two. I had no idea it was causing discontent.'

'Oh,' Tamsin said hastily, 'it is not so bad as that. Straws in the wind, that's all. But perhaps, another time . . . ?'

'I'll bear it in mind,' Chyrose promised, and there the matter ended.

Afterwards, Tamsin felt a little ashamed of herself. It had been rather petty. It must be the strain of the past few weeks. Though, she consoled herself, it was all for the best. It *could* have led to difficulty. And you couldn't go on allowing the girl to hang around the Hospital without even a proper uniform. It lowered the tone.

The next morning she wrote a note to Mrs Rouncewell, explaining that, unfortunately, Miss Beswetherick found it impossible to accede to her request. She required her uniform, and was therefore unable to offer it for sale.

The French drizzle had lifted enough to permit flying. Ashton lowered himself into the cockpit.

The familiar clothes: the flying jacket, the goggles, the scarf, the gloves. For the past few weeks, ever since he had arrived in France, he had spent every available hour in the air, 'putting in time', flying, flying, flying.

The station commander at St Omer had echoed Paddy Lowe's words. 'Sixteen hours? My dear boy, you'll be no use to me until you can fly this old crate by the seat of your pants. Treat the thing as your own. Get up there and find out how to fly.'

And he had flown. Every time the weather permitted, until he felt he could fly the aeroplane in his sleep. Not quite the fifty hours that Paddy Lowe had suggested, but more than half that, and he was beginning to feel like an old hand. He had even learned to loop.

It had been amazing that first time. Take her speed up to a hundred. Ninety. Ninety-five – Tamsin was right, the wings would fall off! No, a hundred! Now. Take her over. More. More. Would she ever go? Yes, now, engine off. God, God, right rudder before she spins. And then wonderfully, miraculously, he was out of it, riding the clouds again. He glided in, so exhilarated by his achievement that he almost forgot to switch on the engine again, so that he came in too steep and almost wiped a wheel off the aeroplane.

Paddy Lowe was watching as he slewed to a halt. 'Bloody fine aviator you are! Come on in and I'll buy you a drink.'

But that had been St Omer and last week. This was not St Omer, it was Quellieu, to the south, and this was not a practice flight. He, Ashton Masters, was flying today over the enemy. There was a camera fixed to his aeroplane and he was to fly out, over the lines, and bring back additional photographs of enemy positions.

It was unexpected. He had done a few flights to 'get his bearings', but nothing like as much as men usually did before they flew out in earnest. Quellieu had a regular 'reconnaissance', a two-seater with a gunner-observer in the front seat, but the pilot had flipped his plane on landing the day before and fried the pair of them to a crisp. Ashton tried not to think about that. He turned his attention to the aeroplane.

The familiar controls. Rudder, elevator, ailerons.

'Switches off.' The mechanic swung the propeller to prime the engine. 'Contact.'

He switched on the magneto, and the engine fired and roared. He ran her up, and throttled back. This was it. A cold caterpillar of fear crept up his spine and settled like a lump of ice in his stomach. He could feel the clammy sweat behind his knees. Then, 'Chocks away!' He was off, bumping over the uneven field, lurching into the air, skimming the hedges.

It was better here. The view from the air never failed to thrill him. The tiny houses, like toys. The church spires, pointing to heaven. The smoke of chimneys. The shifting shadows of clouds.

He banked, turned, taking his direction from the thin grey pencil of road – unnaturally long and straight after the meandering ribbons of England. He could see the traffic on it, little ant-people moving to and fro, between the patchwork pattern of fields.

Little by little the landscape changing. A broken building. A deserted farm. A ruined village huddling round its church, whose spire still stood, askew. Leafless, distorted trees. And between them all the road led on, turning from grey to brown, its cargo of ant-men busier than ever. A column of soldiers glanced up as he passed. Gun-carriages, horses, wagon-loads of supplies. Even a motor-lorry ploughing through the mud.

And then, a scene of desolation. The road itself lost in a sea of mire. A rubble of stones that might have been a hamlet, discarded wagons, blackened stumps of trees. And beyond them, slits, gashes in the mud, and ant-men slithered and scuttled into them. The trenches.

That was the Army, down there. British men, hunched behind sandbags and barbed wire, huddled in holes in the ground. And that roar, that grumbling thunder which had grown louder all the way, resolved itself too. Those were the guns, booming to the right and left of him. 'Light guns in this sector.' Thank the Lord for that. But there was still a banshee screeching, or occasionally a high whining whirr, and the ground below him shuddered and threw up mud in gouges all around.

The fear was crawling again, knotting his stomach. He flew on. A dreadful deserted place. Craters and tumults of mud and earth, and everywhere the rusting coils of wire.

And then, more slits, more trenches, facing the other way – but the same ant-men scurrying half-bent along their lengths. He came down lower. A man with a rifle, leaning on a parapet, his helmet by his side. Another, on a firestep, dived into a bolt-hole as he passed.

Whirr-ping! An angry wasp seemed to buzz beside his face. And another. He looked up. Another. A row of neat holes was in the fabric of the wing above. All around him, little puffs of grey smoke exploded with a dull bang. Archie! Anti-aircraft fire. Good Christ! They were shooting at him.

He loosed off his own gun and saw men scamper for safety. He had the presence of mind to arm his camera too, struggling with the plates as the rifles sang around him. Enough. He was turning, weaving, up and away, back over no-man's-land and the British lines, and then there was green in the fields and red roofs and for a moment he thought he was lost. But he followed the road, and – God be praised – there was the airfield. He landed, badly, but without damaging anything.

Paddy Lowe was down before him, and waiting as he climbed shaking from the cockpit.

'Good show, Masters! See you got hit. Spot any German planes?'

He dared not confess that he had not looked for any. First rule of flying – watch for the enemy. 'No. Got a picture or two.'

'Well done. Doing anything later? One or two of us thought we might take a jaunt into Quellieu. Have a "jolly". Care to come?'

Ashton put his hands into his pockets to stop them trembling. 'Love to,' he said, carefully casual.

'Good egg.' And they went in to report.

Chapter Twelve

There were four of them on the 'jolly'. Lowe, of course, and Ashton, and two others whom Ashton knew only slightly. There was 'Chubby' Beresford, a huge strapping Londoner who barely seemed to fit into a cockpit, but who flew like angel, and Goodenough, from Transport, a wiry Cornishman who attached himself to Ashton immediately because they both had connections with Fowey.

Ashton was rather embarrassed by this, the fellow was only an NCO, but Chubby put his mind at rest. 'Bloody good show, Masters. Time someone made our little "Cousin Jack" feel at home. Need him to wangle the transport, don't you know. He can drive the "bus" and let the rest of us concentrate on the ooh la la.' Chubby was like that. Been with the RFC since its formation, knew all the slang, and you could almost hear the quotation marks every time he spoke. Made you feel quite 'in the know' just to be with him.

My God, Ashton thought. The habit must be catching.

The 'bus' this evening was an RFC staff-car, an ancient Siddeley which had been 'liberated' for the evening on some pretext which Goodenough had managed to get signed by the station commander. That was a considerable feat – petrol was scarce, and forays into Quellieu were rare. Not surprising, Ashton thought, as they lurched into town. Quellieu had been dangerously close to the front lines a month or so before, and Ashton was able to see at close quarters the kind of devastation he had glimpsed from the air. Down here, it was the details that struck you. A child's perambulator, full of clothes and saucepans, upturned beside a wall. The carcass of a horse, left rotting where it lay. And the town itself seemed little more than a ruin, with broken buildings turning blind eyes to the sky.

He glanced at Lowe. This was a far cry from St Omer, with its bars and restaurants still open, where you could buy 'deux fines' for a handful of coins. This was like the stage of a theatre, when the cast had gone.

'This way,' Chubby cried, leaning forward in the front seat to direct Goodenough down a narrow street, a mere twisting array of potholes between shattered houses, shuttered against the night. 'We're here.'

He got out and led the way around the corner to a house much like its neighbours. But there was a thin band of light under the heavy door, and nailed to the boarded-up window a piece of paper bearing the pencilled words *'Ici on parle anglais.'* If they spoke English, Ashton thought, why say so in French?

Chubby strode up to the door and knocked. A women opened it. She was small and stout and dressed in the shapeless black which every Frenchwoman over the age of forty seemed to wear.

'Chub-bee!' she greeted him. *'Chéri!* You have come again. It is so long! And your friends, yes? In. In.' She closed the door firmly behind them and ushered them into the room as she spoke – a small dark room, lit by candles, half a dozen tables with red and white chequered cloths. A Frenchman in a waistcoat was playing a battered piano in one corner, and being ignored by the only customers present, another group of fliers from a different unit. They – Australians by the sound of them – had got to the stage of singing.

'Now, *chéri*,' she said, as they sat at a corner table under the boarded-up window, 'your special, yes?'

'Four specials,' Chubby said. 'And none of that gnat's piss you tried to give me last time.'

She laughed, delightedly. 'Sylvie! Four cognacs, specials, for the gentlemen.'

Sylvie came in. She was young, thin and pretty, in a worn sort of way. Ashton recognised her, the daughter of the farm where they were billeted. She brought the 'cognacs', a wild, wicked brew that threatened to blow your head off quicker than any German shell.

'This is your special?' he said to Chubby, when he had got his breath back.

'Make it from plums,' Chubby said. 'Drink up. You'll find it grows on you.'

It certainly seemed to. Ashton had another, and another. Later he had a dim recollection of singing – stirring, moving songs that brought tears to your eyes. Bloody good show. Good ol' Chubby. Won'erful sh-pecials. Won'erful songs. Won'erful evening.

The Australians were gone. Time to go home.

They got to their feet. Something was the matter with the floor. It was dancing. Dancing to the music. It struck Ashton as very funny and he clung to the doorpost laughing.

The fresh air, when it hit him, felt like a cold shower. Where was the car? Somewhere. They set off to find it, blundering in the darkness. Round this corner perhaps?

One of the Australians was there, with Sylvie. He was holding her, pressing his lips to hers. She was struggling. 'No, *m'sieur. Laissez-moi.'*

111

Afterwards, he was never sure what prompted him. That flight perhaps? The 'cognac'? Some dim memory of Tamsin in the lane? Whatever it was, he did not hesitate. He lurched up to them. 'Leave her alone.' He wanted to say something profound, about disgrace to the uniform, but what came out was, 'Anyway, 's mine.' He was thinking of Tamsin, again.

Rather to his surprise the man backed away at once, releasing the girl. 'Oh. Sorry sport. You should have said.' He stretched out a massive hand. 'No offence intended.'

'None taken.' Ashton said. He took the hand, grateful for its support. The girl cast a startled glance at him and scurried away.

'C'mon then, Masters!' Chubby and the others wove into view, arms wound around one another's necks. 'Found the bloody bus. Some fool left it round the corner.'

Somehow, they found their way back to their billet. Ashton let himself into the stuffy little end room that was his. He heard the others shambling off into the night, still singing. He was too tired to undress. He lay down on the iron bedstead with the dusty chicken-smelling mattress and closed his eyes.

When he opened them again there was light in the sky. The door was open.

'M'sieur?'

He sat upright on the instant. 'Sylvie? What are you doing here?' He tried to think of the question in French, but his head ached too much. She came and sat beside him on the bed. 'No, *m'sieur*. Do not concern yourself.' She slipped out of her knitted cardigan and skirt. Underneath, she was naked. '*Maintenant, alors,*' she said, slipping her hand expertly beneath his tunic. 'Now then.'

It was not at all how he had planned that it should be, the first time. His head was a furnace and his mouth tasted foul, but there was enough youth and cognac in his blood to meet the moment. Later, much later, she got to her feet and pulled on her garments.

'You're going?' he said stupidly. Of course she was going, she couldn't stay here. 'Shall I see you again?'

She laughed. '*Oui, chéri.* Of course, if you wish. But tonight, you understand, there will be no charge. Tonight, it is – I do not know how you say – *pour l'amour.*'

It was some time after she left before he understood. Of course. That was why the Australian had backed down so unexpectedly. He had supposed Sylvie had a prior engagement. For a moment he was shamed. He was a fool – his drunken, fumbling attempts to be a knight errant were merely ludicrous.

And then he began to laugh. A flight over enemy lines, a jolly, and a girl. All in one day. Well, he would write to Tamsin tomorrow but – between the military censor and his feelings as a gentleman – he couldn't tell her any of it.

Up at Nanzeal everything seemed to be happening at once. Peter was finally coming home. Merran, assisted by Mother and Hunnicutt, had spent an hour struggling downstairs with a bedstead and washstand, and another struggling up again with the contents of the parlour – the horsehair chairs, the embroidered texts, all Mother's china cats. Even the harmonium, though it weighed a ton and almost got wedged on the landing.

'Be like a big house, it will,' Hunnicutt said, as they carried up the last of the bits and pieces. 'Sitting-room upstairs. Silas Farrington will think he's visiting gentry next time he comes.'

Merran frowned. He glanced at the framed text he was carrying. 'God Bless the House.' 'God Help this House' more like. And it was all Farrington's fault.

Pa had insisted on doing things his way – asparagus, marrows, sugar-beets. Fortunately the government had urged everyone to put in more grain and potatoes, so even Pa had seen sense and turned over two fields to barley and extra earlies. Just as well. Asparagus beds took time to mature, and though the marrows had done splendidly they were not a lot of use without the sugar-beet – and that had been a disaster. The leaves were yellow and withered, and the beets themselves smaller and harder than pebblestones, scarcely worth the labour of lifting and transporting to the refinery.

Farrington was no help. Paid the agreed price all right, so much per ton, but he wouldn't touch the marrow without the beet to match and Pa was left to sell the extra for what he could get – a ha'penny or two a time. Good thing that folk were hungry. There wasn't much call for cartloads of marrows, in the ordinary way.

'Could have told you what would happen to those beets,' Merran stormed at his Pa, after a particularly fruitless day at market. 'Salt and scorch, that's what it is, and the soil up in those fields so thin you could run a comb through it.'

'Shouldn't be, then,' Pa muttered stubbornly, 'I spread 'un regular. That seaweed you brought in, and no end of stuff from the heap.'

The 'heap' was the great pile of muck and sand in the field behind the cowsheds. Took months to build it, a layer of muck and a layer of sand, till it was half as high as a hayrick. All sorts of stuff went in, stubble from the arrish fields, stable sweepings, tops from the beans and parsnips. Kitchen leavings too, though Mother insisted on keeping the heap away from the house because of the smell. Pa even had stinking heads and tails sent up from the fishmarket. It all went in, then more straw, more sand from the beach.

'I told you,' Merran said. 'Too salt for it. What you want up there is a good dose of manure, and then plant potatoes or mangolds. Hardy old crops, not this newfangled nonsense.'

'Besides,' Hunnicutt had been listening and joined in now with his two-pennyworth. 'That heap's never been properly turned for the winter. I've set Liddel on it a score of times, but I've never seen them farm-gates once.'

Merran grinned. It had been a joke, almost, before the war. The heap had to be turned, so that it rotted evenly, and it was a job given to the itinerant workers when they turned up looking for work. The heap was built on a pair of old five-bar hurdles, and the men weren't paid till they'd shifted the pile and could show the gates.

That would have been asking too much of Liddel.

But Pa was not grinning. He was suddenly, unaccountably furious. 'Here,' he said, 'you keep your opinions till you're asked for them. You aren't too old to be turned off, George Hunnicutt, and don't you forget it. This is my farm, and I'll run it how I think fit. And if you two had been watching Hercules, instead of finding fault with other people, perhaps I shouldn't be in danger of losing a valuable horse, with the vet out here every five minutes at a guinea a time.' He turned and stormed away.

Merran and Hunnicutt exchanged glances. It was the first time in his life Merran had ever heard Pa speak to Hunnicutt like that. 'Worried about Hercules,' he said, as a kind of apology.

Hunnicutt shook his head. "Tisn't that, is it? It's that Farrington. Paid your Pa money to take on Liddel, and now he's got him over a barrel, if you ask me. Your Pa's afraid of his life someone will find out.'

Merran frowned. 'Not against the law, is it? Wasn't conscription when Liddel came.'

'Maybe so. But there's plenty wouldn't see that. There's a lot of high feeling – mob burnt down a house, up Cambourne, where they thought a deserter was hiding. And it's not just Liddel. It's my belief

114

your Pa has taken money for this new man. And Farrington won't take it back. There *is* conscription now, and your Pa'd be liable for that. Conspiring to avoid lawful service.'

Merran was appalled. 'But Pa didn't know that at the time.'

'You try telling the conscription tribunal that,' Hunnicutt said. He stomped off to see to Hercules.

Merran might have had a chance to tell them at that. He and Liddel were due before the tribunal the next day – each case was being heard individually now. They took the pony and trap and went in together.

Merran's case was quickly dealt with. Two brothers serving, one wounded, father with half a hand. Himself running the farm. Exempted for twelve months.

Liddel followed. He was shaking as he gave evidence. How long had he been farming? Six months. Previous agricultural experience? No, sir. Anyone from the farm prepared to swear he was indispensable? Liddel looked at Merran. Merran looked away. No, sir. Anything to say why you shouldn't be referred to the military forthwith? Not married are you?

Yes, sir.

Merran gasped.

Elderly wife in need of support, sir. No children, no. How long married? Only a few days, sir, but had intended it much longer. There was a general laugh but there it was. Register to military service, but not liable to immediate call-up. Case to be reviewed.

On the way home Merran challenged Liddel over it. 'What about this wife of yours? First I heard of it.'

Liddel flushed and huddled down on his seat, 'Well, I am married, and all. Last Wednesday.' Merran nodded. Liddel had asked for two half-days together and disappeared from dawn to sundown. 'All legal and above board. She's a widow, out St Buryan way. Special licence, ring and all. Don't have to live with her, though – more than visit once a week, make it legal.'

Suddenly Merran understood. 'Farrington arranged it?' Liddel didn't reply. 'How much did that cost you?'

Liddel flushed again, but he was defiant. 'Fifteen guineas.'

The dreadfulness of it left Merran speechless, and he said nothing more to Liddel the rest of the way home. When he got there he felt even less like chattering.

He had been looking forward to it. Lord Chyrose had promised to bring Peter home in the carriage – but Peter was not in the bedroom they had prepared for him. There was no sign of anyone else either – not in the kitchen, not in the parlour. Merran was beginning to be alarmed, and then Liddel came sidling up to say he had found them in the stable.

'They're all in there,' Liddel went on, 'mooning over that old horse.'

If Liddel had been more of a man, Merran would have hit him. As it was he just shouldered Liddel aside and hurried across the farmyard. They were all there. Peter, Mother, Pa and Hunnicutt, and half a dozen of the neighbours, too. Hercules was lying on the floor and Peter was leaning forward in his wheeled chair, stroking the great head. He looked up and Merran saw that there were tears in his eyes.

Hercules was dead.

It was like losing a friend. It *was* losing a friend. They buried Hercules in the old mine-shaft on Rocky Acre, where he had always loved to graze and where he had given Liddel so many hours of fruitless exercise. Merran felt his own eyes stinging.

They gave him a good send-off. Crowdie from Penvarris was there, and when they went indoors for a drop of cider – or tea for the Methodists – Merran took him aside and struck a deal for the young cart-horse they had borrowed earlier. Jason, his name was, and though he wasn't Hercules, he was a fair animal.

Pa grumbled when he heard. Farrington had offered to find a cart-horse.

'Probably spavined,' Merran said. 'I've heard of people lately cutting the nerves so a horse won't limp. Fools the vets sometimes, and Farrington wouldn't know a horse from a hyena. This is a good horse. It's expensive – with animals so scarce – but it's money well spent, and there's an end on it.'

For once, Pa didn't argue. Merran wondered why, until Peter told him. Farrington had offered to buy Hercules for dog-meat, and to boil down for glue.

So Jason came. The price was ironic too – exactly fifteen guineas.

Little Manor wasn't the same without Peter Jago. With his stubborn lumbering lurch, his furious impatience, he had become a kind of fixture – like the giant tea urn, simmering and unpredictable – and the ward seemed unnaturally quiet and empty without him.

Lizzie said so to Nurse Blight as the two of them were scrubbing down the bedstead with carbolic, and disinfecting the mattress ready for the next casualty. 'Funny thing, I seem to miss him more than some of the easier fellows.'

'Miss his brother, that's what you do,' Nurse Blight said.

That could be true. Without Peter, there was no reason why Merran should ever come to the Hospital now. And without Merran she would have no opportunity to talk about Mike. She enjoyed doing that, just mentioning his name. It was no good trying to talk to Daisy about anything – the Jagos were still a tactless subject with her, although she was taken up these days with Abel Hoskins, the boy with the damaged hand. Lizzie would miss Merran.

'I suppose I could go up there,' she said half to herself. 'Sunday afternoon when the shop is closed – see how Peter is getting on.' A lot of the other Volunteer Ladies did 'home visits' to the amputees.

Nurse Blight surprised her. 'I'll come with you if you like.' Lizzie glanced at her and saw that her friend had turned redder than the cross on her uniform. 'I'm not working Sunday, and it would be nice. A bit of a walk, in company.'

Lizzie had no objection. In fact, it saved her an embarrassment. She hadn't been up to Nanzeal since Daisy broke her engagement. And it was easier to call with two.

It was a long walk, even over stiles and it was warm in the summer sun. The two girls were soon chattering away like old friends. Lizzie found herself telling Nurse Blight – Nell, her name was, it turned out – about Michael and how he was writing off everywhere for an overseas commission. 'Fed up, he is, stuck on the Isle of Wight running these training courses. Too much use where he is, Peter says, and his CO won't let him go.'

'Did Peter use to work on the farm then?' Nell said, and turned that ripe tomato colour again. 'His mother won't mind us calling, will she?'

'Soon see,' Lizzie said. 'We're here.' And she led the way down the lane.

Mrs Jago made them very welcome, gave them buttermilk, and a slice of home-made tart with jam in it – a strange watery, tasteless, kind of jam. 'Marrow,' Mrs Jago said, and looked daggers at her husband, who went out scowling and slammed the door.

'Don't you take any notice of him,' she said. 'You come and see Peter. Merran's made him a little cart, so he can be pulled down the field and weed the rows, but it wears him out something cruel. He's in here.'

Peter was lying on the bed, looking exhausted, but he was

delighted to see them. 'Quite perked up,' Merran said, when he arrived a few minutes later. He sat on the chair and chatted to Lizzie, while Nell talked to Peter.

After that, it became quite an established thing between them. Every week or two, when Nell Blight could arrange her day off, she and Lizzie walked over to Nanzeal for an hour or so of a Sunday. Sometimes Peter would be in the kitchen, or in his chair, and then Merran would take Lizzie out to 'see the pigs' or 'give the dogs an outing' – to leave the two together, Lizzie guessed.

'Thought any more about the Land Army, have you?' Merran said, one afternoon as they leaned over a gate and scratched the old boar, Egbert, behind his ear with a piece of straw.

Lizzie shook her head. 'I can't rightly. Mam's ... under the weather, and I'm needed home.' She sighed. 'Oh dear, that sounds selfish I know, but I just want to account for something.'

'You count for something with me. With us.'

She grinned at him. 'I know. And I care about you two and all. Only I feel trapped, sometimes.'

He nodded. 'So do I. Stuck here and made to watch while Silas Farrington ruins this farm, when I want to go and knock spots off the people who shot Peter. Both caught, you and I.'

She smiled, grateful for his understanding. 'Michael feels it too,' she said, and saw his face fall a little. 'Think he'll ever get a posting, do you?'

'Might do.'

'They're awful short of men,' Lizzie said. 'They've started calling up married fellows now. Here – whatever's the matter with you?'

Merran explained, laughing until he cried. But Liddel didn't go into the Army. They turned him down at the medical because he had bad feet.

PART THREE:
DECEMBER 1916 – EASTER 1917

Chapter Thirteen

Lizzie walked up Causewayhead, bending her head against the rain. She was beginning to wish she had never come to town at all. Her boots were letting in water and the drizzle was getting under her hood, and it would never do to turn up at Little Manor with her feet leaking and her hair in dripping rats-tails. Only she had been hoarding a few pennies to buy some little Christmas treats for the younger ones, and things were so busy, what with the shop and the Hospital, she couldn't see when she would have another opportunity.

Not that there was much Christmas cheer about. A few shops had decorated their windows with artificial snow and ribbons, but there was no heart in it. The whole town was grey – grey pavements, grey faces, grey buildings, and even the 'fashionable' colours in the dress-shop window – thrush or oyster, dove or sand – were only browny-grey when you came right down to it. The real people – scuttling for cover under the awnings – were mostly in mourning for somebody and muffled in black waterproof crepe. It was as if War had squeezed the colour out of the world. And every little luxury with it.

She went to the sweet-shop, thinking of Aggie's sweet tooth, but it was no longer the old Aladdin's cave: aniseed balls, sherbets, pear drops, boiled fruits clear and colourful as stained glass, pink and white peppermint walking-sticks. This year there were only a few dull caramels and cough sweets lurking at the bottom of the big glass-stoppered jars. Lizzie had to settle for a couple of penny clay pipes for her 'treats'.

'They children can blow bubbles with them,' the shopwoman said, scrabbling for them in a big bottom drawer full of sawdust, so that her petticoats showed.

Lizzie hurried out, pocketing her pipes. A shame for the children not to have their bit of Christmas, but there was little on offer, even for those that could afford to buy. Even the hotel on the corner, which already had 'meatless days', had a new notice in the window. 'Maximum two ounces of bread or cake per customer.'

And it was awful bread! Made with 'national flour' which was anything but wheat, and the price so high there had been deputations to parliament. But whatever you paid for it, it was the same bread, whether you were Mrs Nobody or Lady Beswetherick herself. Even the bread was grey!

At least, Lizzie thought as she walked up the drive to Little Manor, the Treloweths – being butchers – did not actually go hungry. She gave herself a little shake, partly to pull herself together and partly to shrug off the worst of the wet, wiped her boots carefully and let herself into the Hospital.

It was a different world. No shortages here. The stuffy warmth hit you as soon as you walked in, and the men who were able were already receiving lunch. Eggs – delivered fresh every week by the Wounded Serviceman's Collection – meat, vegetables, even cake and chocolate provided by well-wishers. Visitors cast longing eyes on Matron's tray as it passed, with its fresh jam and butter and two sugar lumps on the saucer.

Colour too. Blue and white pyjamas. Knitted bedspreads every colour of the rainbow. Red dressing-gowns for the 'ambulant', with nurses in green, or Red Cross blue, with scarlet crosses on their apron fronts.

Life seemed to be like that, divided into separate compartments. There was the everyday world of home and the shop, Mam's backache, and people worrying over letting down hems and getting enough to eat. And there was Little Manor: the smell of pain, disinfectant, blood and beeswax, hushed voices, starched sheets, and shoes squeaking on polished linoleum.

But there was no time to loiter. The Somme offensive had begun on 1st July and since then the Hospital had been busier than ever. Men arrived back on every boat from the dressing stations and front line hospitals, and Little Manor was crammed to the skirting boards with eighty-five beds. And still they came.

Mrs Rouncewell came down the ward now. 'Ah, there you are, gel. I need you to come with me in the ambulance! We have two new patients arriving.'

So Lizzie had to go straight back out in the rain again. She was glad she did. On the station she walked slap-bang into Michael Jago.

When Lizzie looked up and saw him she went quite weak at the knees with surprise. My heavens, he was some handsome in that uniform. He came hustling over at once. His eyes were laughing, and he was smiling broadly as he put his hands on her waist and swung her round him like a child. 'I say, Lizzie, here's a piece of luck. Fancy seeing you. Here I am home, all at a moment's notice, and there you are on the station. I was going to come up and find you. Must be my lucky day.'

She disengaged herself, smoothing her apron and cap, and tried to look more decorous than she felt. 'Here! Whatever will people think? And me on duty, too.'

'Think the truth more than like. An officer's come home and found his girl waiting for him when neither of them were expecting it.'

His girl! She was 'his girl'. She felt her heart skip a beat and the colour flood to her cheeks. 'You're in some high spirits, then.'

'High spirits. I should think so, too. You know what? I've done it Lizzie. Got a posting at last.'

The joy left her like water tipped from a bucket. 'Oh?'

'Yes! Soon as ever this next training course is over. Adjutant to an old friend of mine who has got his first command. So what do you think of that?'

What did she think of it? She could see Mrs Rouncewell helping the first casualty into the ambulance – a boy with a hideous bloodstained bandage where his eyes had used to be. What could she think of it – when that might be Michael himself in a week or two?

She could not say so. She had a duty, too. All the posters screamed it at you. '*Women of Britain say "Go!"*'

She found her voice somehow. 'Of course I'm pleased, Michael. If that's what you want.' It sounded grudging. She had to do better, for his sake. He must know the dangers well enough. 'Well done.'

Michael was still looking at her, his hand on her arm. 'Lizzie?'

She shook her head. 'I'll have to go.'

'But I'll see you? Tomorrow? I'll come down the shop. We need to talk, before I go back. There's something I want to . . . we need to talk.'

'Miss Treloweth!' Mrs Rouncewell's voice rattled the hoardings, so that passers-by stopped to stare. 'When you're *quite* finished . . .'

Still he did not release her arm. 'Tomorrow?'

'Tomorrow.'

'Sorry Mrs Rouncewell, ma'am,' she muttered, and hastened back to help.

Mrs Rouncewell looked daggers all the way back to the Hospital, and Lizzie was summoned to report to Matron's office after duty. But – perhaps because Lizzie's face was truly 'whiter'n a bolster-case' as Nurse Blight said – she did not get quite the dressing down she expected.

Instead she was sent to 'clear up the library' before she went home. It was hard enough (Albert had been loose in there for an hour) but Lizzie knew she had got off lightly. She picked up the torn papers, rearranged the sealing wax and scrubbed up the spilt ink (and other things) from the writing table.

She was grateful. It kept her busy. She unscrewed the handle of the blotting pad and changed the paper as though by concentrating hard enough she too could blot something out – the thought of Michael Jago going overseas.

Merran had felt in his bones that Michael was coming, and when he heard the step at the door he knew without looking who it was. But he didn't guess the truth until he saw Michael's face.

'My dear life,' he said, before Mike had time to speak. 'You've gone and got yourself a posting.'

Michael grinned. 'Managed it at last. Here, Merran – you might look a bit pleased for me. Worse than Lizzie Treloweth you are, with a face longer'n a fiddle – and me bursting with my good news.'

'You've seen Lizzie then?'

Michael nodded. 'Met her on the station . . .'

Merran heard him out, but inwardly he was fuming. Couldn't Mike see how unkind it was, gloating over his posting, while Lizzie looked at her wounded soldiers and saw Michael everywhere? He might have said so, but Mother came in. It was only when she went to call Pa and Pete and find Paul's latest letter that Mike said, 'Merran?'

'Yes?'

'I'm going down to see Lizzie tomorrow. To talk about the future.'

There was no need to say more. Merran knew Mike's feelings about Lizzie. They were the mirror of his own. And Mike knew that too – they were not twins for nothing. Merran felt his heart stop beating and it was a long moment before he managed to say gruffly, 'Well, see you look after her then.'

'You won't . . . mind? Not too much?'

Merran gave an unnatural little laugh. 'Mind? Why should I mind? It's what she wants – it's what you want, when you're not making cow's-eyes at Tamsin Beswetherick. You got over that, at least. No, best thing all round. That's obvious.' His voice was not quite answering his bidding, and he turned away, shrugging into his waterproof coat and jamming his hat down over his eyes. 'I'm off out see to the pigs. You know where I am if you want me.'

'But Merran . . .'

Merran was controlling himself with difficulty, and he whirled to face Mike, holding his twin's eyes with his own. 'Like I said, best thing all round. Now leave it be, Mike, there's a good fellow.' And he went out, glad of the rain on his face.

Mike came out to find him, later, but by that time Merran had recovered himself and was able to talk, quite casually, about the problems Liddel had caused them and how Farrington was promising Pa another man in the New Year. 'Not just a man, seemingly. A whole family. Refugees. They were up at the Poldair estate, but they didn't really suit. Good workers, by all accounts, but the fellow had his own farm in Belgium. He wasn't quite so sweetly grateful as Poldair expected. And his wife and daughter weren't a great success either – had servants of their own at home – so they had no more idea of milking than Tamsin Beswetherick.'

He had no sooner said the name than he regretted it, but Mike only said, 'And what has Silas Farrington to do with that?'

Merran made a face. 'Who knows? Poldair offered him a placement fee perhaps? Farrington isn't doing it for charity – that I'm sure of.'

'At least,' Michael said, leaning over the gate to scratch the boar's back with a stick of wood, 'sounds better than Liddel. A farmer, with a bit of something about him.'

'Yes. Tell you the truth, I've been looking at the idea to see where the flaw is, but I haven't found it yet. There'll be one though, mark my words, if Farrington has a hand in it.'

'Pa still growing everything he says?'

'Worse than ever,' Merran said bitterly. 'He's in a fair way to ruining this farm and that's a fact. And the worst of it is, I think Pa knows it. Only Farrington has got such a hold on him, there's no way out. Borrowed money, I do believe, for all this fancy seed and the new steam-plough – and what happens? Fields are too small – no room to turn the thing around, without you miss ploughing half the ground. Pa's talking of leasing it out but it's the same everywhere. And it ploughs too deep, so you're forever snagging the blades. Three inches down you're into granite, round here, and you can't keep steam light and easy like a horse-plough. Leastways, I can't, and I'm damty sure Farrington couldn't either.'

'Must be bad,' Mike said, 'for you to make such a speech. Still, these new people sound better than Liddel. And there's a daughter?'

Merran rounded on him angrily. 'That's right. Twenty years old. Name of Anna. And I know what you're thinking, Mike, so you can just unthink it. I don't want to discuss it. All right?'

He turned on his heel and stomped back to the house.

Chubby Beresford was cock-a-hoop. 'There!' he said, coming into the billet and slapping something down onto Ashton's pillow. 'Didn't I tell you to leave it to good old Beresford?'

Ashton was sitting at the rickety table under the cobwebby window trying to write a letter by candlelight. 'What is it, now, Chubby?'

Chubby produced a bottle of the Quellieu 'special' from his pocket. 'I told you!' He rummaged in another pocket, took out a chipped enamel mug and a handleless cup with the air of a magician conjuring rabbits, and poured a generous amount of spirit into each. 'A wangle. A wonderful wangle.' He tapped the piece of paper lying on the bed. 'Come on Ashers, drink up. A toast to a truly miraculous wangle. What do you say to a spot of Christmas leave?'

'What?' Ashton jumped up so sharply he almost upset the table. 'You don't mean it?'

'I do. Discovered there are three new "kites" waiting to be delivered from Gosport. They're "string-bags" so they want decent pilots. And there's a ship going back on Monday with a couple of billets on board. Persuaded the CO there's no chance of sorties in this weather,' – he nodded through the window at the grey interminable wall of rain – 'so, with a little help from Paddy Lowe – Bob's your uncle. And it's a delivery flight, so it won't affect your normal leave when you're due it.' He took a deep draught from the mug. 'So just you be grateful to your Uncle Chubby.'

Ashton pushed back his chair and picked up the brimming cup. 'Three planes, you say. Who's the third going?'

Chubby chuckled. 'Who do you think? Paddy, of course. He wants to slip home and see his wife. So what do you say we go to London and paint the town red?'

Ashton took a deep sip of his 'special'. 'I'd love to Chubby, you know that. But the fact of it is, I'm an engaged man. It would be damnably uncivil not to call there, if I'm to be in England at Christmas.'

Chubby topped up his mug with a thoughtful air. 'Thought your Mater was in Belgravia, old fruit? Quite relying on a pied-à-terre there, to tell the truth. My family have all moved to the wilds of Scotland for the duration. The zeppelins were getting too much for them.'

Ashton shook his head. 'Mater's spending Christmas at Gulveylor. She and Aunt Winifred will be having a wonderful time, plotting the wedding. Hundreds of ghastly relatives one hasn't seen for a lifetime, but there, it has to be done I suppose. Still, Sir Gilbert keeps a good table.'

'And a decent cellar too, I suppose?' Chubby laughed. 'You are a lucky blighter, Ashers. Well, I shall just have to enjoy London on my own – I hear the theatres are still open, zeppelins or no.'

'Tell you what, Chubby. Why don't you come down with me for a couple of days. Aunt Winifred would be delighted – entertaining the dashing fliers – you can have a look at Cornwall and drink Sir Gilbert's port to your heart's content, and I would have the benefit of your company.' It was an agreeable prospect, in fact. Tamsin was all very well in her way, but her conversation could be rather limiting. Besides, he hadn't altogether forgiven her for that incident in the lane. It would do her good to have to share him for a while.

Of course, if he was honest, Tamsin was already sharing him much more than she knew. Ashton had seen quite a lot of Sylvie since that night – more of her, really, than he could strictly afford. Still, it was something to look forward to when you were up there, weaving and diving with a Hun on your tail, or playing hide and seek with you in the clouds. It had become almost a talisman for him. When he came down shaking, as he often did, from one of these encounters the first thing he looked for was Sylvie's familiar figure waving her scarf for him on the road beside the airfield.

Not that she was exclusively his. He did not expect it, just as she expected nothing from him. A simple, sweet, warm interchange. An affirmation that tonight, at least, they were both alive. Though he did occasionally have a twinge of guilt about Tamsin.

So when he next saw his fiancée it would, on the whole, be easier to have Chubby along.

'I'll wire to my aunt tonight,' he said, and he was as good as his word.

Winifred replied by telegram before they sailed. Lord and Lady Beswetherick would be delighted to welcome them for Christmas.

Chapter Fourteen

Lizzie could hardly bear to spend the morning in the shop. The time inched past instead of flying, and whenever she looked up at the clock the hands seemed to be standing still. Michael would be here in the early afternoon.

There was plenty to do. Mam, of course, had given up serving in the shop weeks ago and was upstairs now seeing to the hams and helping the younger girls make paper Christmas-chains for the shop-window. Good thing too, Lizzie thought, there was precious little else to give the place a festive air. Everyone was out: Gramps and Eddy out with the wagon, Aggie doing the deliveries, and Daisy and Millie off working. Still with Gan here, it should be possible to steal an hour or so with Michael when he came – take that promised walk perhaps, though the wind was coming in southerly and it would be proper blustery down by the sea. All the same, she had polished her boots, specially.

'What's up with you then?' Mam demanded, when Lizzie slipped upstairs to have her lunch. 'All ahop, like a one-legged blackbird! Fetch me some of that soup while you're about it. My back's some bad this morning.'

It must be, Lizzie thought. It wasn't like Mam to sit down in a chair with half the hams not finished. 'Will I do these?' she said, gesturing to the two still waiting to be boiled.

Mam shook her head. 'I'll see to them later.' She ate the soup cheerfully enough, and by the time Lizzie went back downstairs, was nagging Penny for putting too many red loops together – quite like her old self.

'I'll make her some beef-tea when I go up,' Gan said, when Lizzie explained. 'She'll be feeling a bit peaky, and no surprise. That baby's due in a week or two.'

But it wasn't twenty minutes later that Elsie came downstairs with a face the colour of dripping. 'Here, Gan. Come upstairs quick. There's something the matter with Mam.'

Gan put down the rabbit she was jointing and disappeared faster than light, but a moment later she was back again. 'It's all right, Lizzie my lamb. It's the baby, that's all. Now – I've sent Elsie off to get Mrs Owens and Penny is going to take the little ones down to Aunty Simmins.' Lizzie nodded, the policeman's wife often acted as midwife and 'Aunty Simmins' was Gan's own sister, a thin arthritic old lady who lived at Madron, but who always 'took' the children when there was a birth, or an illness. Lizzie had been 'taken' by Aunty Simmins herself once or twice, and she didn't envy her sisters.

'Agnes will give you a hand when she gets back,' Gan went on. 'And Elsie's old enough to help, for once.' She was interrupted by a moan from upstairs. 'I'd best get back to your mam. Don't you worry about the noise, my handsome. Always the same she is, roaring like a bull. But she'll be right as a trivet once it's over – though I'll shut all the doors – keep it a bit quiet in the shop.'

Lizzie smiled. 'Don't you worry, Gan. I've heard a sight worse up at that hospital – and no, before you start thinking it, you'd be a lot more use up there than I would. One thing you don't learn, in·a soldier's hospital.' The moan came again, louder this time, and a customer coming into the shop looked upwards in dismay. 'Go on then, Gan, you get up there. I can manage here until the girls get back. Now then, Mrs Lambert, what can I get for you . . . ?'

Gan scurried upstairs, and Lizzie went back to her serving. Perhaps it was because she was on her own, or perhaps because it was close to Christmas, but the shop seemed to be busier than ever. Lady Beswetherick sent down for an enormous order, and Lizzie looked round at the half-empty hooks and the few remaining game-birds in dismay. Send out an order like that and there would be nothing left to sell. Some customers hadn't got their orders in at all yet.

She hesitated. There was no one to ask. Judging by the noises from upstairs Gan and Mam had their minds on other things. But she had to do something.

She took up a piece of card and wrote on it, in her best fancy capitals, 'Owing to the present shortage of retail meat . . .' (she was proud of that, it sounded official) 'Treloweth's regret that they are limiting Christmas supplies to . . .' – she hesitated a long time over the amount – 'two guineas an order.' Two guineas – you could feed an army for that – even with meat the price it was, but Lady Beswetherick's order came to a lot more. And half of it would be wasted, so Millie said, fed to the animals – as if the hounds cared whether it was a bit of old neck-end, or the best topside. All the same, her hands were trembling as she hung the notice in the window.

To her surprise, Lady Beswetherick took it very well, sent her girl down again for a shoulder of mutton instead of legs of beef. It was the same with everybody. Didn't affect a lot of people of course, they only spent a few shillings at most, even at Christmas. But most people, like the cook at Trevarnon, who did take their two guineas' worth cheerfully included a couple of rabbits – 'Handsome they'll be, stewed in a bit of wine' – instead of the dearer cuts they might usually have taken.

There were a few grumbles, but there wasn't the jostling and bad-temper there had been once or twice lately, as the good meat went to the big houses and other people were faced with scrag ends or nothing at all. By the middle of the afternoon there were queues forming – other butchers had run out long ago. Lizzie had to put up a second notice promising preference to 'existing customers'. Even when Elsie came back, they were run off their feet trying to keep up with demand, and Agnes had a second round of orders to do.

Michael came. Extraordinary, with everything else she had almost forgotten. She looked up, and there he was, standing behind the crush of people in the shop. She caught his eye and he followed her out into the cold-room when she went to unhook another carcass for the shop.

'I'm some sorry Michael – but you can see how it is. I can't leave the shop this afternoon.' He looked stricken. 'It's Mam, you see.'

The last words were unnecessary. The door at the top of the steps was closed but Mam's laboured groans were coming very quickly now.

He shook his head sadly. 'I've got to catch that train at five. Take for ever as it is.'

'I know.' Her whole heart was in the words, and he must have sensed it. He caught her in his arms and kissed her. She had never been kissed, like this, by a boy and the sweetness and warmth of it took her breath away. He kissed her again, and they blundered backwards into one of the sides of mutton that was hanging from the rail.

It broke the moment. Lizzie smoothed down her apron. 'There's Elsie out there in the shop alone this blessed minute.' Another shuddering moan echoed from upstairs. 'And there's Mam with this baby.'

Michael nodded. 'I can see that. You know what I wanted to say to you, don't you Lizzie?'

She grinned. That kiss had given her confidence, and her old tongue-tied silence had gone. 'Got a pretty good idea, after that!'

He took her hand. 'Well, this isn't the place for it, or the time either. It's a big step – you'll need to think about it. But I'll be home again in six weeks, Lizzie. I'll have my question ready, and you better have your answer.' He grinned. 'But I can hope, can't I?'

Lizzie tried to look remote and thoughtful. 'Perhaps!' But it was ridiculous. She felt impossibly happy. Her heart was dancing and her lips refused to stop smiling. He bent to kiss her again.

'Lizzie?' It was Elsie, at the cold-room door. 'Whatever are you doing in here in the cold? There's Mrs Tavy asking for a bit of pig's head for brawn – her Christmas dinner she says – and I haven't got any to sell her.' Her eyes went from Lizzie to Michael and back again, with an expression of wonder.

'I'm coming,' Lizzie said. 'Michael's just giving me a hand with this side of mutton. No, there's no heads left – that many people have taken them to make up their orders. But she could have a little bit of rabbit belly.' She hurried back into the shop, and Michael followed her, carrying the carcass. Mrs Tavy gave him a strange look, but Michael only grinned, and raised his hand in farewell. 'I'll see you next time.'

She was grinning like a nitwit. 'I'll write.'

'You better had!' He put on his cap and was gone, and Lizzie was back to the mundane world of liver and loin-chops. But her heart was singing. Better than any old walk on the Promenade, that five minutes in the cold-room.

She grinned even harder a minute later. Gan came down, looking hot and flustered, but with a smile that stretched from ear to ear. 'Agnes home with the hand-cart is she?'

It wasn't the greeting Lizzie expected. 'Not yet.'

Gan's smile seemed to widen even further. 'Only we'll need to be getting the paint-pot out, adding another 's' to the sign on it. Treloweth and Sons.'

Lizzie felt her eyes fill with tears of delight. Father would be that pleased!

Mam named the baby Horatio Russell. Horatio for poor Lord Kitchener who was drowned in June, and Russell in memory of the Cat's-meat-man.

Father *was* pleased. His next letter was so bursting with pride, you'd think it would have broken out of the envelope. He praised Lizzie for her 'rationing' too, which was just as well.

Mam had been furious when she found out. Lizzie was getting

'headstrong', she said. But having started they were more or less bound to keep on, at least over Christmas. Soon Eddy came home saying other butchers in the town were doing the same. Father's say-so put the final stamp on it.

It had unexpected bonuses too. On Christmas Day, the Treloweths had a piece of best topside on the table. It had been left unsold – something which hadn't happened for months. There was enough for them all, and a cold slice for the Cat's-meat-man's mother too, so the poor woman had a bit of something.

It was a surprisingly good Christmas, considering. Lizzie gave out her pipes, and hugged Mike's secret to herself like a bed-warmer. Mam had contrived a present for everybody – apples, nuts and a few pennies all round. Eddy had a new cap from the peddler, which covered him like a tea-cosy but tickled him pink. Gan had found a recipe for sugarless carrot cake, and Lizzie came back from early shift at Little Manor with a pocketful of broken chocolates which the men had given her from their Xmas boxes, so Aggie had her treat after all.

At Christmas it was a yearly ritual to visit Aunty Simmins but thanks to Horry's arrival some of them had 'missed out'. As soon as she was well enough Mam took Elsie, Eddy and Agnes up there, and a few days later, on Millie's afternoon off, Lizzie and Millie followed. It wasn't much of a celebration – Aunty Simmins' notion of tea was fish-paste sandwiches and jelly – but she liked to see them, and afterwards Lizzie walked back down to Gulveylor with Millie.

It was a damp, gusty day, with a sharp south-westerly chasing the rain-clouds across the sky, but as Lizzie said goodbye and turned back down the lanes the squalls started in earnest – sudden, savage, driving rain with a touch of sleet in it.

Lizzie stopped and sheltered beside a gatepost, in the lee of the wall, but the wind plucked at her skirt with crooked fingers and sent little spiteful flurries into her face and legs. She hesitated a moment, uncertain whether to wait out the shower or make a dash for it, when she heard the rattle of wheels in the lane.

Lord Beswetherick's brougham lurched past, and she huddled closer to the hedge away from the splashes, but a few yards down the lane the carriage stopped. A door opened, and a cheerful voice called, 'My dear Miss Treloweth. What brings you here? You look half-drowned.'

It was that nice cousin of Tamsin's, better-looking than ever, and she blushed at the thought of her own damp skirts and dishevelled hair. 'I came up with my sister, sir – she's maid to Miss Tamsin – and I was walking home when the rain caught me.' Now, she thought savagely, he'll think me a proper fool – not even the wit to keep in out of the rain. 'Blew up sudden,' she added, by way of explanation.

But Ashton Masters was smiling. 'Well,' he said lightly, 'we can't have that, can we? My little bandager drenched to the skin. I am going to the station to meet my mother – she has been to Fowey for the day – and I can give you a lift that far, if you like. It would prevent you getting any wetter.'

She looked at him stupidly. 'Me?'

He laughed impatiently. 'Of course you. Who else can you see? Only, if you wish to accept, I should be obliged if you would step inside and relieve me of the necessity of getting damp on my own account.'

Lizzie got in and the brougham ambled off. She had never been in a carriage, excepting the stripped-out one which Lord Chyrose had provided as an ambulance. She looked around her in delight, taking in the leather seats, the brass handles, and the little mirror set so that a lady could see her hair. Her own was damp and straggling and she looked away quickly.

'This is some kind of you, Mr Masters sir.'

He leaned back in his seat and smiled at her with those hooded brown eyes. 'You can't call a man "sir" when you've taken off his coat and wrapped bandages around his ears.'

Lizzie couldn't see why not. Lots of the officers at Little Manor were still 'sir' to her, and she had done a lot more than that for some of them. 'No, Mr Masters.'

'So your sister works at Gulveylor, eh? I wonder Tamsin never told me.'

'Never crossed her mind, I shouldn't think. Wouldn't think anything about a maid, would she?' Lizzie was only stating a fact, but when the words were out it sounded terribly rude. 'I mean . . .'

Ashton laughed. 'I know what you mean. Tamsin is inclined to think only of what is in front of her nose.' A little cloud crossed his face. 'And at this moment, my dear Miss Treloweth, that is neither of us.'

There did not seem to be any adequate answer to that, so Lizzie said nothing. After a moment she ventured, 'I thought you were in France, sir . . . Mr Masters.'

He grinned. A nice grin, that drove the sadness out of his eyes. 'And so I should be. I'm here to collect an aeroplane, but in this weather it is impossible and anyway in the wind last week there was slight damage to the aircraft. But as soon as it is ready, I expect a wire, and then I shall be away.'

'Flying?'

'Flying, fighting, yes.'

And Michael too would be out there, fighting, in only a week or two. She could not keep the distress of it from her face, because he said gently, 'That is a charming frown, Miss Treloweth. Is it for me?'

'I was thinking of my young man, sir, that's all.' He caught her eye and she smiled. 'Mr Masters, I should say. My young man.' It was the first time she had said the words aloud, and she came all over pink.

'A lucky young man,' Ashton Masters was saying, 'to have you think of him so. And now, my dear young lady, we have reached the station, so we will put you down here. Besides, I believe the rain has eased.'

It had, and she climbed out gratefully, murmuring her thanks. The carriage trotted round to the station entrance, and she saw him lean forward at the window and wave a cheerful farewell.

A ride home in a brougham. That would be something to tell them at home. And what a nice young gentleman Mr Masters was. Far too nice, some part of her added inwardly, for that Tamsin Beswetherick.

Ashton leaned back in the brougham, smiling. She was engaging, that young woman and a pretty girl too. And the more engaging because she seemed entirely oblivious of it. Unlike Tamsin, he thought a little sourly.

The carriage drew up at the station entrance and Ashton got down, aware of the affronted glances of the elderly coachman. Appalled, no doubt, at the idea of offering rides to a shop-girl. Well, Ashton was accustomed to Sylvie, and social conventions didn't concern him as they used to. Not that he would have stopped if Mater could have seen him, of course.

There she was now, haranguing some unfortunate porter for taking insufficient care with her travelling-case. Why she insisted on taking the thing on a simple trip to Fowey was more than Ashton could fathom, but Mater was never happy unless she had constant access to her powders, paints, combs, pins, fresh hand-kerchiefs, eau de cologne and sal volatile. 'It is a travelling case,

Ashton, and I am travelling,' she said once, when he protested. He had never mentioned it again.

She came towards him now, leaving the porter floundering behind her. 'Ashton, my dear boy, what an age you have been in coming. The train has been in quite five minutes, I declare.' She accepted his arm to help her into the brougham and handed the porter a coin, without looking at him. She turned to Ashton. 'You have left Tamsin and your friend back at Gulveylor, I assume.'

That was like Mater, putting her finger unerringly on the painful spot. Ashton said, with a show of lightness, 'There was little help for it, I fear. Poor Chubby took a tumble from a horse this morning, and has turned his ankle damnably. The doctor fears it is broken, and has ordered complete rest.'

Mater looked out of the window as if she were studying the scenery. 'Which does not, I assume, prevent Tamsin from doing things?'

Ashton found himself smiling. 'Quite the contrary. You remember she has some training as a nurse. She has got out her uniform and appointed herself ministering angel – and is rather enjoying herself, I fancy.'

Mater glanced at him sharply. 'You are cynical, Ashton.'

He laughed. 'Am I? Perhaps so. But she wants to show off her skills.' To impress Beresford, presumably. Tamsin had set out to impress Beresford ever since they had arrived. Ashton had begun to find it irritating. The little-girl flutters as she lost or won at the Christmas games, the lowered eyes and demure blushes, the way she demurred to Chubby at every turn. Not that she did not do the same for Ashton. Indeed, it was piquing. She flirted with them equally, as though they were both old friends, instead of being engaged to one and a near-stranger to the other.

In fact, it was becoming clear to Ashton that the wiles and little feminine ways to which he had so readily succumbed on his last visit were really little more than that – wiles and ways, as much part of her nature as her curly hair. Oh, she wanted to marry him, no doubt of that – but there was nothing personal in it. If some other man had been visiting in the summer, he thought ruefully, Tamsin would doubtless have encouraged *him* with the same enthusiasm and she could not resist flirting with everyone she met.

That fellow in the lane, for instance. No doubt it was, in her mind, as innocent as she said. And now Chubby. But, although she was as charming and pretty as ever, Ashton found to his surprise that he did not altogether care. He was piqued, yes. It hurt a man's pride to find his fiancée smiling at other men, but she was no longer the dream-creature of his fantasy, painted in burning colours by unassuaged desire. Sylvie had quenched the most urgent of his fires, and considered coolly, Tamsin did not rouse him as she once did.

He had tried, briefly, to rekindle the old spark. Taken her walking in the park (though she had complained bitterly of the December chill) and, in the shelter of the summer-house, attempted to take her into his arms. Sylvie, at such a moment, would have turned to him warmly and kissed him with a passion that kindled his own. If Tamsin had done the same, all might have been repaired, but she merely offered a chilly cheek to be pecked as though it were a favour, and when he attempted to insist she pushed him away.

'My dear Ashton. We are not married yet!'

Even then he might have forgiven her. She was young, innocent, he might have to teach her to love him. But she had not been able to disguise, in that moment, a quiver of genuine repugnance and fear. The repugnance was not for him, he realised – an instant later she was her smiling, coquettish self again – but for the intimate contact of the kiss. He remembered that she had drawn away for a moment that night in the library, flinching at his passion, but then he had been too afire, too inexperienced, to care.

But he cared now. He had learned what intimate contact could be, and it was very precious to him. He had nursed to himself private dreams of sharing it with Tamsin, but her instinctive shudder of disgust told him the sorry truth. The little moues and glances, the bared shoulders and offered lips, were not matched by any inner drive. It was all intended to ensnare and enslave, but at a 'romantic' distance, as though they were characters in a penny dreadful and not real people at all. Altogether, he was beginning to fear that he had made a terrible mistake.

Mater was still looking at him. 'You are abstracted, Ashton. Concerned for your friend, perhaps?'

He smiled. 'And well I might be. The poor fellow will be laid up with this foot for a fortnight at least.'

'They will send someone else across to ferry back the aeroplane?'

'I imagine so. If the weather breaks.'

There was a long pause, and then Mater leant forward and tapped his knee sharply with her gloved hand. 'I hope you are not regretting your engagement, Ashton. It would be a great foolishness, I think, to lose the chance of Gulveylor now.'

Drat the woman! Was nothing sacred? Ashton scowled.

'She's very young,' Mater went on, as though she were choosing a puppy. 'I'm sure you could mould her, over time. She is genuinely fond of you, you know, Ashton.'

'Of course,' Ashton said coldly. 'And I think a lot about her.'

But that night, as he watched Tamsin tripping to and fro in her Volunteer's uniform, he was struck again by that air of artifice in her. She was playing at being a nurse. And later when she joined him at supper, and twinkled and smiled for him alone, he felt that her sparkle was false, like the swatch of ringlets she had pinned in her hair.

He went to his bed and found that it was Sylvie whom he 'thought a lot' about. Sylvie, and another young woman, tousled, damp and smiling with not an ounce of artifice about her.

Chapter Fifteen

Merran trotted the farm-trap up Market Jew Street with a mood that matched the weather, bleak, clouded and disagreeable. Altogether it had been a dismal day.

He had just taken Paul back to the station after his leave. It was only the second time Paul had been home in more than two years of war, and saying goodbye again was a sorry wrench – although the visit had been an unexpected strain. Paul was like a stranger in the house, his parents had hidden anxiety under a false, brittle brightness, and Peter – doubly aware of his loss of limbs – sunk in a pit of tormented despair from which not even Nurse Blight could raise him.

Then, just as they were leaving (with a load of winter broccoli for the train – no one took a cart into town any more just to deliver people) Paul had produced his bombshell. He had a present for Pa, he announced proudly, a 'new' coat picked up for a song at St Buryan. There was almost a nasty scene.

It wasn't Paul's fault, of course, even Pa could see that. Paul wasn't to know that St Buryan Bazaar was kept by Tom Liddel these days, 'making a fortune out of other folk's misery' as Pa said, by buying up the unwanted clothes of the men who were not coming back. They were good clothes, most of them, very little worn, and the widows and families were glad of a few pennies, but Pa would rather freeze than wear anything sold by Tom Liddel and Paul's gift almost spoiled their farewells.

Then at the last minute Silas Farrington had arrived with a request for Merran to pick up a lathe from the station while he was there, and of course Pa agreed at once. It seemed a reasonable enough request, but Merran could see how it would be. Farrington had a permit for petrol to move his 'essential supplies'. He would offer Merran sixpence for his trouble and sell the petrol at a profit. The half-hour Merran had spent kicking his heels and then struggling with a heavy lathe was not sweetened by the knowledge that it put money in Farrington's pocket.

And then, this. Seeing Lizzie Treloweth clambering out of Ashton Masters' brougham – around the corner too, as if she knew it was indecorous. And with such an inane grin of pleasure on her face. It was the last straw, as if all the good, simple wholesome things in life were being corrupted.

She glanced towards him as he approached, but he affected not to see her and trotted by without stopping. It was only a few yards to the shop and the rain had eased, but it was a peevish gesture and he drove home doubly irritated by his own ill-nature.

When he arrived, however, there were other things to occupy him. Hunnicutt was waiting in the yard, with a face like thunder, and even as Merran handed down the reins and clambered from the cart he could see through the open door of the stable.

'My stars!' he said. 'Whatever's been going on here?'

But he need hardly have asked. Even without walking into the building he could see that a sort of transformation had taken place. The whole place had been scrubbed and tidied. The cart-house too (which was usually a cheerful jumble of sacks and implements) was swept and clean, the sacks neatly folded and the tools – forks, spades, evals – hung self-consciously from a row of nails newly hammered into the wall.

It was the same in the cow-house next door. Even the little high window had been cleaned of grime and cobwebs, and a thin shaft of grey light fell on the unnaturally organised byre below, the gleaming floor spread with a neat layer of fresh bedding straw.

Hunnicutt glowered. 'That Willi Braun,' he said glumly (he pronounced it 'Willie Brown'). 'Started work this afternoon and went through here like a dose of salts.'

'Done a good job, though,' Merran ventured. 'Except he

shouldn't have used the straw and hay like that. Supposed to be for fodder purposes only with this shortage on.'

Hunnicutt grunted. 'You try telling him that. Said so till I was blue in the face, but he just smiled and went on working like a heathen. My belief the fellow doesn't understand plain English.'

'Perhaps he doesn't,' Merran said. 'He is a foreigner, after all.'

'But he must have known. "That there bain't for beasts laying on," I said. Said it slow and hollered it out besides. An idiot could have understood. But he took no notice.'

Merran had a mental image of the poor Belgian being shouted at in incomprehensible Cornish and for the first time that day he found himself grinning. 'I'll have a word to him myself,' he said. 'We can't afford to use fodder at that rate, and if the Agriculture Commission people come, there will be trouble and no mistake. Where's Braun now?'

Hunnicutt shrugged. 'Your ma's given them that old drying shed, and the refugee committee has been here half the afternoon with bits of furnishings. Gone back there more than like.' He didn't add 'and good riddance' but the meaning was clear enough.

Merran nodded. 'I'll look for him there.' He made his way to the building. It was not big – one large room downstairs, and two smaller attics reached by a steep staircase, but there was a big fireplace and a pump outside, and Mother had spent days scrubbing it ready, so when it was furnished it would be snug enough. All the same he was not prepared for what met his eyes when the door swung open.

There was not much furniture, a big table and three chairs with a sort of lopsided dresser and chest of drawers, but already the room had an indefinably foreign air. Perhaps it was the patterned cloth rug in front of the fire, or the starched white lace runner and brightly painted wooden ornaments on the table, or perhaps it was just the strong, vinegary cooking smell of whatever was bubbling in the pan on the fire. Most of all it was the tall, strapping girl who stood before him in an embroidered apron – her blond hair swept up into plaits over her head. Merran remembered that the Braun daughter had been spat at more than once on suspicion of being German. He could see why.

'My mother, she is not here, excuse,' the girl said. 'She is cheesing.'

Merran was perplexed. 'Choosing? Choosing what?'

The girl laughed. 'She make a cheese. Your mother show her how. You are Merran, yes? Am Anna Braun.'

Merran smiled – the girl was much less formidable when she laughed. 'Hello Anna. I was looking for your father.'

It sounded severe and Anna frowned. 'He work bad?'

'Not bad, no. It is only, he put straw on the floor for bedding, and that is forbidden.'

'Forbedding forbidden?' She sounded so perplexed that Merran laughed.

'Not allowed,' he said. 'For eating, not for sleeping.'

She smiled. 'I tell him. And now, I must to finish here. Only I put up these, yes?' She gestured towards a pile of pictures spread on the floor. They were paintings – bold, simple, primitive almost – but even Merran's untutored eye could see that they had a kind of vibrant life. 'You like them? Or no?'

She had painted them, Merran realised foolishly. 'Yours?' he asked.

She nodded. 'Is Belgium. This our house, this Bruges, this my grandfather. But perhaps you rather see' – she burrowed in the pile and produced a paper, rather shyly – 'this?'

It was a page of cheap paper, and the sketch was in pencil. It was in the same bold style, and the face was obscured in shadow, but there was no mistaking the subject. Smock, cap, leggings, boots, hauling a bucket from the well – it was Hunnicutt to the life.

'It's wonderful,' he said, and her face lit with pleasure.

'Is not finish,' she explained. 'But you like I finish it for you? Is good, when you are sad, this draw. Make you feel better.'

Merran nodded. 'I wish Peter could do something like that,' he said half to himself. She was looking at him quizzically. 'My brother,' he explained.

She brightened. 'I can teach, if you want. In Belgium I a little bit teach.'

Her directness surprised him, and he found himself grinning. 'You will have other duties, I expect.'

She hung her head. 'Yes.' But she sounded so downcast that he decided that he would suggest it, after all. He was sure Mother would agree. Even an hour a week would give Peter something to think about, something he could do even without legs. If he could be persuaded to do it. Perhaps Lizzie could suggest it to him. Or Nurse Blight – Peter listened to her.

The thought of Lizzie recalled the events of the morning, and his smile subsided. 'Well, I've got work to do. Tell your father about the hay.' And he grumbled off to find out what Farrington wanted done with the new lathe.

Sunday seemed to be for ever coming. Being at Nanzeal seemed to bring Michael closer, and Lizzie really looked forward to her weekly visits now, even when the rain was lashing the treetops like today, and the outing would mean a dismal trudge across sticky fields, or through lanes ankle-deep in muddy puddles.

'Don't know what you want to go traipsing out there for, this weather,' Mam grumbled, when they had all come in from church and were sitting down to a warming stew of mutton-ends and carrots. 'Here's Daisy come home with her skirts soaked to her knees, and she's only come on main roads. Missed the bus again, though I'll never know how.'

Lizzie knew how. Selwood's motor-bus ran a special service to Farrington's, whenever there was a shift starting and the ordinary horse-bus didn't run. Cost threepence, but the workers liked it, especially this weather, and the bus was packed tighter than a sardine-can. But Daisy often lingered behind on purpose to walk back with Abel Hoskins, who had a bicycle – and Lizzie suspected that they didn't hurry home at that.

'I'm thinking,' Daisy said, as if she was reading Lizzie's thoughts, 'I might get a bicycle myself.'

Lizzie waited for Mam to say, 'Whatever next?' but it was Gramps who spoke, helping himself to another spoonful of carroty gravy, 'My dear life, Daisy! What are we coming to? Peddling round with your ankles showing! Unbecoming, that's what it is.'

And then of course Mam had to be contrary. 'Well, there's plenty of girls ride bicycles these days Feyther. Quality folks too. There's Rosa Warren up at Trevarnon, bicycling everywhere like an errand-boy, and nobody thinks anything about it. Patriotic, that's what it is – save the horses for war-work.'

Gramps snorted, but Daisy pressed home her unexpected advantage. 'And talking of errand-boys, it wouldn't come amiss to have a bicycle for the shop. Get one with a basket, and we can take it out with the orders. Save no end of time. Be a good thing, all round, a bicycle.'

Then Mam did say, 'And what are you going to use for money, Daisy Treloweth? Mutton bones? We're pinching as it is with meat so scarce. I'm thinking we'll have to buy in some of that Australian beef that's come to Plymouth. Supposing the Food Ministry doesn't insist on unloading in London and sending the ship back to sea for the Germans to sink it – like they did with that wheat last month.'

'Mind you,' Gan said, collecting up plates and forks and setting a jar of plums on the table, 'folks are a sight worse off in London. Down here we've got the farms at least, and the fishermen are working seven days now, Sabbath and all.'

Mam tutted. 'Wouldn't have done that, before the War. And have you seen what they're bringing in? Eels and dog-fish – stuff that Christian folk would have been ashamed to eat, one time.' The Treloweths of course didn't often eat fish without it was Good Friday. 'And the price! There's some poor miners up Penvarris taking home twopence a week. Hit a poor seam, see, and still got to buy candles and explosives. It was all in the papers. And then you find fishermen asking fivepence apiece for hake. Profiteering, that's what it is.'

Gan doled out a plum each with a slotted spoon. 'Fishermen got a living to make, same as you. There's been demonstrations some places against butchers, don't forget.'

'That's different,' Mam said. 'All right, the price of beef has doubled. But how many carcasses do we see these days? Doesn't take a genius to figure out we're still taking much less than we used to. And there's a lot more work too, with people taking smaller joints.'

'If I had a bicycle,' Daisy said, returning to the fray, 'I could maybe bring home a rabbit or two from the farms on my way.'

Lizzie looked up, with her mouth full of plum. 'Did I tell you Pa Jago was saying he'd send home a few chicken for the shop? Government directive. People have got to kill off half their chickens to preserve the grain supplies.'

'Can't be right,' Gan said. 'Where do they think the eggs are coming from? And people won't do it, mark my words. Afraid there'll be a famine, whatever the Government says. Still, we'll be glad of the extra poultry and no mistake. I don't know how to fill the orders, sometimes, even with Lizzie's rationing system.' She cut the remaining plums carefully into quarters and doled them out – one piece for each of the girls and two for Gramps and Eddy. 'And talking of rationing, mind you make the most of these plums. Pre-war they are, and there's only the one jar left.'

'Honestly,' Agnes said, 'nobody talks about anything but food these days.' Aggie felt the lack of sweet things more than any of them.

'I'm not talking about food,' Daisy protested. 'I'm talking about bicycles. Silas Farrington has got hold of three and he's willing to sell them to anyone in the works, so much a week off your wages.'

'I wouldn't buy a dead cat from Farrington,' Gramps said, 'for fear it was faulty.'

Daisy tossed her head. 'Well, the Government do. We had a new lathe delivered last week and we're going to start in on making aircraft tails. Top rates. I've volunteered.'

'I thought you were cutting screw-threads,' Lizzie said.

Daisy flushed. 'Well, I was. But we're getting men now, directed from the register. The ones who aren't A1. Die-cutting was man's work before the War, so the women have to get equal rates for it. He's putting the men on that job, and getting we girls to do other things.'

Lizzie did some frantic calculations. If they were directing men from the register, how long before they sent her somewhere? And what about Eddy? They'd have him in the Army as soon as he was eighteen, if the War went on like this, and send some fellow from the register to work in the slaughteryard. They might take Merran too, for that matter. She couldn't bear to think about it.

Daisy was looking at her fingers. 'Besides, it's hard on your hands, cutting threads. Metal splinters all over and that rough you could grate cheese on them.'

'I'll bet Abel Hoskins doesn't like that,' Eddy said.

Daisy ignored him. 'Anyway, if we don't take that poultry, Silas Farrington will. He's been round the farms offering to take all they kill, for the canteen. Cut out the butcher's profit, he says.'

Mam put down her spoon sharply. 'He never did?' and Gramps said, 'I'll profit him when I catch him, underhanded blackguard.'

'Here,' Gan said, 'not in front of the children. Now, you lot run along and let your mother feed Horry, and me and Agnes will deal with this cloam. Lizzie, you'd best be off or Nurse Blight will be drowned dead waiting.' Mam went off with the baby and the younger children scrambled down from their chairs. Lizzie put on her coat and bonnet.

'What you need is for me to have this bicycle,' Daisy said.

'Fat chance I'd have of using it,' Lizzie retorted, stooping to lift little Dot down off her perch. 'You'd be off out with your Abel every chance you got.'

Daisy flushed, but she didn't deny it. 'And I suppose you wouldn't go out riding with Michael Jago supposing he asked you?'

'She'd sooner be in the cold-room,' Elsie said with a giggle, and everyone turned to stare at her. Drat the child! It was Lizzie's turn to burn scarlet.

Gan twinkled at her, 'What's all this then?'

'It's nothing. At least, it's nothing yet. When he comes home next there might be something to tell you – though he'll want to talk to Father, first.'

Gan said, 'Oh, Lizzie!' with such delight that Lizzie held up her hand.

'Like I said, there's nothing yet, so don't you go saying nothing to Mam. Right, I'm off.'

She went out, but as she closed the door softly, she heard Daisy muttering to Agnes. 'I'll have to get Abel up to the mark, or Lizzie'll be married before me.'

Married! It made her heart pound louder than Penvarris stamps, and all the way to Nanzeal her soul was singing, in spite of the rain.

The weather did not trouble Chubby Beresford. He was enjoying himself, lying in comfort on a deep sofa in front of a blazing fire at Gulveylor.

It had been plumb foolish of course to try to take that nag for a canter. He had been raised in London and though he could ride, obviously, he had never really liked it. Since the day he was twelve years old and his father brought home a motor-car, Chubby had heartily preferred horse-power to horse-flesh.

It was almost mutual, this love affair with machinery. Motor-buses and motor-cars which snarled and died in the hands of lesser drivers purred into life at Chubby's touch. There was no motor-bicycle on the whole station at Quellieu that he hadn't ridden at some time or other, and he could coax miracles from an aeroplane.

But horses! That was a different matter altogether. He would not have ridden one at all, in fact, if it hadn't been for Ashton. Chubby was fond of his friend, in a lazy, good-natured sort of way, but he didn't care to be outshone at anything, not even something as trivial as riding. Especially not when there was a damned pretty girl in the case. He had acquitted himself well, on the whole, until he attempted a canter, but the wretched horse had a mind of its own, and, since Chubby's attention was occupied with something else (the bewitching rise and fall of Tamsin Beswetherick's breasts under her riding habit), accidents were not altogether surprising.

The mishap had been vexing at first – his foot puffed up like a purple pillow, and he had been rather impatient of all the fuss. But when Tamsin appointed herself his personal angel of mercy, and decked herself out in her nursing uniform to tend him hand and foot, his attitude changed. His injured ankle rapidly came to require a great many hot and cold fomentations and a good deal of lying about on sofas with his foot on a cushion. By the time the expected wire arrived summoning Ashton back to Gosport to collect and deliver his aeroplane, Chubby was beginning to fear that the nursing would have been too effective, and the doctor would order him back at the same time.

But it had worked out splendidly. Another week at least, before it would take his weight, and a second before he could safely fly. Ashton set off (accompanied by his mother, who was making her way back to London) and Chubby was obliged to stay behind.

It cost him a real pang for a moment, watching Ashers go. Chubby did love his flying. He managed to console himself, though, with the promise of a fortnight and more of Tamsin's undivided company. She was a damned attractive little filly, and though Ashers was a pleasant enough fellow in his way, he didn't altogether deserve her – or appreciate her, Chubby thought.

When Ashton left, Tamsin was charmingly distraught, and Chubby seized the opportunity to offer her a little gentle comfort.

'You are very fond of him?' he asked, when she came in that evening. He was half-lying on the couch with his foot on a footstool and she set a supper-tray on the table beside him. He had developed a special voice for the sickroom, a soft tone – brave but plaintive. 'Think he's tickety-boo, all that sort of thing?'

Tamsin picked up a cup of beef-tea and guided it to his lips. Chubby eyed it doubtfully, disgusting stuff, but he swallowed a mouthful for duty's sake. 'Oh Charles,' she sighed. (He loved it when she called him Charles.) 'I suppose I do.'

He was on to that in a moment. 'Only "suppose"? Now see here, old thing, it isn't quite the ticket, you know, marrying a fellow when you only "suppose" you're fond of him.'

Tamsin dropped her eyes, toyed with her hair, and smiled at him from under her lashes. Little hussy: he was sure she knew the effectiveness of those actions. It was enough to make a man forget himself. Chubby shifted a little on his pillows and mastered his voice with difficulty.

'You can tell Chubby,' he said, doing his best to sound as much as possible like an animated, harmless, amiable teddy-bear. 'Bit cut up,

I daresay? Not feeling quite the thing?'

Tamsin said in her little-girl voice. 'Yes, it's terrible to see him go.' She met his eye and coloured again. 'Except,' she went on in a more normal tone, 'that he's so . . .'

He reached up with his hands and grasped hers. She did not withdraw them. 'So . . . what?'

She shook her head, her face redder than the hearth-rug. 'It is nothing.' She went to move away but he held her wrists fast. 'Only – I don't know – he will touch me so.'

'Touch you!' Chubby was so astonished that he almost released his grasp. He would have laid money on old Ashers behaving every inch like a gentleman – though you could hardly blame the chap. Tamsin seemed sometimes positively to invite seduction. He composed his face into a concerned frown. 'Fellow's a scoundrel. You mean he's been . . .' – he sought for a word – 'untoward?' Dashed dark horse, old Ashers – to look at him you'd think butter wouldn't melt in his mouth.

She shook her head, 'No, no nothing like that. It was only that Mama left us alone for a moment, on purpose I'm sure to say goodbye . . .'

'And what did he do?'

She shook her head again. 'Nothing. Kissed me. Held my hand. Stroked my hair. But it's not romantic any more. He's so . . . I don't know . . . so urgent!'

Urgent, was he? Well what the devil did she expect, he was engaged to the girl. Scared her, more like. No more than half an idea of what to expect. While Ashton, of course, had that girl in France. The thought of Sylvie quelled his qualms. Ashers had other interests and, by Jupiter, it wasn't fair to Tamsin. Still, all this gave a man a cue how to behave. He was still holding her hands and he raised them reverently to his lips. 'Urgent?'

'Always . . . pawing me.' She seemed unconscious of any irony. Her eyes met his and he was alarmed to see tears in them. 'Oh, Charles, he frightens me sometimes.'

He pulled her gently down onto the couch beside him. 'My poor Tamsin.' He found a clean handkerchief from his dressing-jacket, and handed it to her. She dabbed her eyes with a corner of it and smiled at him through her tears. Chubby fidgeted again on his pillows, but he kept his voice light, 'Now see here, old thing, don't cry. It's bound to be a bit . . . well . . . worrying, d'you see? Sweet young thing like you. But can't blame a chap, when he's engaged to be married, and he's going away to war next minute. After all, when you *are* married . . .'

That made its point. She turned away from him and stood up sharply. 'I know,' she said, after a moment. 'And I don't think . . . Oh, Charles. What am I to do?'

'Now, listen to your Uncle Chubby,' he said, patting the seat beside him. She sat down. 'See here, my dear old thing, you mustn't be frightened. Old Ashers is a good fellow – only he's a bit hasty that's all. There he was – going away – he doesn't know if he'll ever see you again. It's forgivable.' He glanced at Tamsin, but she was looking at him soberly with her green eyes very wide. He made a daring move. 'I can understand any man being carried away, looking at you.'

She coloured, pink and pretty. If he was Masters, he thought, he'd have done a lot more than hold her hand and stroke her hair. And she would have liked it too, by God. He would have seen to that.

'Don't be absurd, Charles.'

'Not absurd,' he said seriously. 'Foolish perhaps. Hopeless. But not absurd. Any man might . . .' – he was going to say 'desire' but he amended it '. . . yearn for you. Though others, perhaps, know how to be less pressing.'

That pleased her, you could read it in her face. He might have kissed her then, but better, far better to bide his time. Though it was deucedly tempting. He took up his cup of beef-tea and swallowed it at a gulp, before allowing himself one final shot in the assault. 'Just as well I'm getting stronger by the hour and shall soon be gone myself. With a nurse like you it's almost a pleasure to be ill.'

She said, 'Oh, Charles!' with a little laugh and the moment was over. But after that he planned his campaign with meticulous care.

Chapter Sixteen

Daisy got her bicycle, but she never really got the hang of it. She went out on her afternoons off, wobbling down the lanes with Abel Hoskins. It didn't improve her bicycle riding, but it did bring Abel 'up to the mark' and before the bicycle was half paid for, or February half-over, Daisy came home saying they wanted to wed.

Mam was not displeased. She had met Abel, when he came calling for Daisy and her bicycle, but Lizzie hardly knew him because she was always at Little Manor when he came. It was half-deliberate. She could never quite forget that Daisy should have been marrying Peter. Even when Father wrote, giving his blessing, the whole idea made her uncomfortable.

All the same, the wedding date was fixed. First Saturday after Easter. Abel and Daisy changed to the early shift, too, so they could have a whole day before they went back to work. Daisy already had that blouse half-made and her bonnet trimmed from last time. It troubled Lizzie, but Daisy did not seem to mind.

'Told the Jagos have you?' Lizzie said one evening as they sat together in front of the fire. Everyone else was either in bed or busy downstairs so the two sisters had a rare moment of peace.

Daisy looked up from the dusters she was hemming. She was going to move in with Mrs Hoskins, after the wedding, but she was sewing for her household chest all the same. 'No.' There was a tell-tale spot of crimson in her cheeks. 'Think I ought to, do you?'

Lizzie put down the sock she was darning – one of Eddy's, more hole than stocking. 'Course you ought to. My hat, Daisy you're a queer one sometimes.'

Daisy went back to her stitching. 'Well, it's awkward Lizzie. You can see it is. But I've got Abel, and Peter's got this Nell Blight of yours. So where's the point of making folks unhappy?'

'They've got to know some time. And I'm fixing to marry Michael, as you well know. What do you think? They ought to hear it from Hunnicutt, or one of the dealers down the market?'

Daisy flung down her duster. 'Well, what am I to do? March up there and knock on the door? "Please Mrs Jago, I've come to say I'm getting married"? It isn't as if it is ordinary times and we could ask them to the wedding. There'll be fifteen of us to the feast as it is. Mam's in a proper taking over the food.' It was true. Gan and Agnes were staying home to mind Horry and the shop, but everyone else would be there. Even Millie had a half-day. And then there was Aunty Simmins, and Mrs Hoskins and Abel's married sister – though his brothers were both away at the Front. A lot to feed. Mam was already making plans for a pressed tongue, and Gan was putting by a bit of flour each week to make a 'drop of cake' for the wedding. Saffron more than like – there wasn't enough sugar for anything fancy.

''Tis difficult, I suppose,' Lizzie said frowning as she wove the needle in and out to make a darn.

'You tell them,' Daisy said. 'It won't seem half so bad coming from you.'

Lizzie didn't want to, but in the end she agreed.

She tried to do it the next time she was up at Nanzeal, but every time she opened her mouth she felt so dreadful that she promptly shut it again, and it was late afternoon before she plucked up the courage to confide her news to Merran. They had gone out to 'see the pigs' although the day was raw and the salt wind from the sea stung their faces. As they struggled up to Rocky Acre the gale was almost blowing them backwards.

'If this weather doesn't break soon,' Merran shouted to her against the wind, 'it'll kill off the winter wheat – and then where will we be?'

Lizzie shook her head. 'Where?'

'In a proper famine, that's where. Here, come on over here out of the wind.' He led her into the lee of the ruined mine-building.

It was quiet there, the roar and buffeting ceased, and they could hear themselves speak without having their words whirled away on the wind. But Merran didn't say anything, just looked at her for a long moment in silence. 'You're going to marry Michael then?' he said at last.

She evaded his eyes. Funny to raise the subject now. Merran must have known for weeks – he and Mike had no secrets. 'If he'll have me.'

'Oh, he'll have you.' Merran said. 'But I wanted to know what you thought. Though I suppose I needn't ask. You've always loved him, haven't you?'

She nodded. 'Always.' If love was the right name for that crazy, confused feeling she always felt when Michael was near.

There was another silence. 'Well then,' he said at last. 'Best thing. But I want you to know, Lizzie – if you ever need anything, you can count on me.'

He sounded wretched, and for some reason she felt suddenly miserable herself, as if the door into some beloved, secret garden had been closed for ever. 'I know that,' she said. 'You are my dearest friend.'

'Then that will have to do,' he said, and made no effort to explain. 'Come on then, before it's dark.' He led the way out into the wind again.

But something in the exchange had given her courage. 'There is one thing, Merran.'

149

He whirled to face her, his face suddenly alight. 'What's that?'

'It's Daisy. She's to marry Abel Hoskins from the factory. She wanted me to tell Peter. Only I can't do it.' Lizzie had not met his eyes as she spoke, and when she did look up his expression surprised her. He looked as if she had slapped him.

His voice too was pained. 'And you want me to do it for you?' She nodded, and he went on more gently. 'Well, I will of course. Anything for you, Lizzie. You know that.'

She reached out and squeezed his hand. 'Thank you, Merran. Don't know how ever I'd manage without you. Only it doesn't seem right somehow, Daisy marrying one man when she'd promised another.'

They went back to the farmhouse, but Merran seemed more cast down than ever. She didn't like to mention that they had never got as far as the pigs.

Peter took the news badly, with a kind of fierce and morose depression. Not that he still hankered after Daisy, or even begrudged her happiness, Merran knew, just that it brought home his own condition more forcibly than ever.

'Never even came up here to bring the news her own self,' Peter said bitterly. 'Better things to do these days than think of me.'

'You might find better things to do yourself, if you'd a mind to,' Merran said. He had learned long ago that the best way to deal with Peter was never to sympathise. 'There's Anna Braun ready and willing to teach you painting whenever you're willing. Don't need feet for that job.'

Peter said 'pah!' with disgust and disdain, as he always did when the subject was mentioned. 'Painting. All very well for women, but what sort of occupation is that for a man?'

It was Silas Farrington, oddly enough, who changed his mind, one afternoon a few days later. He came in to see Pa – people all over the town were turning lawns and golf-courses into these allotments, and they were willing to pay to have it ploughed. Silas had a scheme for leasing out Merran or Hunnicutt with the steam-plough and he wouldn't listen to Merran's misgivings about the difficulties.

'You're wrong there, Master Merran,' in that singing-kettle whistle of his, 'but I can't stay to discuss it this evening, I'm due to go up to Trevarnon House for a Charity Evening in aid of Little Manor. There's a fellow giving a lantern slide lecture and an exhibition of war paintings. Lord Chyrose heard him in London and was very impressed.'

'Paintings?' Merran said wickedly. 'A woman, is he?' He looked sidewise at Peter, who gave a reluctant grin.

Farrington looked baffled. 'Dear me, no. Senior man in the Home Establishment, something to do with public information. He was an official artist in the African War – that's what the pictures are about, I understand.' His little pink eyes wrinkled into a condescending smile. (You couldn't call them 'piggy eyes', Merran thought dispassionately – he was very fond of pigs.) 'Anyway, Master Merran, you couldn't have a woman doing war paintings, could you? Need to *be* there to capture the flavour of it.'

'Something in that, I suppose,' Peter said. 'I wouldn't mind seeing those.'

Merran stared. 'Private function, I imagine?'

Farrington nodded. 'Subscription supper tonight – but if you're interested in the paintings, they'll still be there Saturday. Mrs Trevarnon is having a supper for the convalescents and the hospital supporters. Perhaps your brother could go – he's war wounded after all. Though it might be difficult, getting him there, I suppose.' He always talked about Peter as if he wasn't there.

'I'd get him there,' Merran said grimly. 'But we can't just turn up uninvited. It's a pity.'

Farrington looked at him. 'I might be able to arrange it,' he said, rubbing his hands as if he hoped to produce the invitation from the air, like a magician. 'Only, I promised Mrs Trevarnon a couple of chickens for the supper. If you could see your way clear . . .'

It was blatant bribery, and Merran was about to refuse angrily, but Pa had been listening. 'I've got to get rid of some anyway, and I'd just as soon they went to Little Manor as to some farmer in Brittany on this resettlement scheme. So you have them and welcome. But if the Government wants me to start killing ducks, I shan't be doing it. Stop the cows catching liver-fluke, they do. Eat the snails, see, and that's what carries the disease.'

'Really?' Farrington said, without interest. 'Shall I take those fowls now?'

It wouldn't have surprised Merran if Farrington simply took the birds and that was the last they heard, but he must have arranged something with Mrs Trevarnon, because the next day the postboy brought a charming note from her. She would be delighted to entertain them at the tea, and would send her own carriage for them, 'since I am sure your own transport is required on the farm.' It was delicately done – though there was no mention of chickens. Merran smiled wryly. Mrs Trevarnon would certainly have acknowledged them if she knew where they came from.

All the same, the exhibition was a great success. Merran went with Peter, the first 'time off' he had had for months. He could be spared now, because Willi Braun was a hard worker – though he did what he thought, rather than what anyone told him – and Mother had the two Braun women to help. When his time was up to go to the tribunal again, Merran thought, he'd be sent to the Army. And a good thing too. He burned to get out there and 'pay someone back' for Peter's legs, and there was getting to be less and less for him at home. Mother and Pa were always at hammer and tongs these days, and with Peter sunk in this bleak despair the mood at Nanzeal was dreadful.

If only Peter would rouse himself out of it. This exhibition might help. Peter was genuinely interested.

'Fellow can't paint horses,' he said to Merran. 'Look at those legs, all going in the wrong direction.' His face was animated, more alive than Merran had seen him since he came home. Then Nurse Blight came over – she was with the Little Manor party – and Merran wandered off and left them alone together for a little. That would do Peter good, too.

He looked around for Lizzie, but she was not there.

Anyway, he thought miserably, Lizzie was going to marry Michael. He ought to be pleased for her, but he felt sick at heart. Time he went in the Army, did something, before this terrible mire of despondency sucked him in too.

He could scarcely eat the tea provided, though it was delicious – sweet cakes, and potted meat which he hadn't seen for months. But it was worth going to the exhibition after all. When they got home, Peter consented to have Anna Braun come and show him how to paint.

Tamsin attended the Charity Evening, too. A tedious affair with those horrid paintings – all blood and battles and people falling out of saddles – and the lantern-slide lecture bored her almost to weeping. As liaison lady for the Linen League, however, she could scarcely avoid the occasion, and at least her uniform won her some gratifying attention.

Rosa Warren was there, naturally, since Trevarnon House was her home. Tamsin had hoped for a little girlish gossip, but Rosa seemed genuinely interested in the exhibition and spent most of the evening in animated conversation about it with Lord Chyrose. Tamsin found herself obliged to mingle with the other guests. She knew many of them, but they were not the kind of people one mixed with at Gulveylor.

There were so many guests, and so few men present, that she might have been obliged to fetch her own supper if Silas Farrington hadn't presented himself at her side and offered to escort her to the buffet. He was an odious little man, so globular and unctuous that he reminded her somehow of candlegrease. But there was no one else, not even Papa – he had gone to Truro for some dreary meeting about allotments. She took Farrington's arm with the best grace she could muster, but altogether it was turning into a most disagreeable evening.

If only Charles could have been there. He was up and about now, hardly even hobbling on his stick, and the doctor was talking of signing him off 'fit for flying' very soon. But his foot still swelled if he stood too long, and he couldn't get his boot off. So he had stayed at home.

She missed his company. Charles had a boisterous enthusiasm for everything which made her laugh. She could imagine now what he would say about Farrington, smiling and bowing, and buttoned into a dress-suit and waistcoat that were absurdly tight. 'Not quite the ticket, old thing – fellow looks like a badly upholstered chair.'

The idea made her smile, and Farrington – thinking the smile was for him – was plainly flattered. That made her smile even more, which pleased him further, but he broke the spell by saying in that hissing whistle of his, 'Something pleases you?'

'I was thinking of someone,' Tamsin said. It was not polite, but the man could not be allowed false impressions.

Farrington leered knowingly. 'Of course. Your fiancé. You must miss him sadly. But since he is not with us, you can suffer me as escort?'

Tamsin flinched. Not only because talking to the wretched man was like conversing with a rainstorm, but because she had not in fact given a thought to Ashton all the evening. More than that, she realised, she was deliberately putting her cousin out of her mind.

She did not want to marry him. It had to be faced. Ashton was nice – handsome, charming, cultivated – and she had enjoyed her romance. When it *was* a romance. But that had all changed, recently, to that flushed urgency that frightened her so. If only he were more like Charles.

When Charles kissed her – well, yes he had kissed her once or twice when she was helping him take his daily exercise around the rose-garden – it was so different. His lips were cool and reverent, and this morning when he had lifted back her sleeve and run a ripple of kisses down her inner arm and onto her shoulder it had been nothing but enchantment and delight. He had raised her hair and touched the nape of her neck with his tongue so gently it had felt like a moth landing and sent the most delicious shivers of pleasure down her back. If only Ashton could behave like that instead of all that disagreeable passion.

'Is there anything more you wish?' Farrington's voice brought her back to the present, and she was so irritated that she abandoned supper and insisted on being taken to the gallery again. Even then, she could not bring herself to be civil to him, and pretended to be absorbed in the wretched paintings until Mother sent the carriage for her and she was able to excuse herself and get away.

The next day she told Charles about it. He was amused, and amusing, but his response lacked the sparkle that she had come to expect. They were in the summer-house, having walked round the lily-pond, and Charles sat down to rest his foot.

She looked at him, 'What is it Charles? You are melancholy.'

He grinned. 'Am I? Sorry, old thing. Got to keep one's pecker up and all that. Only, you see the sawbones dropped in last evening, took a dekko at me. Fit to leave next week he says.'

She felt her face fall. 'Charles!'

'Here, no, don't cry old girl. That's what airmen are for, isn't it? To fly. Only, you know I shall miss you most damnably. Shouldn't say so, when you are someone else's girl, but there's the truth of it.' He reached out a finger and twined it gently in her hair. 'If you weren't Ashers' girl, you know what I should do with you?'

She almost stopped breathing. 'What?'

'This.' He leant forward, and his hands were undoing her buttons. She was shocked. She went to push him off, but he caught her hands and kissed them gently, so gently that she ceased to protest, even when he reached into her camisole and brought out her breasts, cupped in his palms like ripe melons.

'Beautiful,' he said, 'so beautiful.' And then he was kissing them, those fluttering moth-kisses. It wasn't at all proper, but it was rather nice.

A little later, when he went to lift her skirts, she did move to prevent him, but he was too strong for her. 'I shall leave so soon,' he said, pinning her hands, and then the moth was on her thighs and between her thighs.

When he loosened his trousers she was horrified by the sight of him, and the pain when he entered her was a fearful, rude awakening; but by then it was too late. He was panting and groaning within her, then it was all over and he let her go.

She staggered away from him, clutching her garments around her. She felt shocked, ravaged. He had hurt her and there was blood on her petticoats.

Chubby came and took her in his arms, gentle as ever. She could not reconcile him with that lunging, grunting thing of a moment before. He kissed her, but she was numb. 'Now see here, old thing, that is what it's about. It's always bad, first time – but you will like it, when you get used to it. And it won't be so bad now, with Ashton.'

She raised her head, and looked at him with tear-filled eyes. 'Ashton. Will he . . . know?'

Chubby raised his eyebrows. 'Shouldn't think so. How could he know? You're not going to tell him, and I'm certainly not.'

'But I can't marry him now.'

He looked at her, 'Of course you can, my dear old thing. If that's what you want to do. D'you think you'd be the first?'

'I couldn't bear it, him doing . . . that to me!' She was actually crying now. Chubby cradled her in his arms, and she let him do it, as if it was someone else who had caused her tears.

'Tamsin, Tamsin, it's all right! People do it all the time. And believe me, it is never so painful again. Now, here, dry your eyes. We'll have to go in, and we can't have your mother see you like this.'

'I can't face Mama!'

'Of course you can!'

So she dried her tears and adjusted her clothes, dutifully. But when they got inside, she felt she really could not face her mother at dinner, and she pleaded a stomach-ache – to explain the state of her petticoats – and had a tray sent to her room.

Chapter Seventeen

It was positively provoking. Michael had been getting weekend passes, regularly, every time a training course was over, but now that he had something special to come home for, his leave had been cancelled twice. And when he did manage to get back Lizzie had only a day's notice, so it was too late to alter her shift at Little Manor. In fact, she would not have heard about it then, if Merran hadn't stopped by at the shop after market, on purpose to tell her. The Jagos had got a wire that morning.

It was not fair, she thought furiously, as she worked through the familiar routine of the wards – breakfast, beds, bottles, bandages. Michael would be arriving in Penzance any minute and she could not even be there to meet him. She had not even had the pleasure of anticipation – though admittedly she wouldn't have dared look forward to his visit too much, in case it was cancelled again.

Perhaps she ought not to wish him home at all, she thought, as she took the temperature of the new admission with shrapnel in his shoulder (105, poor boy, the wound was infected). The sooner he came, the sooner he would be posted abroad, and then it might be Michael lying here, with his eyes rolling and his face livid with pain. Or even worse, one of those men the patients still saw in their nightmares – wounded and moaning on the wire, beyond human reach. It made Lizzie sweat to think about it. Better dead than that. Oh, Michael, Michael. Why must you go?

She pulled herself together and settled the wounded captain a little more easily on his pillows. He murmured 'Thank you' through ashen lips, and she marvelled, for the thousandth time at the patience and fortitude of these men. Ordinary men, like Michael, uprooted from home and family – to this.

'Miss Treloweth,' Mrs Rouncewell's voice rang through the ward like a bugle. 'When you have quite finished here you may bring a tray of tea to my office. And biscuits. I have a visitor.'

Lizzie sighed. Silas Farrington again, no doubt, with his offer of 'cheap' vegetables and poultry. That man had more irons in the fire than Falmouth Laundry. Why did Matron waste hard-to-come-by biscuits on the likes of him?

Why couldn't they call *him* up for the Army? Serve the Germans right, she thought with a grin, having Farrington loose on them. Buy their guns for sixpence and sell them back for a shilling.

She popped the thermometer into disinfectant and hurried off to make the tea. A proper china pot for Matron, with milk in a jug and four precious sugar-lumps nestling in a sugar-basin. She put it all on a tray, with a starched white cloth and took it down to Matron's room.

Mrs Rouncewell came out to meet her. 'Ah, there you are at last, child. Now, I have something urgent to attend to. Take it in please, and see my guest is served. I shall not be long.'

Lizzie grimaced inwardly. She did not like Silas Farrington and the prospect of being alone in his company made her uncomfortable. But there was no appeal from Mrs Rouncewell. She said, 'Yes, Matron,' meekly enough.

'Well, get on with it, gel,' Mrs Rouncewell said. 'Don't stand about idle, like a train in a siding.' She disappeared in the direction of the dispensary.

Lizzie hesitated a moment longer and then plucked up courage and opened the door. She was aware of the man, staring out of the window with his back towards her, but she avoided looking at him, 'Tea, sir?'

'Lizzie?'

It was as well she had put the tray on the table or she would have dropped it all.

'Michael!' And then he was beside her, showering her face with kisses.

For a moment she revelled in it, but then she pulled back. 'But, Matron . . .'

Michael laughed. 'This was her idea. I came up hoping to see you, and she invited me in. Pretended it was to talk about Peter's legs, but it's my belief she did it on purpose for you to bring the tea.'

Lizzie stared at him, 'She wouldn't!'

He laughed again. 'Wouldn't she though? She's got a soft heart under that starched apron. And I've only got twenty-four hours.'

She felt her heart sink. 'And then you are going? To France?'

He traced her cheek with a finger. 'Not quite yet.' He sighed. 'It's absurd, Lizzie. Here they are "combing out" all kinds of occupations – miners, policemen, all sorts – to get men to the Front. And here's me, willing to go, begging to go, and they are going to send me on a blinking course before they send me. Something new about Mills bombs. So I have another ten weeks to wait.'

There were tears in her eyes, she could not help it. 'I wish you weren't going,' she said. 'I'm sorry Michael, but there it is. You are safe where you are, and you are working for the war effort, everyone says so.'

He took her shoulders and turned her to face him. 'I must go, can't you see that? I must. Every time I see a man with a wound-stripe, I feel guilty. I have to play my part in it. What do you want me to do? Shirk it, like Tom Liddel?'

She shook her head slowly. 'No, you are no coward. But I am. I am afraid for you.'

He put a hand under her chin and tilted her face upwards. 'Ah Lizzie, I have a charmed life. I must do, because I have you, don't I? You will be my wife?'

'Of course I will. If you come back.'

'Why shouldn't I come back? Look at your father, Paul – even the boys in this hospital – they have all come back, after a fashion. Even Peter. And you would not leave me, Lizzie, legs or not.'

'No,' she said, and knew that it was true. 'But we are lucky, Michael. So many people have died.'

He took her into his arms. 'I told you. We are charmed. Can't you feel it?' But she could not answer, because he was kissing her in real earnest.

There was a noise at the door, unnecessarily loud, and they leapt apart as Matron came into the office. Lizzie smoothed down her apron and tried to calm her thumping heart.

'Why, gel, you have not poured Mr Jago his tea,' Mrs Rouncewell said, severely.

Lizzie looked at her in dismay. 'Yes, ma'am. I mean, no, ma'am. Only Mr Jago and I are to be married.' There, she had said it. Announced it to the world.

Mrs Rouncewell did not smile. 'Very nice, I'm sure. But you are here to work, not to stand and chit-chat. So you may run along smartly and blanket-bath the patient in bed nine. Mr Jago and I have matters to discuss. Oh, and Miss Treloweth . . .'

'Yes, ma'am?'

'Straighten your cap before you go. Anyone might think you had been courting!' Matron's voice was stony, but there was the suspicion of a twinkle in her eyes.

When Lizzie finished her shift, Michael was waiting for her, offering the shelter of his umbrella against the rain. 'Some nice of you,' she said. 'But you ought to have gone on home. Your family will be wondering where you are.'

Michael smiled. 'Merran'll work it out,' he said. 'And anyway, I've got to go down and tell your family. And I'll write your father. What do you think he'll say?'

'Something daft more than like, but he'll be delighted. They all will. But I wonder what your pa will make of it, you wanting to marry a Treloweth, after that business with Daisy and all.'

'Oh, he'll understand. You aren't Daisy and never were. There's a rogue pig in every litter.'

'Thanks very much,' Lizzie said. 'So I'm an old sow, am I?' They laughed and they wandered together down the lane to Penzance, oblivious to the weather. Strange how once she'd been so nervous of this man, who now seemed as comfortable as Merran to be with.

That reminded her and she said, softly, 'And what will Merran say?'

He frowned then. 'He'll wish us happy. But don't let's stand here guessing about it, let's go and tell them. And what do you say to a wedding first leave I get? Soon as may be without spoiling Daisy's?'

She grinned up at him. 'I say, yes,' and she floated up the granite steps as if she were made of cloud, insubstantial with happiness.

'Pillowcases, hemmed squares, padded dressings, eye-patches and slings. That's all this week, Matron, I think.' Tamsin ticked off the items and snapped her notebook shut. 'Not such a big pile this time, but the Sewing Circle are as devoted as ever. Several of the ladies have adopted the uniform now.' There was no reason for telling the Matron that, except that it rankled rather. Tamsin was rapidly losing her special status, and if Papa would only have let her, she would have considered giving up her liaison role altogether.

Matron poured her a cup of tea. It was served in a horrid thick china cup and accompanied by one of those cheap bought biscuits. She sipped at it a little, as convention demanded, and then set the cup back on the tray.

'I regret Matron that I cannot stay longer this afternoon. We have an injured serviceman of our own, you know, and he is to leave us tomorrow. I must get home in good time to wash and change for dinner.'

In fact it was not 'dinner' which Tamsin wanted to be home for. It was a cold afternoon, but fine, and if she hurried there would be time for one last walk around the estate with Chubby Beresford. There was no real excuse for an unchaperoned stroll, now he was recovered, but she had accompanied him so often as his nurse that no one any longer thought anything of it.

And the walk would undoubtedly lead on to other things. Tamsin was not so keen on that, but it didn't last long, and it made Charles so attentive. He was so agreeably romantic before the event, and so very flattering afterwards, that – apart from those disagreeable few minutes – she had come to look forward to their little rambles.

She had not really intended to repeat the experience.

Indeed, after that first occasion in the summer-house she had been so ashamed and shocked that she had tried to avoid Chubby altogether. But as an invalid it was easy for him to ask for her, and it would have caused awkward questions if she had refused.

Charles had made his feelings clear.

'I can't,' she said. 'I can't! I won't!'

He took her hands and looked up into her face. 'Tamsin, my beautiful Tamsin. Don't say that, old thing, or we shall both be in deep water. I couldn't bear to stay, you know, if you insist on saying that. Not after what has happened. I couldn't trust myself, d'you see, to be so near you and have to keep away. I couldn't do it. I should have to take myself off, foot or no foot. Your parents would want to know why. And what could I say? Unless I told them the truth, of course. Whereas, if you are a sensible girl . . .'

He was threatening her. She felt the helpless tears rising, and suddenly he was the old, gentle, romantic Chubby once again. 'I'm sorry, Tamsin old girl, but you see how it is. You can't snatch a glass of water from a dying man. And that's how I feel, Tamsin. Desperate. I'll do anything – anything – but I must have you again. You can't blame a fellow. You're so ravishing. It's enough to drive any man mad.'

'But . . . I can't!'

'You can. You have. How can it make any difference now? I know it is not the same for women, but it means so much to me. And you'll have to do it, you know, when you marry Ashers.'

The name descended on her like a candle-snuffer. 'Ashton!'

He put a finger to her lips. 'Yes, Ashton. He'll be full of fire, and he won't want his little lady turning away whenever he goes anywhere near her. So think of yourself as doing it for him. If you're accustomed to it now, you won't mind it so much then.'

It was so outrageous that she almost laughed. She began to protest, but he interrupted her.

'And I should hate to have to leave, and explain everything to your mother. So come on, old thing, we're supposed to be tootling around the jolly old garden. Do this foot of mine a bit of good. Among other things.'

So he had cajoled and persuaded and teased and bullied her into compliance. Not once, but again. And again. It became quite an established thing between them whenever they went for a walk. Charles was thoughtfully quick about it, and once it was over he never alluded to it again. And the rest of the time he was so courteous, so attentive, so charmingly flattering. It was a price to pay – that was what marriage was about, she supposed.

And Chubby was quite right about one thing. After that first time it was never so bad again. No more actual pain, or blood. In fact, even the tiresome bleeding which used to plague her every few weeks or so seemed to have stopped, since. So there were compensations.

'Are you all right, Miss Tamsin?' Mrs Rouncewell's voice brought her back to the present.

Tamsin gave her a bright smile. 'Perfectly well, thank you. Only I was a little abstracted. And now I must go, thank you again for the tea.'

As she bowled down the lane with the donkey-cart she passed Michael Jago with Lizzie Treloweth on his arm. Did *they* do that, she wondered. Probably not. Lizzie was such a respectable creature with her lumpy skirts and drab Sunday blouses. The thought gave her a frisson of unexpected delight. Tamsin Beswetherick, secret adventuress. She went home to Chubby and her walk, and there was, this time, a certain charm about it.

And when, next morning, Charles set off for the train, so masculine in his uniform, with the hint of a romantic limp, she found she could not help the tears. She could hardly weep in public for a man who was merely Ashton's guest, and she was compelled to scramble her goodbyes and hurry to her room to hide her swollen eyes.

Her eyes were still pink when she went down for luncheon. Mama noticed it at once. She set down the letter she had been reading and said, 'Are you quite well, Tamsin?'

Tamsin swallowed. 'Quite well, Mama, only that I have a slight . . . feminine indisposition.' There, that should put a stop to unfortunate questions.

It did. 'I see, well lie down this afternoon and Millie shall bring you up something on a tray. But here is something that will revive you at once. A letter from Helena. She has arranged leave and she is bringing this doctor of hers home to meet your father. They wish to be married.'

'Helena!'

Mama smiled, 'Yes! Your father will be delighted. We had quite despaired, you know, of Helena ever making a match. Too many modern ideas about education and votes for women. Not like you, my dear, you might have had anyone you chose.'

Tamsin seized the moment. 'As to that, Mama, there is something I wish to speak to you about.'

161

Her mother stiffened. 'Well?'

It was too late now. Tamsin had to say what had been in her mind for a fortnight. 'I am not sure, Mama, that I wish to marry Ashton after all.' It took an effort, but now that the words were out she felt ridiculously relieved. 'I am sorry, after all the plans you have made for the wedding, but if you have Helena to wed perhaps it will not be a complete waste after all.'

Mama said nothing for a moment, but her face had gone very pink. When she spoke her tone was severe. 'This is my fault, I left you too much alone with that Beresford fellow. Your father was right. He said there was a danger you were falling for your patient. Well, here is a how-d'you-do. No doubt you hope that we will simply sit back and allow you to transfer your affections? Well, I am sorry Tamsin, I have no intention of permitting anything of the kind. What would Alice Masters say!'

Tamsin shook her head. 'This has nothing to do with Chubby.'

'If it has nothing to do with Charles – which is I suppose what you mean by that ridiculous nickname – would you be kind enough to tell me what it does mean?'

Tamsin felt the colour rise to her face. 'It is nothing to do with Charles, Mama. I have felt this way before – you will remember that Ashton left abruptly, the last time he was home. The truth of the matter is Mama, he is so . . . importunate . . . and I cannot like it. Even before he offered for me . . .' She trailed off.

Mama let out a long breath and sat back in her chair. That was a clever plea, Tamsin thought. Her mother would certainly remember occasions when Ashton had been indecorously pressing. And besides, it was the truth. After Chubby, she could not bear the thought of having Ashton touch her. She said, with genuine feeling, 'I cannot bear it.'

Mama sighed again. 'I see. And Charles Beresford?'

Tamsin had to scotch that idea very quickly. 'Oh, don't be absurd, Mama. Do you suppose I would accept attentions from Charles if I will not accept them from my own cousin? No, the fact of it is I do not want to marry anyone. At least, not yet. I do not feel ready for . . . all that, and with Ashton away at the War . . .'

Her mother nodded slowly. 'I see. That is a pity. Well, we shall see what your father says. It will look an unfortunate coincidence, I think, since Mr Beresford has been so much in your company.'

Tamsin coloured, 'Yes. I did like to talk to him. He could tell me so much about Ashton.' That was cunning. 'All about France, and

162

everything.' She cast about for some anecdote to relate, and remembered something Ashton himself had said. 'There is a French girl – Sophie? Sylvie? – the daughter of the farmer where they stay. Chubby says she waits for Ashton whenever he comes back after a sortie.'

A look of comprehension dawned on Mama's face. 'Ah! I see. That does put a different complexion on it. I cannot blame you, Tamsin, for being hurt by that. And a foreign woman too. Though it was not discreet to discuss it with his friend. And young men, you know, will be young men and sow their wild oats. But perhaps, as you say, it would be wise to wait. There would be much to be said for marrying when the War was over – supposing that it ever is over. I will speak to your father tonight, but he might agree, at least, to your seeking a postponement.'

Tamsin was secretly appalled. She had imagined Sylvie as a small child, with a girlish admiration for an airman. Nothing else had ever entered her mind and the idea was horrifying. Ashton could surely not have preferred another woman? When Papa came home her agitation on the subject was so self-evident that he agreed to her writing at once.

Tamsin Beswetherick regretted that although she remained fond of him, because of the uncertainties of war, she felt obliged to ask Mr Masters to release her from their understanding – at least until the cessation of hostilities.

The letter got to Quellieu about ten days after Chubby did.

Ashton was ridiculously piqued to receive it. Ridiculous because he himself had been casting around ever since he got back for a way to write a very similar letter to Tamsin. Five minutes of Sylvie's company had been enough to convince him that his engagement was a terrible mistake. But when release was handed to him on a plate, as it were, he felt slighted. He was sitting on his bed in the billet, still frowning over it when Chubby came in.

'What's the matter, old fruit? Not looking very pukka this morning. Bad news?' He patted a pocket. 'I've got just the remedy for that. Dr Beresford's special recipe. Care for a nip?'

'Not bad news, exactly,' Ashton said. 'It's from Tamsin. She wants to call off the wedding. Goes waffling on about "after hostilities" but that's what it comes down to. Wants to cancel the whole thing.'

Chubby paused in the act of pouring the brandy. 'Does she, by Jove?'

'Mater will have something to say,' Ashton said wryly. 'She knew I was having doubts of my own. She'll insist it was my fault and go on and on about losing Gulveylor. But better like this, I suppose.'

'She doesn't . . . ?' Chubby was devoting scrupulous care to pouring out that glassful. 'Tamsin that is – she doesn't mention me at all?'

'No.' Ashton was perplexed. 'Why should she?'

Chubby handed the glass without looking at him. 'No reason. I just – wondered.' He was uncomfortable, anyone could see that.

Ashton got to his feet. 'Look here, Beresford, have I got you to thank for this?'

Chubby took a gulp of special. 'Don't be idiotic, Ashers. As if I would. Here, drink this up and have another.'

Ashton pushed the glass aside angrily. 'As if you would what?'

'Oh Ashers, for heaven's sake. You were tired of the girl yourself, you as good as told me so. She must have sensed it, that's all.'

Ashton sat down but he was still glowering. 'Or had it pointed out to her.'

Chubby drained his glass. 'Now look here, Ashton, be reasonable. Your cousin is a dashed pretty girl – none prettier – and I can't pretend I wouldn't have liked to hold her hand. But she's got all the warmth of an Arctic iceberg when it comes to things like that.'

That was true, Ashton thought bitterly. But how the deuce did Beresford know?

'All right,' Chubby said, spreading his hands in a gesture of innocence, 'I tried to kiss her once. Heavens above, Masters, you ought to understand that. Don't catch you behaving like a monk when your fiancée is not there. But it got me nowhere.'

'Call yourself a gentleman!' Ashton found that he was unreasonably angry. 'We were engaged to be married.'

'But you didn't want to be,' Chubby persisted. 'And neither, apparently, did she. And in any case, as I said, nothing came of it. It was foolish, I suppose, but she seemed so unhappy after you'd left. Oh come on, Ashers, there's no harm done. And you shouldn't get yourself worked up into a tizzy like this. The weather's clearing and we may be flying later on.'

'Then you shouldn't be drinking,' Ashton said sourly and stomped out of the room.

The weather did clear, as it happened. They went out, six of them, in the way they had practised – single file, in line astern like a single, enormous insect taking the air. They were the best, the last, the survivors. Most pilots survived, on average, three or four weeks, and over Christmas most of the older hands had been posted away to Home Defence, or Training. On his return Ashton had found few familiar faces.

Ironic then, to take his place in airborne formation next to Chubby. He glanced over and Chubby gave a sardonic wave. Ashton looked away. He was still furious. He busied himself with the aeroplane.

They were to fly out at intervals over the lines to 'range' the guns – tell the gunners where to shoot – and Ashton fanned off south as directed. There was a bank of cloud, horrible white blindness – no horizon and no direction – and climb as he would he could not get out of it. He fought down panic – forcing himself to believe the 'level bubble', and not trust to his senses and send the aeroplane into a spin, but today the cloud seemed to go on for ever.

Then, suddenly he was out of the 'white darkness' and into sunlight – completely lost – and there were two German scouts below him. Bright red. Part of the Richthoven circus. They had seen him.

Kill or be killed, he thought grimly and dived, getting one of them in his sights. He pressed the trigger of his Vickers gun. Nothing. It had jammed. But there was still the Lewis gun and he pressed home the pursuit. It fired once and then it, too, failed.

Hell and damnation! Here was a pretty pickle. He slewed away, wrestling with the Vickers jam but he could not clear it. The German turned steeply and he followed, still working at the guns. He slid the Lewis gun down to try to clear it and reload, but it would neither come down cleanly, nor slide back to its place on the top wing.

Outnumbered and unarmed. By now the second scout had gained height and began to dive towards him.

He twisted, turned, but he heard the bark of guns and felt the airframe shudder as bullets tore into the wing-fabric. And then, suddenly, there was a shadow over him and he closed his eyes, waiting for death. There was the stutter of fire.

But a moment later it was the German scout that was spiralling earthwards in a plume of smoke and the plane that had been above him swooped alongside and the pilot gave him a cheerful wave.

Chubby!

There was no time to think of that. There was still the other scout – but Chubby was off in pursuit. Ashton took stock and looked around. He could see the river below him – he must have wandered miles off course in that cloud. One wing felt floppy and the jammed Lewis gun was still pointing uselessly to heaven. There was nothing for it. He banked, turned, and nursed the wounded plane homewards. He was still shaking, and whether it was because of that or the damaged wing he never afterwards knew, but as he touched down he managed to lurch disastrously.

One wing-tip buried itself in the soft earth of the grass beside the airstrip and the plane did a gentle pirouette around it. Ashton stumbled out of the cockpit as Paddy Lowe came over.

'All right, Masters? Nasty arm you've got there.'

Ashton looked down. There was blood on his sleeve and his arm was burning and throbbing. He hadn't noticed it before. They helped him towards First Aid.

'Bad time of it?' Lowe asked, and Ashton nodded. After all this, he thought, Tamsin's letter seemed strangely unimportant. And Chubby had saved his life. He reported the 'kill' to the CO and went back to his billet to write to Gulveylor – a warm, generous letter, releasing Tamsin and wishing her happiness. Then he wandered off to the mess to down a pint. Buy one for Chubby when he came in.

Chubby didn't come in with the others. One of the boys reported seeing his plane, nose-downwards but otherwise apparently unharmed, in a cabbage field this side of the lines. Ashton grinned. Lucky blighter. Chubby was always doing this. He would get his drink all right, probably in some comfortable billet, and ring up in the morning demanding transport, while the poor ground crew went out to a muddy field and attempted to rescue his bent machine.

But the morning passed without news of him. And the next. Days lengthened into weeks.

Chubby didn't come back.

Chapter Eighteen

Lizzie was still nervous about what Michael's family would say to their wedding – though he swore they were 'happier than squirrels in a nut-tree'. She delayed going up to Nanzeal for a little, pleading that Alice had a fever and she was needed home. But when she did go, one Sunday with Nurse Blight, she found there was no need to worry.

'My dear girl,' Ma Jago said, planting a warm kiss on her cheek, 'I couldn't be more pleased if I found a pig in my pudding.'

Pa Jago nodded gruffly and said, 'There you are then!' as if you had just proved him right in an argument, and Old Hunnicutt beamed so hard he seemed in danger of splitting his face, though he did mutter about 'One man's meat being another man's poison,' whatever that was supposed to mean.

Even Peter, whom she had been most afraid of, seemed too occupied with his new hobby to be upset. He had been doing painting, seemingly, with Anna Braun and when Lizzie saw the results she had to admit that they took her breath away.

It wasn't painting as she knew it. No delicate water-colours, or prim portraits of people looking improbably grand in upright armchairs. Not even pictures of Cornish life like you occasionally saw down at the Newlyn galleries before the war.

These were different. They were crude, dark paintings – all reds and blacks and browns – and the scenes they depicted might have been made in hell. Men with no faces dragged leaden feet down corridors of mud. Another man, all scream, leapt backwards off a parapet. One picture, called 'gas attack' was a swirling mass of greens and browns, where shadowy shapes groped writhing. Lizzie had seen men like that, coughing their lungs into buckets, and though the painting repelled her she could scarcely tear her eyes from it.

'Ugly, that's what it is,' Ma Jago confided, misinterpreting her glance. 'But it seems to be doing Peter good, that's the funny thing. As if he's painting the poison out of himself. Even Pa can see it. Anna Braun says they are good. He could sell them, she thinks, but who'd want a thing like that? Make you feel ill, looking.'

Perhaps that was the point, Lizzie thought, but she did not say so. Instead she said to Peter when he wheeled himself in, 'I looked at your paintings. They are very . . . strong.'

The word pleased him. 'You think so? There is something there, but it is not quite right. I can't get the violence somehow.'

It left Lizzie shaken. She went back to the canvases and tried to imagine Michael there, real flesh and blood among the horror. But she could not, and she knew that it was just as well.

The Brauns came in with Merran, for some crowst, and Lizzie was introduced to them. They did not work on Sundays as a rule,

Merran explained, except for the milking. They were devout people in their own way, though it was some heathenish foreign kind of Christianity – not Methodist, or church, or even Roman Catholic which at least Lizzie would have understood. But at the moment it was essential to set the potatoes and summer corn before people and horses started to starve to death.

Lizzie had not met the Brauns before and they stood before her politely in a line: Willi, a little round turnip of a man in a hessian apron, Mrs Braun, formidable and foreign, and Anna, looking more German than the Kaiser. No wonder she had been set on in the town.

'You are the artist?' Lizzie said to Anna, feeling like a school inspector dispensing prizes on speech-day.

Anna nodded. 'A little. But Peter is more. I tell him, should sell these for money. But he not listen. But Merran think so, yes?' She smiled at Merran and he grinned back cheerfully.

Lizzie felt an unexpected little twist of pain, almost like jealousy.

'Well,' Merran said. 'Gilbert Beswetherick might advise us there. He's on the committee for these new allotments they're arranging, and he's coming up here, any day, to see about hiring the steam-plough. Some decent-sized fields have been released, and the Government's issuing seed potatoes – so perhaps that steam-plough of Farrington's will come in useful yet.'

''Tisn't Farrington's plough,' Pa Jago said darkly. 'It's my plough and don't you forget it. Though why I should hire it out so people can grow their own food and do we farmers out of a job, I'm sure I don't know.'

'Do you out of a job?' Merran retorted. 'Save you from ruination, more like. Perhaps now you'll see the sense of growing proper crops instead of messing about with all this fancy muck. And if you won't do it, the Ministry'll take the fields for allotments, or let your neighbours farm them for you. Don't you forget it.'

'Here,' Ma Jago said sharply. 'Not in front of callers. Lizzie and Nurse Blight don't want to be hearing our troubles.'

'They'll be Lizzie's troubles too, soon enough,' Merran broke off. 'Aaahhh!' He slumped into a chair, clutching at his stomach.

'Why, Merran, whatever is to do?' his mother cried.

Merran shook his head, his face whiter than chalk, as if he had no strength for words. Then, 'Nothing. I don't know. Seems to have passed. Sorry. I'm all right now.' But he was clearly shaken.

'Hungry, I dare swear,' Ma Jago said. 'Time you had some crowst.

That bread's new-baked, though I can't answer for it. Flour's that poor it isn't fit to make paste with. There's a bit of butter here, and a little something to put on it.'

Lizzie knew what that would be – marrow jam.

A little later, as they were walking home, Nell Blight said sadly, 'He's very taken with Anna Braun, isn't he?'

That little stab of jealousy again. 'Merran? Yes, he seems to be.'

Nell Blight stared at her. 'Merran? I'm talking about Peter. All this painting. Awful things, too.'

'It's not pretty,' Lizzie said. 'But it's good. Must be, or we wouldn't mind it so much.'

'It isn't the painting I mind,' Nell said crossly. 'It's Anna Braun. Too fond of her by half. Didn't you notice?'

Lizzie had to laugh. 'And I thought it was Merran she was keen on.'

Nell brightened. 'Can't both be right, can us? What was the matter with Merran back there, anyway?'

Lizzie shook her head. 'I don't know. Seemed to take him sudden, didn't it? And over it just as quick. Nothing serious, whatever it was.'

She was to remember those words later, when she knew.

Tamsin looked at her sister in horror. 'You can't mean it!'

Helena laughed. 'Of course I mean it. It happens when women are expecting a happy event. So you tell your friend, whoever it is, not to worry at all. It is all perfectly normal. More than likely she'll start to feel a bit sick too, in the mornings.'

Tamsin began to feel that the ground was sinking under her feet. She *had* felt sick, twice lately.

Helena was still smiling at her. 'Don't look so startled, Tamsin. I'm sure your friend and her husband will be perfectly delighted. After all that is what people get married for.'

My God. So that was it. Of course it was. Tamsin had never understood the cause and effect before. She didn't believe that babies were really found under gooseberry bushes, of course: and she knew there was something shocking about it, because everyone avoided the subject, but the terrible truth left her almost paralysed with fear.

She sat down heavily. It was no good, she thought helplessly. If there was to be a – she couldn't bring herself to think it – a baby, everyone would know. There would be disgrace, scandal. Papa would be furious. He might even disown her. And as for Mama! She closed her eyes in misery. It didn't bear thinking about.

'Whatever is it Tamsin?'

She found her tongue. 'It's . . . my friend,' she blurted out. 'She hasn't got a husband. He's . . . missing. Maybe killed. In the Army. Just before the wedding.' She was inventing wildly. What had she done? Whatever had she done?

Helena looked sober. 'Oh, poor girl. Still, it is partly her own fault. They should have waited. Millions of couples have to.'

'But what is she to do?' Tamsin wailed.

Helena shook her head. 'Do? There is really nothing *to* do. She had better throw herself on her parents and hope they will support her. It is to be hoped they do, or she may end up like poor Fanny Selwood.'

Terror on terror. Everyone knew what had happened to Fanny Selwood. Went mad, had a child and was locked up in an institution. At least, Tamsin realised with horror, everyone *said* she went mad. Dear God. What could she do? Appeal to Mrs Masters? No, Ashton would certainly disown the child. Would he marry her in any case? Not after that accursed letter she had sent. And Chubby – who might have rescued her, who would have rescued her with a little persuasion from Papa – was dead, missing. A letter from Ashton this very morning had brought the news. She was too miserable even to cry for him.

'Tell her to come and talk to me,' Helena was saying kindly. 'She works at the hospital, you say? She should not go on nursing much longer. It is heavy work. She might leave the district altogether – I really think that would be best. Unless he does come back, of course, or she can find someone else to marry before it is too late. Though that is hardly likely. May I know, Tamsin, who is this unfortunate creature? Or should I not ask?'

Tamsin did not blush. Rather she felt herself pale. 'Perhaps it is better not.'

Helena said, 'Ah,' and picked up her tapestry. She changed the subject, 'Well, what do you think of Stephen? He is a brilliant doctor, Tamsin. Tell me you like him, do.'

Tamsin's mind was on other things. 'I am sure he is very nice.'

Helena was all apology. 'Oh, my poor Tamsin. How thoughtless of me. Running on about my own plans when you have so recently cancelled your own. I know it was your own choosing, but you must still feel it sorely.'

'More than you know,' Tamsin said bitterly. A hundred wild plans were racing through her head. A letter to Ashton. An appeal to Papa. She could take a little jewellery, and run away – to London perhaps, where no one knew her and she could pass herself as a war widow. But what would become of her in London? What would become of her anywhere? Perhaps she should just go out to Penvarris Head and fling herself off. They would all be sorry then.

Helena seemed to have read her thoughts. 'Stephen and I are going to Penvarris later, with Papa. He wants to hire the steam-plough, and Stephen is anxious to meet Peter Jago, to see how a double amputee manages. You have nursed Peter Jago, perhaps you should come with us. You are looking pale, and the sea air would do you good.'

Tamsin sat up abruptly. Of course. Michael Jago. 'Another man to marry her.' No! It was unthinkable, a miserable farmer's son with the daughter of Gulveylor. But when you considered the alter-natives! He was an officer, at least. And he adored her. He would be flattered, probably, when she asked him. Only she couldn't ask him of course, just like that. She would have to let him think of it himself, approach him gently. In a roundabout fashion.

She smiled up at Helena. 'Of course I'll come with you. As you say, it will do me good. And I have something to deliver too, for one of the twins. A book that I wanted to lend him – about King Arthur and the Knights. We were talking of it once, at the bandaging classes.' The story of Galahad – that should do the trick. She remembered the last time they had met. If only she had not been so unpleasant to him in the lane.

She went upstairs and found the book. This was no time for misunderstandings, she must make her meaning clear. After a little hesitation she slipped a note into the pages. 'My most gallant knight. I wanted you to have this. I have important news since our last meeting. I have broken my engagement with Ashton Masters and am now a free woman. I have learned where my true happiness lies. Your own Tamsin.'

There, she thought bitterly, she had as good as thrown herself at him. She toyed with the idea of adding something further – an invitation to call – but decided against it. It was humiliating enough as it was.

All the same, she felt better for having taken action and she joined the others in the carriage with quite an exhibition of good grace. Michael Jago had regular leave – he might be home any moment – so there was no time to be lost. She would get his mother to give him the book as soon as he arrived.

When they arrived at Nanzeal her resolution wavered. To marry into this – a smelly farmyard with horrible animals under your very walls, and Mrs Jago bustling from the dairy, up to her wrists in milk. It was, taken all around, an appalling mess, but anything was better than the fate of Fanny Selwood.

She steeled herself, and while Papa was arguing with Farrington about the plough, and the others went off to talk to Peter, she allowed herself to be invited into the 'downstairs parlour' with Mrs Jago.

'Used to be the nursery, one time, before Peter came home,' Mrs Jago said, throwing open the door, 'but Pa's done it out special, give ourselves somewhere to sit. We've got a parlour upstairs, but Peter can't get up there, without Merran carries him. Now, you sit down, my dear, and I'll fetch us a drop of tea.'

Tamsin stole a look at her surroundings and her heart sank. It was such a dreadful little room, dark and poky with a horrible kind of stamped earth floor, and nothing but a couple of rag rugs to stop the draughts. Plain whitewashed walls. Even the furniture was ghastly. Nasty horsehair chairs which pricked your legs, and hideous heavy ornaments. Worst of all, though, no amount of beeswax and dried lavender could mask the proximity of the cow-byres.

She reminded herself that the alternative might be the madhouse, and when Mrs Jago came in she accepted the brackish brew with a genuine smile. She took a small sip, and a deep breath and then asked outright for Michael's address. 'Or perhaps you could see that he gets it? I wish to send him this.' She indicated the parcel.

Mrs Jago beamed. 'That's some good of you, Miss Tamsin. For his wedding, is it? Heard about it up Little Manor, did you? Didn't know Lizzie had told anyone.'

Tamsin felt the world spinning again. Wedding! She had not allowed for this. She put down her cup carefully and took a deep breath.

Well, it was unfortunate. Lizzie would be disappointed – she must remember to make some little gesture towards her – but the butcher's daughter could not be allowed to marry Michael Jago. Not under the circumstances. Papa should see to it. Not that there was much chance of it anyway, once Michael had seen the note. She must get it to him as soon as possible. Mrs Jago's next words gave her renewed hope.

'Of course I'll give it to him. He'll be here soon. We had word this morning. Made a fuss about not getting his overseas posting, and they've put it through, unexpected.' She was between smiling and crying, pride and anxiety. Tamsin gave her the parcel gratefully.

'What's all this then?' That was the other twin, Merran, striding into the room. 'Where's Pa to?'

'Talking to Sir Gilbert and Silas Farrington about the plough,' Mrs Jago said, and he went out again, looking like thunder. 'You must excuse Merran,' she went on. 'He's been like that all day. Had some sort of turn yesterday, and he's been grimmer than Bodmin Jail ever since. You can't get out of him what's the matter. Have a split, my dear, with a bit of this jam?' And Tamsin had to refuse hurriedly.

Presently Merran came back with Peter, the boy with no legs, in a sort of cart. Dreadful to think that this might be her brother-in-law.

'Here,' Peter said, and you could hear the delight and pleasure in his voice. 'You'll never guess. Dr Macready's offering to buy one of my paintings. Five guineas, he says. That's a month's wage. I'll give it to him, of course, for a wedding present. But he says I could sell no end if·I'd a mind to.'

Merran said, 'Anna has been telling you that for weeks.'

'Wish I could get a few up to London. Earn a bit of something useful, instead of lying about like pooked corn.'

'Well,' Merran said sourly, 'ask Silas Farrington to take them there. He'd do anything if there's money in it.'

Papa came in a moment later, looking irritated. He had struck a deal with Farrington over the steam-plough, but it obviously didn't please him, and he was anxious to get away. Helena and Stephen had their picture – a ghastly green and grey thing with no artistic merit whatever that Tamsin could see. They climbed back into the carriage and rattled off towards Gulveylor – too fast, because Papa had had words with the coachman.

As they lurched down Market Jew Street they passed Treloweth's shop. There were queues, like there always were these days, and a big notice in the window. 'No beef left today.'

'I was thinking,' she said idly, 'I might give Lizzie Treloweth my uniform now that I am giving up my liaison position.'

Helena looked at her sharply. 'Why's that then?'

Tamsin flushed. 'Oh nothing. Only she has wanted a uniform for months, and I feel rather sorry for her about something.'

'I see,' Helena said, with a meaningful look. But of course, she didn't understand at all.

*

'My dearest Lizzie,' the letter ran, 'I have just had the news I have been awaiting for so long. My posting has come through, and I am to be overseas by Friday. At any other time I should have been dancing for joy, but now there is you and all I can see is your unhappy face as you read this letter. Try not to grieve, my love, but know that I will come back soon and we will be together for always.' There was a great deal more then, about books he had been reading. Lizzie had not heard of half of them, but she relished every word. He was sharing his very thoughts with her.

At the end was a hurried note, scribbled in pencil. 'I have just learned that I may, after all, be able to get down to Penzance to see you before I leave. Forty-eight hours' embarkation leave beginning Tuesday – so this letter will scarcely be there before me. I shall, if at all possible, be on the evening train. Try to meet me Lizzie my love, or if not I will find you wherever you are. I have spoken to the padre – we'll get a special licence on my very next leave.'

Lizzie read the letter for the thousandth time. It had only arrived this morning, and already it was wearing across the creases. She put it in her pocket tenderly and looked at herself in the glass. Her Sunday skirt, neat and pressed, that was all right – pity her good blouse was in the wash and she'd have to wear her old one. Best stockings, neatly darned, and her boots polished dazzling. Her good coat, bought from the second-hand bazaar for a shilling. And her 'new' bonnet.

It was a wonderful hat. Beautiful quality – Millie had brought it home from Gulveylor. Little rosebuds and ribbons. It made her coat and skirt look more faded than ever. Still, never mind. She sneaked a little of Daisy's scent and dabbed it on the roses. 'Wild Violets' but that didn't matter. It made her feel special, all the same.

Her heart was thumping as she waited for the train to come in. Really thumping, so loudly that it almost drowned the hubbub on the station. 'Czar abdicates' the newsboy shouted, but she scarcely heard him. And then, far off she saw the rising plume of smoke from the approaching train.

'Lizzie?' She barely registered the word. 'Lizzie?'

She turned. It was Merran. He looked terrible, gaunt and grim.

'Lizzie,' he said again. Suddenly, she knew.

'Michael?' she said. 'What's happened?'

The train was pulling in by now, and people were rushing forward. Happier people. Real people. People whose world had not just fallen apart around them.

174

'We had a wire. There was an accident with a bomb. Someone was demonstrating it, and pulled the fuse carelessly. Michael flung himself forward, saved the rest. They're giving him a medal.'

She didn't care. 'But he's dead.'

'Died instantly. I don't know why it took so long to wire us.'

Dead. Michael was dead. All day, while she had been reading her precious letter it was already from a dead man. She bowed her head, and the cheap scent of violets filled her eyes with tears.

'I'm sorry, Lizzie.'

She stared at him. 'And you knew, didn't you. Sunday, up at the farm, when you clutched your stomach. You knew then.'

His eyes were full of pain. 'I knew . . . something. But what could I tell you, Lizzie? A crazy fancy?'

'You knew,' she said again, 'and you didn't tell me.'

He put out his hand to her, but she swerved away, past him. Out into the road and running, sobbing, her bonnet in her hands. All the way up Market Jew Street where people, including Helena Beswetherick, turned after her to stare.

When she got home she shut herself away and lay, with sobbing breath, until the children came and wanted their bed, but she was too shocked for real tears. It was only much later, when everyone else was asleep that she talked to Gan about it and the weeping truly began.

Merran Jago called twice, but she refused to see him. She could not bear anything connected with Michael.

She went up to Little Manor and did her duties but she was like an automaton, no sense and no feeling. At home she wrapped herself in silence. It was almost a fortnight before she began to come out of her shocked state.

Nell Blight called with news. Silas Farrington had sold three of Peter's pictures to a dealer. But the Jagos were too numbed to care. And Merran . . .

'Decided there was nothing here for him any more,' Nell said sadly. 'And furious with the Germans. Didn't even wait for his next exemption hearing to come up. Went straight down to the recruiting office and volunteered. Left this morning. Near drove his mother crazy with it.'

So she had missed him too. Lizzie turned away, to a world so empty that it seemed as if all the fallen millions had been her especial loss.

She never wore the rosebud bonnet again.

PART FOUR:
EASTER – SUMMER 1917

Chapter Nineteen

'No!'

Tamsin stood in front of the long mirror in her bedroom and stared at herself in horror. This couldn't be happening. Not to her. The carefully planned scene in her imagination had all gone disastrously wrong.

She had seen herself in something simple but fetching (her new blue muslin, perhaps, which flattered her new-found curves, and the blue poke bonnet with the satin trim). Michael Jago came to meet her, tall and handsome in his uniform. He felt the social difference between them (he was certain to do that) but she graciously allowed him to kiss her – and he was so grateful and eager that he protested his love for her at once. It was only necessary to get him to . . . well . . . do what Chubby did . . . as soon as possible. And that would be that.

To be sure there was Lizzie Treloweth, but no man halfway willing could fail to choose Tamsin Beswetherick and the Gulveylor fortune over a butcher's daughter and a dingy shop. And Michael Jago was more than halfway willing, he had shown her that.

Papa would have to be told. Not about the child, if she could help it, but about her wish to marry Michael. She had prepared a little speech about the course of true love being divided – worthy of Romeo and Juliet she thought. Scandalous, naturally, but romantic: the young gentlewoman losing her heart to the poor but dashing hero. She was half in love with the idea herself. Papa would be furious, of course, but she could bring him around on most things, and if absolutely necessary, she could tell him 'the truth'. In the dream it was all so simple.

But it hadn't turned out like that. There had been no answer to her note, although almost two weeks had passed. That was worrying, but there was absolutely nothing she could do about it. Helena's young doctor – such an earnest, boring young man – had occupied them all at home and it was impossible to call on the Jagos or even make any enquiries. The gossip of the town had passed them by. Until today.

That maidservant had let it slip, talking about something else entirely.

Michael was dead.

Dead. Even now she didn't believe it. She was expecting a baby and Michael – her last hope – was dead. Ashton would never have her back: she had tried, but he had returned her two despairing letters, unopened. Whatever was she to do now?

She put out her hand and touched the mirror. It felt frighteningly cold: substantial and solid. It was her own flesh which seemed unreal, as if her reflection was the true Tamsin and she was the illusion.

She felt hollow, a cold empty pit of panic, and she watched with a kind of detachment as her reflection began to cry. Great hopeless tears of despair and self-pity. It made her look very ugly. Oh this confounded war. Look what it had done now!

'All right, are you, Miss Tamsin?'

Tamsin whirled around. That wretched maid, hovering in the doorway with an armful of laundered garments. How humiliating, to be caught like this by the servants, with her face flushed and puffy, snivelling like a child. She took control of herself.

'Quite well, thank you. Only I have a headache. You can fetch me some hot water and balsam.' And then, as the girl hesitated, 'Well, what are you waiting for?'

Millie, or whatever her name was, flushed. 'Only – excuse me, miss, you looked so pale and faint. And you were so unwell earlier this morning. I thought perhaps . . . your mother? Or, a doctor?'

A doctor. That was the last thing she wanted. 'Don't be impertinent. I am upset, that is all. I have received bad news of a friend.' That was better. Everyone heard bad news from time to time these days. And she must disguise the truth.

Millie nodded. 'Yes, Miss Tamsin. I'll fetch your water.' Even then she stopped at the door. 'And . . . I'm very sorry.'

Tamsin snapped, 'And so you should be!' before she realised that the girl was offering condolences, not apology. But it was too late, the child had gone.

Tamsin sat down on the dressing-stool and dabbed at her swollen face with eau de cologne. This would not do. Gossip spread around the servants' hall in minutes. She could cry once – everyone was allowed to cry once – but she must not let her feelings get the better of her again. As it was, the whole staff would be speculating about her 'news'. She composed a face to meet Millie when she came back

180

with the water, and when she heard the tap at the door she was able to say firmly, 'Come in', very much as usual.

It was the balsam inhalation, but the person carrying the tray wasn't the maid. It was Helena.

'Tammy?'

The name almost brought Tamsin to tears again. Helena had not called her that since they were children. She looked up at her sister in the mirror, and glimpsed again her own reddened eyes and flushed face. It was obvious that she had been crying. She wanted to say something, but words deserted her and she simply shook her head helplessly.

Helena set down the tray on the dressing-table and perched on the stool beside her. 'I met the girl on the stairs. She said you were ill, so I came to see. I thought you needed a real nurse. She seemed quite alarmed about you.'

Tamsin blurted her excuse again. 'There was no need. I have had some bad news, that is all.'

Helena frowned anxiously. 'Not from Ashton, surely?' That was the trouble with Helena, she would expect to know everyone Tamsin knew.

She shook her head. 'Not Ashton. It's just – the Jago boy that's all. He came to my classes, and he used to visit his brother at Little Manor. And now he's been killed. He was engaged to Lizzie Treloweth. It . . . upset me.'

'Oh, Tammy. I don't mean to tease – especially now. Of course, you have been good to them. I remember now. You took a wedding present to Nanzeal for them, didn't you, when no one else even knew about it. And you were thinking to let Lizzie have your uniform. No wonder you are upset. She must be taking it hard.'

Somehow, that made it worse. Lizzie, Lizzie, Lizzie. It was all anyone ever talked about. Tamsin felt her voice shake as she burst out, 'Good to her? Lizzie Treloweth? Well, why not? Everyone always is. And as for the uniform, I wish I'd *given* it to her – might as well have done. Stupid thing won't fit much longer anyway.'

Helena looked at her sharply. 'So that's it? You are feeling sorry for not being generous when you had a chance? That is nice of you, Tammy, I didn't think you so tender-hearted.' She reached across and pressed Tamsin's hand. 'But why should your uniform not fit?'

It was said so gently that for a weak moment Tamsin was tempted. It would be such a relief to confide in someone. With Michael gone, there was no possible husband in sight so Helena would have to

181

know some time. She said, hesitantly, 'You won't believe this, Helena. It isn't just guilt about the stupid uniform. It's much more than that.' She took a deep breath. 'There's going to be a baby.'

Helena gazed at her in amazement, and when she spoke her voice was shaky with shock. 'You mean . . . that's what you were asking me about the other day? When you talked about your "friend"?'

Tamsin nodded. The relief of the confession left her weak, and she dabbed at her eyes again. 'You see, if Michael hadn't died . . .'

'It would have had a father,' Helena finished grimly. 'And that would have stopped the gossip.' She sighed. 'People can be so cruel. But I'm surprised to hear this from you, Tamsin. I always thought you the very voice of social respectability. Mama would be appalled.'

It was a much milder rebuke than Tamsin expected, but the last words threw her into fresh panic. 'You won't say anything will you? Promise. Not to Mama. Not to anyone. Not until we've worked out what to do.'

Helena shook her head. 'What is there to do? Go away and have the baby of course – get it adopted perhaps. That would be best. There are ways of getting rid of it, but that's far too dangerous. Don't let her try that, will you Tamsin? It could kill her. Oh, the poor creature. No wonder you were so upset for her, Tammy.'

Tamsin looked at her sister in dismay. Surely she had understood? But Helena rushed on. 'Her mother might take the child, I suppose, and she could go and find a position somewhere she is not known – if she can find someone to give her a character. Mrs Rouncewell might do it – she was always fond of the girl. Lizzie is a good worker, and after all it was not quite a casual liaison. They were engaged to marry. But you are quite right, Tamsin, we must not mention it to Mama. She would very likely dismiss Millie at once – as if one could catch immorality, like measles.'

Tamsin was still opening and closing her mouth like a fish, too shocked for tears. She made one more attempt. 'No, Helena . . . I . . .'

'What?'

Tamsin shook her head. It was impossible. 'I shouldn't have said anything,' she said miserably.

Helena smiled. 'I'm glad you did. I think I sometimes misjudge you, Tamsin – I still think of you as a silly child, inclined to be vain and selfish. But the War has obviously changed you – you are developing into a different person.'

'You are right about that, at least,' Tamsin said, fervently. 'You certainly are.' And if there was any irony in her tone, she buried it in a bowl of steaming balsam.

Up at the Hospital there was some kind of infectious germ abroad. Half the men were coughing and wheezing and complaining of aches in their limbs. Mrs Rouncewell was run off her feet, fetching camphor and poultices – the last thing she wanted this afternoon was a social call.

However, the Beswethericks were important people, and subscribers to the Hospital. Mrs Rouncewell sighed, rammed her hair back under her veil, sent Nurse Blight out to the kitchens for a tray of tea, and sailed out to meet her visitor.

'Miss Beswetherick. What an unlooked for pleasure.'

Helena Beswetherick looked at her squarely and Mrs Rouncewell saw a flicker of amusement in those clear grey eyes. This gel, she thought ruefully, was not taken in for a moment: she knew perfectly well that this visit was an unwelcome nuisance. At least, however, this obviously wasn't the usual aimless benefactors' visit, just to 'take an interest' and be shown over the Hospital. Miss Beswetherick was wearing her VAD uniform, badges and all.

Helena extended a firm, gloved hand. 'My dear Matron, you are very kind, but I know perfectly how busy you must be. I should not have burst upon you like this, unannounced, but there is some urgency in the matter I wish to discuss with you, and I return to my own duties in a day or two.'

Mrs Rouncewell found herself smiling with genuine warmth, 'Yes, we're very busy. The men are sicker, and we seem to have more arrivals than Clapham Junction. But there is always time for you, Miss Beswetherick – you might even care to have a short tour of the wards.' Now, why on earth had she said that? A moment ago it was the very thing she feared.

Helena Beswetherick, though, was genuinely interested, and a few minutes later found them walking from bed to bed.

'Now,' Mrs Rouncewell said. 'You've been at a Base Hospital, haven't you? What do you think about this?' They went to the conservatory ward (passing a startled Nurse Blight with a tea-tray) where the poor lieutenant who had lost his eyes was still moaning every time he moved.

'His wound has festered. The doctor cauterized it, a week ago, but the pain is dreadful. We're giving him chloroform gas every few hours – a few drops on a cloth inhaled through a gauze mask.' You

183

could tell. The room swam with the smell of it. 'What do you do at the Front, with cases like that?'

'Opium, if we have it, or gas, like you. Very often there isn't much we can give them, and we have to save that for the ones that are – saveable.'

Mrs Rouncewell nodded. She knew what that meant. The hopelessly injured would be taken aside, somewhere, and left to die, and the scarce drugs saved for the men who had a chance of living. It was one of the crueller aspects of the War.

'We give brandy here, three-hourly if the doctor recommends it. Or cigarettes, if the pain is less severe. It does seem to comfort the men.'

Helena said, 'My friend . . . Stephen . . . Dr Macready . . . says brandy opens the veins and makes the bleeding worse. He uses aspirin, that they introduced for headaches before the War.'

Mrs Rouncewell smiled inwardly. She had heard quite a deal about Dr Macready in the last few minutes. But Matron was not afraid to learn new ways, when old methods failed. She said thoughtfully, 'I suppose your Dr Macready has no clever modern cure for a common old-fashioned ailment like a cough? Just listen to these boys. I am at my wits' end with it. They have enough to suffer with burns and wounds and trench-foot, without coughing all night as well.'

Helena looked doubtful. 'Stephen does have rather advanced views on that subject,' she said doubtfully. 'He believes that smoking tobacco may somehow cause it.'

Mrs Rouncewell stared. 'Nonsense! The latest advice is that cigarettes help to ward off infection. In any case, the men have always smoked, here and everywhere else – except the gas cases. We've never had coughing like this before.'

'Perhaps . . .' Helena began, and then broke off with a laugh. 'You would not welcome the opinion, I am sure, but Stephen has an idea that parrots can sometimes transmit a disease. I have known him say so to sailors with respiratory problems. It occured to me . . . perhaps . . .'

Albert, she meant. It was absurd. Albert!

Mrs Rouncewell suddenly wished the interview over. 'I fear you were correct, Miss Beswetherick. I do not welcome the opinion. In fact, I find it preposterous. And now, since we have finished in the wards, perhaps we could go down and see what Nurse Blight has done with our tea.'

It was cold of course, which did not improve her temper, and when – a little later and very discreetly and hesitantly – the subject of Lizzie Treloweth was raised, she was in no mood to compromise.

'Do you wish to tell me, Miss Beswetherick, that one of my nurses – a gel I have singled out for consideration – has rewarded me by getting herself into trouble?'

That was unfair, of course. Helena had said nothing so indiscreet. She had merely hinted that Lizzie might have future distress from the loss of her young man – but Mrs Rouncewell could accept an inference when it was offered to her.

Helena flushed. 'Not at all, Matron. I meant no more than I said. Anything else would be the merest conjecture.'

'But there are grounds for conjecture?'

'As to that, I cannot say. I have heard nothing from Lizzie herself. It was only that I felt, should there be any difficulties of that kind, you might be prepared to assist her – give her a character, perhaps? It would be very hard for her, otherwise, especially with a child. She could not return to Penzance, clearly, so you would not be in the position of recommending her to anyone who might know the history. But I should not have approached you – it is simple speculation. My sister was concerned for the girl.'

Mrs Rouncewell nodded grimly. So that was the source of the information. She could imagine that Tamsin would take a perverse delight in passing it on. It made her feel a little more sympathetic towards Lizzie. After all, she could see how it might happen. Lizzie was very wrapped up in her young man, and with him going off to war . . .

Mrs Rouncewell could remember a time, long ago, when Captain Rouncewell was ordered suddenly to sea. She coughed.

'Well,' she said severely, 'I will see what I can do. Obviously, if I learned for certain that the gel was no better than she should be, I should have to say so. But up to now I know of nothing against her.'

Helena rewarded her with the warmest of smiles. 'Thank you, Matron, I knew that you would understand.'

'I make no undertaking, of course,' Mrs Rouncewell said hastily. 'And I can't have her here if there is the slightest scandal attaching to her. Not in my hospital.'

Helena rose to her feet, 'I am sure that there is none, at the present, Matron. And as I say, there may be nothing whatever in the suggestion. But I am glad we understand each other.' She extended the gloved hand again. 'And thank you for the tour of the hospital. I will speak to my father – and to Stephen too. Perhaps we can arrange for some aspirin to reach you.'

It was a kind offer. Mrs Rouncewell said goodbye cordially enough. Perhaps, next Friday, when Lizzie came to Little Manor again, she would have a word to the gel.

But it was something else which haunted her as she tossed restlessly that night on her pillow. All this business about parrots. It was too preposterous for words of course, but when she came to think of it, Captain Rouncewell *had* died – rather unexpectedly – of an infection of the lungs.

The summons to 'see Matron in her office' came immediately after Lizzie arrived for duty on Friday morning. It alarmed her, really the first time she had felt anything since Michael died. It puzzled her too. Formal interviews of this kind were usually reserved for serious breaches of discipline – running in the corridor, 'lounging' in the wards on duty, or (Mrs Rouncewell's favourite) 'answering back'. But Lizzie was not guilty of any of these, as far as she knew.

'My life!' she said to Nurse Blight, as she straightened her apron frantically, and rubbed her boots against her stockinged legs to clean them. 'I feel low enough losing Michael, without having all this. Whatever do you suppose I've gone and done now?'

Nurse Blight sighed. 'Goodness knows. Breathed in the wrong tone of voice, more than likely. She's been crosser than two sticks ever since Helena Beswetherick came here Wednesday. We've all had it. I got a jawing myself because I was told to bring tea – quick smart, you know what she's like, by the time she's told you it's already too late – then she went round the Hospital with Miss Beswetherick for half an hour. Well of course the tea was cold and I got the fault for it.'

Lizzie frowned. 'That isn't like Matron – hard she may be, but she's fair, as a rule.'

Nurse Blight shook her head. 'I don't know what's got into her, but something has. Even poor old Albert's been banished – he's shut up in her room and nobody's allowed to fetch him. So I shouldn't worry. You probably haven't done anything.'

Lizzie flashed her a grateful smile and hurried off to Matron's room.

A half an hour later, though, she was back. She was feeling something now, all right – angry, pale and shaken. Nurse Blight was scrubbing bedpans in the sluice-room, but she saw Lizzie's face and risked Mrs Rouncewell's wrath by slipping out to speak.

'My word, Lizzie, whatever is the matter. You're whiter than a bedsheet.'

Lizzie wanted to reply, but no words came. She shook her head bitterly.

Her friend looked at her anxiously. 'Here, come and give me a hand with these bedpans and tell me all about it.'

And then Lizzie did find her voice. 'No,' she said, 'I shan't be doing that. Not now, and not ever.'

Nell Blight gaped. 'She's never turned you off?'

Lizzie shook her head. 'Not that exactly, but she as good as suggested I left. If I went now, she said, she could give me a character, but if I stayed much longer she wouldn't be able to.' Even as she spoke the words they tasted like acid on her tongue. 'My condition would be obvious.'

'Your condition?'

'That's what she said,' Lizzie replied. 'I didn't understand what she was talking about, first off, but then she started on about was I eating enough, and was I feeling sick in the morning – and then of course I realised.' Nurse Blight was still looking puzzled, so she spelt it out, although the very words made her cheeks blaze. 'She thought I was – you know – in an interesting condition.'

Nurse Blight's colour matched her own. 'You never are?'

'Of course I'm not.'

'Have you told her that?'

Lizzie felt suddenly that she might cry with shame and frustration. 'No, I haven't,' she burst out, and her voice was shaking. 'She was going on and on about how her "gels" had to be above suspicion, and how she was disappointed to think such a thing of me – and . . .' Lizzie was so furious and distressed she didn't want to dwell on it any more, even to Nell. 'I was that mad – what with Michael and everything else – I just said if that was what she thought of me she could go on thinking it, and I wouldn't be an embarrassment to her any more because I was leaving, right then and there.' She could taste the tears as she spoke. She pulled out her handkerchief and gave her nose a good blow. 'So, that's that.'

Nurse Blight gazed at her in disbelief. 'But you can't . . . you love nursing.'

Lizzie gave her eyes a final dab and lifted her head high. 'Well, I shan't be loving it any more. I've thought for a long time about going away to the Land Army, and that's what I shall do.'

'But if you go away,' Nell said, 'it'll only make things worse.'

Lizzie looked at her for a long moment. 'Michael's dead,' she said at last. 'Merran's gone to the Army. I've as good as lost my reputation. How could things possibly get worse?'

As it happened, she was shortly to find out.

Chapter Twenty

Suspected of being a loose woman! Whatever would Mam say? Lizzie walked home, her eyes and cheeks burning, feeling as though the whole of Penzance was peering at her behind its curtains.

When she got home Daisy was there.

That was a surprise. Daisy had not come home unannounced since she became Mrs Abel Hoskins, but there she was now sitting at the kitchen table, clutching an enormous mug of Gan's dandelion wine. That was a double surprise – Gan's brew was wicked, and kept only for special occasions and emergencies.

Gan took one look at Lizzie's face and handed her a cupful, too.

Daisy though was oblivious. Her face was like chalk and she was trembling. 'Awful it was,' she kept saying, over and over. 'Awful. Them screams – I can hear them now.' She shut her eyes as if to block out the pictures and took another swig from her mug. 'Using a drilling machine, she was – same one I used to have. Nothing to it really – you just put the piece in the hole and the machine cuts it. But she hadn't a cap, see. Supposed to, of course, but Mr Farrington isn't all that particular, and a lot of the girls don't bother, seeing what they cost. Anyway, turned her head – half a second, that's all – and that was that. Caught her hair in it and dragged her right down in the machine. Scream? You could have heard her up London – and when they did get her loose . . .'

The picture was so horrible that Lizzie almost forgot her own troubles for a moment. Daisy swallowed another gulping mouthful. 'Pulled it out, see, by the roots, skin and all, and her poor face black and blue where she'd been dragged on the metal. Passed out with the pain of it, in the end. But Mr Farrington, he wouldn't stop the work. Only that one machine – had it taken off so they could clean it – and everyone was back to work as usual. I was painting tail-planes – I'd only gone in the cutting-room for some more screws – but it shook me so bad I couldn't handle the brush tidy, and they sent me home before I spoilt something.'

Lizzie nodded. Daisy was working in the paint shop now, 'doping' the stretched canvas. Better pay, but the fumes got into your skin and hair, and Daisy's beautiful reddish curls were yellowing and thin, and there was a faint Chinese tinge to her face and hands. 'Shock, that's what it is,' she said, with feeling. She had some inkling herself of what shock could do.

'Anyway,' Daisy finished, 'Abel's ma is off up to her sister's this week, so Abel said to come home here. Glad I did, and all. Been missing you all something chronic.' She turned to Lizzie. 'Never expected to see you home, though. Finished early, have you?'

So then Lizzie did tell them. 'I haven't finished early. I've finished altogether! Mrs Rouncewell's got hold of some tale about me from somewhere – thinks I got myself in trouble with Michael – and I was that mad I gave my notice, then and there. Won't pay me anything this week more than like, though I worked Tuesday, but I haven't rightly got time to work out like a lot of people.'

'And she let you go, just like that?' Mam exclaimed. 'Well, more fool she. And listening to silly stories like that. You're better off out of it, my girl. That's what you get for getting mixed up with fancy folk. Happens all the time with them, I shouldn't be surprised. Prancing around all day with all those young men in their pyjamas.' Lizzie had expected an outcry, but instead Mam seemed bent on finding fault with Mrs Rouncewell.

Relief made her feel quite weak, although it was such a ridiculous picture of Little Manor that she could not help smiling. All the same, she had never felt less cheerful in her life. Bad enough losing Michael, but that had been grief, simple and unsullied. This was different, a hopeless misery and anger that made you feel unclean.

'Want to come up the factory with me, do you?' Daisy said, brightening. 'Not much of a recommendation, me coming home with tales like this, but it's all right if you're careful.'

'I was thinking of the Land Army,' Lizzie said. 'Had the form upstairs for ages. Training and all they give you.'

Gan pursed her lips. 'I shouldn't rush into anything, Lizzie. There's gossip around, or Mrs Rouncewell would never have said anything. You go dashing off somewhere, you'll only add fuel to their fire. Better to stay home and face it out – soon see they were mistaken then.' The family took it for granted, Lizzie thought gratefully, that Mrs Rouncewell's suggestion was a baseless slur.

Mam, though, had objections of her own. 'Land Army? You? Whatever next? People will have something to talk about then, you going off to live the Dear Lord knows where, working with strange men on the farms, and wearing britches as well! Unseemly, that's what it is.'

'Folks'll talk anyway,' Lizzie said bitterly. 'Even if they see me every day between now and Christmas. No smoke without fire, that's what they'll say. And as to the Land Army, it's all properly supervised. Government wouldn't allow it else.'

'And what man is ever going to look at you,' Mam said, 'when you've been clodhopping round like a farmboy?'

'I already lost the man I wanted,' Lizzie said, feeling the tears start again. She didn't say that she had discussed the idea, long ago, with Merran.

'Here, my handsome,' Mam said, 'I didn't mean it like that. Only, it doesn't seem ladylike to me. Why don't you write your father and see what he thinks?'

'Trouble is,' Daisy said, 'you'd need a character. Might be hard to get one, now, right off.'

Lizzie sighed. 'That's what Mrs Rouncewell said. Said if I left now, she'd give me one – but if I left it too late she couldn't.'

Gan said, thoughtfully, 'Well, Lizzie, strikes me she was trying to do her best by you. If you were in any trouble, it would have been a handsome gesture. But why didn't you tell her, straight?'

Lizzie shook her head in misery. 'I don't know. Only I felt that low, with Michael and everything – it seemed like the last straw. Anyway, too late now.'

'Shouldn't have walked out like that though,' Mam said. 'She'll never give you that character now.'

But, before the next week was out, a package arrived. A reference commending Lizzie Treloweth as 'honest, industrious and intelligent, and to the best of my knowledge, of good character'. There was even the money for Tuesday's shift. Mrs Rouncewell had done what she could.

Days edged by. Morning after morning Tamsin awoke to the realisation that this was not a dream, but a pressing reality – a problem from which charm and wealth and position could not rescue her. By ignoring it, she could not make it go away.

At least Helena had gone, at last. That was a relief. Helena's smiling enquiries after 'your poor friend' and general air of sisterly conspiracy was enough to try anyone's patience, and the fact of it being so embarrassingly misguided made it a thousand times more difficult to bear. When Helena set off for the station, full of plans for her Christmas wedding, Tamsin was actually able to feel a little lightening of her spirits.

But not for long. One thing Tamsin had understood from her sister, it could be a matter of very little time before the fact of her condition would become evident, at least to her dressmaker. Something would have to be done before that terrible event. Somehow, Mama would have to be told.

She plotted to do it a dozen times. She began lingering discussions over the breakfast table, or interrupted her mother in the library for cosy tête-à-têtes. But somehow when it came to it, the moment was never quite appropriate.

When she did blurt it out it was not at all as she intended. Mama was sitting in the drawing-room with her diary, fretting over the difficulty of arranging a charity dinner these days.

'I assure you, it is quite impossible to "seat" a table properly, for there are quite three women to every presentable man, and one is reduced to inviting the most unsuitable people. I shall have to ask that appalling Silas Farrington, simply to make the numbers. Then there is the problem of food. And as for finding anything to wear, I shall soon be reduced to wearing a bed-sheet, for one can't get good material, and the fashions today are so skimpy I wonder that any woman over thirty dares to be seen in them.'

Tamsin, thinking sourly that wearing a bed-sheet might prove an answer to her problems, said nothing.

Her mother sighed. 'Still, I suppose one must make the effort, since it is in aid of the wounded. Though what we shall offer for entertainment I'm sure I don't know – we cannot ask people to sit through another of Maud's dreary recitals. I wish you would get up a "stunt", Tamsin, as Lady Poldair did at her supper last week. It was just a pageant, representing the countries of the Empire. You know a great many young women, from your hospital work. I'm sure you might do something quite as striking, if you chose. There is still four weeks before the dinner.'

Tamsin calculated with horror that, by that time, she might find difficulty in getting into any balldress, skimpy or not.

Mama set down the notebook and peered at her over her pincenez. 'Are you attending to me Tamsin? A pretty little tableau, perhaps representing the Home Front. The women of Britain? Now, there is a notion. We might borrow a uniform from one of the maids, and then there are your nurses, and doubtless Silas Farrington would lend us a costume from one of his factory girls. There! I'm sure it would be the greatest fun. What shall you represent, Tamsin?'

Tamsin muttered that she did not know, but she was certain that an excellent tableau could be arranged without her.

'Nonsense,' her mother snapped. 'I do not know what is the matter with you this morning, Tamsin. You refuse to put your mind to this, and yet it is the kind of matter in which you excel. And of course, if the tableau is here, you must be the centre of it. Something patriotic, perhaps? Britannia?'

Tamsin raised her head. This chatter about costume in her present state was almost more than she could bear. 'I do not wish to be Britannia.'

'Well, your eggshell taffeta, then, with red roses in your hair, and a letter in your hand. "The Waiting Woman". What do you say to that?' Her mother was quite carried away by enthusiasm for her scheme.

'Oh, I shall be a waiting woman, all right,' Tamsin cried, suddenly losing patience. 'The waiting mothers of England. Perhaps I could represent that.'

Her mother stared at her. 'Whatever do you mean, Tamsin?'

'I mean,' said Tamsin, 'that I am to be a mother. There, it's out, and there's an end of it. So I shall not be in your stupid pageant, as Britannia or anything else.'

She was too defiant for tears, but looking up, she realised the enormity of what she had said. Mama had turned deathly white, even her lips were pale. Only two little bright patches of red burned in her cheeks. She sat very still.

'Is this some nonsense, Tamsin?'

Tamsin's defiance began to ebb away, and she found herself trembling. 'No,' she said, in a small voice. 'It is not nonsense. I should have told you before, but I did not know how to begin.'

There was a pause.

'It isn't . . .' Tamsin began.

'Silence!' Her mother's fury shocked her. 'How dare you address me. You may go to your room, and stay there, until I have spoken to your father. Your meals will be sent to you.'

'But, Mama . . .'

'Don't "Mama" me! I disown you. Go to your room until you are sent for. You may reflect a little on the disgrace you have brought upon this family, while your father and I decide what is to be done with you.'

Tamsin hesitated.

'Will you go,' her mother asked, 'or shall I call the stableman to put you out of doors?'

So Tamsin unwillingly went, and a few minutes later heard the scrape of a key in the lock. She was a prisoner in her room.

What followed was the longest day of her life. The fate of Fanny Selwood danced before her. The asylum! She could see the great gates locking behind her, the dribbling, unwashed, babbling company. No dances, no dresses, no books – only the terrible certainty that you would never escape from those grim grey walls again! The thought was so horrible that Tamsin even thought, briefly, of flinging herself wildly from her window and onto the gravelled drive below.

Millie brought lunch, a frugal plate of cold meats and a bowl of fruit. Tamsin attempted to remonstrate but the girl shook her head helplessly.

'I'm sorry, Miss Tamsin, but it is what the mistress ordered. And I'm not to talk to you, miss, but to go back downstairs as quick as may be.' And she was gone, securing the door behind her.

Tamsin was angry, frightened, despairing and remorseful by turns. She paced the room, hurled her shoes one after the other at the bedpost, and finally flung herself down upon her bed in a frenzy of hopeless sobbing.

She was still there, much later, when her parents came into the room. She got up, startled. She could not remember having seen her father in her bedroom since she was a tiny child. She looked at him hopelessly. Her hair was tumbled, her face was streaked and swollen with tears, and her clothes were awry, but she was past caring.

'Well, Tamsin,' he said. 'What your mother tells me is true, I see.'

She gave a great ugly sniff, like a fishwife. She tried to say, 'Yes,' but all that escaped her was a gulping sob.

'Your mother blames Ashton, but I have different ideas. This, I presume, is why you decided *not* to marry your cousin.'

It was not quite the truth, but it was simpler to mutter, humbly, 'Yes.'

'And who is the young man? I shall have him horsewhipped. One of your young convalescents, I suppose? Well, he will have to marry you, that is all. And quickly too.'

Tamsin shut her eyes, almost giddy with relief. Marry her. Papa was making plans. She was not, after all, to be sent to the asylum, or turned out on the streets. But the danger was not over yet. She shook her head. 'He can't.'

'My God! He is not *married*, surely?'

She shook her head again. 'Not married. Dead.' Somehow after the idea of a married man, it didn't sound so bad. 'It was Charles Beresford, and we might have been engaged if he had lived.' In fact Chubby had never given her any such expectation, but he was not here to deny it.

Her mother's face was steely. 'Beresford? Under our very roof! I should have known what to make of your denials! And you engaged to another man. How shall I ever hold up my head to Alice Masters again. Marry you, would he? Then you may apply to his family for support. Sir Gilbert shall write to them tonight.'

For a moment a hundred new nightmares danced before Tamsin's eyes, and then her father said wearily, 'Don't be absurd, Winifred. Writing to them will not bring Tamsin a husband, and they have enough to bear with their son dead. The fewer people who know of this, the better. We have allowed her too much liberty, my dear, and there's an end to it. The question is, what are we to do with her now? She cannot continue to stay here, that is obvious.'

Tamsin's knees failed her, and she sat down heavily on the bed.

'I won't have her in the house,' Mama said. 'She can pack her bags and go where she pleases.'

'Winifred, my dear, I understand that you are upset. But if we are to avert a scandal, this is a moment for rational thought. I could wish that you had not already made such an exhibition in front of the servants. Now, Tamsin must be moved, and soon, to a place where she is not known. We need someone to whom she can go until – afterwards. We shall have the child adopted, and then we shall see.'

Visions of the mad-house wavered and died, and Tamsin, in a positive frenzy of relief, did something she had not done since she was very small. She flung her arms around her father's neck and kissed him.

'Oh Papa, you are very good. Thank you. Thank you.'

He pushed her away awkwardly and said, with a return to his usual manner, 'Very well. But you need not suppose, young lady, that I condone your behaviour. It is merely that I see no occasion to make bad worse.'

'We might ask Alice, I suppose,' Mama said. 'It is a little awkward, considering that you were engaged to Ashton, but I can think of no one else. She would be discreet, at least. And in London Tamsin would be quite unknown. Yes, Gilbert, I really think that would be best. We could put it about that Tamsin was going to London to nurse an aged relative.'

'Then, after a little I can come back,' Tamsin said. 'If she is very aged, it will be supposed that she has . . .' She trailed off.

'Precisely,' her father said drily. 'I see that your predicament has not taught you discretion, Tamsin. But you are quite right. And since you have done some nursing here it will seem quite natural to send you.'

'I will write to Alice tonight,' Mama said.

'But not, I think, for Tamsin to go at once. The servants would gossip. Tamsin has clearly been the subject of acute displeasure today. Better, I think, to delay for a week or two. Then perhaps, we can ask Alice to wire for her.'

'After your charity dinner, perhaps,' Tamsin said. 'Perhaps after all I could get up a stunt for it. That should help to allay suspicion.'

Already her mind was racing. The worst was over. At the very outside she would go to London. And in the meantime she had four weeks. Surely in that time she could find someone – anyone – to marry her.

'Well, well, Mr Jago *now* what have you done?' The regimental sergeant-major's voice boomed out, for the whole parade-ground to hear. He delighted in showing up the young subalterns when they made a mess of things. He seemed to take a particular pleasure in singling out Merran and Lewis, a taciturn Welshman from a farm near Rhyll. Because they were only farmers perhaps. Always called them 'Mr So-and-So', but held them up to ridicule all the same.

He looked at Merran's latest attempt at directing the drill. 'We'll have that battalion in routing order, shall we, not drooping about like pigs in a market? In your own time, Mr Jago, in your own time, but don't take too long about it or Fritz will have gone home before your men have unscrambled their feet.'

Merran felt a flicker of stubborn defiance. 'Like pigs in a market' was it? Well, if he could organise pigs, he could organise men. He squared his shoulders.

'Right,' he told his men. 'Fall out. Now, take that again. In single file, by the right, fall . . . in!'

It was not at all what he had joined the Army to do. He had wanted action, almost revenge. Instead the training seemed to be designed to remove initiative, reduce them all to mindless, faceless machines. He understood, as never before, Mike's impatience to be posted overseas.

He watched the battalion struggle through the drill. An unlikely collection. Fresh-faced youngsters, just out of school. Older men 'combed out' of the reserved occupations, grizzled and cynical. Evaders and avoiders, sullenly unwilling. Weaker than water most of them. Not even the strength to pull a strap tight on a horse's girth, and if the animal puffed itself up – as they often did with strangers – the case was hopeless. Only Lewis seemed to have the least idea how to handle a horse.

The RSM boomed up. 'Well, Mr Jago that is a little better. We'll have some rifle drill then, shall we?' And then there was an hour of pointless marching, presenting and shouldering arms – half the ranks with sticks because the rifles had not arrived yet.

Life in the training camp was made up of this. Parades and drills, bayonet-practice and target shooting, route-marches and mock-attacks on country roads (to the distraction of the motorists), and retreats down muddy ditches. And in the evening, lectures and demonstrations for the officers in which imaginary battles were fought with neat crosses on the map.

'All this talk about "open warfare",' Lewis whispered, during a talk on the new, magic 'tanks'. 'Lot of nonsense, that is. We'll be stuck in the mud until there is only one soldier left, look. Then, if that soldier is British, we'll have won, I suppose.'

Merran frowned. 'Not what you think, the Army, is it?'

Lewis laughed. 'Learned that, have you boyo? A long way from the farm, isn't it?'

It was a long way from Nanzeal and the quiet surge of surf beyond the cornfields. Merran nodded.

They had learned a good deal. How to use an entrenching tool and build a blast wall out of sandbags: to sleep on a palliasse: to eat bully beef and drink disgusting tea, which was doped (so everyone said) to 'curb desires', but was certainly laced with 'jollop' since the Army seemed to believe that all its recruits required daily purging.

'That's why they call it the "regular" Army, look,' Lewis remarked, and Merran smiled grimly.

After the lecture, they went back to their task, a 'tactical exercise' planning an advance on a fictitious village, a painted canvas displayed on a trestle. Merran and Lewis exchanged glances at the cheerful talk of 'running forward across farmland, taking advantage of natural cover'. They had never seen a battleground but they had some idea of what it was like to run across ploughed fields.

Merran was not a drinker, but he went with Lewis to the bar. The mindless monotony of it all was past endurance.

Then suddenly it was over, and there was a precious pause. Thirty-six hours of 'embarkation leave', and then France – where the battles were real ones, fought with blood and sweat and stench, and any reveille was likely to be your last.

Lewis went down to the station with Merran. 'Afraid, boyo?'

Merran looked at him.

'Nothing to be ashamed of,' Lewis said. 'Everyone's afraid. You can see it in their eyes, boyo.' He gestured towards a group of privates, sitting together on a station-bench, singing 'Mademoiselle from Armentieres' with drunken gusto. 'Look at them, now. It's fear they're wanting to drown with their songs and laughter. The dreadful whisper of fear. They talk too loud, because they know that if they are silent even for a moment, they'll hear the whisper.'

He was a bit of a poet, Lewis. Merran watched him onto his train.

Then he was off home himself. An officer, with a rail-warrant for first class travel in his pocket, and an ache in his heart. Lewis was right. He was afraid. He knew what he would do. It was Friday, so first thing, before he even went to Nanzeal, he would go up to Little Manor and speak to Lizzie.

It was hopeless, he knew that. She had loved Michael and she wouldn't transfer her affections lightly. But he had to tell her for his own sake, before it was too late.

If he never came home again, at least she would know that he'd loved her.

Chapter Twenty-One

Lizzie was in the backyard washing tripes when Merran arrived. It was a job she hated – horrible, slippery, smelly things that had to be rinsed and rinsed again till your fingers were as wrinkled and white as the tripes themselves – but she was so miserable with grief and shame she didn't care what she did.

It was true what she had said to Daisy. Rumours spread like wild-fire in a little town like Penzance. Everyone was talking about her. You could tell, though they didn't come right out and say anything to your face, of course. People in the shop smiled knowingly and stared, or asked meaningfully after her health. Lizzie tried to hold her head up and ignore it, but it was difficult, especially when some people, like Mrs Tavy, refused to let her serve them at all and asked pointedly for Aggie or Gan instead.

More and more she had retreated to the back shop, and found herself tasks like washing the tripes. Like this morning. Two customers, left alone in the shop, had been nodding and whispering, but stopped scarlet-faced when she came in. She knew what they were whispering, and she was miserable and furious. If only she could get away to the Land Army, but Mam wouldn't have it without Father's say-so, and though she had written a fortnight ago there had been no reply. She bent over the horrible tripes again.

No leaving tripes to the Cat's-meat-man now. Now that there was a limit, not on how much you could buy, but on how much you could spend in the shop, lots of respectable households were asking for them. And for the brains and giblets which once would only have found their way into the poorer baskets.

But how many fine ladies would eat the tripes, she wondered, if they could see the contents of her bucket now?

At first she paid no attention to the man half-hovering near the back door of the shop. Khaki was so commonplace these days, even in Penzance, that one scarcely glanced twice: and since Michael had gone, Lizzie had deliberately avoided looking at people in uniform. It reminded her too much.

'Lizzie?' the familiar voice almost made her drop her bucket.

'Merran! I did not recognise you. You look so . . . so . . .' She wanted to say 'so like Michael', though of course he didn't really. She managed, 'So military! When did you come home?' Suddenly the terrible day did not seem quite so grey.

'Lizzie,' he said, urgently, ignoring her questions. 'I must talk to you. Privately.'

He sounded so serious, that she did not protest but led the way immediately out through the back gate and into the lane.

She turned to face him. 'Merran, what is it? Bad news?'

'Lizzie, I have just come from Little Manor. I went to look for you, but you were not there. I met one of the nurses and she told me that you had been . . . sent away.' He scanned her face. 'She told me why, Lizzie.'

198

Lizzie felt colder than her tripe-water. Naturally the rumour was all over the Hospital now. 'What did she say?'

'That you were . . .' – he hesitated – 'expecting a child.' You could see the shock on his face.

'I see.'

'My poor Lizzie. I'm so sorry.'

His sympathy brought the tears to her own eyes. Someone, at least, understood how she was feeling. She turned to him, stretched out a hand and squeezed his arm. 'It's all right, Merran. It's not your fault. There's nothing you can possibly do about it.'

She saw the cloud cross his face then, and there was a little silence. Then he said, 'Of course there is not, Lizzie, if that is how you feel. But there is one thing that I want you to know. Michael was my twin, as near to me as it is possible to be. If you wish it, Lizzie, I am willing to marry you, take the child as my own.'

The bluntness of it shocked her. It had not occurred to her that Merran, of all people, would believe that malicious nonsense. She went to protest again, 'Merran, you don't understand. I do not need you to marry me . . .'

He looked at her bleakly and when he spoke his voice was bitter. 'I understand perfectly, Lizzie. Well, so be it. I realise that you have never wanted me, but I felt I might at least offer you the protection of my name. It would make the child a Jago at least.'

She felt his words like a physical blow. Merran – even Merran – thought she was the trollop they called her. She was furious, desolated, speechless with despair. For a moment she struggled with tears of impotent rage, and then she raised her eyes and faced him squarely. 'You,' she said slowly, each word dropping like a stone into the silence, 'think . . . that . . . of . . . me?'

He was perplexed. 'I think only what I am told. What should I think?'

'Well,' she said furiously, 'I should think you would know better! You, of all people. And if you didn't know me better than that, you might know your own brother!'

He looked away. 'He was human, Lizzie. We are all of us human.'

'What is that supposed to mean?'

'I can see how anyone might be tempted, Lizzie, going away to War.'

He seemed embarrassed, as if he was confessing something. She burst out, 'What did Michael say to you?'

'Nothing, Lizzie.'

'Perhaps that's because there was nothing to say. I don't know how you could ever suppose such a thing. It was bad enough Mrs Rouncewell and half the town thinking it, but you too! Well, I aren't expecting a child, and even if I were I wouldn't marry you, Merran Jago. I don't want to be wedded out of pity, to you or anyone else.'

She turned on her heel and fled back through the gate into the yard, feeling the hot tears on her face.

'Lizzie!' she heard him call. 'Lizzie! Come back.'

But she did not go back. She bolted the gate and raced upstairs to her room, to weep with grief and helplessness, frustration and shame. Not even Gan, for all her pleadings, could persuade her to come down again. Not until Merran Jago had gone.

Mam was furious, because Agnes had to finish the tripes. She never washed them half so thoroughly as Lizzie.

Merran tried to concentrate on the present. France. This was what he enlisted for.

It was not a bit as he had imagined it – and there was no resemblance at all to those painted landscapes of the Training Camp.

Nothing had prepared him for the vastness of it: the great sweep of the horizon, the endless straight monotony of the roads, the fields so large you could lose the whole of Nanzeal in any one of them.

They had one evening in Etaples, and he walked about briefly, with Lewis, glad to be on dry land, after the pitching misery of the troop-ship. There was an indefinable foreignness about the town, not merely in the buildings, and the language of which he did not understand a word – but in the very people. Old women, dressed in faded black and huge, improbable starched lace caps, huddled in dusty doorways, eternally knitting. Priests, in the same long belted black, peddled on bicycles, like two-wheeled religious crows.

They went to a church. Merran – whose notion of a church was St Evan, at Penvarris, prim stained-glass and polished brass – looked at the agonised painted saints, the gashed, tortured, bleeding Christ at the altar, and was shocked by the physicality of it.

'Something the matter, boyo?' Lewis said, as they made their way back. 'You're more miserable than the camp itself.' It was a dreary place, all tents, sidings and warehouses.

Merran shook his head. Lizzie's angry rejection of him was not to be shared, even with Lewis. He was glad of the crowded discomfort of his billet.

Next day it was into a train and a slow, tedious crawl across seemingly endless countryside, and even Merran, who was enjoying the misery because it matched his mood, began to wish that it was over. He was an officer at least. What a journey it must be for the men, herded into hot compartments, hearing already the growl of guns, and thinking of those last few hours at home.

Well he would not think of it. That memory was the most dismal part of this whole dismal war. But he could not drive it from his mind. Lizzie, turning away from him with that exclamation of despair. His own fault, he should never have listened to gossip. And he had never told her of his feelings, as he intended, only blurted out his clumsy offer, and heard her turn it down in disgust.

He tried to think of other things. Nanzeal. Though that wasn't much better. Merran had been gone for only a few short weeks, and already Farrington had put his stamp on the place, and there was Pa messing around with Jerusalem artichokes instead of getting in the late carrots. Merran had had words with him, Mother and Peter had joined in, and there had been an almighty row, finishing with Pa slamming the door and going out to spend the night in the cow-house.

He was apologetic next morning, but the mood was still strained, even when it was time to say goodbye. The long and short of it was, Merran thought, that Farrington was within a hair's-breadth of ruining Nanzeal. It wasn't one thing, it was a hundred little things, like Farrington selling all the hay to the Army. Pa had gone along with it, to Merran's disgust, looking for a quick penny and relying on the early grass. Now with the late season, his own beasts were needing it, and he was obliged to buy his own hay back at a premium. Farrington, of course, had got his percentage. It was Nanzeal that suffered.

Well, it was too late now. That was Nanzeal, and he was here in France.

They were coming into a dusty station, with two staff officers important on the platform. This was truly the last stop before the War, the trainlines east were already rusting and ragged with grass. The luggage was disgorged, a huge straggling heap, and he located his valise with difficulty. The platform heaved with humanity.

201

Most of the men were marched away. His orders were different. He and Lewis were to take the light railway to a neighbouring town, and thence via the regimental mess-wagon, to Brigade Headquarters, an ancient farmhouse behind Doumiens.

'They call it "Do-me-in",' Lewis said, 'or "Doomy-ends". Makes you feel comfortable that, doesn't it?' Even Merran had to smile.

It was not a comfortable feeling, though, especially as the wagon took them past a colonnade of trees and a stone wall where a casual shell had ripped a gaping hole the day before.

'Nearly took the pants off the padre,' the sergeant-wagoner told them cheerfully, and then as Merran winced at the crash of guns behind them. 'That's nothing, only a couple of our heavies. Fire over the top of here, they do. Long range, see. You'll get used to it.' Merran and Lewis exchanged glances.

But there was no time to get used to anything. The commanding officer greeted them, unsmiling, and informed them they were to 'go up with the rations'; Lewis to the support trenches, Merran to the front line.

The 'rations' went up after dark, a jolting collection of wagons and limbers, with Merran and Lewis in the midst of them, down a road pockmarked with craters, illuminated every now and then by distant flame from the howitzers or the crimson burst of a shell. They halted at a cellar where yellow light filtered through a blanket, and the rations were unloaded onto smaller trolleys to be pushed on up the track by waiting soldiers.

The two newcomers followed clumsily, giving a helping hand now and then when one of the trolleys toppled off its narrow wooden rails.

'Nearly there,' one of the men said, after what seemed an age of stumbling over pot-holes. At that instant something fast and buzzing zipped past Merran's ear. He flapped a hand at it, thinking of insects, but a split-second later he heard the pop of a rifle in the darkness ahead, and something else buzzed by. Their first taste of the War. They cowered behind the trolley, feeling hopelessly exposed, until they could scamper over a rampart and into the dugout.

It was literally 'dug-out' – a simple earth cave, with walls of canvas. Lewis was to stop here, but for Merran the journey was not over. It gave him an odd wrench to say goodbye. He had known Lewis only a few weeks, but he seemed like an old friend.

'This way.' It was time to follow his guide again, bent double now, along a muddy duckboard in a shallow trench lined with sandbags. They passed parties of men: sentries, lookouts, men with shovels, and others with heavy bloodstained sacks which Merran did not care to examine closely. Then out into the moonlight.

It was a strange, ghostly, ghastly world. This was war, Merran thought. This was what he had come to. They crossed another trench – abandoned, silent and formidable. There was a dreadful stench, of marshes and charnelhouses, and in the drying mud Merran saw what looked like giant mushrooms, gleaming whitely in the gloom.

He looked closer. Skulls. It was a dreadful place. The sky was lit with a hideous, infernal glare, and the crack and thud of guns vibrated everything.

Merran stopped again, appalled at the sight of an arm still clutching a gun, though the rest of the body was nowhere in view, but his guide hustled him on, as though finding such piteous remains were a normal part of an evening stroll.

Merran stumbled after him, across wire and wet grass and finally on a wooden track, until they came to the firestep of Cover Trench and tumbled in.

It was deeper than the reserve trench, and busier. Sentries, mining parties, observation patrols everywhere; bullets and shells whined, droned and pinged incessantly overhead. They pressed on, down dark muddy recesses to a narrow hole with chairs and a lantern on a table. This was company headquarters. Merran was introduced, and given a mug of tea and a plate of rations.

He found, to his surprise that he was shaking with fatigue, and when they showed him a space in the dugout – a mere ledge in the wall where he might wrap himself in his British warm with his valise for a pillow – he was ready to fall into it and would have been asleep in an instant, shells or no.

As he was preparing to do so, however, he heard his name called. A messenger had come running. 'The Major wants to see you, right away.'

'What, now?' Merran said stupidly, scrabbling to his feet again.

'Now,' said a familiar voice. And amazingly, unbelievably, it was Paul, coming towards him with his hand outstretched, and calling him by the nickname he had not heard since childhood. 'Hello, St Merran. Welcome to hell.'

After Merran's visit, Lizzie withdrew even further into herself. She refused even to go into the shop. There were dreadful queues now, and Mam was mad as hops to start with – it wasn't like Lizzie to be disobedient – but soon even she stopped fussing and began to worry.

Lizzie couldn't explain it. It was as if she could feel gossip lurking outside for her, waiting to enfold her in clammy fingers like a mist. Even the long-delayed answer from Father failed to rouse her.

He didn't exactly encourage the idea of the Land Army, but he didn't discourage it either. 'I can't help feeling, Lizzie, that you'd be better off doing what Gan says and facing it out. But if you want to go for a Land Girl, I won't prevent you. You always were happiest looking after somebody or something, so a farm might suit you. If you do decide to go, go with my blessing and tell your Mam I said so.'

But perversely, Lizzie didn't do it. Instead, she busied herself in the household, all the unpleasant, tiring tasks, scrubbing the floors, blacking the stove, and boiling the clothes in the heavy copper.

Mam was delighted by this frenzy of activity, but Gan was thoughtful.

'It will do no good, my girl. You can't blot things out like that. You got to stop some time, and when you stop the grief will still be there waiting.'

And it was. Every night as soon as she shut her eyes, she lived it again. Michael dead. The town, whispering behind its doors, and Merran – Merran! – offering to 'take her on', as though she were second-hand goods on Tom Liddel's stall.

Then Millie came home one weekend with news of her own. She was to be put off, she said, and was working out her notice. Not that she hadn't given satisfaction, but Miss Tamsin was going to London, to nurse an ailing aunt.

'Though it's my belief,' Millie said, privately to Lizzie and Agnes, as they sat together peeling potatoes for tea, 'that it's a lot of nonsense. There's something funny going on, and that's a fact. Why, one day last week, Miss Tamsin and her mother had such a set-to! Sent her to her room all day and locked her in. Crying her eyes out, she was, when I went in. And I wasn't to speak, or anything. Course, when Sir Gilbert came home, it was all sorted out, and now Miss Tamsin is all over the place wanting to borrow uniforms, if you ever heard anything like it, for some tableau she's arranging for her mother's dinner party. But there is something going on, all the same. All the girls say the same – we're up there tiptoeing around, afraid to blink in case we do it wrong.'

'I suppose they're angry about her breaking her engagement,' Agnes said. 'Mr Masters' mother won't like it either.'

''Tisn't that,' Millie retorted. 'They've been thicker than thieves with Mrs Masters. No end of letters and even telephone calls. In fact,' – she put down the potato she was peeling and looked at her sisters dramatically – 'it's my belief that's where Tamsin's going to in London, and there isn't any "frail relative" at all.'

'Don't be so wet,' Aggie said. 'Why would they say so else?'

Millie tossed her head. 'No one in the house has ever heard of this aunt, and one day when I was passing I heard Sir Gilbert on the telephone, plain as day. 'You'll wire for her then, in a fortnight, Alice?' he said, and then he saw me and pretended to be talking air-raids. I didn't say anything, up there. More than my job's worth, if anyone thought I'd been listening. But that's what he said, all right. Makes you think, doesn't it?'

'Think what?' Lizzie said dully.

'Well, she's being sent away, that's clear. Wonder what she's done. Here,' – she cast a sideways glance at Lizzie – 'you know what I think? Her being sick in the mornings, and off her food – reminds me of Mam before Horry was born. And I do her clothes, and there hasn't been any – you know – for months. That's supposed to be a sign, Cook says. I think it is *her* expecting this baby Mrs Rouncewell was on about.'

Lizzie put down her knife. 'Don't be so wet! A lady like Tamsin Beswetherick!'

'Don't be so sure. Quite worried about her I was, one day, but when I suggested a doctor, she snapped my head off that quick! Hiding something, that I'm sure of.'

'Can't be,' Lizzie said. 'Or if she was, she'd be marrying her cousin double-quick, instead of breaking the engagement.'

'I think she's tried,' Millie said. 'Written to him two or three times, but he sent the letters back. She thinks no one's noticed, but I've seen her pick them up from the post-tray. Got tired of her ways, if you ask me. Make up to anyone, she would.'

'Yes,' Lizzie said, remembering Tamsin's manner with Michael. 'But a baby! That's different. You shouldn't be talking like this, Millie. That's how rumours start, and there may be nothing in it at all.' She had suffered enough from baseless gossip herself.

'Except that she's going away,' Millie said, obviously determined to have the last word, 'to her Aunt Alice, and not to nurse any aged relative. But you are right. It doesn't prove anything.'

And there the matter might have rested, if it hadn't been for an unexpected visitor.

Chapter Twenty-Two

Since Michael's death Lizzie had avoided any contact at all with Nanzeal. She wouldn't even go up with Nurse Blight on her weekly visit. She simply couldn't bear to be reminded. So it was a surprise, one Friday, when Gan came up and summoned her down into the shop. Mrs Jago wanted to see her.

Lizzie couldn't avoid the meeting. She felt herself burning brick red as she went into the shop, and a dozen customers stopped to stare.

Mrs Jago was aware of it. 'Shall we go out the back, my handsome? Away from prying eyes?' And they went through the shop and out into the yard.

'First off, Lizzie,' the woman said, 'I wanted to tell you that, whatever stupid stories the town is telling, we Jagos don't believe a word of it. And second, you are always welcome at Nanzeal. I know what happened with Merran – he told me. It was stupid of him, blundering in like that – and then blurting out his feelings when you were still grieving for Michael. I can't blame Merran, he's been sweet on you for years, but I can see how it would upset you, so soon after losing Michael. I'd feel the same myself. So you mustn't feel that you can't come and see us, because you turned him down. We're all fond of you, my dear, and would be in any case, for Michael's sake.'

Lizzie's face flamed scarlet. The last thing she expected Merran to do was tell his family about that terrible conversation. And as for turning him down, she hadn't really thought of it like that. It was just, she wasn't a fallen woman needing to be 'rescued'.

But Mrs Jago was rushing on. 'Speaking of Michael, I think you should have this.' She reached into her basket and brought out a packet. 'It was given him by Tamsin Beswetherick – for a wedding gift. I thought about sending it back, one time, but then I thought

206

no, if it was a marriage gift it was to both of you and you should have it. Or if you feel you should send it back, that's up to you.'

Lizzie eyed the parcel doubtfully. 'A wedding present? From Tamsin Beswetherick? How did she know there was even going to be a wedding?'

'I couldn't say my dear, I supposed you must have told her. Or maybe Michael did. She used to chat to him sometimes.'

'He must have said something,' Lizzie said. It gave her a little inward glow. Michael, claiming her in public. That would put a stop to Tamsin's flirtatious ways. 'It wasn't me.' She took the package, smiling. 'Nice of her. What is it?'

Mrs Jago shrugged again. 'A book, by the looks of it. Funny sort of wedding present, but they've got odd ways, some of these gentry. Anyway, have a look at it, and see what you think. And do come out and see us next week, Lizzie. Peter's done some more paintings, and Dr Macready wants him to exhibit them in London.'

'I will.' Lizzie felt suddenly more able to face the world. 'Next time Nell comes, I'll come too.' But she never did.

Once in the privacy of her room, she undid the parcel. It *was* a book. A story book, all about King Arthur. As Mrs Jago said, a funny sort of wedding present.

There was a letter too. Lizzie picked it up.

'My most gallant knight. I wanted you to have this. I have important news since our last meeting. I have broken my engagement with Ashton Masters and am now a free woman. I have learned where my true happiness lies.' It was signed, 'Your own Tamsin'.

She had read in stories of the room spinning around you, and for a moment it really did seem to be dancing about her, tilting and swaying, as if she were caught up in a nightmare that someone else was dreaming.

Tamsin Beswetherick. Tamsin Beswetherick and Michael. All those lingering looks at the bandaging classes – they were not just another of Tamsin's silly flirtations. And Michael's infatuation had not been a passing, childish fancy. It was all in earnest. Her mind was racing, trying not to believe the evidence of her own eyes.

But it explained everything. Why Tamsin had so suddenly broken off her engagement. Why she was being suddenly packed off to London – Gilbert Beswetherick would move heaven and earth to get her right away from such an unsuitable romance! Yet all the same, Tamsin had contrived to smuggle a note to Michael – letting him know that she had made herself free and was now able to marry him.

It all made perfect, terrible sense.

No, her heart said. No, it was impossible. Michael had loved her. Or was she only second best? She could not believe it. And yet – the letter. There must be some innocent explanation! Well, there was one way to find out. And by heaven, she would do it too. Go to Gulveylor herself and confront Tamsin Beswetherick in person.

It was unheard-of, of course. Impossible in the ordinary way. But since Michael's death everything had taken on an air of unreality, and now – with this letter – normal life seemed to have stopped altogether. Anything was possible, and nothing familiar and ordinary seemed to matter any more.

She watched herself, in a kind of dream, put on her bonnet and cape: the fingers that tied the ribbons seemed to belong to someone else. She picked up the book – returning that gave her the semblance of an excuse to call – tucked Tamsin's letter into her pocket and walked steadily down the granite steps to the yard.

Ma saw her come. 'My dear Lizzie, whatever's the matter?'

Lizzie heard herself say, 'I'm going out.'

'Where to?' Ma said, but then she saw Lizzie's face and stood back without waiting for an answer, as Lizzie went out through the shop.

Lizzie walked on, driven by a dull, grey purpose – down the street and out of town towards Gulveylor, scarcely aware of the pavements and roads beneath her feet. At the great gates, though, she did stop, and gazed down the drive towards the imposing frontage, struck for the first time by the full enormity of what she was proposing. For a moment she almost wavered.

Then she felt the letter in her pocket and, holding her head high, marched down the drive, up the front steps before she could think better of it, and boldly rang the bell.

The appearance of an elderly footman in uniform unnerved her. She said, flustered, 'I have come to see Miss Tamsin. I have a book to return to her.'

He extended a hand. 'I will take it to her.' But Lizzie, having come this far, was not to be deflected now.

'I wish to speak to her in person. I know she is here – working on her tableau, I believe,' she said, blessing Millie for the information.

'Ah,' the man said, 'the tableau. In that case, perhaps . . .' He led the way inside. Lizzie had just time to glimpse Millie's appalled and startled face on the staircase, before she found herself shown into a large room, so full of velvet and gilt that she was half-afraid to breathe out for fear of tarnishing something. It was all immensely grand. Never, from Millie's descriptions, had she ever imagined anything like this.

The gold-coloured clock with the cherubs ticked the minutes loudly. She began to wish that she had never come.

And then Tamsin came in, bustling in figured pink silk, with a tasselled notebook in her hand. There was something about her, the expensive elegance, the unconscious air of authority, that gave Lizzie a sudden furious courage. Of course Tamsin would have taken Michael if she wanted. She had always had everything she wanted. It went with being called Beswetherick and living in a house like this.

Lizzie raised her head defiantly and looked her rival in the eye.

'Why, it is you!' The smile froze on Tamsin's face. 'They told me it was about the tableau.'

Lizzie said nothing. There seemed to be nothing to say.

'Have you come about the uniform? If so . . .'

'The uniform?' Lizzie burst out. It was the first time in her life she had ever interrupted her 'betters'. 'No, I haven't come about the wretched uniform. It is no use to me, in any case, because I have been effectively dismissed from the Hospital – as I am sure you know, since the whole town is talking about it.' Her voice was shaking and she took control of herself with an effort. 'So, no, I haven't come about the uniform. I've come about . . . this.' She slammed the book down on the little carved table, so hard that the legs rattled.

Tamsin looked at the book, and a patch of dull red appeared in her cheeks.

There was a silence. The cherub clock seemed to tick louder than ever.

Tamsin studied her fingers. 'Where did you get that?'

Lizzie could hear her own heart beating. 'Mrs Jago gave it to me,' she said. 'Said it was for a wedding present. But it wasn't, was it? There was a letter in it . . .'

'You have no right to read my letter,' Tamsin was scarlet now. 'It was personal.'

'Personal, I should think it was! And he was engaged to me! I loved him. Why were you writing to my young man, Tamsin Beswetherick? I have to know. It is important for me to know.' Now that the words were out, Lizzie was almost shaking.

'Hush!' Tamsin said urgently. 'Keep your voice down. The servants will hear us.'

She was genuinely afraid, Lizzie realised. That could only mean one thing – there was no innocent explanation of that note. Everything was as terrible as she feared. The knowledge gave her a terrible recklessness. 'I don't care,' she said, slowly and deliberately, 'if they hear me all the way to Plymouth Sound. I want the truth. And don't try to put me off with excuses. I know exactly why you wrote that letter. You wanted to marry him, didn't you?' She stopped, appalled by her own effrontery.

But the effect of this outburst on Tamsin was astounding. All the colour had drained from her face, and there were tears of genuine anguish in her eyes. 'You know?'

Lizzie nodded, too full for words. It was true then. Tamsin's obvious distress was more proof than any words. She said, bitterly, 'But why? That is what I don't understand. Why Michael? Why a farmer's son when you could have had any man in the county?'

Tamsin was staring at her. 'But surely it is obvious if you know the truth? I would never have written to Michael, if it had not been for . . . this.' She patted her waist. 'You'd have done the same thing, Lizzie. Anyone would. Surely you understand?'

Lizzie looked at her, at the figured silk waistline cut unfashionably wide, and all at once, she did understand. Only too well. She closed her eyes, and grabbed at the back of the chair to support her, or her knees would have betrayed her.

Of course, of course, Millie was right. A baby! It was 'Tamsin Beswetherick and Michael' more than she could ever have imagined. It explained everything. The rumours. Mrs Rouncewell. Merran. Michael had obviously confided that he had got a girl into trouble. Only no one had ever thought of it being Tamsin. They had thought, as she herself had thought, that Lizzie Treloweth was Michael Jago's girl.

She was consumed, suddenly, by an overwhelming desire to get out of this house, to get away. The last few weeks had been dreadful enough: grief for Michael, and humiliation over the rumours. But this was a thousand times worse.

Tamsin was speaking. 'What is it you want? Money, I suppose?'

Lizzie flinched. Money! Did Tamsin suppose that money would somehow help? But before she had time to utter a word, Tamsin snatched up the book and went on, 'Well, I haven't any to give you, and if I had I shouldn't do it. I've got the book now. You shan't spread stories about me – Papa would soon put a stop to them anyway – and who would believe you, a girl without a character?' She paused. 'And how did you learn of this, in any case? That sister of yours, I suppose. Well, she shall be dismissed at once, immediately my parents get home. And as for that odious shop of yours, I shall see to it that no good family in Penzance ever buys anything from you again. And don't think I couldn't do it, because I can. How dare you come here trying to blackmail me.'

Lizzie was too stunned to speak. Everything she had ever loved and wanted lay in ruins around her. Michael had betrayed her – with Tamsin of all people. And now – this. She had brought trouble to Millie and the shop, besides. Or – perhaps not. The letter was still in her pocket. She summoned the tatters of dignity from despair.

'You are wrong, Tamsin Beswetherick, I do not want your money. I wanted, or thought I wanted, only the truth, though I would sooner have died with him, I think, than know what I know now. But your secret is safe with me. Not for your sake, but for his.' That was true, not even Gan must know the dreadful truth. 'Keep your book, Miss Beswetherick, and welcome. But I still have the letter. And if Millie is dismissed one day early, or if I hear a murmur – a single murmur – of your bringing any trouble to the shop, I shall see to it that the whole town knows what you wrote and why. And don't think I couldn't do it, because I will!' She looked at Tamsin's astonished face. 'Otherwise, you need fear nothing from me. I am going away, as far as possible away from you and everything about you. And now, if you will excuse me, I will see myself out.'

She went home, shaken by her own forwardness. The Land Army form was still in the bottom drawer, creased and faded, but intact. Lizzie took an indelible pencil and filled it in, added Mrs Rouncewell's testimonial, and went down, then and there, to deliver it in person to the War Service Registry.

She didn't tell the family until she got back, and then – although it was only Friday – insisted that Gramps lit up the copper and heated some water for a long hot bath.

'Masters! Masters! Damn the fellow. Wake up man!' Paddy Lowe's voice, urgent through the mists of sleep, and a rough hand on his shoulder shaking him awake.

Ashton half-opened his eyes. His limbs were heavy and his mouth thick and furred with last night's 'jolly'. Ever since his release from Tamsin and the loss of Chubby he had joined every 'jolly' on the base. It was one way to forget. 'What is it? D flight is on respite today. Go away, Paddy, there's a good fellow, and let a man sleep.'

'Masters! For God's sake. Get up. We're moving out. The Germans have broken through the line behind Quellieu and they'll have the range of us any minute.'

'What?' He was fully awake now, pulling on his tunic and belt. His clothes were rank with old smoke and sweat. 'What happened?'

Lowe shrugged. 'Who knows. Captured an old communication trench, is one rumour. Anyway, they've pushed right through to Doumiens, and brought up a couple of heavy guns. They started this at first light and it hasn't let up since.'

The thumping, crashing roar, which in his dreams had been a stampede of elephants, resolved itself into the crunch and thud of artillery. He glanced through the grimy narrow window. The courtyard was full of horses, wagons, motor-bikes, and motor-lorries, and men were streaming to and fro with supplies and possessions.

'My God,' he said, picking up his flying jacket, and stuffing everything else frantically into his carryall. 'You should have called me.'

'We've been trying to, for half an hour. But if this didn't wake you, what would?'

Ashton was still stupid with sleep. 'But, the kites . . .'

'Exactly, old fruit. That's why you don't get your beauty sleep. There's another airfield a mile or two west of here, Quellieu-le-Hameau. We're to take them there, out of harm's way, until this fuss dies down.'

Ashton groaned. 'But my poor old crate is hardly fit for the air. The riggers were dealing with her. I took some light Archie yesterday, coming back from the lines, and I've got a fractured strut and a hole in the nacelle. Lucky it didn't hit anything vital.'

'Well,' Lowe began, but a sickening 'crump' interrupted him, and they both flung themselves down on the bed with their arms covering their heads. The old farmhouse shivered, and pieces of ancient plaster showered around them.

'My God.' Ashton got to his feet, shaking dust from his hair. 'That was close.'

'Some way off yet,' Lowe remarked. 'They've hit Quellieu once or twice. One or two stragglers missed the transport last night and were caught in it. One "reccy" pilot is still missing. But it is us they're after, so brigade thinks. We had a couple of German scouts over earlier, taking a shufti. Our ground gunners took a pot at them but they got away.'

Another blast shivered the building. 'If this is "some way off",' Ashton said fervently, 'God preserve us when they get the range. Right. I'm ready. Let's see what can be done to rescue those kites.'

Outside the early morning air was crisp and cold, the grey sky streaked with the yellow-gold of sunrise. He had that strange clarity of vision again, as though every detail were etched on his eyes: a tethered horse with flattened ears and rolling eyes; a man with teetering boxes of papers; a pile of apples rotting by the gate. Then from the east, a roar and a boom, the sky lit with flame and fury like the mouth of hell. There was a whistle, a distant thud, and the ground rocked again.

'Come on!' Lowe cried, and they thrust the kitbag into a lorry, and seized a motor-bicycle from a startled messenger. The billet was not far from the airfield but the road was an impenetrable mass of horses, men and vehicles.

'The back road,' Ashton shouted, and they roared away, down a narrow lane.

They were moving towards the bombardment now, and it seemed as if every shell must hit them, but they skittered onward, bouncing over stones and treeroots, while the guns shook twigs and branches from the trees. Then they turned a corner and Lowe brought the motor-bike to a halt. 'My God.'

A procession was coming towards them, shambling down the lane from Quellieu. There were perhaps twenty of them, with perambulators, hand-carts, ancient bicycles piled high with pathetic belongings: saucepans, mattresses, baskets of chickens. Absurdly, a sewing machine and an accordion. One old grandmother, pushed in a cart, clutched a squealing piglet in her arms. Ashton had never seen anything so pitiful.

As they came nearer, he recognised some of them. The villagers of Quellieu. Madame, her sparkle gone: the piano player bent double under a mattress on his back.

They shuffled past, eyes averted, as though they were strangers. Ashton called out to her. 'Madame?' She did not even raise her head, and he called again, more urgently. 'Madame. Sylvie, where is she?' It was suddenly very important to know. He had left her last night at the bar with the others.

Then at last Madame did meet his gaze, and her eyes were hopeless. '*Dommage, monsieur.* The barn, it is destroyed. She was there . . .' She gestured helplessly towards the distance where a plume of smoke and dust trembled. He heard the tears in her voice. She turned away from him and resumed her despairing shuffle away from the guns and danger – and everything she had ever known.

He knew the barn, he had been there many times with Sylvie. 'Come on!'

'But the kites . . .' Lowe hesitated for a moment. 'We'll be court-martialled for this.' But he turned the motor-bike down the side lane in the direction of Quellieu.

There was desolation here. A party of men, routed from the ridge, had floundered back through the lines, and were regrouping outside a ruined building, dazed and exhausted. Some were wounded, with makeshift bandages around arms or heads, or limped along with tattered boots, their uniforms caked with dirt. They had no idea where they were. Lowe stopped to help them, stabbing with his finger at a ragged map.

Ashton left him to it and pressed on, possessed by a desperate sense of purpose. He must find Sylvie. Past other gaggles of men, sitting at the roadside, too weary to move another step – regardless of the gunfire. Two, he noticed, were even stretched out in the thin grass at the crossroads, their helmets over their faces, peacefully asleep.

There was the barn. It had not burnt, as he had first thought. A shell had fallen close by and the frail old building had collapsed inwards like a pack of cards. What he had taken for smoke was a pall of dust, still heavy in the air.

He looked at the wreckage. Great twisted timbers, fragments of broken brick – they brought tears of rage to his eyes. Sylvie. Little Sylvie.

'Sylvie!' he bellowed. Futile.

But there was, surely, something? An answering knock, a whimper?

'Sylvie!' he called again. He was already on his hands and knees, scrabbling among the debris, while behind him the sky exploded again into fire and thunder. Two soldiers came to his aid: not asking, merely burrowing beside him, lifting the broken brick, the pieces of wall.

Lowe came, lumbering up on foot, adding his hands to theirs. Then Ashton saw it. A leg, under a great baulk of wood, lying jagged at an angle.

214

The wood had saved her, for though its weight had trapped her, it had formed a cave, propping up the great slab of wall that rested on it. It took them, all four of them, every ounce of strength to lift it, toppling the broken wall away and clear, and then gingerly lifting the dead weight of the great timber truss.

Sylvie was there, her legs twisted and broken. She knew him, briefly, pressing his hand, but as soon as they moved the weight from her legs she fainted from the pain. There was a man with her, unconscious, his head laid open from flying stone. Ashton knew him, the missing fellow airman. He turned away.

Another salvo shook the ground. 'Moving range,' one of the soldiers remarked.

'The airfield!' Paddy Lowe said, and they left the army stretcher-bearers to it.

It was an appalling ride, but they arrived at last. Most of the planes had gone, but Ashton's was there, roughly patched and mended. There were still mechanics in the sheds, tumbling spares and pieces into a motor-lorry.

'Took you long enough,' one of the fitters grumbled.

'Had to come the back way,' Paddy Lowe said, but there was no more time for words. The aircraft were trundled out, started up, and they were away, bouncing across the grass and up as the air thundered and roared behind them. The gunners though had still not found the range.

Quellieu-le-Hameau. Taxiing in. The CO glad to see them. 'No problems, then? Good show. Only one plane's not arrived. Into the mess, then, they are waiting for you.'

But on the way over, Paddy Lowe said, 'You know whose crate that is?'

Ashton nodded, a wild daring impulse forming. 'He won't be flying it, will he?'

Lowe looked at him. 'Shall we?'

And they commandeered a vehicle, and a mechanic, and bumped back down the lanes to the old airfield. It was late afternoon when they arrived. The plane was still there, camouflaged among the sheds. Her rigger had refused to leave her.

'I lit a big bonfire this afternoon,' he said. 'Since then the Germans have left us alone. Reckon they think they hit the fuel store.'

They took the kite. Ashton flew it, with Lowe in the observer's seat, and the others returned in the lorry. That night he slept sweeter than he had slept for weeks.

215

It was all in vain, as it turned out. A week – and a thousand men – later, Doumiens was recaptured, the communication trench taken, and the war moved back to a comfortable distance, where it had been before.

The squadron moved back, a day or two after. Ashton went into the village as soon as he was able, to find news of Sylvie, but the place was deserted. Only, at the crossroads, the two soldiers, helmets over their faces, slept peacefully on. Ashton saw the blue-bottles that buzzed around them.

And understood.

Life was so damnably short.

The days since Lizzie's visit had been a nightmare for Tamsin. Imagine, that odious girl, coming in here and making such a scene. It was as well that the rest of the family had been out. She tried not to think about it. In fact, looking back, she could hardly believe that it had happened at all.

It was hard to know what the girl had wanted. Tamsin had waited, hourly, for some dreadful occurrence, or at least the sudden dearth of callers and invitations, which would mean that her reputation had been lost. But nothing happened. Millie, when discreetly questioned, seemed genuinely surprised and touched by Tamsin's sudden interest in her sister, and confirmed that Lizzie had indeed applied to join the Land Army.

Of course, she told herself, she had handled that dreadful situation rather deftly (threatening to withdraw their custom from the shop had been a clever touch) and, provided she herself did not carry out her threats – which, in any case, it would have been difficult to do – perhaps trouble had been averted, at least from that quarter. Finding a suitable husband, however, had been made more urgent than ever.

In the meantime, she busied herself with the tableau. Finding the costumes gave her something to do, and provided a welcome diversion from her other problems.

Britannia, she had decided, might reasonably wear a tunic, cape and breastplate. That would effectively disguise any thickening of the waistline. Nursing uniform posed no problems, and it had been an easy matter to obtain dresses and caps from the various staff at Gulveylor. The rest of the costumes were proving more of a head-ache: one could hardly walk up and ask a female ticket-collector or police constable for her clothes.

There remained the question of the munitions workers. There was only one possible source for that. The next time she met him, a hospital fête and sale of work at Trevarnon House, Tamsin approached Silas Farrington about it.

'Mr Farrington?'

He was walking dejectedly around the stalls, looking without interest at the potted jam, the beaded sugar-covers and the knitted gloves. He brightened when he saw her.

'Miss Tamsin. My dear young lady. This is indeed a pleasure. I had not expected to see you here. But, of course, like me you are a supporter of the Hospital.'

He was a disagreeable creature, Tamsin thought. So pink and portly and so obsequious somehow, bowing and smirking over his hat, and hissing as he talked. However, she knew how to be charming when she wanted something.

'Dear me, yes, Mr Farrington. I was liaison lady for the Linen League until very recently. So I am aware what a friend you have been to Little Manor. All those pillows you found for us, and the chickens and vegetable jam.'

He was flattered, as she had intended. 'My dear young lady. One must do what one can, mustn't one, in times like these?' He picked up the smallest bottle of relish on Mrs Owens' stall and solemnly counted out three halfpence for it. That was to persuade her of his liberality, Tamsin thought, for he could never have intended to eat it. It was horrible yellow, lumpy stuff – which, lacking enough sugar, had failed to set.

She bestowed a gracious smile on him. 'And now here you are supporting the stalls. You are very good, Mr Farrington.' That pleased him, you could see from his self-satisfied smile. She decided to strike while the iron was hot. 'You make other contributions to the war effort too. You have a munitions works, I understand.'

The pink face creased with pleasure. 'Indeed I do, my dear young lady, indeed I do. Though it isn't strictly munitions, you know. Essential war supplies, that's what it is. Started small, just screws and bits and pieces, and now we have moved on to making tails for aeroplanes. Not that I wouldn't think of filling shells too, if I had the premises.'

She couldn't stand here all afternoon, Tamsin thought. She looked around for relief, and saw it.

'Fascinating, Mr Farrington. Do please, accompany me to the tea-tent, where we may sit down and you can tell me all about it.'

He did tell her all about it, over refreshments – though his generosity extended only to a cup of tea and a gingerbread – and Tamsin listened with an appearance of absorbed interest to his accounts of quotas and quality inspections and visits from the Ministry. At last, when she felt she had nodded often enough, she ventured her request.

'Mr Farrington, I wonder. I am getting up a little tableau, for my mother's charity. You are not to breathe a word, of course, it is the greatest secret, but if I were to require a munitionette's overall and cap – for the tableau – might you be able to oblige me?'

He looked startled, but he rallied at once. 'My dear Miss Tamsin, with the greatest of pleasure. I'm sure one of our girls . . .'

Tamsin almost gasped. Imagine. Wearing a sweaty uniform that some factory girl had been working in. 'We should need to keep it for some time, I'm afraid. For rehearsals and so forth. I thought perhaps – a new one?'

'Ah,' Farrington said, 'there might be a little difficulty there. We haven't any new overalls at the moment, a temporary difficulty with our supplier.'

Tamsin gazed at him, failing to understand his meaning. 'Difficulty?'

Farrington seemed to wish the words unsaid. 'A temporary one, that is all. A number of unfortunate events together. We had a little accident in the factory – lost a machine and people had to be sent home, and then the Government insisted we plant seed potatoes when I had laid out a great deal on Jerusalem artichokes. But you don't want to hear all this, my dear young lady. You are interested in your uniforms.' He reached out his pudgy fingers to pat her hand. 'Leave it to me. I'm sure something can be arranged.'

He meant he had not paid his supplier, she realised, and was being refused credit. It was ill-bred of him, first all this talk about money, and then the over-familiarity of the pat. She stood up to bring the interview to a close, but she was careful to keep smiling. 'I'm sure I can rely on you, Mr Farrington.' She leaned forward and added, to soften her departure, 'And don't forget. Not a word to anyone. This tableau is our little secret.'

It seemed to work too, because she overheard him a little later saying to Lord Chyrose, 'Charming creature, isn't she, that Tamsin Beswetherick? Favoured me with her most particular attention this afternoon.'

Tamsin felt that, despite his 'temporary difficulty' the provision of her overalls was quite secure.

Chapter Twenty-Three

Silas Farrington looked after the retreating figure with approval. There had never been a great deal of time in his career for what he always referred to as 'the fairer sex', but he was not insensible of their attractions. On the contrary, he had always had a lively interest in the curve of a neat waist, but he had not on the whole had much success with the ladies.

Perhaps it was partly because he had never dared. His mother, whom he dimly remembered as gentle and pretty, had died young and penniless, and he had been raised by a resentful, wealthy aunt, who reminded him constantly of how much she was doing for him, and how much he was costing her. He had learned, very early, that to lack money was to commit an unforgivable social indiscretion, and he had devoted himself ever since to ensuring that it never happened again. But, though he had amassed a considerable sum, and had fingers in every pie, he could never quite lose the feeling that he was somehow, fundamentally, inferior, and he envied the Beswethericks and their effortless self-assurance with all his heart.

There had been women, once or twice, who had shown an enthusiasm for his bank balance, and one or two of the factory girls had made it clear that they would welcome his company, but the very fact of their willingness had reduced them in his eyes. Real ladies, he told himself, kept themselves aloof, and a man of substance should be interested in a real lady or none at all.

Not that he was interested in Tamsin Beswetherick. Naturally not. That would have been presumptuous. She was the daughter of gentry, with expectations which must run into thousands, even if she was the second child. A liaison like that would exceed his wildest dreams.

It did not prevent a man from looking, however. He had to admit that he would not have objected to a bit of that waiting for him when he came home of an evening. Damned attractive girl, a bit of 'all right' in all departments. The thought of all that money, too, did nothing to decrease her charms. Farrington ran a longing tongue around his lips. Well, a man might dream. And she had shown him the most particular attention.

In the meantime there was the problem of the uniforms. If she had asked him only a week ago there wouldn't have been the slightest difficulty, but now there was this awkward business with the bank. Refused to honour his bill to the supplier, and once news like that spread you could whistle for credit. He had overstretched himself, that was the trouble: laid out too much capital for the new house he was building behind the factory at Penvarris and had been unable to resist the offer of some 'under-the-counter' explosives and a bankrupt shop-premises. If he only could get the shell-filling enterprise off the ground.

Still that didn't answer the question of the overalls. He didn't have any new ones in stock, the girls all 'bought their own' by having it stopped from their wages. That one who pulled her hair out, now, he might be able to get hers back. Once it was laundered and pressed, no one would ever know the difference. Or he might apply to Tom Liddel. Amazing the stuff that turned up second-hand these days. If Tamsin Beswetherick wanted uniforms, he might be able to oblige her. Liddel owed him a favour or two.

The thought of Tom Liddel reminded him that he had business at Nanzeal, and he turned the car towards it. Lucky to have the car, really, with these shortages, but he was entitled to a certain amount of petroleum for 'essential purposes'. Perhaps, if he could arrange something with Liddel, Miss Tamsin Beswetherick might be persuaded to take a turn out to St Buryan and see what she wanted. Young ladies went about so much more unchaperoned than they used to, and even if her dreadful mother came, it was a price worth paying.

He was so pleased with his deliberations that he was able to listen to Jago's complaints with equanimity. Some of the local farmers were threatening to form a committee and take over Rocky Acre for potatoes and grain, under the Government directive.

'They reckon sugar-beet will never do no good up there,' Jago said sourly. 'For all your fancy fertilising mixture.'

'Well, even if the beets aren't big enough for the factories again, I've found a buyer for them. The Army'll take them, for the horses,' Farrington said. It had cost him a great deal of time and effort to negotiate that contract, but he had found someone, in the end, who was prepared to let him have a little paraffin on the quiet, apart from the agreed price. He didn't say that to Jago of course.

On the way back to the car, he met Willi Braun. The fellow always supposed that, because he had paid a small fee for someone to smooth the way for his placement, he now had an automatic right to Farrington's time.

'All right then?' Farrington said, briskly, busying himself with the car.

'Is better,' Braun muttered. 'But I not understand these farmers. In bottom field, where the stream, is good wheat. Another three inches with the plough we maybe double. But Mr Jago, he say no. Three inches only. Three inches, pah! What can you grow in three inches.'

Silas made a mental calculation. Even if the yield was only a quarter up, let's see, half an acre at sixpence a bushel. He beamed at Braun. 'You are sure of this?'

Braun shrugged. 'I have been a farmer ten, twenty years. On my farm, I tell you, I plough this twice as deep.'

Farrington smiled. 'Well then, you go ahead and do it. And if he argues, say it was me that told you. Afraid of change, that's his trouble.' He fished into his pocket and took out the pot of relish. 'A little token,' he said, 'to thank you for telling me.' The relish looked so disagreeable, he wouldn't have eaten it himself. But foreigners liked these things, and it was a shame to waste it.

Braun was overcome with gratitude. A good move, Farrington thought. He turned down the lane towards the factory with a very good opinion of himself.

Lizzie had expected to leave at once, but it all seemed to take an eternity.

Posters everywhere were urging you to join the Land Army. 'Could You Do This?' they thundered, alongside pictures of young women milking cows or harvesting grain. But when you had put your name down, they seemed to put every kind of obstacle in your way.

You needed a doctor's letter for a start, which meant a visit, and you had to be vaccinated for all sorts of things and get a certificate for that. Then you had to send away forms so you could collect your footwear (two pairs of boots, two pairs of gaiters, one pair of clogs). They only offered sizes four to eight, so it was as well she didn't have very small feet, like Aggie.

Then you indented for your uniform. Three sizes for everyone, small, medium or large. Lizzie decided that she was 'medium', though she wished she hadn't, because when she got them the breeches were too loose and the overalls too long.

Mam couldn't say much, after Father's letter, but she still didn't like the idea of a girl wearing trousers, and she made all kinds of difficulties when it came to buying the underwear. You provided that yourself, two sets of it, regulation long bloomers and woollen stockings, and a man's khaki shirt which all had to be named and marked for the laundry. It did put rather a strain on the finances, and Lizzie could not have bought them all, if it wasn't for Gan's help.

At last however, the formalities were over. Lizzie solemnly made her four promises – to behave quietly, to respect the uniform, to avoid conversation with German prisoners, and, oddly, to get eight hours' rest each night – signed away a year of her life, and was a probationary member of the LAAS. Her travel warrant arrived, and her shoulder flashes, and she was away to Hendra Farm, up near Truro, for training.

For the first time in her life she was an independent being. She liked it from the first, and found herself too busy to grieve.

There were seven others in the group. Four, like Lizzie, had some idea of what they were about, but the others were 'townies' who had never been on a farm before. One of them, a big, good-natured girl called Belinda, was so shocked when she saw where an egg came from that she wouldn't eat one for a week.

Unlike some training courses, Hendra provided accommodation on the farm. The 'gang' lived all together in a kind of dormitory above the old stables, eight iron bedsteads all in a row, with a locker each, and a rickety washstand in the corner. It felt extremely odd to Lizzie. She had always shared a bed, ever since she could remember, but she had never shared a room with a stranger, and certainly never undressed in public – and in daylight too! Yet there was no help for it. They were expected to be in bed nine o'clock sharp, and up at five next morning to help with the cows. Lizzie soon became adept at wriggling out of her clothes under cover of her night-gown.

Next door, in a sort of annexe, slept the supervisor, Miss Swann, small, stout and waddling. 'Looks more like a duck to me,' Belinda said and made them all grin. You couldn't help grinning, with Belinda.

When it came to eyes, though, Miss Swann was a hawk. The slightest wrinkle in your stockings, a hat worn at an 'unseemly' angle, or bedclothes that were not pulled as flat as planks, and you were 'spoken to', a process that reduced several of the girls to tears. Lizzie was glad of her bed-making experience at Little Manor. Without it she would never have escaped a wigging.

Training was a mixture of comedy and common sense. Most of the time it consisted of being shown how to do something, and then trying it yourself. Some of the jobs appealed to Lizzie at once. The animals, in particular – gave her something to care for as Father said – and, despite her sorrow and upset, it brought her a kind of peace. She loved bringing the cows in, for example: their warm, slow bodies friendly in the sharp morning air, the smell and sound of them oddly familiar and comforting.

Belinda couldn't understand it. When it was her turn, she edged around the cows nervously, as though they were German bombs in danger of going off, and if one turned and nuzzled her, as they sometimes did, she would stand stock still with her eyes closed – a perfect personification of terror. At least Lizzie, being a butcher's daughter, was not afraid of cows.

She did not care so much for feeding the chickens. It was a strange smelly slop they were fed, with grain so scarce, but the chickens seemed to like it, and would rush towards you, pecking your legs and ankles in their eagerness to get at the bucket. Much nicer to collect the eggs, searching for them in the grass and under bushes, or slipping a hand under the warm feathered bodies in the roost.

There were things she knew already, like how to stook corn, but she had never before learned to rick it into mows, piling the slippery sheaves heads innermost, into a neat stack, and fanning the top to keep the rain off. It was hard work, and made your arms and shoulders ache. Lizzie had watched Merran Jago make a mow, and she felt a new respect for his skills.

It was when it came to milking, though, that Lizzie really began to shine. Perhaps it was her confidence with beasts, or Little Manor had given her a gentle touch, but certainly Lizzie could coax the animals to let down their milk. She would sit beside them, half-resting against their warmth, while her fingers moved in a smooth, dreamy rhythm, and the creamy liquid squirted into the bucket below. Her dreams of 'doing something' herself seemed to be coming true.

Some of the others, however, were too funny to laugh at. The cows would stand on the girls' toes, overturn their buckets, or simply stand stolidly facing the wall and refuse to give any milk at all. Most people got the hang of it, more or less, in the end, except Belinda. She never did master it completely, even though Miss Swann took to letting her practise with a leather glove filled with water. Belinda could manage the glove perfectly, but as soon as she got near a cow, there would be a howl of anguish as a well-manured tail flicked across her face.

'They do it on purpose,' Belinda wailed, and Lizzie secretly agreed. Cows were cleverer creatures than you supposed. Like Buttercup – always rushing to the milking sheds, and snatching a mouthful of hay from every stall before the others arrived. Just like Dottie at Christmas, stealing a spoonful of pudding from everyone's plate.

There was precious little pudding for the War Workers. Meals were provided according to the National Economy League booklets so there was a lot of sardines and turnips or haricot beans and dripping, and not a great deal of anything else, although you never went hungry. Two of the girls secretly smoked cigarettes, though it was expressly forbidden in public, and Lizzie was fascinated by their daring. She and Belinda tried it once, feeling like scarlet women, but it made them so queasy that they never did it again. All the same, it gave Lizzie a strange, heady sensation of freedom ever to have tried such a thing.

After the first few weeks there was a 'practical phase'. They went to surrounding farms, all travelling together by bus, like a Sunday School outing, while the children shouted and jeered after them. The men at some farms were not much better, leaving the trickiest jobs for the girls and mocking unmercifully if they failed, but other farmers were more helpful and seemed genuinely glad of extra hands. Lizzie learned to drive a binder, after a fashion, and she could work a thresher with the best of them. 'Whatever would Mam say,' she wondered, climbing up to the high seat in her britches and operating the heavy machine like a man.

She worked hard at it, though, because at the end of the training there was an Efficiency Test, and if you passed that you could be sent out on a placement, and get paid. Good pay too, even if you did have to find your National Insurance and your keep out of it. Twenty shillings a week – no wonder people were leaving trades like tailoring and domestic service and starting to work for the Government. Lizzie had never in her life had a whole pound note, all of her own. Lodgings were dear, and she would have to send something home of course, but even so it was a wonderful prospect.

She would never have believed it, after the dreadful happenings of the past few months, but altogether, she was beginning to enjoy herself.

*

Helena had been sent for. Tamsin didn't want her, and Helena had tried to resist the summons at first.

'How can you casually require me to come, when my work here is sometimes a question of life and death?' she wrote indignantly.

But on this matter Mama was immovable. Helena must be told, and in person too, lest some unguarded remark should accidentally reveal that no 'Great-Aunt Enid' ever existed. There was a family crisis, she wired back, and Helena must return at once.

She came at last on 'compassionate leave of absence', with the understanding that she would go back immediately she could be spared. Tamsin saw her arrive, but there was no chance of the quiet word she had hoped for. Helena was bundled upstairs immediately to see Father.

She emerged half an hour later, white-faced and angry. Tamsin was waiting. Remembering how Helena had reacted over Lizzie, she was hoping for a similar sympathy, but her sister's first words disabused her.

'Tamsin, how could you be so wicked?'

Tamsin was startled by this greeting. 'It was not so very wicked, Lena. We would have married, if he had lived, and you said yourself . . .'

Helena silenced her with a look. 'Oh, as to that, Tammy, it shows a complete want of morality. It is foolish and wanton, but it is not cruel. But to allow me to suppose that it was poor Lizzie Treloweth you spoke of, that was unforgivable. I presume she is not, after all, in a similar case?'

For a moment temptation flickered, then Tamsin said dully. 'Not that I know.'

Helena shook her head, 'And to think that I went up to Little Manor.'

Tamsin gazed at her, aghast. 'Helena. You didn't?' She really had not known of that. It had never occurred to her to wonder how the rumours about Lizzie had begun.

Her sister gave her a steely glance. 'Ah, but I did. I supposed that I was doing a discreet favour, both to yourself and to your friend. All I have done, I see, is bid fair to destroy the poor girl's reputation. And my own. Mrs Rouncewell will wonder what I was about, since I imagine by now Lizzie has denied it.'

Tamsin avoided her eyes.

'What is it Tamsin? What has happened?'

'It is not my fault,' Tamsin cried. 'She has gone away, that's all.'

'Gone away? Why? Because of this, you mean? Because of you?'

'Not because of me,' Tamsin said. 'There were . . . rumours.'

'Well then,' Helena said. 'I must go up there at once and put a stop to them. I seem to have started it – unwittingly.'

'No,' Tamsin could not disguise the urgency in her voice. 'You can't.'

'Oh, I won't tell her about you, Tamsin. Just confess that I've made a terrible mistake.'

Tamsin shook her head. 'It isn't that, it's just . . . You can't, that's all. Not after what I said.'

Helena looked at her slowly. 'You don't mean, Tamsin, that you have been encouraging these rumours? I can't believe it of you.'

'I didn't say anything that wasn't true,' Tamsin protested. 'It's just, when someone asked me, was it true about Lizzie Treloweth, I said . . . I just said . . .'

'What?'

'I said I'd heard something of the kind,' Tamsin burst out. 'Well, it was true. Everyone was talking about it.'

Helena was still staring at her. 'Sometimes, Tamsin, I find it hard to believe that you are my flesh and blood. How could you do anything so . . . so spiteful? What is going to become of Lizzie, now?'

'What's going to become of me?'

'Whatever happens to you, Tamsin, you brought upon yourself. Lizzie has done nothing at all to deserve this. I might have had some sympathy for you if you had confessed honestly. Getting yourself in this situation was stupid, but it was human. Deliberately setting out to tarnish another person's character, that is calculated. Calculated, cruel and heartless.'

'I didn't mean to,' Tamsin protested. 'I was trying to tell you about me, and you jumped to your own conclusions. If anyone was quick to tarnish Lizzie's reputation it wasn't me. I didn't ask you to go and speak to Mrs Rouncewell, and start spreading these stories.'

Helena was still staring at her. 'You twist things, Tamsin. You always do. But there is some truth in what you say. This is my doing, and I must put a stop to it. I shall go and see Mrs Rouncewell directly.'

'But what about me? Have you no sympathy?'

'Tamsin, we are in the midst of a war. Men are dying, suffering hideously, every day. You have behaved appallingly – you have betrayed Ashton, disgraced the family, and deprived poor Lizzie

Treloweth of her reputation. You will go to Aunt Alice, and no doubt contrive to be cosseted. On the whole, I do not feel that I have pity left to waste on you. If you wish to make amends, you will come with me now to Little Manor and try to repair what you have done. If you do not, I will go alone.'

'But you can't. What will Mama say?'

'Mama can say what she wishes. This has to be done. I will not implicate you, Tamsin, unless I have to, but I cannot allow this to continue, when it is my doing.'

Tamsin shut her eyes. If Helena went to Little Manor there was no knowing what she might say. Yet there was no way to prevent it. Papa might have stopped it, but Helena would certainly tell him of her own little, well, excursions from the truth, and there were few things Papa hated more than deliberate dishonesty. She took a deep breath. If she accompanied her sister, at least she could keep some check on what was being said.

If only they didn't have to go now, while Helena was so hot under the collar, but try as she would Tamsin could think of no reasonable excuse to delay the visit, even for an hour or two.

She sighed and got to her feet.

'I'll come with you,' she said. At that moment, the doorbell rang.

Chapter Twenty-Four

As the motor-car turned into Gulveylor, the curtains twitched in the coachman's cottage at the gate. Silas Farrington smiled. The whole town would know tomorrow that he was on calling terms with the Beswethericks. And a private visit, too.

It was daring, of course. He had debated with himself for a long time whether to come at all, rather than write, but decided at last that he had a reasonable excuse. Tom Liddel had managed to secure half a dozen assorted women's uniforms – everything from a London ambulance driver to a cinema organist, and the 'shell overalls' too – so the 'essential war work' this afternoon included a visit to let Tamsin Beswetherick know. If he was very lucky he might have the chance of a few words with the lady herself.

He rang the bell in a mood of pleasurable anxiety, but his reception was beyond his wildest dreams. He had been prepared for a long wait, or a 'thank you' note brought by a servant, but Miss Tamsin herself came down almost at once. What is more, she sent down for a tray of tea and muffins and had the fire made up in the drawing-room.

He took the seat she indicated, feeling flushed and anxious. Should he have brought some tea or sugar – it was the expected thing, nowadays. Or perhaps he should offer a bit of his under-the-counter butter or coal? He did not know how a great house like this would respond to such an offer. It was a dilemma. He had not expected to be invited to tea, like a long-lost friend.

'My dear Mr Farrington, do please make yourself at ease.' There could be no doubting the warmth, almost the delight in her manner. She turned to the maid. 'Please tell my sister that I have a visitor. It is impossible for us to visit Mrs Rouncewell just now. Ask her to wait. I know it is inconvenient, but it is imperative that I talk to Mr Farrington.'

Silas felt himself glow. Tamsin Beswetherick, delaying a social engagement on his account. It was decidedly flattering.

She seemed determined too, to spend as much time as possible in his company. Instead of getting straight down to business, as he had expected, she talked about other things. Asked a hundred questions about his factories, for instance, and positively encouraged him to talk about his hopes and plans. It was astonishing. No one in all his life had ever shown so much warm interest in his concerns. And when it did come to the uniforms, she was enchantingly grateful.

'My dear Mr Farrington, six, no seven costumes for my little pageant. You are too good. Do pray, have another cup of tea and a muffin. Millie, bring up some more hot water and sugar at once.' She gave him one of her dazzling smiles, and Silas plucked up courage to suggest that visit to St Buryan to see them for herself.

Once again, her reaction astounded him. 'Mr Farrington, that would be delightful. When could we manage it, do you think? Time is slipping by, you see, and the dinner party is only a week or two away.'

By heaven she was positively encouraging him. And she was such a beautiful girl, the thought of the drive made his mouth actually water. He said, greatly daring, 'I am at your service at any time, my dear lady. I have a car outside at this very moment, if you would care to accompany me now.' It sounded presumptuous, even to his own ears, and he added quickly, 'And your mother, or your sister too, if she is free.'

She clapped her hands like a child. 'Splendid. What a capital notion. And tomorrow I shall have some of my chums come up for a rehearsal and we shall see what fits them. Mr Farrington, I am more grateful than I can say. Excuse me for a moment, and I will speak to my sister about it.' She went out, leaving him alone.

He looked around the drawing-room not knowing quite how to comport himself. The furnishings themselves made him feel small. Why the silk carpet alone must represent a small fortune, without the Wedgwood and silver displayed on the shelves, or the paintings on the walls. How the wealthy live, he thought to himself, and made a mental note to invest in some gilt and brocade chairs, and a pair of long gilded mirrors for his own new drawing-room, when the time came.

Still nobody came. He moved to the window, moving aside the heavy blue curtains, and affected to be looking at the garden. Tamsin's voice floated down from somewhere above him.

'Don't be so disagreeable, Helena. I'm sure Mr Farrington is very pleasant when you come to know him. And of course we must go. He has come on purpose, and he has gone to so much trouble on Mama's account. I mean to go with him, even if you do not!'

Just then, the maid came in for the tea-tray and Silas moved hastily, but already he was walking on air. 'Mr Farrington is very pleasant . . . I mean to go with him, even if you do not.' He had not imagined it. Tamsin Beswetherick welcomed his advances.

When the sisters came down – they did both come down, so there was no opportunity to speak to Tamsin alone – he set out to be as attentive and charming as he could possibly be. He drove to St Buryan more carefully, and more courteously than any coachman. He even refused to take a penny for any of the uniforms, though she wanted them all and it would cost him a shilling or two to square matters with Liddel.

He was rewarded. Tamsin was delighted with them, and, when her sister wasn't listening, even suggested a detour to see how his new house was progressing. He was a little worried at that – the road was dreadful – but fortunately a mine-wagon from Penvarris had recently flattened the worst of it. Tamsin seemed enchanted. So much so, that later, as he was handing her down from the car and passing her the uniforms from the trunk, he plucked up the courage to say, 'Miss Tamsin . . . I have a pair of tickets for the charity concert at the town hall on Friday afternoon. You wouldn't, I suppose . . . care to . . . ?'

There was a frightful pause. I have gone too far, he thought, desperately, but then Tamsin smiled. She was looking at him with a sudden, alert interest, as if she had just seen him for the first time, or seen him in an entirely new light.

'Why, yes, Mr Farrington, I should be delighted.' She glanced at her sister, and added, 'Though perhaps, if you wish to escort me in public, you should have a word with my parents first. My father has strong views about entanglements.'

Entanglements. Silas felt his heart thump painfully. The idea filled him with such a sudden wild desire that it was almost embarrassingly visible, and he was obliged to move the uniforms on his arm to cover it.

'I'll ask them to see you, straight away,' she promised, and he was shown into the drawing-room again.

Things were moving faster than he had bargained for. He was really anxious now, his palms were sweating. What had he let himself in for? Helena, clearly, disapproved, he could hear her raised voice on the stairs, and the prospect of facing the parents terrified him. He mopped the moisture from his brow with his handkerchief and was almost ready to bolt for it, but Tamsin came back, smiling with a warmth that gave him hope. Sir Gilbert was not in, but Lady Beswetherick would receive him.

She did receive him – cordially too. She accepted, indeed, welcomed his invitation to Tamsin with evident delight, and even invited him to lunch before the concert.

Silas Farrington, he told himself, as the car lurched home to Penvarris, you can hold your head up with anyone now. You have arrived, my son.

Lizzie gained top marks in her Efficiency examination. Ninety per cent, which was an 'A'. Most of the girls got 'Bs' and even Belinda, to her delight and astonishment, achieved the minimum mark and was entitled to put up her badges.

Then there came a wait for a placement. The girls had been warned that there might be a short delay, a lot of farmers would still sooner have a prisoner of war than a woman, even if he was a German shoemaker who'd never seen a farm, and she had her certificate of Efficiency, with special merit in dairying.

Lizzie went home to wait. She did not want to go. It would be nice to be home, of course, but since that dreadful meeting with Tamsin, Lizzie had tried to think about Penzance as little as possible. All those terrible rumours. And supposing she should meet one of the Jagos? Or worse, run into Tamsin Beswetherick somewhere in the street?

230

It was a wretched journey. Not only was the carriage crammed (there weren't the trains, with coal wanted for the war effort), but the clackety-clack of the wheels sang 'Tamsin's baby. Michael's baby', until she felt the whole compartment could hear it. When she got to Penzance the town, too, was wreathed in unseasonable mist. The damp grey misery of it reached into her very soul.

But there was a warm welcome at home. Gan's elderflower wine was brought out again, and nothing would do but Lizzie must read the latest letter from Father, admire Penny's schoolwork, and look at Horry's newest trick, before she had time to take off her cap. Gan hugged her fit to burst, and even Mam, who wasn't given to 'scenes' blew her nose sharply on a handkerchief and said gruffly that Lizzie was 'a sight for sore eyes' in her uniform, britches or no.

Even this, however, did not lift her spirits. Things seemed to have changed so much in a few short weeks. Horry had grown out of recognition, and the house – by contrast – seemed to have shrunk. She had never realised before how crowded it was, with never a private moment – without you went into Mam's bedroom and hid, and even then you were apt to run into somebody else with the same idea. It was strange sharing a bed again, and Lizzie spent her first night huddled uncomfortably in a corner afraid to move in case she disturbed somebody.

The next afternoon, though, brought Millie and with her some astounding news. She was still working at Gulveylor – her period of notice before Tamsin 'went to her aunt in London' had been unexpectedly extended – to Lizzie's no great surprise.

'When are they putting you off then?' Lizzie said, after tea, filling the kettle from the water-bucket, and preparing to wash up. 'Tamsin must be leaving any time now?'

Millie almost dropped the cups in surprise. 'My lor, Lizzie, haven't you heard? I'm surprised someone haven't told you. Didn't Mam say, when she wrote?'

'Say what?' Lizzie asked. There had been little news in Mam's letters except the shortage of beef and Horry's teeth.

'About Tamsin Beswetherick? Got herself engaged again, hasn't she? So I'm to stay on, after all, and go with her soon as her house is ready. Due to be married in a week or two. All very hurried and hush-hush.'

Lizzie stared. 'But wasn't she . . . ?' Michael, she was thinking. Wasn't she hoping to marry Michael.

'Course she is,' Millie answered, misinterpreting her words. 'That's why she's in such an all-fire hurry to get herself wed.'

'And Ashton?' Lizzie said. 'What does he think?' Poor Ashton, doubtless roped into doing the decent thing to save the family name. Still, Tamsin was not a Beswetherick for nothing, she thought bitterly.

'Ashton? Nothing to do with Ashton,' Millie said. 'Be the talk of Penwith, I should think, when word gets around. We're all sworn to secrecy. It'll be a quiet affair. Just the family and a few friends. Not at all the grand occasion they were planning before.'

'Not much of a secret is it, if you're telling me?' Lizzie said.

'Well, you're family,' Millie said. 'Anyway, it'll be common knowledge soon. They're reading the banns, Sunday. Sir Gilbert didn't like it at first – there were some right ding-dongs about it – but he came round in the end. Saw the sense of it, I daresay. There aren't many men would take on a girl in her condition. It will give her a name, and she won't be short of money. Mind you I wouldn't marry him, for all the tea in China.'

'Marry who?' Lizzie demanded, almost beside herself with curiosity.

'Why Farrington, of course. Almost pulled out of it, apparently, when he heard about the baby, but Sir Gilbert is giving them an allowance. Cook's cousin works down at Tavy's, the solicitor, and he witnessed the agreement.'

But Lizzie wasn't listening. 'Farrington!' She could hardly believe her ears. What would Michael have made of that? Farrington, who had almost ruined Nanzeal! But better for the child to have any father, even Farrington, than bear the stigma of having no father at all. She would try to be glad, for Michael's sake. But – 'Farrington!'

Millie giggled. 'I know. Awful, isn't it? And you'd have thought she could have had anyone she wanted.'

'Yes,' Lizzie said grimly, and couldn't help adding, 'even Michael Jago.'

'Don't be so wet, of course she couldn't!' Millie said. Lizzie had never mentioned Tamsin's letter to anyone. 'Though I see what you mean. He was a bit smitten at one stage, wasn't he. And she cried her eyes out when she heard he was killed, I heard Helena say. Oh and that's something else, Lizzie. Something you'll be glad to hear.'

Lizzie had thought that she was over the agony of Michael, but Millie's idle chatter had awakened such pain that she couldn't imagine being glad about anything. She said, 'What?' dully.

'Helena. Went up to see Mrs Rouncewell and told her she'd made a mistake about you – listened to malicious gossip, she said, and had come to apologise. There was quite a scene. All over the Hospital in five minutes. Nurse Blight came and told us.'

'Helena did?'

'Yes. Though I don't suppose it signifies now. You're home, and you've clearly been in the Land Army. People will be able to see with their own eyes that there was nothing in the rumour.'

Millie seemed to be right. Folk went out of their way to be warm to her – even Mrs Tavy – all the time she was home. But she was not home for long.

It was less than a week before a letter came. It was a typed form, giving an address near Hayle. She would be met at the station off the first train Friday, and would be in a private billet with one other recruit, charged with 'general farm duties'. A rail warrant was enclosed.

Her posting had arrived.

Mater was furious about Tamsin's wedding. It was the first thing she mentioned when Ashton walked in on leave, and she returned to it time and again over supper. It didn't seem to occur to her that he might have feelings on the subject. His one-time fiancée, carrying another man's child.

Perhaps he should have been angry. He would have been, once, but since that day at Quellieu none of this seemed terribly important. It did not even surprise him very much. He had half-suspected something, from Chubby's manner.

Tamsin's choice of bridegroom, however, left him thunderstruck.

But Mater had other concerns. 'It is too bad, Ashton. To think that you might have had Gulveylor! To be sure there is this awkward business of the child. I suppose you are quite right – it was impossible to marry her under the circumstances – and one could hardly have allowed the child to inherit. But to lose Gulveylor! Really, it is too bad of Tamsin!'

'Yes, Mater,' he said, wryly. 'The observation had struck me!'

'And now there is the problem of the wedding. If we go it will appear bravado and if we do not we shall seem rancorous. I feel it very keenly, Ashton and so must you.'

In fact, Ashton found to his surprise that he really didn't feel anything at all, except perhaps relief that he wasn't involved himself. It wasn't that he was heartless – the dog-fight and that business of Sylvie and the barn had taught him that he could feel very acutely indeed – it was just that his relations with Tamsin had never really engaged his heart. His blood, his loins, his self-esteem perhaps. They had been such children, then.

'What ought we to do, Ashton?' his mother persisted. 'You move in officer circles these days. What do you say?'

He regarded her with detachment. All this concern for social niceties. Mater built her whole life around them, yet in the end they did not matter at all. Those men lying in the grass at Quellieu – did it matter to them if one of the officers wore the wrong tie to a function, or served the wrong wine with the soup? Not that his mother would understand that. He said, 'I have come to the conclusion, Mater, that I am very well out of that liaison. We should not have made each other happy, Gulveylor or not. And as for the wedding, I have no objection to going. My heart is unbroken, I assure you, and not to attend might suggest that I had taken it ill.'

So they went. The ceremony was a strange, unsatisfactory affair. It was conducted at St Evan, a small, draughty barren little church at Penvarris, with the merest handful of guests, and the reception – although lavish – was equally small. Mater affected sympathy for Winifred, but secretly Ashton could tell that she was a little gratified too. If it had been his wedding, she was thinking, things would have been quite different.

Tamsin looked portly and peevish, in a wedding dress of sorts. It was made of some inferior stuff – material was hard to come by – and was ivory, not white, which rather matched her complexion. She looked pale, tense and drawn, and although she once or twice smiled charmingly enough, Ashton noticed that the smile never reached her eyes.

Farrington, though, seemed genuinely delighted – though whether with himself or with his bride it was hard to see – and managed during the reception to be everywhere at once, wringing hands, proposing toasts, eating too much cake, and generally contriving to be both hearty and obsequious in that hissing voice of his. Altogether, Ashton could find it in his heart to feel quite sorry for Tamsin, when she was finally bundled into the motor-car and driven off towards Penvarris and her new home, which was only three parts completed. Mrs Silas Farrington.

Ashton and Mater stayed at Gulveylor for a few days. Sir Gilbert attempted to be hearty, but there was a despondent mood on the whole party. Winifred was vexed at the paucity of wedding gifts, and Mater – pretending to believe it was all on account of the shortages – was helping her to send carefully worded letters of thanks to the donors.

On the whole, Ashton was glad to get back to the War.

PART FIVE
AUTUMN 1917 – 1918

Chapter Twenty-Five

'Lizzie? She's here somewhere. Out with the cows, I believe.'

It was a bright autumn day, the sun glinting on the furze bushes and a fresh wind combing the grasses. Lizzie was out on Far Field and she hardly heard the shouted summons, which was in any case danced away by the breeze.

She loved it here. The small hillocky fields, huddled behind tall stone 'hedges' as if to hide from the wind, the thin blanket of green pasture pierced here and there by the granite which still lurked under the stern earth. And over there, beyond the hedge, the unfenced lands – gold and purple with heather and furze – where ferns and 'hurty-berries' grew, and a glory of grey cliffs tumbled down to the wild sea below. No gossiping whispers, no painful memories here, only the choughs and the cows, and a quietness which soothed her soul.

At first it had seemed eerily strange and silent. Lizzie was used to the bustle of a town, and a house full of family, and even at Hendra there had been the other girls. But here there was nothing but Bengarra Farm and the widow who farmed it – it was the death of her son which had made her apply for Land Army help.

It was not a big farm, but it was hard work for three women. Lizzie didn't mind. Long hours and weary limbs dulled the bitter ache of betrayal and loss. Here she could forget about Tamsin and Michael, and lose herself in the long, slow rhythms of the year.

It had been a busy summer. The other 'recruit' turned out to be Belinda, to Lizzie's joy, and she suspected Miss Swann's hand in the placement, especially as the widow was called Swann too, a sort of distant cousin. It had worked out very well. Lizzie could do anything with animals, and Belinda had developed an unexpected talent for thatching and 'tashing' – cutting the prickly furze and wrapping it together to make faggots for the fire. Perhaps it was because she had worked as a milliner, but Belinda could cut two branches of 'gorse', as she called it, lay them flat with her hobnailed boots, and twine them into a tash better than Mrs Swann herself. And when they came in of an evening, the smell and crackle of the fire, with its furze and turves and the occasional 'stog' of old wood was something wonderful to Lizzie.

Not that they lived on the farm. Each evening brought a mile walk to their billet, with the postmistress who lived in Bengarra 'village'. She was called Miss Stamp, which reduced Belinda to giggles, and she kept a double-fronted shop: post office on one side and teas, honey and knitting wool on the other. How she made a living Lizzie couldn't see, there were only a half-dozen cottages in Bengarra and they didn't go out to tea, but the rooms were pretty, neat and clean. Too clean sometimes, for young women who had walked home across farm fields.

Belinda was good company, and Lizzie was glad of it, especially in the early days when the stillness and solitude kept her awake, listening to the silence and the little noises of the night, the distant murmur of wind and tide. Belinda, today, had the back-breaking job of lifting the last potatoes while Lizzie went out to Far Fields with a bunch of hay on her shoulder and a stool under her arm, to catch and milk Buttercup and Daisy, Mrs Swann's two cows.

Mrs Swann milked everything – cows, goats and ewes – and was famous for her cheesemaking, but she didn't bring the animals in as a rule. There were little stone shelters on the cliff where you could sit and milk out of the wind and rain, and Lizzie loved the late afternoon milking – though the early morning, when half the Atlantic was blowing into your eyes and down your neck, was a lot less pleasant. Still Mrs Swann had only the two cows and a couple of heifers, and there was no late calving at Bengarra, so the milk would soon dry up for winter and Mrs Swann would put away her cheese-cloths till the spring. In fact, when the hens stopped laying, Lizzie was beginning to wonder what there would be for the pair of LAAS girls to do.

'Lizzie? Drat the girl, I believe she's fallen off the end of the earth.' Mrs Swann's voice in the distance, followed very shortly by Mrs Swann herself, short, stumpy and arthritic, her boots unlaced to 'save' her swollen ankles, and her grey hair and weather-beaten face framed by a tattered scarf.

'Oh, there you are, my lover. Wonder you never heard me – I near burst me lungs 'ollering. Here, you leave that cow to me – there's someone to see you down at the house.'

'Finished anyway,' Lizzie said. She put the lid on the pail and wiped her hands in her sacking 'towser' apron. 'Who's come then?'

Mrs Swann gave her a meaningful glance. 'Someone you'll be glad to see, I'll be bound. You're a dark one, aren't you? Nice-looking fellow like that, and you never breathed a word.' And that was all the answer Lizzie could get.

She hurried back to the farmhouse, balancing her bucket over stiles, spurred by a sudden hope. Merran? Who else could it be?

'There you are then,' Mrs Swann said, pushing open the stable-style door into the back kitchen. 'As if you didn't know.'

She knew him, of course, but she could not have been more astonished to find the King himself. 'Mr Masters!'

'Miss Treloweth . . . Lizzie. I heard you were here. I have just learned from my cousin Helena about the rumours that drove you from Little Manor. My family's doing, I understand. I was sorry to hear it. You loved it there, I know.'

'I love it here,' Lizzie said. There was a pause.

'I felt,' he said, awkwardly, 'that we owed you something. An apology at least. Tamsin seems to have behaved abominably . . .' – Lizzie secretly whispered an 'amen' to that – 'I wanted . . . to apologise. If there is anything I can do . . .'

Lizzie was about to say, 'Thank you, but there is nothing I need,' when Mrs Swann broke in.

'Well now, you might walk her home, sir, since you have come so far. Lizzie, you knock off now. Belinda and I will finish here. She's a good little worker, this,' she said turning to their visitor. 'Make a good little wife to someone, when the War's over, you mark my words.'

Lizzie devoutly wished that the stone floor would open up and swallow her, but it remained obstinately solid.

'I'm sure of it,' he replied, and made her blush pinker than ever.

She hardly knew how to put on her cap and get ready to go. Imagine him finding her like this – in breeches and muddy boots. But Mr Masters didn't seem to care. On the contrary he treated her like a lady, offering her his arm to step over stiles and opening the lane-gate for her to go through, as if she were Helena Beswetherick herself. It was a bit daft really, she could manage the five-bar hurdle better than he could, but it was nice all the same.

'It's some good of you,' she said, to break the awkwardness, 'coming all this way to see me. I'm truly grateful, but you needn't have worried. I'm doing very well as you can see.'

'I am sorry you let the rumours drive you away. Penzance is poorer without you, and it was cruel of Tamsin. Helena went to Mrs Rouncewell on your account – and of course that made it worse. She meant it kindly.'

'So it was Tamsin's doing?' Lizzie could not keep the bitterness from her voice.

He put a finger under her chin and lifted her face towards him, 'Oh my poor Lizzie. Tears? Did it hurt you so much? All this talk?'

She shook her head, pulling her face away. 'Not the rumours, no. It's only . . . it doesn't seem fair, when she's the one expecting a baby herself.'

'You knew about that? But of course, your sister is a maid at Gulveylor, isn't she?'

Lizzie flushed. Now he would think that Millie had been telling tales. It was what Tamsin had thought, too. ''Tisn't Millie, sir. I knew the father, that's all.' Her voice trembled as she spoke.

He stared at her in astonishment. 'You did? How in the world did you come across Chubby Beresford? I thought he had been almost a prisoner at Gulveylor.'

It was her turn to stare. 'Chubby Beresford? Who on earth is Chubby Beresford? You mean that airman who broke his leg, Christmas?' She shook her head, hardly daring to believe what she was hearing. 'You think he was . . . the father?'

Her companion nodded. 'I know he was. Tamsin has admitted it, and Beresford as good as told me so himself. From what Aunt Winifred tells me, it is a wonder half of Penzance didn't guess the truth, although Farrington is claiming the child as his own, I understand.'

'Beresford?' Lizzie said, as if by repeating it she could make herself understand. Beresford. Not Michael Jago. Beresford.

'Lost, poor fellow, in a flying accident.'

Lizzie closed her eyes. It all made sense. Of course it did. Tamsin Beswetherick had never even known of Michael's engagement. The letter in the book had been a ploy, an undignified last attempt to find a husband. That was why she had been so guilty and confused about it. There had been no betrayal. Michael had wanted Lizzie Treloweth, as he said he did. A great, grey dismal blanket of misery lifted from Lizzie's heart. Mike was gone, but he had been hers. All the love and grief and feeling which she had locked away poured over her in a torrent.

She could even feel sympathy. Poor, silly, spoiled Tamsin. She must have been desperate. Desperate enough in the end to marry that awful Silas Farrington. 'Beresford!' Lizzie said again.

'Beresford,' he returned, with a bemused smile, and suddenly she was drunk with joy and relief. It must have been a headier potion even than Gan's dandelion wine, otherwise she would never have done anything so outrageous. She flung her arms around Ashton Masters and hugged him with delight. She didn't realise the dreadful impropriety of it until she found his arms around her, answering her embrace.

240

She attempted to disengage herself. 'Mr Masters, sir, I'm that sorry. I don't know what I'm thinking of.' Her face burned scarlet.

He did not let her go. 'Lizzie, Lizzie if only you knew. We have been victims, both of us, of the same sorry story. Why should you push me away?'

'I didn't mean . . .'

'I know you didn't. You acted out of simple innocence of heart, and I'm glad. Otherwise I should never have had the courage to hold you, yet I've dreamt of doing it a hundred times.'

'Mr Masters!'

He let her go then. 'I won't lie to you Lizzie. I won't tell you any nonsense about how you have filled my dreams ever since I met you. There was another girl. Not Tamsin. French – a farmer's daughter. She was unaffected, good-hearted, beautiful – like you. I loved her, Lizzie, after a fashion, and after I lost her I did begin to think of you. You are alike, in many ways.'

'What happened to her?'

'There was an attack. I found her with her legs broken in a ruined building. Saved her life, I believe. But she disappeared. I never saw her again.'

The pain in his eyes was real. Lizzie squeezed his arm. He turned to her.

'Let me come and see you again, Lizzie. Please? I have so little time – only a few days. I won't pester you, more than you like, but it would mean so much to me. I am weary of Gulveylor, all that fuss and rigmarole. I want something simple, something honest. We could go somewhere, if you like, or walk. When you have a day off.'

'I don't get many of those,' Lizzie said, doubtfully. 'But I am free, Friday afternoon. You could come then, if you like. But don't go reading anything into it, mind. Just a walk, with a friend.'

He smiled at her. 'It's settled then. Friday. And Lizzie?'

'Yes?'

'If I'm a friend – shouldn't you call me Ashton?'

'I couldn't,' she said, feeling herself colour. But after that day she never thought of him as anything else.

He went back to Gulveylor in high spirits. Even Mater noticed the change in him.

'I am glad you have not entirely forgotten how to smile, Ashton. You have been sunk in gloom ever since you arrived.'

The truth was, he did not enjoy being at Gulveylor these days. As he said to Lizzie, the stiff, cumbersome machinery of social convention irked him. He would not be here, but the powers that be had sent him back on attachment to Training Command. They 'rested' everyone, after a certain number of sorties, and there was good sense in that – the strain of flying day after day led to costly mistakes, and there were few enough seasoned pilots in the service as it was, without losing them from simple fatigue.

So, for a little while, his job was training pilots. It was not altogether a respite. Ashton sometimes joked that they had threatened his life more often than the Germans, but really it was no laughing matter. The need for airmen was so great that they were sent out after only twelve hours, sometimes – operational pretty well as soon as they could take off and land reliably without breaking something. The luckier ones survived long enough to learn on the job. He shook his head grimly – mere boys, that was all. He was barely twenty himself, but he felt centuries older than they were.

The Home posting meant extra leave of course, and Mater had abandoned the house in Belgravia, on account of the zeppelins and air-raids, and had taken up residence in Gulveylor. Supporting Winifred, she said, following Tamsin's marriage, but it left Ashton in an uncomfortable position. He could hardly refuse to visit, yet the whole business was awkward.

He had set about finding things to do with himself which would take him out of the house, and once he had heard the full story from Helena, the idea of seeking out Lizzie Treloweth had occurred to him at once. It had been harder than he anticipated but, perversely, the very difficulty of the search had whetted his appetite for it, and by the time he had found out where she was, seeing her again had become a kind of obsession.

Finding her had not dispelled it, as he expected. He had become a realist. He knew that he had painted for himself a romantic picture – her prettiness, her innocence, that freshness about her that he had always found so enchanting – and he was ready to be disappointed. But he was not. Lizzie in person was so unaffected, so unexpectedly attractive in those absurdly masculine breeches that if he had not been obsessed before, he assuredly was now.

He was looking forward to Friday, like a child waiting for Christmas. But before it came there was an unexpected summons. Tamsin had been brought to bed, before her time, and was safely delivered of a daughter. Ashton was faced with the excruciating necessity of a family duty dinner at Penvarris.

*

Tamsin lay back in bed, propped against her pillows. If she wasn't so tired and pale, she would have hurled the bedclothes to the floor and kicked in frustration.

How dare this happen to her. It had been terrible, simply and literally shocking. She had been attended by nurses and a doctor – Silas had insisted on it – but they had been worse than useless. She had told them – begged them – to make it stop, and all they had done was smile and say it would get worse before it got better. And it had. She tried not to cry out, but in the end she gave in and roared and screamed and lashed out at her attendants – furious at the pain and at the way they were all looking under her night-clothes at her swollen shapeless body. Just as though she were a peasant, or nobody at all. It was so humiliating.

They brought her the child. A big baby, they said. Just as well it had been born early, or the birth would not have been so easy. Easy! She should have dismissed them for impudence, then and there, but of course she couldn't. She was sure they knew her secret. The earliness of the birth was not altogether accidental. It would have been 'early' in any case, but she had hurried it along.

Her dressmaker had given her the idea, one day when she came in to measure her for yet another horrible voluminous skirt. 'Spot of castor oil, my dear, when the pains start, that's the ticket. Get it going nicely, and then you won't be racked with it for days. Just between ourselves, mind you. Doctor wouldn't like it. Think the pains are a judgement of God, most of them. I'll get a bottle in, and you can take some when the time comes.'

Only she hadn't waited. She was so bored with being huge and swollen, with being confined to the house and seeing nobody – for of course you couldn't be seen in that condition, and the roads around the house were so dreadful that Silas had forbidden her to go out, even in the motor-car. They way he fussed over her, you would think it was really his own child, and when the girl was born, he was prouder than Tamsin herself.

It was a nice enough baby. A bit long and thin, but quite a pretty little thing, once the first few hours were over and it had 'pulled through'. Only it seemed to have nothing whatever to do with her. When they brought it to her and suggested that she 'put it to the breast, to bring the milk in', she had looked at them with such blank disbelief that they abandoned the idea, and brought a bottle for it. It was weak anyway, and needed the nourishment, doctor said.

Silas had spirited up some pretty baby clothes, and things for her too, in spite of the shortages. He was wonderful like that. She had overheard one of the nurses saying, 'Two of us, and a doctor, in wartime – and she a perfectly healthy girl with no complications! I don't know how he does it.'

Tamsin had not thought of that. She sat up in her new satin and swansdown wrap and learned to give the child its bottle. It was like a doll, in its lace dress and knitted cap. She quite enjoyed holding it.

And now Silas was giving a dinner party. Just the family, in view of the circumstances, but it was the first real entertainment Farrington House had ever attempted. He had managed to acquire a baron of beef, cream, autumn raspberries, champagne – all sorts of luxuries. And she was not even to be present. Instead she was expected to lie here, stiff, sore – still swollen under the swansdown – and be prettily grateful while the family sat down to an excellent meal and helped Silas celebrate the birth of his daughter. *His* daughter!

She protested about it when he came up to see her, 'Silas it is too bad. I am to be stuck here, like a prisoner – pecking at a tray, while you have all the fun.'

'It wouldn't be seemly, Tamsin. Anyway, you're to rest, the nurses say so.' His eyes flickered over her. 'I am glad you like your swansdown, my dear.'

Instinctively she clutched it around her. One of the unexpected bonuses of her marriage was that Silas had not once, ever, attempted to . . . well . . . act like Chubby. She had dreaded that, all her wedding day. That lunging and grunting had been barely tolerable with Charles, a disagreeable but necessary price to pay for the rest of his attentions. But the thought of Silas – fat, oily, ugly Silas – doing those things to her, was appalling. She had been ready to bear it only to escape disgrace.

But Chubby it seemed had been wrong. Married people didn't necessarily do 'that'. On the contrary, Silas had treated her like a piece of delicate china, and had not even suggested it, once. He had been quite gallant.

A gallant knight. Well, she was quite safe now. Safe from wagging tongues, beyond the reach of Lizzie Treloweth and that infernal letter.

Thank goodness she had not addressed it to Michael by name. Only to 'my most gallant knight'. That might apply to anyone – even to Silas. And, indeed, Silas had proved himself to be surprisingly chivalrous, even agreeing (with a little help from Papa) to accept the child. Perhaps he could still be persuaded to allow her down to dinner. She smiled at him. She had grown quite fond of her husband, in a remote kind of way.

She did not, however, care for the way he was looking at her now. Perhaps that smile had been a mistake.

'Yes, that swansdown is most becoming.'

'Nonsense, Silas,' she said, and added, 'my dear.' She had discovered long ago that by offering some endearment she was more likely to get her own way. 'I am sure I am quite strong enough to attend the dinner. I should so like to, you know, with it being our first entertainment. I have been out of bed. Look!'

She swung her legs over the side and took a step or two towards him, but she did feel a little weak. She sat down hastily.

'You see?' he said. 'It would never do. All the same,' – he came over to sit beside her – 'I am glad you are on your feet again. We must start to think of creating an heir of our own. A son, this time.' He reached over and squeezed her breast. Just like that. Casually, as if he owned it.

Tamsin was outraged. He had never touched her before. 'How dare you!'

He flushed. She hated it when he did that. It made him so unattractive – the pink face even pinker, the little piggy eyes watering. His voice when he spoke, seemed more whistling than ever. 'I am sorry, Tamsin. It is too soon, I see that. But I have waited a long time.'

She clasped her hands across her chest as if protecting herself. 'Well, you'll have to wait a lot longer. I can't . . . I won't . . .'

He looked at her, and spoke with unexpected dignity. 'Tamsin, I have been patient. I have respected your condition – and, of course, I will respect it now. But in a month, or six weeks – understand me – I shall expect my due.'

'Your due!'

'Oh yes. I have given you a name, respectability. A home for your child, too. But in return I shall expect my rights. I would like a son – as I say. Fortunately, this child was a girl, so there is no awkwardness there. So as soon as you are well, my dearest, I shall expect a summons. The doctor says it will only be a few weeks at most. In the meantime, I shall look forward to it. I purchased this bed for you – a fine big old bed, isn't it? – on purpose.' There was a rattle from the lane. 'And now I believe I hear the carriage. Your mother shall come and see you, directly. I have registered the birth, by the bye. She is to be called Prudence, after my mother.'

'Prudence!' If it were not so unexpected, it would be laughable, under the circumstances. 'But I wanted to call her Charlotta.'

'And have the town gossip? No, dearest. In any case, the thing is done.'

Mama, when she came up, was gratifyingly solicitous; and even Papa looked in to growl, 'Glad to see Farrington is looking after you. Genuinely fond of you, I do believe. All worked out better than I feared.'

Tamsin, thinking of her husband's fat pink hands and the intimate indignities that lay in store, could do nothing except rage inwardly while 'grandmama' held Prudence up to be admired.

Chapter Twenty-Six

'Had the baby has she? What's it like then? And the house? Nellie Blight says it's no end of a place.'

They were sitting on a stone stile, looking across the small stony field to the sea. No bigger than the courtyard at Gulveylor, yet it had been painstakingly turned and furrowed, and set with rows of skinny-looking plants.

Lizzie followed his glance. 'Don't belong to plough this as a rule, but we had it down to potatoes, see – under the food plan – so Mrs Swann thought we might put in a few broccoli. Awful thin ground, and that much granite you wonder plants could find room to grow. But it's coming on.' She grinned. 'But what about Silas Farrington and this house then?'

'It's a big house, certainly,' Ashton said. He had looked forward to this moment all week, and now it had come he was not disappointed. She was so touching, sitting there decked out in her 'best' clothes for his benefit, prattling artlessly about Penvarris as though they were old friends. He toyed with the idea of slipping an arm around her waist. It was deucedly tempting. However, she might not have welcomed that, and he did not want to spoil the moment. He settled for covering her hand with his own, and she did not draw away.

She looked at him enquiringly, and he realised that she was still waiting for him to tell her about the house. He recollected himself. 'Almost finished now – though goodness knows how Farrington got hold of the materials. Good furnishings too – a bit vulgar, all velvet and gilt – but he's got hold of some nice pieces and one or two really good paintings.'

'Velvet and gilt,' Lizzie said dreamily. 'Sounds lovely.' It was endearing, her enthusiasm for simple things which Ashton had always taken for granted. 'Can't imagine Tamsin Beswetherick with a house of her own. Or a baby either.'

'I don't know much about babies,' he confessed, with a smile, 'and I'm not sure Tamsin does.'

Lizzie laughed. 'That's what Millie said. She's going up there from Gulveylor, soon. They've had a local girl, coming in daily, but Miss Tamsin – Mrs Farrington I should say – always planned to have proper staff, soon as ever the servants' quarters were ready. Millie's quite dreading it. It's a long way out there, and Silas Farrington's as mean as mustard.'

It had never occurred to Ashton that servants might have opinions about their employers. He made a mental note to treat his own man with a little more consideration in future. 'She needn't worry about that,' he said. 'Farrington isn't mean where his wife's concerned. Nothing's too good for her, as far as I can see.'

In fact that had been his overwhelming impression of that appalling evening. Farrington, pink and portly, horrifying Mater by talking about money all through dinner and passing the port in the wrong direction, but absurdly proud and possessive of his new wife. Tamsin didn't seem aware of it. She was petulant and dissatisfied. Farrington was too good for her, Ashton thought, and astonished himself at the idea.

'Well, 'tisn't only Mr Farrington,' Lizzie said with a smile. 'There's a gardener's boy up Gulveylor Millie's got her eye on. Put on his age to get in the Army, but Sir Gilbert told them different and they sent him back. 'Tisn't as easy to fool them as it was, with the register and everything. Still, you don't want to hear about them. You're still enjoying the flying, are you?'

He made a face. 'I'd rather fly myself than watch others do it,' he said ruefully. 'But when you are in the Army you do what they tell you. Though they are talking of changing that, making it "The Air Force" with its own command.'

'And its own uniform too, I expect,' Lizzie said with a laugh. 'Probably sky blue. Or sky grey, if you live round here.'

He was to remember that, when the uniform did appear. For the moment though, he was thinking of other things. He said, 'To tell the truth, Lizzie, I'd wish I was back in France, doing some proper flying, except for one thing.'

'What's that, then?' she asked, as he knew she would.

'I think you know.'

He did slip his arm around her waist at last, and she did not resist.

247

She made no move towards him either, and they sat like that, cheerfully chattering, until it was time for him to catch his train and go.

Like brother and sister, he thought. It made him feel very tender. It wasn't an emotion he was accustomed to.

Merran too was 'on respite'. Not on leave, back in 'blighty' – he had not put in for that – but at Etaples on 'rest and recreation', where they had given him a battalion to drill for a week or two.

It was insane of course. The last thing men needed, after weeks at the Front, was the crushing boredom and futility of marching point-lessly to and fro in a barrack yard. Yet it was, after all, a relief from the ever-present threat of death and for that small mercy they were grateful. They blocked their minds to the terrors awaiting and lived each moment in a kind of grey numbness.

He had known horses like that, on the fire-cart at Penvarris. Fit them with blinkers and they would stumble on, looking straight ahead, though they could smell the smoke and feel the heat. But let them have their head and look at the flames and you'd lost them.

Merran had learned to wear blinkers in his head. Or rather, he had learned to be two Merrans. One was the real Merran who laughed and loved and worried about Lizzie and Peter and Pa – the Merran who had joined the Army, full of hopes and courage. The other was the Merran that the Army had made him: numb, doing his duty, refusing to feel because the things around him would drive a feeling man insane.

Life itself was insanity. One week in the front line trenches, one in the second line, two weeks in the reserve trenches, then back to the Front somewhere else. That was insane if you like. The men who moved to the front line knew nothing of the place, and the terrible losses were multiplied by ignorance. Yet a week was enough. No man could have stood much more of it: mud, terror, lice, rain, shells, bullets, and everywhere the moans and shrieks of the wounded and the stinking, unburied dead. Merran realised that he had become part of the insanity the day he hung his rifle nonchalantly on the toe of a corpse sticking out of the parapet, and the new young officer relieving fainted at his feet.

Worse was to follow. Moving up to a newly dug trench one day to take over from the exhausted men who were holding it, Merran found himself face to face with Lewis . They hadn't seen each other since the day they arrived, but they felt like old friends.

Lewis had a new pair of boots he was very proud of. He had been 'curing' them for days, with cold tea and other more personal liquids.

He wanted to show them off – and a photograph he had received from his wife. Merran had to nip along and find the CO with the sealed orders, but promised to return for a cup of cocoa boiled on the little paraffin stove in the dugout before Lewis and his men pulled back.

He was longer than he intended. The CO had been wounded near the wire and the second officer was out leading a stretcher party to rescue him under cover of darkness. There was nothing to do but wait. Merran was beginning to fear that he would miss Lewis altogether.

By the time the stretcher party returned – too late, the man was dead – it was an hour later. Merran made his way back down the slippery duckboards towards Lewis's post. He was looking forward to his cocoa.

The dugout was demolished.

A shell had landed on the firestep and the blast had blown inwards, ploughing up gouges of mud and splintering the table to matchwood. The air was still full of choking mud and dust, and a handful of survivors from further down the tunnel were coughing and groping towards him. Merran wasted several minutes searching for Lewis amongst them, before he spotted a boot beside the shattered duckboard, with part of Lewis still in it.

He needed the blinkers very much, that night.

After that, a kind of cold fury possessed him. Everything – Michael, Lewis, Peter's legs, even Silas Farrington and the farm – seemed to become a single event, driving him onwards. He did not expect to live, and did not care if he died, but wherever there was a daring mission, he was in the thick of it. He did insane things, rushed a crater single-handed and brought back three embarrassed and embarrassing prisoners: went out with a mining party and blew up a machine-gun post.

Most of all he developed a mania about the wounded. Time and again he went out, in broad moonlight, to drag back a man who was moaning in no-man's-land. And far from relaxing now he had pulled back in his turn, he found himself, like a restless horse, champing and chafing to be allowed to start again.

It wasn't natural. Perhaps, after all, he had become a little mad. Certainly, he had become a legend. Like all fools, he seemed charmed. Men who valued their lives fell around him, but Merran walked unscathed. They gave him a medal. Two. He did not care. Each man snatched from the jaws of death was a victory for Michael. Nothing else mattered.

And now, here he was, obliged to drill a pack of men who needed nothing more than to be allowed to sleep, to get clean and dry, to eat and drink and then to sleep again. He did his best for them. Took them on 'route marches' in riverside meadows, where willows dropped their leafy heads into still waters and the first leaves of autumn rusted overhead. The men did not care. They appreciated his efforts, but they did not care. They just knew, with stoic terror, that when the week was over, they would go back to the trenches, and like the leaves would flutter, fall and die.

After the drill session he walked into the town, to see the Americans arriving. Coming to join in a war which was half a world away, as though it were some kind of jolly game. More insanity.

He went back to camp. There was a letter awaiting him, and he found a quiet place to sit and read. Letters from home were the only things that roused him, a precious link with the real, feeling world. One thing about Etaples, the mail arrived regularly and there was no chance of being blown to smithereens before you had a chance to read it.

It was from Ma. Just reading it made his eyes smart, reminding him of an existence where mud meant only a turnip field, and men measured their lives in years, not hours. Gossip about Mrs Farrington, expecting her baby 'any day, by the time you get this'. Peter had sold two more pictures in London, and for a lot of money too. 'Just as well,' Ma wrote, with her idiosyncratic spelling, 'that Willy Brown has been down with the ploughshare trying to dig up Daisy Bottoms. Says Farrington told him to. No more sense than to try and plough through a great granite rock. Jarred the horse and spoilt the plough-share so we shall have to buy new. But Peter says he'll pay for it. Quite perked him up – make a contribution he says.'

Merran read and reread that paragraph, revelling in the dear warm pictures it created. If he ever got out of this war alive, he thought, he would go back to Nanzeal and plant himself there, like the apple tree at the door, sending great deep roots into the Cornish soil and granite, and never, never be moved again.

There was more news in the letter – about the chickens, and Nell Blight, and 'Mrs Rouncewell has got some bee in her bonnet about that parrot, and is trying to find somebody to take it for her. Silas Farrington wanted *us* to have it, but I put my foot down.' Then, tucked away at the end, the news he was really waiting for. 'Lizzie is loving it out at Bengarra. Nell sees her sometimes, and she asks after you. I look for your letters. Our love to Paul if you see him.'

Merran wrote back that very night. Two letters, since he enclosed a note for Nell to take to Lizzie. He thought a long time about that one. If he was to be an apple tree he wanted Lizzie planted alongside him and it was time she knew. But the censor would read it, and he couldn't bear that. He had censored a few letters himself and he knew what could happen. He didn't want his words to Lizzie to be read aloud and scoffed at.

'Dear Lizzie,' he wrote, finally, 'I am well here. There is something very important I want to tell you. I didn't know how to do it, but you are a Land Army girl now, and will understand if I write like Hunnicutt. Last time I saw 'ee I put my girt foot'n it, like a cow in a cream bucket, but fact is, my maid, I'm more mazed be 'ee than a sow in a mangold-field. I aren't Mike and I never could be, but what I am I be, and 'tis yourn if 'ee want 'un. Please write. Merran.'

There, he thought grinning, the censor would never understand that.

He didn't either. The duty censor was a pleasant conscientious young man from the Midlands, and he read the letter twice without making sense of it. He hesitated for a long time and then took his black pencil and put a dutiful line through all but the first and last sentences. It was obviously in a kind of code. When it came to security one could never be too careful.

Autumn drew on, but there was still plenty to do at Bengarra. In fact, Mrs Swann applied to the Ministry, and was allowed to keep her landgirls a little longer. Feeding the animals was a daily chore. The cob had the best of everything – crushed oats and hay if Mrs Swann could get it, but the girls had to chop straw and mangolds for the cows and sheep, and then there was the swill to make for the pigs and chickens. The goats, of course, ate anything – even your breeches buttons if you didn't watch them – and there was quite a scene one day when Belinda left the garden gate open and they ate all the shoots of Mrs Swann's wallflowers.

Then there were hedges to mend, turves to dry, fields to dress. The pile of grain in the grain-store had to be turned regular, heavy work with a shovel, or it would get hot and rot, or go mildew and cake together. She and Belinda turned the grain last thing, by the light of the oil-lamp, and then there would be a cup of cocoa by the turf fire, and a long cold cheerless walk home in the dark and wet. Lizzie rarely saw her billet by daylight now.

All the same, she was content, almost happy. She had come to love the farm, and Penzance, on her occasional visits, seemed nothing but grim, grey bustle. And at home things seemed to be going from bad to worse. Mam was at her wits' end, trying to make ends meet and she was crosser than two sticks half of the time. Even when Father came home again briefly, he was dreadfully altered, a strange silent shadow of himself – though he was thrilled to death with Horry.

There was trouble in the shop, too. There simply was not enough meat, and several times Mam'd had to shut the shop altogether. Closed for days, sometimes, and then there were crowds of people outside, protesting. It wasn't Mam's fault, of course, you couldn't sell meat you didn't have, and then if you did get a rabbit or a chicken or two it only made matters worse. Small animals went nowhere among a crowd that size, and more than once Mam kept the shop doors firmly locked and simply jugged the creature for the family, or swapped it for bread or sugar, jam or cheese. The mood was nasty, though. People were shouting after the Treloweths in the street, and once someone shied a stone at the shop-front, making a cobweb of cracks in the fanlight over the door.

Then when there was a beast, there would be a queue halfway down the street and folks would be nicer than pie.

Altogether, Lizzie was thankful to be out of it and up at Bengarra, where there was always fresh milk, home-cured bacon and pickled eggs, and where Miss Stamp seemed to have a lifetime's collection of home-made jam, put aside in case any teashop customers ever came.

There were sometimes customers now. Nell Blight came, several times, and had Lizzie crying with laughter over the gossip from Little Manor. Mrs Rouncewell, it seemed, was having all kinds of problems with her parrot. 'Someone told her it could spread disease,' Nell said, tucking into one of Miss Stamp's splits and blackberry jam as if food was going out of fashion. 'She keeps sending it away. But the blessed thing keeps coming back.'

'No?'

'Mrs Trevarnon had it, first,' Nell said, 'but you know what Albert's like. Got out of a window and flew away. Poor Mrs Trevarnon was in a real taking, had the whole household out looking – and you know where he turned up? Perched on the door at Little Manor, calm as you please. Come home, see. Well, Mrs Rouncewell got him down and then Lord Chyrose took him. Thought if he went further off, he might settle, but a fortnight later he went missing again. Lost him for three days that time, and Mrs Rouncewell near broke her heart, but one morning sure enough, there he was squatting on the porch. Nobody knew he was there until he baptised one of the Ladies' League, coming in with the linen.'

'Wasn't Tamsin Beswetherick, was it? Is she still doing the linen?' Lizzie asked, wiping the tears of laughter from her eyes.

'Tamsin Farrington, you mean,' Nell said. 'No not she. Got a new trick, she has. You know how Mrs Trevarnon used to organise "motor treats" for the convalescents? Jaunts round the country, and then tea on the lawn? Well, Tamsin's started doing that. Comes in every week or so, picks out one or two of the best-looking men, and whisks them off for the afternoon. Mr Farrington doesn't seem to mind – keeping up with the gentry, I suppose. She's learned to drive that motor-car of his, and you should see her, standing there all helpless while the poor fellow turns the starting-handle, and then batting her eyelids at him all the way down the drive. Still, I can hardly blame her. Who'd be married to that horrible man, for all his money?'

Lizzie was following her own train of thought. 'Seen the baby have you? Millie says it's a pretty little thing.'

Nell gave a scornful laugh. 'Don't be so daft. Doesn't bring that with her. Leaves it at Gulveylor I should think. Lady Beswetherick is quite besotted with it.'

Lizzie nodded. 'All she talks about, Millie says, apart from this wedding of Helena's.'

'Speaking of weddings,' Nell turned bright pink and glanced at Lizzie from under her lashes. 'Peter Jago and me are fixing to get married too, in the New Year. Nothing grand, but we'll try and fix it for a Friday so you can get there if you've a mind. I'd be some glad to have you come.'

'Delighted,' Lizzie said. 'Live at Nanzeal, will you? You won't go on nursing, of course.' She tried to imagine Nell Blight presiding over the farmhouse at Nanzeal and felt a sharp pang of jealousy. Foolish really. Michael was dead, and anyway it wasn't likely that Peter would inherit the farm, now, being how he was. Paul probably, when he got married. Or Merran.

That was an awful thought. She put down her tea-cup sharply. Of course, Merran had as good a right to get married as anyone else. It was just . . . well . . . he was Merran, that's all. She had no right to be jealous. It wasn't as if she wanted to marry him herself. In fact, he had offered for her once, and she had turned him down. But telling herself all this only made her feel worse, if anything.

Nell misinterpreted her sigh. 'It's good of you to worry, Lizzie, but we shall be all right. There's a man up Plymouth, saw one of Peter's paintings, and has written to offer him a commission – painting horses.

Regular, it'll be, for postcards and things, so we're very lucky. Lots of amputees end up on the street selling matches and papers, or just plain begging for food. Chance like this, we'd be fools not to take it. It'll mean moving to Plymouth, but we've got our eye on a room there. Nice to start off on your own, if you can, and Nanzeal is no treat, these days. That Belgian is creating trouble again – I don't know the half of it.'

'You'll write though?' Lizzie said.

'Course I will,' Nell said. 'Oh, and that reminds me, I've got a letter for you. More black lines than letter, but here it is.'

It was from Merran. A strange sort of letter. 'Dear Lizzie. I am well. Please write.' The rest had been censored. Typical Merran – on about his socialist nonsense, 'Not Cornwall's War' more than likely, or giving hints where his battalion was, instead of just saying 'somewhere in France' like he was supposed to. Well, she'd never know now. All the same it was ridiculously comforting to have a note, even a note as short as this, as if a friendly arm had slipped around her shoulders.

'You coming to Penzance at all?' Nell asked. 'Only you could pop up and see the Jagos. Or come to Little Manor and see us.'

Lizzie made a face. 'No. Not for a month or so, anyway. Mam's promised to let Aggie come up here for the day, soon, and I've promised her a drop of tea and a honey split here in the teashop. I can't afford that and my train ticket too. I can't disappoint her. She doesn't get many treats with this war on. Mind, I never had an outing and a bought tea like that when I was young.'

'Well, I'll see you before Christmas, anyway, I hope,' Nell said, getting to her feet and finding the twopence for her tea. 'I'd better be getting back. It's coming to rain, and it's a long walk to the station.'

Lizzie watched her go, with a faint feeling of guilt. It was true what she had said about Aggie, but that was not the whole story. The fact was there was another visitor expected at Bengarra, a visitor who had already called more than once. Ashton Masters.

She couldn't say anything to Nell, of course. It would be all over the Hospital before you could say wink. And she particularly didn't want gossip reaching Nanzeal.

Not that there was anything improper about it. He was a friend, that was all. People wouldn't understand that, a gentleman like him and a girl like her. But he *was* a friend. He wasn't Merran exactly, but he made her feel looked-after. He was amusing and charming and he made her laugh.

There was no doubt that she was looking forward to seeing him.

254

Chapter Twenty-Seven

'Albert! Albert! Come down this minute, you wretched bird.' Nurse Blight, perched precariously on a chair, made a wild grab for the parrot and missed.

Albert looked at them malevolently and flew a little further up the roof.

'I'm sorry, Mrs Rouncewell, ma'am,' the young woman said, sucking her pecked finger. 'But he won't let me catch him.'

Mrs Rouncewell sighed. There was nothing for it. She would have to fetch a ladder and climb up to collect Albert herself. It was most regrettable, and undignified – she could just imagine the gels sniggering behind their hands. Bad enough at any time, but it was particularly unseemly, at the moment.

The Hospital was supposed to be in mourning. Poor Major Trevarnon had been killed by a zeppelin in London, and Little Manor, being on his estate, was naturally expected to observe respect. Mrs Rouncewell had arranged for a crape muffler on the door-knocker, and all the nurses had worn black armbands for a week. And now here she was proposing to shin up a ladder like a chimney sweep. It was just as well that all the men who could be moved were up at Trevarnon House for the singing!

There had been a lot of singing lately. There had been Major Trevarnon's memorial service last week, with prayers in the chapel and funeral cake after, and a choir. Mrs Rouncewell had naturally attended that. But today was something else entirely, a concert at the new Trevarnon wing, under the supervision of Rosa Warren.

The new wing was Mrs Trevarnon's doing. She had taken her loss very hard – gone to Truro to stay with her stepdaughter – but she had been very good to the Hospital. She gave instructions for the furniture to go into storage, and offered half the House as extra wards. But it was hard to supervise. Trevarnon House was a long way from Little Manor, though they were in the same grounds.

Lord Chyrose suggested the solution. 'Send the more recovered men up there, and leave it in Rosa's hands. She is competent enough, if there is no skilled nursing, and it would work out nicely, since Trevarnon House is her home.'

Matron had agreed at once. It freed her to devote attention to more critical cases. And, as it turned out, to Albert.

She set the ladder against the wall and began to climb. The dratted bird was turning out to be more trouble than the patients – more like a homing pigeon than a parrot. There was something touching about it – you couldn't help feeling a little bit sentimental about the way he kept coming back to her – but she couldn't keep climbing about in this undignified manner to rescue him. People were watching. Something more satisfactory would have to be done.

'Albert!' she called, and the parrot fluttered onto her shoulder, as if it had never had another intention in the world.

She was halfway down the ladder when the Farringtons' car bumped down the drive.

Drat. If there was one person she did not want to find her in this preposterous position, it was Silas Farrington. He had been very helpful, admittedly, when it came to equipping the new ward. Knew somebody who knew somebody who supplied the mattresses, and with the help of a flag day the thing was organised and ready to run in a week. Before you knew it, there was Rosa with her opening concert, planning egg-and-spoon races on the lawn.

But Farrington had promised to call on another matter, and she particularly did not want to be found at a disadvantage.

It was about food. The Food Controller had suggested consumption limits, and set a fixed price for things, but you still had to find them. The Charities for the Wounded did their best, and the Hospital had a priority rating in the shops. But first choice of nothing was still nothing, and there were so many shortages – tea, butter, milk, bacon, pork, rice, currants, raisins, beer and spirits – it made you wonder how there was ever going to be any festive season at all.

That was why she had agreed to see Silas Farrington. He could get you most things, at a price. Mrs Rouncewell didn't approve of it, but her boys came first. She had to do something. Half the butchers in the county were closed, and she hadn't seen dried fruit for months.

It wouldn't be long, Mrs Rouncewell thought, before the Government introduced rationing. Some shop-keepers, like the Treloweths, were already doing it privately, and a good thing too. It made you mad, knowing that Farrington could still lay his hands on ham and cream and plum cake, when her poor nurses were getting by on National bread and thin soup.

But, now she came to look, it wasn't Silas. It was Tamsin Farrington, bringing back one of the young officers from a motor outing. Mrs Rouncewell climbed carefully down the last few rungs and went to meet them. She wasn't at all sure she approved of this either. The boy looked very flushed and happy.

Don't be absurd, Phyllis Rouncewell, she said to herself. Tamsin Farrington is a married woman, and a mother. Besides that particular young man had been wounded in the groin.

Mrs Farrington smiled. 'Excuse our coming here, Matron. We did not wish to disturb the concert. Instead we have interrupted you, I see.'

Mrs Rouncewell said, with as much dignity as possible, 'I have been fetching down my parrot. He will keep escaping, though I am trying to find a home for him. The trouble is, he pines if you keep him caged all day.'

Tamsin looked at Albert doubtfully. 'Does he bite?' She stretched out a finger towards his head feathers.

'Careful!' Mrs Rouncewell said, but she was too late. Albert gave a startled squawk and was off, up to the top of the roof ridge this time.

Tamsin pressed a hand to her mouth. 'I'm terribly sorry,' she said, but she couldn't stop giggling. It was ill-mannered, in the circumstances, and she attempted to make amends. 'I can see that it is a problem. I'll speak to my husband about it if you like. He might know someone who wants a parrot.'

That might cost a shilling or two, Mrs Rouncewell thought, but it would be worth it to think of Albert settled and loved. She nodded.

'If you would do that, Mrs Farrington, I should be most grateful.'

Tamsin was still smiling as she turned down the lane past the factory and towards the house. Imagine finding that dreadful woman halfway up a ladder just to get a parrot. And the way the thing had flown off, so it had to be rescued again. It was a long time since the humiliation of the concertina bandages, but revenge was certainly sweet.

She gripped the steering wheel grimly as the car lurched over the rutted track. If only Silas would do something about the road. What was the use of a grand house, if visitors were shaken to pieces before they ever reached it. Not that they had many visitors, apart from family – and her officers of course.

She called them her 'double double-yoos' – walking wounded, she told Silas, but privately they were her 'wonderful warriors'. Mrs Farrington's motor treats were becoming quite famous at the Hospital. Trips up to Farrington House for afternoon teas and recitals by Maud Preston on the piano, and then home via Penvarris, on lonely lanes where they could 'look at the sea and talk'.

It was talk, too, most of the time. Her new status as a married woman gave her a charmed life. It was just the situation she loved. The men were wonderfully flattered and attentive but they did no more than kiss her hand, or stroke her hair, which she had always found delightful. Until this one – a young fellow called Goodenough, who held a field commission in the Flying Corps and turned out to be a friend of Chubby's.

She had made a particular point of inviting him, to chat about Charles, but he knew Ashton too, which was unfortunate. Ironically, though, Goodenough was the one soldier who didn't want to talk at all. He slipped a hand under her blouse, and then under her skirts and she discovered, to her surprise, that she liked it.

It was Silas's fault, of course. If he didn't keep insisting on blundering into her bedroom and thrusting his oily fatness onto and into her, she would never have been tempted. But with that disgusting indignity awaiting her every night, was it any wonder that she sought comfort from someone more skilful, more attractive? Anyone would do the same.

She couldn't do it cold-bloodedly. Goodenough enjoyed a drink of brandy, and she found that a nip or two gave her courage too. Hiding a bottle and a couple of glasses in the car made her feel deliciously wicked, like Mata Hari. She had discovered where Silas kept his 'stores', all sorts of under-the-counter supplies, in a ramshackle old mine shed next to the one where he garaged the car. There were several cases of cognac there. She had found the shed-key hidden in a drawer, and after that she and Goodenough had visited it a number of times – not only to replenish the brandy.

She went home now and up to the nursery. Prudence was there with her nursemaid, and Tamsin dandled the child a moment, before going downstairs to dine with her husband. He was full of himself this evening, pleased with some deal he had struck for galvanised iron. He would sell it to the farmers, he said, to cover their ricks since thatching-straw was scarce.

She said, 'Very nice, dear,' dutifully, though these considerations bored her to distraction. However, when he was feeling expansive he often opened a bottle of wine, and if he drank enough of it, could be relied upon to fall asleep snoring on the sofa, and so spare her a pawing. The trick was to make him drink enough – too little and it inflamed his desire.

'You are clever, dear,' she said again, motioning the servant to pour another glass. 'And there was something I wanted to ask you. I told Mrs Rouncewell you might be able to help.' She outlined the problem of the parrot.

He was preening. He always liked it when she appeared to rely on

258

him for something. That was excellent. She wanted the car and some petrol for Monday, so she needed him in a good humour.

That much was easy. He was mellow with wine and full of schemes for the parrot – Tom Liddel would have it, he said, and Mrs Rouncewell could pay for its keep – so he agreed to her borrowing the Bean without demur. Afterwards, in the drawing-room, she patted the chair beside her. 'Have a nice glass of whisky dear, and tell me about your ricks.'

It was a waste of effort, as it happened. Someone came to see him about purchasing some paraffin, and Silas went out with him, leaving the whisky untouched. Later, he came to her bed.

She shut her eyes and tried to occupy herself by mentally designing her new winter coat. Burgundy with white fur trim, she decided, and by that time he had finished.

Ashton bumped the motor-bike along the narrow road to Bengarra, whistling. Lizzie was not expecting him – he was due to go back to France, in fact – but the weather was keeping him grounded and he had wangled last-minute leave for Helena's wedding. It was the same bike. Silas had not charged this time, 'Since you are family now,' and instead had demanded an extortionate price for the can of petrol which was strapped to the carrier.

But who cared. He grinned cheerfully. What would they say at Gulveylor if they could see him now?

Not that they spared him a thought. The whole house was a turmoil of wedding-lists and dressmakers, rooms billowed with lace tulle and crêpe de Chine, and every door seemed to open on some earnest consultation on hats or hymns or seating arrangements.

Helena had resigned her nursing and come home for good, seeming aghast herself at the fuss, and Sir Gilbert – having solved the meat problem at a stroke by buying a complete pig from Silas Farrington who also had it slaughtered for him – hid himself in the estate office and stayed there.

'Good idea, my boy,' he had confided to Ashton this morning. 'Get out of the place for the day.' He glanced ruefully at the buffet table which had been commandeered for wedding presents. 'I'd do the same thing, if I could.'

So Ashton had gone. Bought a meagre meatless lunch at a country inn, and meandered down country lanes, past granite churches and trickling streams. The roads were rutted and muddy, slippery with fallen leaves, and there was mist in the air but it still seemed to him perfection. The rugged intimacy of Cornwall before the sprawling vastness of France.

He had not, consciously, intended to come to Bengarra. But his wanderings turned in this direction until he was forced to acknowledge his own inner purpose. So here he was juddering down the lane to the farm, looking out for the familiar figure over every stone hedge and gateway.

It had not crossed his mind that she would not be there. But the place was deserted. When at last he did find somebody – big stout Belinda, struggling into the yard with a barrowload of turnips – the news was vague.

'Gone off somewhere for the afternoon. Half-day, see, and she's got a visitor.'

The sharpness of his jealousy surprised him. The thought of Lizzie's 'half-day' had been partly what had drawn him, but he had never expected her to spend it with anyone else. The girl laughed.

'Don't look so put about, sir, it's only her sister. But where they've gone to, I couldn't say. Out for a walk, Lizzie said, but I don't know where to, this weather.'

Her sister! The flood of relief that washed over him was quite as great as if one of his trainees had pulled off a tricky landing without buckling a wheel.

'I'll find her,' he said. He left the motor-bike outside the post office and went off looking on foot.

He tried all the places they had gone to together, over the last few months. Out to the cliffs, where they had walked in the sunshine hand in hand, laughing and talking. Down in the valley by the stream where they had sheltered from the rain under the bridge and smiled at the fishes doing the same. Out on the heath, where she had refused to let him eat the blackberries, because it was October and 'the devil had touched them'. She was nowhere to be seen, and the thought of not finding her was a physical ache. It surprised him.

Don't be a fool, Masters, he told himself. She's a farm girl, a butcher's daughter. She's a woman, his heart answered, and he had no reply to that.

He found her at last where he had least expected, in the post office tearoom among the knitting wool and preserves. She was sitting at a table with a small wiry girl, who was spreading honey on a split with all the rapt attention of a craftsman moulding clay.

Lizzie looked up and saw him. 'Ashton! Mr Masters!' She got up so sharply she almost overset the tray. She had coloured – with pleasure, surely – and looked so delightfully cast about that he had to suppress a desire to reach out and hug her then and there.

The younger child gazed at him, her mouth full of split and her eyes full of curiosity. 'Your sister?' he said.

Lizzie was all apology. 'Dear me, what am I thinking of? Ashton, this is my sister Agnes. Aggie, this is Mr Masters, cousin to Mrs Farrington.'

Aggie's eyes opened even wider. ''llo' she said, through the honey.

'Won't you join us?' Lizzie said. 'Sorry if we weren't here when you were looking, but I took Aggie down to the goats.'

'How are they then?' he said, remembering to ask after them all by name. He felt that wave of tenderness again. Imagine Tamsin, or any of the other young ladies he knew, finding such pleasure in looking at a few goats, and spending their hard earned pennies to buy treats for a sister. 'I will join you,' he said, and had Miss Stamp bring out a sixpenny tea: sandwiches, seedcake and fresh splits and cream, to Aggie's delight. He paid the bill for them all – it was less than a shilling – and walked with them to the station to put Aggie on the train.

'Here, Ashton, you're some good, but you didn't ought to have done that,' Lizzie said on the way back. 'Tenpence halfpenny is a lot of money.'

He supposed it was, to her. He looked at her anew, acutely conscious of her nearness, as he helped her over the stiles, and when they came to a muddy puddle he swooped her up playfully and carried her over it – though she wore thick boots and his own were smart ones.

'Put me down, you daft thing,' she said, laughing up at him, but he didn't. Instead, impulse got the better of him. He bent over and kissed her – first gently, then passionately, pouring burning kisses on her face, her throat, her lips.

'Here! Ashton!' she protested. She had turned the colour of a pillar-box, but she did not look displeased.

He set her down softly and took her in his arms. This time she returned his kiss, shyly, awkwardly, like a child.

When he let her go, they walked back to Bengarra in silence as though the kisses prevented speech. It was the first time they had ever acknowledged the intimacy between them. His pulse was thudding.

This was more to him than Tamsin had ever been. Or Sylvie either. He put his hand on the bike. 'Lizzie,' he said intently, 'what are we to do?'

She looked at him and there were tears in her eyes. 'Do? Why, what can we do? Nothing. Foolish, that was. I can't say it wasn't precious, because it was, but it was foolish all the same. And we've spoilt everything, besides. We were good friends, you and I, but we can't

261

pretend it's only that, any more, can we?' She faced him, forlorn but resolute. 'Just as well you are off overseas any minute. You better not come here any more.'

She might have slapped him with less effect. 'Not come? But Lizzie . . . !'

She shook her head. 'What? You care for me, is that what you are going to say? Well, perhaps you do. But what good is that? You aren't intending to marry a farm girl, I suppose, and if you aren't – then, begging your pardon Mr Masters, if you care for me at all, then you'll go away and leave me alone before there's more harm done. Aggie will have the town talking as it is.'

My God. He hadn't thought of that. She was right. 'But Lizzie! Don't you care for me at all?'

She looked at him squarely then, though her face was beseeching. 'Of course I do, I shouldn't have kissed you else. Only I care for my good name more. And yours too, come to that. I don't want to be your guilty secret, and what else could I be? Think of it, Ashton. What would become of me?'

She was right again of course, and he was ashamed of himself. He sighed. 'I wish I hadn't kissed you.'

'Do you?'

He looked at her. 'No.' She was so lovely, it was impossible to believe she was beyond his reach. 'No, I don't. If I had never done it, I would never have known what I was missing. I want you. I must see you again.' He reached for her hand, but she snatched it away.

'No Ashton, don't. Don't spoil it. There's lots of things we want but we can't have. Give me a last smile and say goodbye.'

'Goodbye, Lizzie.'

He mounted the motor-bike and drove away with a sinking heart. At the corner he looked back. She was still standing, watching him. He went to wave, but she turned and disappeared into the house. He rode away, possessed by gloom.

If he had been a butcher's boy, she would have kissed him gladly. If she had been a lady he could take her for his wife. But he could not have her – and her acceptance of that galled him. But, he thought suddenly, that was part of the pattern. Lizzie was accustomed to knowing there were things she could not have.

He needed all of his petrol before he reached Gulveylor and it rained on him most of the way. It gave him an excuse to take an early bath and have a tray sent to his room without the disagreeable necessity of making conversation with anyone.

Chapter Twenty-Eight

Lizzie had intended to watch him out of sight, but when he turned and looked at her she felt she could not bear it, and fled upstairs into her room.

She was in turmoil.

'If only he hadn't done that!' she told her reflection, but the face that looked back at her from the brown mottled mirror refused to look decently penitent.

It was impossible, of course, a girl like her and Ashton Masters, but she couldn't altogether be sorry for it. He had kissed her, kissed her with skill and passion. It wasn't like kissing Michael. That was sweet, fumbling – a childhood romance. This was different, dangerous, adult.

Odd that she hadn't seen it coming, but he had always seemed so natural in her company – so much just a good friend – that she had been able to laugh off Mrs Swann's sideways looks and Belinda's teasing. Or, perhaps, had refused to acknowledge what she secretly knew.

She stripped off her best clothes – worn in Aggie's honour – and poured cold water from the hand-jug into the washstand bowl.

Well, it was over now. She meant what she had said to him. A friendly arm around her shoulders was one thing, though that was daring enough, when you came to think. Kissing was quite another. Friendship was growing swiftly into dangerous romance, and it was important to pull up that little seedling before it had a chance to develop.

She splashed the water onto her face and arms, and rubbed herself with Miss Stamp's goose-grease soap as if she was trying to wash away temptation. Because she could fall for Ashton Masters. She knew that. She did not love him, exactly – none of that heart-pounding excitement which she had felt for Michael – but she cared for him, liked him enormously, and yes, he was a very attractive man.

And he desired her. She knew that too. Not as an innocent friend but as a woman. It was that, more than the stinging cold of the water which brought the glow to her cheeks and made her heart beat faster.

She picked up the rough towel and rubbed herself glowing. She was right to send him away, of course she was. Obviously, she would have to keep out of his way from now on. But she would miss him. He had

263

taught her that it was possible to feel again. The past few months had been so dreadful, she had begun to believe that all her emotions and femininity were dried up and lifeless like straw in the cowhouse. She hoped she would not regret today, as she regretted that day of the tripes.

She put on her skirt and felt in her pocket for Merran's faded, folded note. She didn't know why she kept it really. When Nell first brought it, she had been so pleased. Merran had been her best and oldest friend and she had written back joyfully – a long newsy letter, hoping the dear, dependable friendship could be renewed. But his reply had been so formal and remote, that she hardly knew how to answer, and in the end she had taken her tone from his and written cool, cheerful notes enclosing useful items like knitted socks and toothpaste.

If only she could put the clock back, and the terrible day of the tripes had never happened. She needed advice about Ashton Masters. What would Merran say? That she had been right? But she could hardly put that in a letter. If only he was here, so they could talk it over. How comfortable and comforting that would be.

'Oh, you're here are you?' That was Belinda, sticking a windswept head around the door. 'Miss Stamp said you were in, only I knocked twice and you never answered. Dreaming about that young man of yours – oh, don't deny it, I can tell that by that gone-out look on your face. I don't know why you don't get him to marry you and have done with it – save us a lot of waiting, and him a lot of traipsing around in the mud.'

'Ashton?' Lizzie cried. 'Don't be so wet. He wouldn't marry me! His family wouldn't have it.'

'Don't you be so sure,' Belinda said. 'Do anything for you. That's plain as day. And you're just as bad, by the way you were mooning about when I came in. Never saw anyone more lovelorn in my life. Anyway, Miss Stamp says supper's ready. Egg croquettes and carrots, so don't let it get cold.'

'Coming,' Lizzie said. There was no point in arguing with Belinda. Funny thing was, she hadn't been thinking about Ashton at all.

Helena's wedding was purgatory to Tamsin. It was everything that Tamsin's was not. Helena even wore 'her' dress, altered – since she hadn't worn it herself, and it was impossible to get material – and the family sat down to a proper wedding feast at Gulveylor with a hundred guests in spite of the War. Silas had even arranged champagne.

264

What made it even harder to bear was the fact that Helena didn't want it. In fact there had almost been a scene the day before, according to Mama's dressmaker who came to fit Tamsin for her own outfit.

'I declare, Mrs Farrington, she was almost ready to run off and be married in the registry. Your father had to plead with her, that it would make your mother happy. Criminal, all this waste with a war on, she said – she'd rather wear her uniform – and I believe she would. Not like you, Mrs Farrington. You appreciate good clothes.'

It *was* a smart little outfit, with a nipped waist and a dear little hat with a feather – much nicer than the shapeless satin sack she had worn at her own wedding. Only of course it was such a depressing wine colour, a married woman couldn't well wear pastels. Still with her new burgundy coat – the one with the white fur trim – she looked well enough on the day.

Except that no one spared her a glance. They were all looking at Helena, or at Rosa Warren and the other attendants, decked out in green silk like spring lettuce. It wasn't until after the ceremony, when the nursemaid brought in Prudence, that anyone paid the Farringtons any attention at all.

And when the new Mrs Macready departed for a first-class carriage and a weekend honeymoon at the Dorchester, Tamsin found it quite difficult to keep from scowling. Ashton seemed to notice. He had attended, looking wry and aloof, and he came over to stand at her side as the orchestra struck up again.

'So, Aunt Winifred has presided over her grand wedding after all. Helena did not look as if she cared for it. Or you either, cousin.'

Tamsin flushed. It was hard enough watching all this without being reminded that, if it were not for her own foolishness, this might have been her wedding. Marrying Ashton, too, instead of the fat pink oaf she was shackled to for life. She glanced at her cousin. Perhaps, even now, it was not entirely too late. Politeness more or less decreed that he should ask her to dance.

'Oh Ashton,' she said piteously, looking up at him under lowered lids, 'if only you knew. It is so dreadfully easy, to be deflected from one's first true love.'

It was succeeding. She could see the interest dawning in his face. 'One will always regret it, if one allows happiness to slip through one's fingers.' She smiled into his eyes, aware that Silas was frowning ferociously at her.

Ashton was looking at her quizzically. 'You know, Tamsin,' he said coolly. 'Just for once, I believe you may be right. Now, if you will excuse me. I don't dance, and your husband is here to claim you . . .' He went away to talk to his mother.

He had snubbed her, positively snubbed her. She said crossly, 'Silas, I have a headache. Do, please, send for the car and drive me home.'

She had never felt such a nobody.

Soon, she promised herself, she would have her revenge. A long afternoon with Goodenough, where she should be the centre of attention, entertained and flattered to her heart's content. He knew how to appreciate her. She knew the very place, up on the cliffs at Penvarris. Perhaps even a late pass and a picnic in the dusk. She would have to be quick, Goodenough was almost well enough to be discharged and sent back to the fighting.

Well, she would apply to Rosa Warren for an extended 'outing', just as soon as this wretched festive season was over.

It was a grim Christmas. Mrs Swann let her go home for the day and sent a basket of potatoes, carrots and pickled eggs with her. Mam wept tears of joy when she saw.

It would have been a sorry feast without them. With the new price restrictions on meat there was hardly a penny profit, and beasts were so scarce that the shop had been shut altogether for a week. The price of everything else seemed to be going up like a skyrocket. It was no joke feeding ten people on a soldier's allowance, even with the eldest girls sending something home. Lizzie handed over her ten shillings with the sinking feeling that she had become the chief provider for them all.

No Christmas treat this year, beyond the fact that Mrs Jago, who was still milking, sent down some cream and butter from Nanzeal. Even Eddy, who was painfully in need of boots, had to make do with mended army ones from the Government stores. Mam couldn't afford new.

The family wasn't even together. Aggie was there, but got into a flounce when she teased Lizzie about her 'young man' and got snapped at for her pains. Millie and Daisy were away, anyway, and Elsie and Alice had come home from school with spots and had to be bundled off to Aunty Simmins before it went through the family. Aunty Simmins's paste sandwiches and jelly probably tasted a lot better when there was only the same at home: but the place seemed empty, and Lizzie missed Father worse than ever.

Still, there were others much worse off than they were. Gan had called in during Christmas week to see Mrs Richards, the Cat's-meat-man's mother, and found the poor soul in a state of collapse. Sold every stick of furniture to buy coal, poor woman, and nothing in the house to eat but one old onion. Gan bundled her up in her own coat and brought her home – and there she was now, propped up on the settle, looking a bit livelier with a drop of soup inside her.

'Going to stay and give a hand around the place,' Mam said firmly. 'I've made up a bed in the back shop, until the weather's warmer. And if they bring in ration cards, like they're talking of doing next year, an extra bit of fat and sugar will come in handy.' She didn't say that there would also be another mouth to eat them, or that even rations had to be paid for.

Lizzie nodded. Mam had a sharp tongue, but she was good-hearted.

'Going up Little Manor while you're home, are you?' Gramps said, helping himself to another spoonful of swede and the smidgen of chicken-skin which was left on the dish. 'Only I was up there the other day with the order. How they stretch it I don't know – there's only a pound and a half of meat a week for each man – that's with every-thing, sausages, bacon, the lot – and half those poor fellows need beef tea and liver and all sorts of strengthening food.'

'They get donations, mind,' Lizzie said. 'And I daresay Silas Farring-ton will find them something. The Beswethericks will see to that.'

'I expect so, and all,' Gramps agreed, scraping the last morsel off his plate. 'His sister-in-law is up there now. Helena Beswetherick as was. Couldn't bear to sit home idle she said, and she's gone to help Rosa Warren with the convalescents. Getting on like a house on fire, from what I hear, and making a fist of it, too. It's a good hospital, and always something doing. There's a carol concert up the convalescent wing, this afternoon.'

'I shan't be going,' Lizzie said quickly. Little Manor held too many memories. Michael, waiting for her in the rain. The confrontation with Mrs Rouncewell. Going up herself to confront Tamsin. Even now the thought of that was enough to make her squirm with shame. Besides, Tamsin also reminded her of Ashton Masters. Not that, these days, she needed much reminding.

She felt her cheeks glow. Gan was looking at her quizzically. What would Gan say if she knew that Lizzie had been kissing a gentleman? And supposing, just supposing, Ashton did come back and offer for her honourably, as Belinda was always suggesting, what would Gan say then? What would Lizzie herself say? She had asked herself dozens of times, without resolving it. He was a nice man, a good man. She had no prospects and no suitors of her own. How could she possibly say anything but 'yes'?

Gan brought her back to reality. 'Well, don't go if you don't want, of course,' and Lizzie realised that her refusal to go to Little Manor had sounded very abrupt.

She smiled, and said hurriedly. 'I already went to Sung Service with the children, and it's colder than Greenland out there. Next time, perhaps. I'll be down in a week or two, see Nell Blight wed.'

Mama beamed. 'Well, if you do, see can you bring down a bit of fresh vegetable for our Daisy. Expecting a happy event, she is, and could do with a bit of building up.'

'Daisy is?'

Mam nodded. 'Early days yet though, so don't you go saying. But come next summer I'll be a grandmother and Horry here will be an uncle.'

'Well, I aren't going up there for tea next Christmas, uncle or not,' Eddy said. 'Our Daisy can't bake to save her life.'

They all laughed, but there was no mirth in it. Next Christmas, if things went on like this, there would be nothing for Daisy to cook even if she could, and they'd all be half-starving like poor Mrs Richards.

Besides, Lizzie realised with a horrible start, before then Eddy would be eighteen and liable for call-up. Over with Father and Ashton and Merran in the horror that was France. Everyone she loved. The thought cast a terrible pall over the rest of the day.

Chapter Twenty-Nine

Merran spent Christmas in the trenches. A year or two back there had been a Christmas Truce, even fraternisation across the lines, but there was nothing of that kind now. The shells whined dismally overhead as though it were any other day, and freezing rain and sleet added to the misery.

There were Christmas rations. Well-wishers had sent food parcels for the troops, although people had no sense about things, and half the gifts were rotting and stinking by the time they were delivered. Maiden ladies sent bottles of jam which broke in transit, or hand-knitted comforts, which were usually designed to fit either midgets or giants.

Merran, for instance, had a pair of balaclavas which he had sewn up and now wore one on either hand, like a pair of outsize mittens.

No man living could have got his head into either one of them, but he was glad of them all the same. He had also saved, as a kind of Christmas treat, the warm socks which Lizzie had sent him, and he took off his boots and pulled them on, grateful for the momentary warmth and dryness, though by tonight they too would be mud-smeared and sodden. His feet, he noticed, were beginning to turn white and flaky from the eternal damp.

He could not even feel concerned about that. He could not feel anything. That terrible unreal numbness had returned, and he accepted everything with a dull, dreary fatalism. He had come to life, for a few days, when he first sent that letter to Lizzie. He had permitted himself, briefly, the luxury of feeling. First his affection for Lizzie, which he had allowed himself to express, and then the worst of all emotions – hope. But it had come to nothing. She had written back, true, but without even acknowledging what he had said. He sank back into that damp, dreary no-man's-land of the soul.

The Army, though, had done its best. Extra rations of tinned beef and jam pudding, and a little tin box with crossed flags on top containing – among other things – chocolate and cigarettes. Merran didn't smoke, but he swapped his for plum jam. Better yet, someone from Base Headquarters had looted a cellar somewhere and sent down a whole case of wine. A lot of the men didn't care for it – filthy foreign stuff, they said, and preferred their rum ration – but Merran did. A good measure of that in his tin mug, and a slice of the fruit cake Ma had sent, put a little warmth into his bones.

Then a message came through that a patrol was wanted, to repair the wires.

He went out with them into the gnawing cold, slithering through mud treacherous with frost, and desolation eerie in moonlight. Hell is water, someone said, and he believed it. Craters yawned around them, waist-deep in icy mire, but they stumbled on. They fumbled at the wire, their fingers numb with frost, between the bodies of the sleepless dead. Then, cold, wet, exhausted, they floundered back.

And that was Christmas.

Farrington House celebrated Christmas in some style. Silas had managed to arrange a big tree, and – through the judicious barter of nails and timber – acquired a whole box of Christmas decorations. Little wooden rocking-horses and tinsel angels, painted soldiers and tiny gilt boxes intended for cachous and nuts. Set off by dozens of lighted candles (exchanged for a bottle of spirits from his secret store) it was a festive tree worthy of any house in the duchy.

Tamsin didn't seem to care for it, especially. He was disappointed, but she had been raised to such things and perhaps for her it was commonplace. Privately, though, he was enchanted. Everything he had always wanted was suddenly available to him. A great tree. A grand dinner with half the dignitaries in the town sitting at his table to goose and wine – and the comfortable knowledge that, with the War on, there was probably no better feast available in the whole of Penwith.

And no prettier wife. He loved to see her as she was now, laughing and smiling, in the crushed russet velvet he had obtained for her, his Christmas gifts to her glinting at her wrists and throat. Some of the 'blue boys' from the convalescent ward had been invited for an after-dinner entertainment – another sign that Silas Farrington had joined the gentry – and he was aware of the admiring looks they were casting at Tamsin. He gloried in it. Other men were jealous, overtly jealous, of what he had.

He was aware, almost for the first time, that he was happy.

He had engaged a fiddler, at some expense, and the fellow was tuning up. It sounded like cats in torment, but nothing could displease Silas this evening. He went over to his wife and placed a proprietorial hand on her shoulder.

She flushed and would have shrugged him away – Tamsin never cared for public demonstrations of affection – but he gripped her arm firmly.

'Come, my dear,' he said, smiling. 'We should lead the dancing.'

She gazed at him. 'Surely, Silas, you do not intend to . . . cavort?'

He did not relinquish his grasp. 'Indeed, I do, my dear, and I intend that you shall cavort – as you call it – with me.'

'But Silas, it is no real orchestra. Dancing to a fiddler, like country-folk on Midsummer night. Whatever will people think?'

She seemed determined to deny his contentment, and it made him stubborn. 'They may think what they will, my dear. This is my house and if I choose to dance with my wife, I shall. Besides, I am sure this young man . . .' He turned to the officer with whom Tamsin had been talking, 'Captain . . . ?'

'Goodenough,' the young man supplied.

'Captain Goodenough, would have no objection to "cavorting" in his turn, should his wound permit it.'

Goodenough bowed slightly, and coloured. 'I should be honoured.'

'There you are, you see? There can be no possible objection.' He took Tamsin firmly by the elbow and escorted her to the floor.

He did not dance well. He had never been properly taught, and had learned the rudiments merely by shuffling awkwardly around the floor with his aunt. But with Tamsin it was impossible to be awkward. She floated in his arms like thistledown, and he hardly trod upon her toes once.

He was flushed and beaming as he led her back from the floor, and handed her to Goodenough, who was waiting to claim her.

'If Mrs Farrington does not care for fiddlers,' Goodenough said, 'perhaps she should see the first-class little novelty my parents have sent to me for Christmas. It is called a "gramophone", perhaps you have heard of it? You wind a handle, and there is a cylinder affair which revolves against a needle and plays "Me and My Gal" through a loud-speaker. It is played by a real band, not just picked out mechanically. How they do it, I don't know. Deuced clever. It is a capital little device, better than an orchestra, for it never tires.'

Tamsin was gazing at him, wide-eyed. Goodenough was a good-looking boy, especially when he smiled. Silas was beginning to regret having offered Tamsin so cavalierly as a dancing partner. He said, rather waspishly, 'And do you not weary of hearing the same tune?'

'Ah,' Goodenough said, 'that is the agreeable thing. It is not merely a music box. With a "gramophone", one may exchange the cylinder and so vary the song. You must hear it, Mrs Farrington.'

Tamsin breathed, 'Oh yes, I should adore that,' and Goodenough bore her off in triumph to dance. They made a handsome couple.

Silas felt aggrieved, as though the evening had somehow lost its gloss. He stomped off to speak to his other guests.

Gilbert Beswetherick looked up mildly as he approached. 'Evening, Silas, decent drop of brandy you have here.' He indicated his glass.

Silas glowed. 'Glad you like it, sir. It's French. Not easy to come by, these days. I sent some up to Little Manor,' he added, anxious that Sir Gilbert should know of his generosity. 'Give a little Christmas cheer to the boys.'

Beswetherick nodded. 'Damned sporting of you. If I had a bottle or two of this in my cellar I'd be inclined to keep it for myself. Though I daresay Tamsin keeps you up to the mark, eh? Very keen on her

271

convalescents.' He was looking at his daughter as he spoke, watching her dance with her face aglow and her eyes asparkle. Silas wondered if his father-in-law was being facetious. He decided not.

'She is,' he agreed soberly.

'You were looking for a home for that damned parrot, Winifred tells me. Did you succeed in the end?'

'Yes,' Silas said. In fact the parrot was a sore subject. He had taken it to Tom Liddel, as agreed – the man could hardly refuse him a favour – but it had not worked out smoothly. Mrs Liddel, who ruled the house with a rod of iron, positively disliked Albert, and the parrot seemed to sense it. He would fly up behind her and nip her ears when she wasn't looking, or settle on her best bonnet and peck the artificial cherries off it, one by one. It did not endear him to the lady.

'Have to keep it caged,' Beswetherick said, when Silas explained.

Silas smiled grimly. They had tried that, but Albert drooped and pined so much that Mrs Rouncewell threatened to take him elsewhere. Silas could not permit that: Mrs Rouncewell paid handsomely for the parrot's 'lodging'. All the same, any visit to St Buryan these days was likely to involve a diatribe from Mrs Liddel on the subject of parrots, and another from Liddel himself, on the subject of wives. The problem, Silas knew, was not solved.

'Well,' he said, 'I should dance with my sister-in-law.' And off he went to offer Helena his arm, and listen, with very little interest, to her stories about Dr Macready and the wonderful work he was doing at the Casualty Clearing Station.

When Ashton arrived in Quellieu it was almost New Year. It had taken him an unconscionably long time. First there had been weeks of waiting for a suitable berth – the weather was too bad for flying. Then, when he got to Southampton, the ship he was to have taken had been sunk by a submarine, and there were more days kicking his heels in a dreary billet.

There was little festivity about it. He went, once, to the local public house, but it was such a drab, dreary place, with its restrictions on buying beer and its cheerless notices about the war effort, that he never went again. He did agree to eating Christmas dinner with a friendly household, but it was a paltry affair, and such an obvious strain on the family finances that he heartily wished he had gone back to the mess, where there was at least no shortage of brandy and beer.

Afterwards, he went to London for the weekend. That was better. He took in a music hall and quite enjoyed its cheerful vulgarity – the comic songs, the topical jokes about Bolsheviks, and at the end, the whole audience roaring out 'Goodbye-ee' at the top of their tuneless voices. When he got back to Southampton, though, it was to discover that he had missed Paddy Lowe, who was also on his way back to Quellieu, but who had managed to wangle a plane to deliver and had taken off and gone, in spite of the weather.

It made Ashton wish he had never gone to London at all.

A few days later it was his own turn to leave. He had never been on a ship before, and thirty minutes of it – pitching and bucketing, with half the Channel roaring in if you opened the hatches and a stuffy, sick-making stench if you did not – was enough to convince him that he never wished to be on one again. In the end he staggered out on deck and clung to a stanchion for the entire journey, seasick, drenched, miserable and cold, but at least breathing clean, fresh air. What it must have been like for the men herded like animals below decks he couldn't imagine.

Then the long winding train journey to Quellieu, where there was transport waiting. It was snowing and bleak, yet it felt like coming home.

There was a 'bash' in progress when he arrived. There was no flying in this weather, and a good many of the pilots were letting their hair down, drunk with youth and exuberance as much as with alcohol. There were cheers when they saw Ashton. The CO came over to grasp him by the hand, former pupils thumped him on the back, and someone thrust a drink into his hand. The air was thick with cigarette smoke, and the whole room seemed to vibrate with noise. Laughter, shouting, someone thumping out 'If you were the only girl in the world' while a group of airmen leaned on each other's shoulders and attempted to sing. Ashton grinned, swallowed his drink, and motioned for another.

This was where he belonged. A million miles from Tamsin and her frightful husband, from Mater and her appalling travelling-case, away from the temptations of socially unsuitable butcher's daughters.

One of the younger pilots was talking – with enthusiastic but biologically unlikely detail – of the things he hoped to do to the first woman who would let him. He was acting it out, uninhibited with drink, and it was very funny – especially when you had swallowed another brandy or two in your turn, on an empty stomach. Ashton found himself joining in the cheering, thumping the table and demanding 'More! More!' with the others, in a kind of spiritous stupor.

It occurred to him dimly that he had not bought a drink for Paddy, and he ordered one and returned to his seat, a brimming glass in each hand, with the exaggerated carefulness of the drunken. He set down the glasses without spilling a drop, to cheers and catcalls, and good-natured clapping.

'For Paddy,' he explained thickly. 'Paddy bloody Lowe. Where is he anyhow? Should be here by this time.'

Men were still shouting, laughing, singing, but the group around the table fell awkwardly silent. Their drunkenness seemed to have disappeared.

'You haven't heard?' someone said. 'Paddy didn't make it. Wind was too strong for him and he flipped the kite on landing. Bought it, I'm afraid.'

Ashton set down his glass. 'Paddy?'

The man nodded. 'Sorry old man. Bit of a shocker, I'm afraid. Friend of yours, was he?'

Ashton shook his head, not in denial, but in disbelief. 'Paddy!' he said again, as if by repeating the word he could understand it better.

The whole room had fallen quiet now.

Ashton got up and went out. Outside the night was cold and crisp, with a pale moon silvering the clouds. It was very still, and the black shapes of trees and buildings reared silhouettes, their tops touched white by snow-fall.

Ashton peered up at the sky. It seemed very remote and empty. Impossible to think that Paddy would never soar those clouds again, never come roaring in with barely a foot to spare over the trees, and then land with a cheerful chuckle. 'Good egg.' Never again.

The cold chilled the hot teardrops on his face, and he turned away, desolate. Chubby. Sylvie. The two dead soldiers by the hedge. And now Paddy. Life was so precious, so terribly frail. To hell with what Mater and her friends would say. A man had to seize happiness where he could. Before it was too late.

Inside the hall, the raucous singing had begun again. The next night, Ashton was among them, singing loudest of them all.

PART SIX: 1918

Chapter Thirty

1918 dawned. Another new year, but none of the new hope that generally went with it.

Lizzie, in Miss Stamp's little bedroom, awoke to a day of perishing chill, the water in the wash-jug cold enough to bite you, and the wind outside so bitter that it nipped your legs and backside, even through your breeches and two pairs of warm knickers.

'My lor,' she said to Belinda, as they struggled down the lane against the gale. 'Some New Year this looks set to be. Any more of this weather and there'll be no spring crops to speak of, and then where shall we be?'

Belinda shot her a look. 'What's up with you then Lizzie? You don't belong to look on the black side, as a rule.'

Lizzie shrugged, 'Oh, I don't know. It's all right for us, we've got enough to eat and money in our pockets, but there's plenty that hasn't. And what is there to look forward to? Only more of the same. There's no sign that this war is ever going to end.'

'Over by Christmas,' Belinda said, as everyone always did.

'Christmas 1950, at this rate,' Lizzie retorted. 'Before we know it we shall have Horry called up and in the trenches.'

Belinda pulled a sympathetic face. 'You're worrying about Eddy, that's what.'

In fact, at that moment, Lizzie was thinking of Ashton and Merran but she didn't say that to Belinda. 'Well,' she said. 'Eddy'll have to go, sure as eggs. Shop needs a butcher, but now they're offering Mam a wounded serviceman to "help". Anyhow, there's that little slaughtering to do nowadays, I believe Gramps could manage single-handed. Half what Mam's selling is ready-killed – chilled stuff from Australia. Won't need butchers at all, soon. Unless we start selling horse-flesh, like they're doing up the country.'

Belinda stared at her wide-eyed. 'Horses! We'll be like Germany next. Eat babies and all sorts, over there. It was in the paper.'

'Get off!' Lizzie said, derisively. 'You don't want to believe all you read. But you mark my words, there isn't the call for butchers that there used to be. Half the time we're only killing poultry, and anyone could do that.'

They had reached Bengarra by this time and Belinda looked doubtfully at the geese, ducks and chickens clucking at the gate. 'I couldn't,' she said, with such a comical face that Lizzie laughed.

But a few minutes later, when the smelly swill was prepared, and the birds were swarming around her to get at the pail, she called across to Lizzie who was cutting feed from the rick. 'I take it all back,' she shouted, her voice whirled away by the wind. 'If another one of these beaks comes anywhere near my legs, I'll wring the creature's dratted neck myself.'

Lizzie laughed, but it was not the chickens that were in danger that day. Mrs Swann came up from the cow-house in distress. 'It's Buttercup,' she said, her round face pink with anxiety. 'Done something to 'er foot she has, and it's swoll up nasty. And I can't afford for her to have the vet, with things how they are.'

Lizzie knew enough about farming to realise that 'things' at Bengarra were never likely to permit the expenditure of a vet's fee on a humble cow, but one glance at Mrs Swann, her stumpy frame shaking with emotion, persuaded Lizzie that something had to be done.

'Well,' she said. 'Let me have a look. I used to be a nurse, once.'

Mrs Swann looked doubtful. ''Tisn't a person, though, is it. Cows are different.'

Lizzie grinned. 'More legs, for a start.'

A thin smile crossed Mrs Swann's face. 'Can't do any harm, I suppose, just looking.'

But when it came to it, there was much more than just looking. Poor Buttercup was in a sorry state. The leg had swollen hugely overnight, hot and festering, and the cow was obviously in pain. She looked at the three women with a rolling, beseeching eye.

'I don't know whatever is up with her,' Mrs Swann said. 'She was right as a trivet a day or two ago, then she seemed to go off her food, and now – this.'

'Get a halter round her,' Lizzie said, suddenly. 'And rope her other leg. I don't fancy being kicked to death.' She must have sounded authoritative because the other two leapt to her command. 'Now then, girl.' She ran a hand gently down the animal's shin. It was hot and tight. The cow flinched, and a frenzied tail flicked manure across Lizzie's face, but she had found what she was looking for.

'I thought so,' she said. 'She's got something stuck into her.' She quested with her fingers. 'A nail, by the feel of it. Got a pincers, have you, and a knife?'

'Got a pliers,' Mrs Swann said, producing some from her pile of tools.

Lizzie took her courage in both hands. She had enough experience with shrapnel to know what was required. Ignoring the bellowing from Buttercup she worked with the knife, and after some difficulty, located the end of the nail and pulled it out. A spurting stream of blood and pus followed it. The cow roared and lurched, stamping onto Belinda's foot. 'Warm water,' Lizzie said, 'and salt.'

Buttercup, relieved of the immediate pain, seemed to realise that the bathing was for her own good, and she submitted patiently enough. Lizzie had no antiseptic, but she remembered something her father used to do with Kitty, and she bathed the wound in turpentine, and bound it up. Mrs Rouncewell would have been proud of that bandage.

It was some time before the swelling went altogether, and Buttercup always walked a bit lopsided after, but she was feeding greedily within an hour, and after a few days was lolloping about the yard again – as good as new.

Mrs Swann must have told everyone in the district, because after that, whenever there was a cow in trouble, they brought it to Lizzie. She tried the tricks they had seen in training: rubbing a distended stomach to ease the gas when the beasts 'blew themselves out' with new grass; or, when a cow had mastitis, blowing up the teats with a bicycle pump and binding them with tape – lost quarter of the udder very often, but usually saved the cow.

The tricks worked, more often than not. 'Better nor a vet, that girl.'

Ashton found himself in a sort of dream, going through the motions required of him without permitting himself to think. It was easy to do, because these days, he seemed to be set apart from the other airmen on the base. He was the most experienced, by a long way, and the younger, newer men treated him with a kind of awed respect, as if he had dropped from the moon.

They clustered to buy him drinks and laughed at his jokes, but he sensed that they had made him into a kind of talisman. No one teased him now, or cut him down to size, as Paddy had always done, and his most casual opinions were treated with solemn deference, at least to his face.

It was unnerving.

He was Major Masters now, with medal ribbons on his tunic, and commanding the whole Pursuit Wing at Quellieu, instead of merely D flight, as before. Besides, the squadron was flying Camels, these days, and some of the youngsters were finding them a handful. Marvellous machines in a scrap – the Camel would go anywhere in the hands of an experienced pilot – but they could side-slip nastily if you weren't used to them, and they had to be flown carefully round a loop with exactly the right amount of left rudder, or the whole thing would rear over, hang bottom-side up, then inexorably flop and spin. They could catch even experienced fliers that way.

Ashton would have welcomed action, to lose himself in, but it was a relatively quiet time for the Quellieu base. Not much activity on that part of the line. A bit of practice flying when the weather permitted – and goodness knows some of the new lads needed that! – a few mock 'ground-strafe' attacks at targets marked out on the field, and that was that. Not much need to venture over the enemy, no dawn patrols and hard-boiled eggs at first light. Ashton made work for himself by personally trying out every aeroplane on the base. It kept him occupied. Helped him to forget.

He took up a newly delivered machine one day and put it through its paces. It was a good aeroplane, well-balanced and responsive, and he made a mental note to reserve that one for himself, if he could. Aeroplanes were like that. They had personalities, and though two Camels might look the same, they each had individual peculiarities. That was why men preferred to fly their 'own' machines. Why Paddy Lowe, presumably, had managed to flip a strange kite on landing. Ashton would have backed Paddy to land his own machine safely on a cabbage patch in a fog.

Dammit, he had not meant to start thinking about Paddy. It was too uncomfortably close. Ashton was a good pilot, but Paddy had been a better one, and whatever happened to Paddy could easily happen to him, too. It made him feel absurdly and suddenly mortal. He had always known, intellectually, that any patrol might be his last, that it might be his place empty at breakfast tomorrow, but he had never really believed it, until now.

He took the plane up a little higher as if by doing so he could rise above his thoughts. It was a bleak day, but up here it was beautiful. Banks and valleys of enchanted cloud, landscapes of billowing pink and purple, edged with light as the weak sun caught them, and once, improbably, an entire circular rainbow shining on the cloud below.

His spirits lifted as they did when he was flying. It was good to be alive. Yet, being up here put things into perspective. People looked so small, so insignificant. Which they were, he supposed. Life was very fragile. All one could do was live as fully as possible, while the chance remained.

He swooped down to skim a cloud-bank, watching the shadow of the aeroplane moving on the soft mist, like a ghostly companion in the empty sky.

He had been stupid, he told himself. He loved Lizzie, and he had let her go. He thought about her, sitting beside him on the stile. 'You aren't thinking to marry a farmgirl, I suppose.' So artlessly and unselfconsciously lovely. Why hadn't he offered for her, there and then? Because of Mater, of course. Because of Aunt Winifred and the Beswethericks. Because of what people would say.

His own mental cowardice sickened him.

What did it matter? One false move, one putter of guns, and he would be gone for ever, like Paddy Lowe. Why not enjoy her, while he lived – and if he survived, so much the better. She would make a better wife to him than ever Tamsin would have done. In some ways, she was more of a lady, too. She would never have 'let herself down' with Chubby, like that. Anyway, class was not everything – Sylvie had taught him that.

Well, it was not too late. Lizzie might have him yet. Did she love him? A little, perhaps. Certainly he was attractive to her. And he would make her happy. Buy her some of the things she 'wanted and couldn't have'. What would her family say? That girl, all eyes, thrilled with a bit of honey on a split? And the 'in-laws' – living in that dreadful shop? For a moment he hesitated, and then he thought again of Paddy Lowe. What did it signify? A man must seize happiness where he could find it.

He would do it. He would. As soon as ever he got back to his billet he would write to Bengarra, asking her to marry him. He imagined her face as she opened the envelope. What would she say? He smiled. Plead for time, more than likely. It did not matter. The very next leave he would go and see her. He remembered the warmth of her lips against his. He would bring her round.

The decision made him feel suddenly light-hearted with joy. Wonderful. It was freedom, he realised, freedom from convention.

Freedom to do what he wanted. He should have done it before. Marvellous. He was king of the sky. He pulled the aeroplane round in a steep turn, delighting in his own skill. He swooped, he soared, he looped.

Not enough left rudder. God, oh God. The Camel reared up. He tried to fight her, throttling back the engine to right her, but it was too late. There was a dreadful moment of hanging – he was not strapped tight enough and he could not pull himself up into his seat – and then the plane was spinning, faster and faster. His buckles would not free. He watched the trees spiralling up to meet him for fully half a minute – before the blood pounding behind his eyes was too much for him, and the light went out.

Tamsin was incredulous when she heard the news. 'Ashton? Missing? How can he possibly be missing?'

'Nonetheless,' her mother said, severely. She had come to Farrington House on purpose to bring the news. 'That is what the letter says. He went out to test a machine and never returned. They found the aeroplane – mercifully it didn't completely burn – but there was no sign of the pilot. Thrown clear they think, and almost certainly dead. Your Aunt Alice is beside herself with grief, as you may imagine. We are to have a family supper tonight – Helena is to be there – I presume you and Silas will come, to lend her a little support.'

Tamsin made a mental grimace. Tonight of all nights, when she wanted to take Peter Goodenough for his last 'outing'. She had planned it so carefully: a walk, a civilised picnic, and – before she drove him back in the early evening – a brief visit to the brandy shed and a sweet and romantic farewell. The weather was even promising for it, sharp but sunny.

She said, doubtfully, 'I had promised to give one of the convalescents an outing.'

Mama pounced on the words. 'Splendid, then you may collect Helena from Trevarnon when you drive him back. She finishes at four, so it will be most convenient.'

Silas cut short any possible objection. 'It will suit me excellently, too. I have business in Penzance, and I need to see Mrs Rouncewell in connection with some blankets, so you may drop me in the town and we can all meet at Little Manor later. We cannot disappoint your aunt at such a time as this.'

Really, Tamsin thought, it was too bad. Goodenough would be

discharged in a day or two, and there would never be another opportunity. But there was no help for it. Mama went upstairs to see Prudence roll over (a new trick, so the nursemaid said) and then went home, leaving Tamsin in a sulky gloom.

Her mood was not even improved by Silas allowing *her* to drive *him* into Penzance, although not many husbands would have permitted it. She let him out at the top of Causewayhead and rattled up the lanes to Trevarnon.

Goodenough was waiting for her. He was such a handsome boy, even in that absurd 'blue boy' uniform, and the slight suspicion of a limp made him look quite distinguished. She helped him in (for the benefit of watching eyes) then retarded the magneto and started the engine, proud of her daring skills.

He was gratifyingly cast down when she told him her news. They were parked primly on the Promenade looking out at the sea. 'Damn it all, Tamsin, it's dashed hard lines on a fellow,' he said. 'I shall be back to the War before the fortnight is out. Am I never to see you again?'

It was rather romantic when you came to think of it, this last meeting blighted by an unkind fate. 'It's destiny,' she murmured, with a wistful smile.

He grasped her hand. 'You are my destiny,' he said. 'I can't live without seeing you again.'

She removed her hand. People might be watching. But it was nice all the same. She gave him her warmest smile. 'Poor boy.'

'I must see you. I can. Listen, I will have a few days' leave before they send me back to the Army. My family lives in Fowey – it is not so far – and I shall have a travel warrant. Suppose I come back, just for the afternoon, before I leave for the Front? No one need ever know. We could have our picnic then, and no Rosa Warren to say I must be back at six.'

'But my husband . . .'

'You could think of something,' he urged. 'A visit to your sister – a concert even. Anything. Saturday night. Say you will.'

She flushed. 'I don't know . . .'

But in the end she agreed. A romantic tryst. She hugged the knowledge to her as she drove to Gulveylor, and was so charmingly solicitous to Aunt Alice that even Silas noticed it.

'Of course you must feel Ashton's death,' he said, as they drove away. 'You were engaged to him once. But I hope you do not too much regret your bargain.'

283

It only served to remind her how sharply she did regret it, and she could not bring herself to address a single word to her husband all the way home.

Chapter Thirty-One

Silas drove to Penvarris in an uneasy frame of mind. His wife's silence disturbed him, as it always did. As she intended that it should. He glanced towards her. She had her eyes closed and a tiny secretive smile played on her lips.

The smile was not for him, he knew that.

He had done his best, really his best, to make her happy. He indulged her shamefully – no wife in the country could be more pampered, more adored. Yet somehow it was never enough. There was only one thing he required – indeed demanded – from her, and she acceded so unwillingly that the act lost half its pleasure. Yet he persisted. She would in the end give him a son and heir, and then perhaps she could have her solitude. Although he doubted it. This was the bargain between them, and though she did not care for it, she was still delectable.

There might be daughters first. Well, there was no great harm. Tamsin was young, and her other child was engaging enough. Indeed, he sometimes felt that he was fonder of Prudence than Tamsin was herself. Tamsin had sometimes to be reminded to look in on the nursery, but he often went. It helped him to imagine having sons of his own.

The prospect of that, and of the act that might lead to it, made him impatient to be home, and he fumed inwardly at the ruts and stones in the lane that hindered their progress. Tamsin was always complaining that he should have the road repaired – gravelled perhaps. Well, maybe he would see to it, if this deal with the blankets succeeded. In the meantime he was chafing at the delay.

He was not best pleased therefore, when he did arrive, to find Tom Liddel waiting for him.

'Mr Farrington, I'm sorry sir to disturb you this time of night. Only it's this parrot, you see.'

Silas groaned inwardly. 'What's the matter now?'

'It's my missus, Mr Farrington. Says she won't stay another night under the same roof with it. Got hold of her knitting it did, and unravelled half a pair of socks. She threatened to lock it out, and me with it, unless I found somewhere else for it to stay. I swear to you Mr Farrington, I regret the day I ever said I'd look after the confounded thing for you.'

Silas was privately feeling something of the same. Tamsin had got him into this, he recalled. He said, 'Well, you aren't looking after it for me. You're looking after it for two shillings a week. A wage, that used to be.'

Liddel shook his head. 'It isn't worth it, Mr Farrington. I don't care if it was half a crown, that blessed bird is more trouble than it's worth. Anyhow, what am I to do with it now, that's the question?'

Silas toyed for a moment with the idea of taking it to Farrington House, but he could imagine what Tamsin would say to that. Besides, he knew something Tom Liddel did not. Mrs Rouncewell was concerned that the parrot might be a danger to health, and he couldn't allow his wife and child to be subjected to that.

'Well,' he said with a sigh. 'You'd better put it in one of the sheds, I suppose, at least in the meanwhile. I'll put a notice up in the factory tomorrow and see if we can't find somebody who'll take it. Of course, you can't expect to be paid for this month, since you have broken your agreement.'

He had expected an argument, but Liddel said, 'Of course not, Mr Farrington,' with a readiness that made Silas wish he'd asked for a 'dispensation fee'.

'And in the meantime, you'll have to feed it.'

Again Liddel said, 'Of course, Mr Farrington. You get the key and I'll fetch the parrot.'

It was cold and musty inside the building, and Albert protested vigorously until Liddel put the cover on the cage. There was a final sulky squawk, and the bird fell silent.

'He'll be all right now, for the night.' Liddel said. 'I'll come down in the morning and let him out.'

'Let him out? But there's no end of stuff in here.'

'Well, he won't do more than fly about and peck at it,' Liddel said reasonably. 'These cans are too heavy for him to overturn. And if you keep him cooped up, he mopes and pulls his feathers out, and then no one will have him.'

'Oh very well,' Silas said. 'For tomorrow. No longer mind.'

'Of course, Mr Farrington,' maddeningly.

By the time Silas got to the house, Tamsin was in bed and asleep. He did not disturb her.

Lizzie got a weekend off and went to Nell Blight's wedding. It was quite a 'do', considering, because Mrs Jago had put aside enough sugar and eggs to make a proper cake, and Nell had been given dried sugar-plums from one of the soldiers to put in it. Crowdie had got hold of some proper flour from somewhere and brought down a loaf of real white bread, and there was Nanzeal cheese and butter. So what with that, and cold pork and pickles, it was a better feast than most people had seen for a long time.

'And to think next month there's going to be ration cards,' Nell said. 'Only so much fat and sugar each week, and never mind who you are. And the same with bread and meat soon.'

'Can't get much anyhow,' Lizzie replied. 'You know butter's nigh on half a crown a pound? Have to be a millionaire to eat at all, the rate things are going.'

Nell looked down at her laden plate and grinned. 'Or have the sense to marry a farmer's son. Mrs Jago! I daresay I'll get used to it in time.'

'Still look like Nurse Blight to me,' Lizzie teased. Nell had worn her uniform for the ceremony. New clothes were hard to come by. Lizzie herself was wearing the outfit Daisy had for her wedding. It was a bit cold for January, and a bit big besides, but a fleece vest under it took up most of the slack, and Lizzie felt quite 'the thing' in her borrowed finery. She hadn't anything 'fancy' of her own.

'Wear it and welcome, Lizzie my handsome,' Daisy had insisted. 'I aren't wanting it, in my condition. I'm at my wits' end just trying to find an overall big enough to go round me. Besides, you can come back here after and tell me all about it.'

So Gan's piece of pink silk had gone to Peter Jago's wedding after all. It was a happy gathering, except for Anna Braun who had always liked Peter, and went out halfway through supper with a face like a fiddle.

She came back in no time, though, in great agitation, looking for Pa Jago. He listened, frowning, unnaturally neat in his Sunday suit, then put down his plate at once. 'Nell, my lover, I shall have to go. One of the cows is in trouble, calving. So, I'll say goodbye, and my blessing on you both. I daresay Ma'll write, and you'll let us know how Peter's doing with his pictures.' He hovered a moment, as if he was thinking of dropping a peck on Nell's cheek, but in the end he tipped an imaginary cap. 'Well, I'm off.' And he was gone.

Ma Jago frowned. 'Think I should go too, do you? Only it's the red brindle, our best milker, and we've lost half a dozen cows calving, this last year. Never known anything like it. And those Brauns are handy enough in some ways, but useless when it comes to cows.'

Lizzie hesitated. It wasn't fitting, with her being a guest, but she said it anyway. 'I could help him, Mrs Jago. I've done a bit with cows, these days.'

'You can't,' Mrs Jago said. 'In your good clothes and all . . .' But she sounded hesitant, and Hunnicutt, who was standing nearby, tucking into pork and pickles, drained his cider glass with a chuckle.

'Well, I'm going out there. Shan't be thanked for it, more than like, for there's nothing I can do right, these days. But I can't abide to see a beast suffer. And if you're minded to come with me, Miss Lizzie, there's an old smock of mine out the stable. Have that and welcome.'

And that was how Lizzie came to spend the rest of the wedding-feast with her arm halfway up a cow. It was a difficult birth, the calf's head was the wrong way, but they turned it at last, and the calf slithered out feeble but alive. The brindle red licked it.

'There,' Pa Jago said, wiping his blood-stained hands on the cold rag in the bowl. 'Reckon they'll do, now.'

'Thanks to Lizzie here,' Hunnicutt put in.

Pa Jago sniffed. 'An extra pair of hands is useful, time like this. Mind, it was you and I did the hard work. Anyone could have done the rest.'

It left Lizzie speechless, but Hunnicutt had his say. 'That's not true and you know it. Tom Liddel couldn't have done it, for one, nor Willie Brown either, without you were shouting instructions all the time, and maybe not then. Miss Lizzie did a grand job, and no mistake. Master Merran was right. Always said she was a girl in a million, and so she is.'

Lizzie stared at him. There was muck in her hair and blood on her face, and Hunnicutt's smock would need a boiling before it was fit to be seen, but she was glowing with pleasure.

'Merran said that?'

'Course he did,' Hunnicutt said. 'Been potty about you since he was old enough to hold a shovel, though he was too stupid to see it. Or you either. All moonstruck over Master Michael, you was, and poor Mr Merran eating his heart out. And now you've got some

287

fancy up-country gentleman chasing after you, I hear.'

Lizzie blushed. Aggie had been telling tales, obviously. Poor Ashton.

Hunnicutt threw her a look. 'Still, what's done's done, and if you won't have him you won't, though I never saw two people more made for each other in my born days.'

She said cautiously, 'I was upset, that day when Merran came to see me. All the town gossiping, and Michael dead. I didn't mean to be so rude.'

Hunnicutt brushed her words aside. 'Oh, wasn't that. Upset him, of course, but he could see it was too soon. No, it was when he wrote you. Thought you might give him a bit of hope then. But there you are. No accounting for folks.'

'When he wrote me?'

'Yes. He told Peter all about it in a letter. Still talks to me, Peter does, though there's some round here think I'm past praying for. Just 'cause I can see what's wrong with this farm, plain as your face.' He scowled in the direction of Pa Jago, who was buttoning himself back into his Sunday shirt and coat. Lizzie had almost forgotten his presence.

She was about to say, 'I've got a letter, home. Nothing but black lines . . .' when Pa Jago cut in.

'Now see here, George Hunnicutt, I'm still master of this farm and don't forget it. I don't need to be told what's what by an old man and a chit of a girl.'

Lizzie was suddenly and unreasoningly furious. She had known Pa Jago for years, of course, him and his opinions, but for some reason she could bear this no longer. 'No, you look,' she said, and the firmness in her voice surprised her. ' "Chit of a girl" I may be, but I can see things you don't seem able to, for all that. Hunnicutt's quite right. This cow now, whatever kind of bull did you put her to?'

Pa Jago scowled, but he answered, 'Why, Lord Poldair's big bull. Silas Farrington arranged it. And before you say anything, there was nothing the matter with that animal. Prize bull he was. Twice the creature of Crowdie's old beast that we used to have.'

Lizzie nodded. 'Exactly. And far too big for your poor cows. Look at that new calf now, half as big as its mother already. No wonder you've been losing them.'

'Too big a bull,' Hunnicutt said reflectively. 'Well, I'll be dashed. Could be right at that. Wonder I never thought of it.'

288

'Well,' Pa Jago said. 'Lizzie here has been trained by the Government. Taught her all sorts, and up to the minute besides.' It was such a sudden change of tack that Lizzie looked at him doubtfully, but he seemed to be quite serious. 'Could teach you a few things, George Hunnicutt, I shouldn't be surprised.'

Lizzie turned to Hunnicutt, ready to protest, but the old man silenced her with a wink. She took off her bloodstained smock, rinsed her face and hands in the kitchen bowl, and went back to the remains of the wedding. Peter and Nell had gone already, to catch the Plymouth train, but a few guests lingered on. Pa Jago was telling them about the calving. To hear him tell it she had done it single-handed.

'I always did say,' he bellowed, over a fresh glass of cider, 'this Land Army training is wonderful. Can't beat British girls for that. These refugees are all very well in their way, but it takes a Cornish girl to understand Cornish ways. Stands to reason.'

Hunnicutt came over to Lizzie. 'Never going back to Penzance tonight, are 'ee?'

Lizzie shook her head. 'Too late now, its blacker than the Earl of Hell's cloak out there. I'll go over to Daisy for the night. I said I'd go, anyhow, take these things back.'

'I'll walk with you, up so far as the road,' Hunnicutt said, and Lizzie knew she had made an ally for life.

Daisy was waiting up for her. 'My lor, Lizzie, wherever have you been? I was beginning to think you were never coming.'

Lizzie explained about the calving. Daisy pulled a face. 'Rather you than me, Lizzie. Why you want to mess around with they smelly creatures when you could be working snug in a factory like me, I'll never know.'

Lizzie looked at her sister's yellowed skin and thinning hair and knew why, but she said nothing, and presently Daisy went on, 'Anyway, it's a pity you weren't here earlier. Millie looked in, see if she could see you, but it was getting so late she had to go back. Had an hour or two off, because Tamsin went off all evening, up to Gulveylor to see her aunt. Unexpected. That cousin of hers – you know, the one who came down to open the factory that time . . .'

Lizzie nodded aware that her lips had turned to clay and would not speak.

'Fell out of his aeroplane in France, and killed hisself,' Daisy said. 'Why they won't let those poor airmen have parachutes, I can't think. We could make them easy – they do them for incendiaries –

but the generals won't have it. Think the pilots'll desert, or something. Here, Lizzie, whatever is it?'

Lizzie had discovered that, if her lips were clay, the rest of her was
jelly, and she sat down heavily, trembling with grief. Ashton,
young vibrant, living Ashton. She couldn't believe it.

'Some kind of curse, I am,' she said softly.

'Here, don't tell me that Aggie was right? She was on about you
and him, before Christmas. I never supposed there was anything in
it – you know what Aggie's like – but I can see there was something,
by your face. Lizzie, there never was? You and a gentleman like
that?'

Lizzie shook her head. 'Not exactly. I told him, if he wouldn't
marry me, that was that.'

Daisy's eyes were like saucers. 'My dear life, Lizzie. Suppose he'd
said yes. You might have been mistress of Gulveylor and all sorts.'

'And have the Beswethericks for kin? Can't see that, can you?
Anyway, he didn't ask me and it's too late now. The poor boy's
gone, and I tell you straight, I shall miss him.' Her voice was
breaking. 'He was a lovely fellow, and he made me laugh. He was
like . . . sunshine, that's what.'

Daisy was looking at her shrewdly. 'You loved him.'

Lizzie shook her head again. 'No. Well, I dunno. Perhaps, in a
way. But, what does it matter now?' There were tears in her eyes, she
could not prevent it.

Daisy gave her a sisterly hug, and talked hurriedly of other things,
but Lizzie could not sleep that night and she woke next day with
dark circles under her swollen eyes.

Daisy said nothing more until Lizzie was leaving. Then, unexpectedly – uncharacteristically, Daisy gave her a kiss, 'I'm some sorry about
Mr Masters, Lizzie, but don't you fret. You'll find someone to make
you happy, see if you don't. You've always had fellows buzzing round
you, like bees round a honey-pot. Michael Jago, Mr Masters. And
there's Merran, never had eyes for anyone else all his life.'

Merran Jago. That was the second time in as many days. She went
home very thoughtfully. Dear, solid, reliable Merran. She wanted
him here, wanted to tell him everything. She took out the faded,
folded note from her apron pocket, but no amount of squinting
revealed anything behind the black lines. And his last letter was so
cool and formal. She didn't know what to do.

In the end she wrote him a long letter telling him all about the
wedding, and the sorrowful news of Ashton. But Merran didn't reply.

Chapter Thirty-Two

The peasant who found Ashton Masters knew nothing about aeroplanes, and even less about First Aid. So, feeling the merest flicker of pulse in a vein he simply scooped up the inert body and carried it home in his cart.

If Ashton had been in the hands of the Medical Corps they would have seen that it was hopeless. They would have known it was impossible to survive such a fall, even if it was broken by trees, and finding him unconscious, injured and blood-stained, would have tied a label around his toe, taken him to the 'hopeless' tent, and left him there to die. They had enough to do, tending the living.

The peasant though, was ignorant of this. Finding the branch impaled in Ashton's side, he simply pulled it out, bathed and bound the wound, propped Ashton in his own bed and dampened his lips with water. He did not know enough to be surprised when, after a few days, his patient stirred faintly and began to moan.

Elsewhere in France another serviceman was reporting to the MO. The order to do so had taken Merran by surprise.

He wasn't injured. He wasn't really ill. It was just that his wretched feet had been going from bad to worse, and finally they'd let him down.

It had been a wretched week. They had moved up to the Front again, after a fortnight spent in a ruined village near Doumiens. He had nearly cured his feet there, with clean socks, daily rubbing with goose-grease, and drying his boots off a bit. His toes had been almost dry for days together.

But as soon as they moved up the line, the old problems returned. The flaking skin was blistering, peeling off and leaving nasty ulcer-like patches behind so that it was agony to walk. It had very nearly got him killed today.

The company was moving up on duckboards. Those were always treacherous in the rain, slippery with mud and filth, but you had to have them – the ground around was a quagmire, pocked with craters full of appalling green-brown slime and rotting remnants of men. His party was carrying ammunition, bombs and grenades, in makeshift haversacks fashioned from sandbags. Merran himself wasn't obliged to carry one, but he never required his men to do what he wouldn't do himself, and he took his share, bent half-double under the weight of the strap on his shoulder and with the pins and rods in the bag digging into him at every step.

They carried a spade too, 'between pack and back' as the RSM said, and that was another misery, because apart from the weight and uncompromising hardness of it, the handle formed a convenient channel for any rain to run down and soak you to the skin. Today it had been raining very hard indeed.

Hard enough to walk at all, under the circumstances, but it was his feet that betrayed him. He was limping slower and slower, becoming a danger to everyone, and the men behind were cursing and muttering at being exposed in the open for so long. In the end he was forced to slither into a shell-hole and let the rest of the party go past him. Fortunately, the expected barrage didn't happen, and very little fell on them but rain.

He followed eventually, the agony of the weight on his shoulder almost eclipsed by the agony of his feet. He was a long way behind, and in his anxiety he missed a junction and lost his route. He nearly ventured into no-man's-land before he realised it and had to pick his way back in the thickening dark, step by tortured step, until a terrified sentry took him for a German scout-patrol in the gloom and shot at him. Only bad aim – and Merran's unmistakably British expletives – saved his life.

Exhausted, he reported to the commanding officer. And was ordered to the MO.

It was absurd. The man looked at his feet and ordered him to hospital, then and there. Merran protested. They were the same feet after all which had taken him nearly into enemy territory that very day.

The MO was a laconic Scot. 'Oh aye, no doubt we could leave it. Another week or two maybe. Then ye'll have gangrene setting in, and we can amputate your feet. Or we can put you in hospital now, and there's a chance you'll be fine fit to serve again in a month or six weeks. So ye'll do as I say, if you've no mind to be walking home on your stumps.'

They painted his toes with gentian violet and iodine, which hurt worse than the infection, and put him on the first troop train to Le Tréport. The hospital was a kind of luxury. Clean sheets and a dry bed, hot food, regular washes, and safety. Everything else – trenches, Michael, Lizzie, Lewis – seemed like an unearthly nightmare. He curled like a child in a crib and slept. He hated to wake, because the nightmare was waiting for him.

His right foot, though, stubbornly refused to heal. They were giving him iodine baths now, and regular purges to 'purify the system', but they were going to send him home. There was still a fear of gangrene, and the putrid smell from his toe alarmed him.

Paul came to see him off, not very well himself. He had a feverish headache, he said, and ached in every limb.

'What I need is a name for it,' he said, laughing. 'You've got Trench Foot. There's been Egyptian tummy, and Arras fever. They'll think of a name for this headache next, then I can come in for a nice soft billet and be sent home for a rest.'

Merran grinned at his fooling, but it was no joking matter as it turned out. A little later they did find the malady a name. They called it Spanish Flu, and in the end it killed more people than the War.

Tamsin looked at her reflection consideringly. Not bad. Not bad at all. She had regained her figure nicely, and her old bluebell-blue outfit had been given a new lease of life with violet banding, and a shortened skirt. One good thing about the War, she thought with satisfaction, as the maid pinned her hair into a fashionable 'French knot', the shortages enabled one to wear styles and colours which would have been unthinkable for a matron like herself a few years ago.

'Thank you, Millie, that will suffice. Oh, and you can pass me that eau-de-cologne my husband gave me last week.'

She took the bottle from the girl's hand and pressed the pink-tasselled bulb herself. Perfume was precious, and even Silas could not be relied upon to provide endless supplies of it. She stretched her neck, revelling in the sensuous spray.

It was to be hoped that Peter Goodenough appreciated it. He usually did.

It was one of their Saturdays. He had not, after all, been sent straight back to the War. No good for marching, with his limp, so they had sent him on a 'general transport' course instead, everything from cold-shoeing to tank-tracks. He hated it, but it kept him in England and they had managed three of these clandestine rendezvous.

They had a system now. She would drive, not to the Hospital and a charity meeting (as she told Silas) but to a discreet spot in the lanes, where Goodenough would be waiting for her. He had complained, at first, but she could hardly collect him at the station – someone might have seen them. Then it was out for a picnic on the cliffs, and she would drop him in Penvarris, in the twilight, in time for the horse-bus and the last train back.

He was waiting for her today, with his kitbag, looking young and masculine, in his officer's cap and belted tunic. It always made her heart beat faster, but he was subdued as he slipped into the car beside her.

'What is it, foolish boy?' she said, making a little moue to blow him a kiss.

'How can you ask that? It is the last time, as you very well know. I am to France on Monday.'

'Of course, but we must not speak of that. Today must be the best, the most enchanted time.' She meant it. She would miss him wretchedly.

He reached over and caressed her knee, smiling now. 'Yes, you are right. And it will be, I promise you.'

It was. Rations or no, Silas had contrived roast beef for the household, and she had brought a slice of it, with bread and butter, apples and cheese and even a piece of seed cake, donated for Little Manor. Silas still boasted to everyone of her 'voluntary work'. Well, she was a willing enough volunteer today.

She had brought brandy, too, and they filled brimming cups of it, and sat side by side in the wind watching the waves break far beneath. She stretched an inviting hand to Goodenough.

'Wait,' he said, 'I have something to show you.' He went to the car and took out his kitbag. 'Don't watch!' he called laughing, and she shut her eyes obediently. There was a grinding and a whirring and then, scratchy but unmistakable, the strains of 'Me and My Gal' floating faintly on the air.

'Your gramophone!' she cried. 'Only think. Out here miles from anywhere and we have our own music.'

'I hope it is stable,' he said, frowning. 'The seat slopes.' He turned to her. 'Now, would madam care to dance?'

It was mad, foolish, thrillingly wicked and romantic, out there among the wind-blown grasses, dancing together on the cliff-top. Tamsin thought she had never been so enchanted. And afterwards, when he pulled her to him, that too was a sweet, sorrowful magic.

They had their picnic, walked and talked (Goodenough fretting about his posting) until it was time to go. Goodenough went to put away the gramophone, but she prevented him. She wanted to dance once more.

'Can we do that again?'

'Of course,' he said, but he was not talking about the music.

Afterwards it was late, really late. They had to light the carbide lamps on the car, and driving along bumpy roads was difficult in the dark. Besides, she had taken rather a lot of brandy. She lurched to a stop for the tenth time in a mile, and peered out to see the road-edges. Goodenough tried to take her in his arms.

'Not now,' she said, pushing him away. 'My husband . . .'

'You're so late,' Goodenough returned, 'a bit more will make no difference. Besides you can twist him around your little finger. Here, have a drop of courage.' He was out of the car and pouring more brandy into a cup.

She hesitated. 'Come on!' But he did not get back in the car, and in the end she got out with him. 'Drinky-drinks,' he said, holding the cup to her lips, and she laughed, pretending to struggle, but she drank it all the same. It was dark on the verge and she lost her footing, and he fell with her, half-deliberately, and pulled her towards him again.

'Not here,' she said, giggling. 'Anyone might come past.'

'Let them,' he said thickly, undoing the bluebell-blue buttons again.

Chapter Thirty-Three

'I've solved it this time, Mr Farrington,' Tom Liddel wheedled. 'There's a woman out Lelant who used to have a parrot of her own. I've been out to see her this very evening, and she's willing to have it, right away, soon as ever we can get it to her. Only I can't walk out there with it, this time of night. Take me long enough to get home as it is.'

Silas sighed. 'Oh, very well. I suppose you can put Albert in the shed again, this once. But if he isn't gone tomorrow I shall take the thing back to Mrs Rouncewell and have done with it.' He would have taken Albert back long ago, but the sum Mrs Rouncewell had given him 'to find the parrot a home' had been laid out on other enterprises. It would be a bit awkward to be asked to repay it just now.

Liddel waved the cage forlornly. 'I shall have to let him out for a bit, Mr Farrington, he's been cooped in his cage all afternoon. He'll start plucking his feathers else, and the woman won't want him if he's half-bald.'

Silas snorted, but he handed over the key and waited while Liddel shut the parrot in the shed. He was back in a few minutes, dangling the cage and cover. 'I'll come back later and put him away.'

'Is Mrs Farrington back yet, with the car?' Silas asked. The Bean was kept in the tin shed next to one he used as a locked store.

Liddel shook his head.

'I don't know where she has got to,' Silas fretted. 'I hope she has not had a problem with the motor.'

'No, she's all right,' Liddel said, and looked as if he could have bitten his tongue.

'What do you mean?'

Liddle shook his head.

'Well?'

'I oughtn't to have said,' Liddel muttered at last. 'Only I saw the car, when I was coming back from seeing that woman about the parrot. Stopped by the verge it was, but there was nobody in it.'

'Didn't you look for her?' Silas demanded. 'She might have been hurt.'

Liddel shook his head. 'Nothing wrong with her, from what I could hear. Giggling, she was.'

'Giggling?' Silas was making no sense of this.

'She wasn't alone,' Liddel said, uncomfortably. 'With that convalescent chappie from the sound of it.'

Silas's world was catapulting about him. 'You thought my wife was giggling in the grass with a soldier, and you did nothing? Didn't even stop?'

'Well, how could I?' Liddel demanded. 'Only glad they didn't seem to notice me, tell you the truth. Walked past as quick as I could without drawing attention to myself. Here, Mr Farrington, don't look like that. There was very likely nothing particular in it – they was old friends after all. They were always around together – everyone knows that. You must have known, giving her the car and all.'

A dreadful certainty was forming in Silas's brain, images more vivid than anything shown in the picture-house. 'I'll give her more than the car when I get hold of her,' he muttered. 'Go on, you get off home. I'll see to this.'

'But Albert . . .' Liddel protested.

'Confound Albert,' Silas said. 'This is my wife. Leave this to me.'

He went into the house and got the gun he always kept in case of intruders. He was not sure what he intended to do with it – fill the bounder with pellets perhaps. He strode down the lane to the sheds, driven by a nameless purpose.

The car-shed was still empty. He would wait in there till she returned, catch her in the act and then confront her. There was a paraffin lamp somewhere. He groped in the dark until he found it, on the shelf beside the matches. Empty. But there was paraffin next door, in the store-shed, somewhere between the ammunition and the brandy.

He still had the key in his pocket. He went to the store-shed and unlocked the door.

Something black and feathered rose up with a squawk and rushed past him in a flutter of wings. Drat! He had completely forgotten Albert. Well, it was too late now. He could already make out the lurch of headlamps in the lane, the noise of the motor, laughter and singing.

He abandoned all thought of hiding and went out to meet them, the gun and the empty lantern still in his hands.

'The bells are ring-ing,' Tamsin carolled, and Goodenough finished, 'For me and my gal.' It was a wonderful song. Best song in the world. Pity she couldn't seem to remember the rest of the words. Never mind. Those were very good words. She sang them again. 'The bells are ringing . . .' and they both giggled.

It was bumpy in the lane. Bump, bump, bump, like a game. It was fun, especially when the car went quickly. Ooops. They skidded sideways on a stone. 'Oops!' her voice sounded very loud in the darkness.

'Sshh,' she said, taking one hand from the wheel to put a finger on her lips, 'wake Silas.'

'Good ol' Silas,' Goodenough said. He was lying back in the seat and smiling beatifically. 'Doesn't deserve you.'

'Doesn't d'serve you,' she agreed, and they both laughed, resting their foreheads together as the car lurched on. 'Oops!' The car rocked again. It was priceless. She couldn't stop laughing.

Goodenough fished in his tunic pocket and brought out a packet of cigarettes. He fumbled two from the pack and put them to his lips. They made a 'v' like teeth, and he lit them with a match. Hot teeth. She tried to tell him, but she was laughing too much.

'Here,' he held out a cigarette.

She shook her head. It wasn't connected to her neck properly. 'Don't smoke.'

'Course you smoke. Should smoke. Wicked girl like you. You're a vamp, that's what you are. Vam-pire. Like Theda Bara in the pictures.'

'What's a vampire?' she took a dizzying puff.

'A big black thing from hell that bites your neck . . . like this.' He bent over and nipped her and she yelped, releasing the wheel. The car swerved dangerously, narrowly missing a ditch. He steadied it with a hand.

'Look out,' he said.

''s all right,' she assured him, 'Nearly here.' The shed and the store shimmered at her in the darkness. They seemed to be dancing. Like the gramophone. 'For me and my girl . . .' she began again, and then something dark and dreadful swooped past her in a rush of wings.

She ducked, screaming, and swerved wildly towards the sheds. The car lurched. And there, suddenly right ahead of them in the glare of the headlights, was a black shape, a person. Silas. They were going to hit him. She screamed, wrenching the car round. Too late, the running-board caught him, toppling him backwards. She swerved away, battling the wheel but it jerked from her hand and they were still lurching onwards.

Everything seemed to happen in slow motion. The car slewed onto a low pile of loose mine-rubble by the shed. She felt one wheel take a block of stone, and the car rocked dangerously, half-turning over. She was thrown sideways, the door flew open and then she was falling, sky and stones tumbling about her, and there was a horrible screeching – her own voice, but she could not stop it. She had a confused vision of the car lurching on down the spoil-heap, of the shed walls shattering inwards, heard the crash and clatter of breaking bottles and Goodenough screaming 'No . .oo . .oo' as he catapulted through the windshield, his cigarette still in his hand.

And then the world exploded.

They heard the blast in Penzance, four miles away.

'I swear to you, Lizzie,' Millie said. 'I was upstairs warming the beds – wondering where on earth they was to, that hour of night – and I heard this great bang. Worse than the blasting out the granite works. First off I thought the Germans had come and were bombing Penvarris. Then, a few minutes after Tom Liddel comes in – all shaking, and his face whiter than suet – and tells us what's happened. That poor officer blown to smithereens and Mr and Mrs Farrington in a terrible way. Tom Liddel went off running for the doctor, and he came straight away – middle of the night – and took them to the hospital in his own carriage, else I don't believe they'd have survived. Poor Mrs Farrington, blood everywhere and all her beautiful dress ruined.'

'What about Mr Farrington?' Agnes asked, with ghoulish relish. They were sitting in the kitchen over the shop, five of the girls, unravelling wool from an old grey pullover of Eddy's and steaming it again for socks.

'I don't know,' Millie said. 'They wouldn't let me see him, but if he'd been any nearer the shed it would've been the end of him. All sorts he had in there – ammunition, petrol and no end – and it went up like an inferno. Where he got it all from is a mystery, but there it is. Didn't do him no good in the end, did it?'

'Serve him right,' Elsie said. She was the littlest, so her job was rewinding the hanks. 'Horrible man, he was, all pink and spitty.'

Aggie giggled, but Millie said, 'He isn't so bad, when you get to know him. He's some good to that child, and he dotes on Tamsin. If he comes out of this he'll never forgive himself for it, I shouldn't think. Though she was lucky – thrown clear, they say.'

'What's going to happen now?' Lizzie asked. She still had an uncomfortable feeling of guilt whenever she thought of Tamsin Farrington.

'Lady Beswetherick wasn't at all happy when she heard. Wanted to have them out of the hospital and nurse them at home – afraid there'll be a scandal, I expect – but the doctor said she'd never get the nurses, with this war on. You should have heard her carrying on – what she wasn't going to do! – but she had to accept it in the end. Took Prudence off to Gulveylor with her, shut down Farrington House, and that was that.'

'There will be a scandal too, I should think,' Aggie said. 'Tamsin going off with soldiers like that.'

Lizzie gave her a warning look not to talk like that in front of Elsie, but Millie said, 'And all that stuff in the shed! War profiteering, that is. People have been had up for less. Though I expect Sir Gilbert will manage to keep it quiet. Cook's cousin says he's taking over Silas's affairs himself – been down to Mr Tavy's already, to get things all signed and sealed, "power of . . . something-'r-other". Keeping the factory ticking over, but giving up everything else – that business with Nanzeal, for instance.'

'That'll be a mercy, anyway,' Lizzie said, wriggling a knot to free it.

'And Lady Beswetherick's happy as a sandboy – running round like a chicken with two heads, looking after the baby. Best thing, probably. Tamsin never seemed to have time. Except they'll ruin that child, if they don't look out.'

'And what about you?' Lizzie wanted to know. 'No job for you, now. At least until Tamsin comes back.'

Millie shook her head. 'Doubt if she will come back. How could they hold their heads up here, after all this? Anyway, I wouldn't go back. Nothing to keep me, now Jack's going in the Navy.'

Lizzie nodded. Jack was the gardener's boy that Millie was keen on.

'Lady Beswetherick offered to have me up there, but I shan't go. No sense being in service these days. Daisy wants me to take her place up the factory, but I don't fancy that either. Too young to turn into a canary and have my hair fall out. Though I might go down the railway, they're wanting women for ticket collectors.'

Lizzie said, 'Come up to Bengarra and see me, if you have time. Never know, you might fancy the Land Army.'

'I'm going engine driving, when it's my turn,' Penny said.

'Mightn't be a war, by that time,' Lizzie pointed out. 'The men'll be back, and they'll be wanting the jobs then.'

'Always supposing they do come back,' Aggie said. 'You heard the latest news about the Jago boys, have you?'

Lizzie stopped unravelling. Or breathing. 'What?'

'Paul Jago,' Aggie said. 'Caught this Spanish Flu, apparently. One minute right as a railroad and three days later he was gone. Terrible. His poor mother's half-demented with grief, and it's near destroyed his Pa.'

Lizzie stared at her, horrified. 'No! Not just like that, surely.'

'True as I'm here. Going about like wild-fire it is,' Aggie said, 'and nothing they can do for it. Fomentations, poultices, hot lemon – nothing seems to help. Even the doctors are getting it. And that's not the worst. Paul went to see Merran – he was in hospital, something to do with his feet – and now he's picked it up and all. Proper poorly by all accounts.'

Lizzie's knees seemed to go from under her, and the wool dropped from her hands. 'He never is?' Merran, sick. Like those boys up at Little Manor. And she had been blaming him because he hadn't written.

'Yes,' Aggie said. 'Poor Mrs Jago. What a thing, isn't it? There's nowhere safe. Guns at the Front, Spanish Flu in the hospitals, bombs in London, and even in Penvarris there's that poor soldier blown to Kingdom Come . . .'

'And there was that parrot,' Millie said, 'supposed to be locked up in the same shed, and it turned up next morning at Little Manor, as right as rain.'

'Tell you who else is at Little Manor,' Aggie put in. 'I was up there yesterday with the meat-order and I heard them say. You'll never guess, Lizzie.'

Lizzie felt the goosepimples rise on her neck. 'Not Merran?'

Aggie shook her head. 'Ashton Masters.'

This time Lizzie's knees did fail her. She sat down. 'Ashton! I thought he was dead.'

'They found him being looked after by some French farmer, apparently, more dead than alive, but they got him out and Lord Chyrose arranged to have him brought home, though he's in a bad way, by all accounts.' Aggie gave Lizzie a sideways look. 'Thought you might want to go and visit.'

Aggie had never forgotten the afternoon of the splits and honey.

Lizzie coloured. She wasn't sure how she felt. Relieved, of course, for Ashton, but uncomfortable too, as if an unresolved question had come back to haunt her. But it would never do to let her sister see that, Aggie was too fond of spreading news. 'Perhaps I will. I'll go on the way home. Now, if we've got enough done for those socks, let's put this away and make some tea. There's better things to do with your day off than spend it running back wool.'

The conversation turned to other things, until it was time for her to go.

Chapter Thirty-Four

She did go to Little Manor. It cost her a little internal battle, but in the end she swallowed her sensibilities and went. She could at least look in at the Hospital she thought, even if she didn't visit Ashton.

One hurdle at a time. But he needn't have worried. Mrs Rouncewell made a great fuss of her.

'My dear Miss Treloweth, how nice to see you. Come and have some tea, gel, and I'll show you around the Hospital. We've made a good many changes.'

They had. It was hard to remember that she, once, had been part of this hushed, harsh, disinfected place. Matron showed her the new nurses' room and said thoughtfully, 'I have always been sorry, Lizzie, that we had to part in that unfortunate way. I should like you to know there will always be a place for you here, should you want it.'

Lizzie flushed. It was as handsome an apology as she was ever likely to get. 'That is very kind, Matron, but I am happy where I am. And it wasn't your fault, Matron. You did your best for me, and I shall always be grateful. Without you the Land Army would never have taken me.'

'It is not kind at all, child. I am thinking of the Hospital. Good nurses are hard to find. Still, doubtless you know your own business best. Supposing you are doing what you want to do, and not just running away from uncomfortable memories.'

Perhaps it was those words, more than anything, which made Lizzie decide that she would, after all, go in to see Ashton.

He was ghastly white and motionless: deeply asleep, or unconscious, she did not know which. Morphia, perhaps. There was a bandage on half his face, and they had his body in a sort of cage, to keep the sheets off his dressings. He looked remote and unreal, as if he had turned into a waxwork. She stood for a long minute, then pressed a kiss to his forehead and made to tiptoe away. She could feel the tears pricking her eyes.

Someone came up beside the bed. Lizzie turned away, wanting to hide her distress, but the words detained her.

'And who might you be?' It was a sharp, imperious voice. Lizzie raised her eyes unwillingly.

Ashton's mother. It had to be. Lizzie had only seen her from a distance but there was no mistaking the similarity. The same features, the same hooded eyes. These eyes, however, were not smiling. 'Well, speak up. How do you come to be so . . . forward with my son?'

'I'm Lizzie Treloweth, ma'am,' Lizzie ventured. What did she hope, that the name might convey something? Clearly, it did not.

'Well? What have you to do with Ashton?' A girl like you. She might as well have said it. The contempt in her tone made the meaning clear.

For a moment Lizzie was tempted to tell her – about the visits, the kiss, everything – but she quelled the impulse. There could be no point: she would not be believed, and it would make his mother furious. Ashton had been hurt enough.

She shook her head, meekly. 'He was my volunteer patient at a bandaging class. I was a nurse once.'

'Ah,' Mrs Masters said. 'A nurse. I suppose that explains it. And you wished to see how he was progressing? Well, thank you for your concern, but now that you have satisfied your curiosity, you will oblige me by not visiting again. I am aware that he is unconscious and cannot be offended, but I hardly feel that what I just witnessed is appropriate behaviour for a mere attendant. I presume you do not have other claims on him? You were not hoping for . . . money?'

It was some seconds before Lizzie realised what she meant. The woman thought she was some loose woman of Ashton's and was offering to pay her off. Why did these people always think you wanted money? It was just like Tamsin all over again.

She turned away, too hurt and humiliated even to be angry. It was true what she had said to Ashton, the gulf between them was deeper and wider than an ocean. At least one could cross oceans. Between them there could be no possible connection. His mother could see that, if Ashton could not.

'No, madam,' she said bitterly. 'Just a nurse. No claims of any kind.'

She went back to Bengarra and tossed all night, tormented. In her dream she was standing again by the bedside. She looked down at the white, unreal and lifeless face. It made her awaken, sweating.

But as the first light of dawn lit the little bedroom, she realised that the man in her dream was not Ashton. It was Merran, and he, too, was sleeping that waxen, unearthly sleep.

Mater was standing by his bedside when he awoke. At first he couldn't understand it – what on earth was Mater doing here in France? – but little by little the reality of pain drifted through to him. There was a cage over him, bedclothes.

He was in hospital then, wounded. And in England, too. Distorted visions of journeys, terrible tormented joltings, rose dimly from his memory. Where was he? Little Manor. He put a tentative hand to his face. Bandages. Yes, he remembered now – Lizzie had put them there, and he had winked at her, and Tamsin – in the carriage – had not been pleased . . .

When he woke again, Mater was gone, and there were nurses in her place. Dreadful times then, while they tore off the bandages and cleaned his wounds, while he swore and struggled, and gripped the bedstead to keep from crying out. But the past was coming back to him, piecemeal, like children's wooden picture-blocks, fragments of pictures here and there. He tried to piece together the fragments into a coherent whole.

How had this happened. Not shot down, no – but flying, looping. He had been celebrating something. Something he had decided.

Lizzie!

He tried to tell Mater about it next time she came.

'Mater . . . something to tell you . . . A girl . . .'

'Don't try to talk now, Ashton. You need to rest.'

He moved, painful in his cage. 'But this is important. I wanted to marry her.'

Mater came over and stood beside him, smiling. 'No really, Ashton. You're dreaming. Don't upset yourself. Go to sleep.'

He made one last effort. 'Not dreaming. Serious. You'll like her, Mater, when you get to know her, though she mightn't be what you expect. Her name is Lizzie Treloweth . . .'

A sharp intake of breath. 'That little nurse?'

He grasped his mother's arm urgently with his undamaged hand. 'You know her? How? Has she been here? Has she been to see me? Is that it?'

Mater flushed. She was looking strained, uncomfortable. Even from his pillows he could distinguish that. She said nothing.

'Tell me!' he insisted eagerly. 'We could get word to her, ask her to come again.'

She sighed. 'Ashton, I should have liked to spare you this, at least till you were stronger. But, since you persist – yes, she did come to see you. But, it is too late. She thought you had been killed, you see – but she told me she was glad you were recovering, and hoped that one day you may be as happy as she has learned to be.' She smiled down at him, maternal and sympathetic. He was ashamed to feel tears upon his face.

'Oh Ashton, I am so sorry to be the bringer of such news. She asked me to tell you that any friendship between you was all over, she was sorry if it caused you any pain, but it would be better if you never saw her again. She wished you well, but if she is to begin a new life she felt it would be kinder like this. To everyone.'

Ashton lay back on his pillows. Poor Lizzie. He could see how it would be. She had met someone 'suitable' and she had come to tell him so. That would fit with her fierce notions of morality. So, he had lost her. It did not altogether surprise him, everything he touched seemed to turn to dust and ashes. Well, so be it. He wished her happy. If only there were a little happiness for him.

Mater was saying something, but he did not answer her. His wounds were paining him. He closed his eyes and did not open them again until Aunt Winifred and Helena came, much later in the afternoon, to pay him a familial visit.

Mama had insisted on bringing Helena home, and Helena – after her husband had died of this terrible flu affair – had not been unwilling. She had been terribly pale and withdrawn at first, but Tamsin was amazed to find how glad she was to have her sister beside her. Helena was such a comfort, throwing herself into her nursing duties – a hundred times better than the girls in that horrid hospital.

It had been dreadful in the hospital, simply dreadful. Tamsin was injured, for one thing – she had never imagined that anything could hurt so much – and then to have to tolerate the lumpy mattress, the horrible coarse bed-clothes and the regular torment of iodine baths! And worse! People had been nothing short of impudent – whispering and gossiping behind their hands, and exchanging such knowing looks in her direction. It was humiliating. As soon as she was well enough Tamsin had wept and begged and pleaded to be taken home.

Papa was adamantine. 'You complain that people gossip, Tamsin, but it is no more than you deserve. You, a married woman, out on a drunken revel with a soldier – no better than a fishwife. And as a result, a man is dead. Be thankful that you are merely in hospital, and not in a prison cell.'

He was exaggerating of course. What happened to Goodenough wasn't her fault. It had just been a most terrible accident. Though, she admitted to herself uneasily, it was perhaps rather more her fault than people seemed to suppose. Somehow the story had got about that Goodenough was driving the car. If Papa had not been so angry, she would have suspected his hand in that.

He did bring her home, very soon afterwards – 'It is my good name, as well as yours,' he said – and Helena was summoned to nurse her. It was good to see her, good to be home in Gulveylor, good to be back in familiar surroundings where she felt secure. Good too, to know that Silas, after a few critical weeks, was beginning to make progress. He had looked so terrible, when they first took her in a wheeled chair to see him – his face all bruised and swollen and his hair singed off from the blast – that for a time she thought it possible that she had killed him too.

Killed him. It came to her sometimes in the night with a horrible clarity. She had killed a man – accidentally, it really wasn't her fault – but killed him all the same. 'Wilfulness, wantonness and stupidity,' Helena had said, and secretly Tamsin welcomed the words. She needed to suffer, to atone.

Sometimes, when she thought about it, she was overwhelmed with remorse. She had caused such trouble – scandal, death, injury. There would very possibly be enquiries about Silas's war activities, too. And it was her fault – well, largely, in any case.

When she had recovered – and she would recover, the leg and shoulder were mending nicely, and the scars on her neck and arms were fading (fortunately there had never been any serious damage to her face) – she would throw herself into a life of repentance. Papa was talking about selling Farrington House, and buying them a little place somewhere, far away where they weren't known. She could picture it.

She would dedicate herself to Silas (his convalescence would take a long time, the doctors said) carrying trays to and from his bedside with her own hands, since they would only have one or two servants. She would sit beside him dutifully, for hours, read or play for him (perhaps Mama would let her take the spinet) – and only leave his side to care for Prudence.

She would change her habits. Be less vain. No more pretty pastels and alluring dresses. She would dress entirely in greys and browns, wear her hair in a bun, and devote herself to charitable works. A Home for Fallen Women, perhaps – that would be appropriate. She would take up needlework for the poor and read improving books.

She was so anxious to begin her life of penance, that she resolved to begin at once, and she made sure that when Helena came up to help her into bed, she was sitting demurely against her pillows, her hands folded in her lap and a copy of Devotional Essays by her side.

Helena, gratifyingly, noticed at once. She took one look at her sister's hair, scraped back severely into an unbecoming style and burst out, 'Why Tamsin, what's the matter? What's all this?'

Tamsin explained. '. . . and I shall shut myself off – give up dinners and dances – I shall devote myself to good works, and never be silly and vain again,' she finished.

'I see,' Helena said.

'You're laughing at me,' Tamsin protested. 'You don't think I mean it.'

'Of course I think you mean it, Tammy,' Helena said gently. 'And I'm very glad you feel it so deeply. It is only that I think there may be more to pleasing your husband than borrowing Mama's spinet. And I am not sure, you know, that frugality is really served by throwing away all your dresses and buying new. Now, is there anything else I can do for you tonight?'

Tamsin thought for a moment. 'Not tonight, no. But tomorrow, if you are going into the town. If I am to start working for good causes – could you call into the stationers and get me one of those sweet little tasselled notebooks?'

Helena dropped a kiss on Tamsin's cheek, but she was shaking her head wryly as she went out of the room and closed the door.

Chapter Thirty-Five

It was Friday afternoon, but Lizzie was not off-duty yet. She was raking out the cow-house – the 'shippon', Mrs Swann called it, though no sheep had ever been near it. Mrs Swann had quaint names for all sorts of things – even the china 'gazunda', with the picture of the Kaiser in the bottom. It 'gazunda' the bed, as she explained.

The cows though, had no such provision, and Lizzie was moving the dirty fern-stalks, and fetching in fresh. It had to be done often, with shortages how they were, fern didn't catch the muck like straw did, and it didn't make good field-manure either.

Still, Buttercup would be calving soon, and Lizzie wanted to clean the cow-house, just in case. She went to the fern-rick, noticing the fresh buds on the fruit-tree, the first shoots of the flowers, that promised that there would be a spring even in 1918. There was a shout from the kitchen.

'Lizzie!' Mrs Swann, scrubbing down the slate benches round the dairy. 'Visitor for you.'

'Coming!' Lizzie called. Drat Millie, she had been promising a visit for weeks, but she might have said she was coming. 'I'll just finish this.'

She took another forkful into her square-sided barrow. That should do it. She would spread that, and then clean herself up and take Millie up to Miss Stamp's for a fourpenny tea. Wasn't easy, with the rations, but Miss Stamp would have something. Hot potato-griddle cakes perhaps and honey. She wheeled the barrow back to the shippon.

'Lizzie?' the voice startled her. She whirled around.

'My dear life! It's you.'

'It's me,' Merran said, and suddenly she was weeping.

He took her into his arms. 'Here, here, what's all this?'

She clung to him, neither surprised nor embarrassed. It just seemed naturally where she belonged. She sniffed. 'I thought . . . I dunno what I thought. I thought I wouldn't see you again. With the Spanish Flu and everything.'

It was true, she realised. It was true. She hadn't dared to think about it, but it was true.

He nodded. 'It was pretty bad. But I'm here. Large as life and twice as ugly. Sent me home for a week, to recuperate. Let me look at you.'

She could have cursed the shippon. Muck on her overalls, filthy boots and hands, bits of fern in her hair. 'I aren't fit to be seen,' she said, unsteadily, wiping a dirty hand across her face and smudging the tears.

'Look grand to me,' he said.

She hadn't seen him since the day of the tripes, and when she came to look, she was shocked at the change in him. He was thinner, strained-looking, and he had aged years. But his eyes were the same, and his smile. She found herself looking at him as if he was food and she was starving.

'You never got my last letter then . . .' she began, at the same time as he said, 'Hunnicutt says . . .' They both stopped, laughing.

'No, you go on,' she said, and he did.

'Hunnicutt tells me you were a wonder with the calf.'

She laughed. 'I like beasts. Brought up to them.' It was ridiculous, telling him that. He knew better than she did. 'Might apply for a place with cattle if they move us from here, supposing they do. I aren't bothered. I love it here.'

'Pity you couldn't come to Nanzeal then,' he said. 'Pa might take a bit of notice of you, and he needs someone. At least this year he's talking about sensible crops instead of that nonsense Farrington used to put him up to, so he might pull the place round yet. But not with just him and Hunnicutt he can't.'

Lizzie frowned. 'You've got those Braun people, haven't you?'

He laughed. 'Not any more. Turns out that last year, when he ploughed so deep, Willi turned up a corner of Lower Daisy that Pa walled off years ago. Thought he was doing right, making a bigger field, but of course, he turned up what was under it. Ploughed it in all over. Arsenic it was, a dump from the old mine.'

Lizzie shut her eyes in horror. It would take years, decades even, before the land would bear again. 'My lor! Lower Daisy too. Best pasture on the place.' Merran squeezed her hand.

'I knew you'd see the folly of it. But of course Pa never suspected. Put stuff in, and it just withered and died. Well, when he realised, that was it. Ordered Willi out that very day. Course, with Silas gone, he could. The Brauns have gone to a fruit-farmer up Devon – where they should have gone in the first place if the committee had any sense. But Pa'll have to find someone, all the same. Someone halfway useful, with some brains, for a change.'

'Won't be me,' Lizzie said, proud that Merran valued her intelligence. 'The LAAS don't send you back home, as a rule. You come from Penzance, they'll send you to Launceston, like as not.'

'I can think of a way,' Merran said.

There was a silence.

She looked at his face, puzzled, and then it dawned. 'You mean . . . ? Marry you?' She sounded as she felt, amazed.

He dropped his eyes, and let her go. 'I shouldn't have said. You made your feelings plain, last time I asked. Only Hunnicutt said, you didn't seem to know . . . how I felt. Seemed to think you'd welcome me. Well, don't worry yourself Lizzie. He was wrong, I can see that. You must've realised what I thought, after my first letter.'

'You mean, this one?' She took the crumpled thing from her pocket. She opened it out, showing the black lines across the page, and he looked at it in dismay. Then, catching her eye, he began to smile in his turn.

'So you didn't know?' And then, as she shook her head. 'Does that mean . . . you might think something of me?'

'You daft thing,' she said, laughing through her tears, 'what do you think I kept it for? Wasn't a lot of reading in it, was there?'

'Lizzie!' he said, and then they didn't say anything for quite a long time. Years and years of separation were in that kiss.

At last she disengaged herself. 'Mind,' she said, 'you just make sure that you survive this war. I couldn't bear to go through all that again.'

'There's a good chance,' he said soberly. 'They're not sending me back to the Front, with my feet. Or even without them.' He grinned. 'They're posting me to Home Establishment.'

'That's no guarantee,' she said. 'Look at poor Major Trevarnon.'

'Well this is Major Jago,' he said, 'and it's better than nothing. Besides, I shall get weekend leave quite regular, and if I get a special licence . . .'

She laughed up at him. Suddenly she was full of confidence. Michael had left her star-struck: Ashton had charmed and flattered her. But this man made her feel cherished, made her – as he had always made her – truly and wholly herself. Her best, her most beloved friend. 'Who said I was going to marry you?' she demanded.

'I did,' he replied. 'And did you know you've got muck on your ear?'

It wasn't the most romantic of proposals, but it would do.

Epilogue: 1927

It was Thursday and Lizzie had come into town with the boys, while Merran took the beasts to market. Two young steers and a cow with a calf at foot, so it should be a profitable day for the Jagos. She called in at the shop.

Mikey, the eldest boy, went out the back with Grandpa. Lizzie loved to see Father herself, only she wished he wouldn't take Mikey out in the slaughteryard, to get his best clothes filthy. And Eddy was as bad, though he spent most of his time in the shop. The bullet-wound he'd caught at Rheims stopped him from doing the heaviest work.

Funny, to see the shop now. Like it used to be, more or less, though the War and the General Strike had taken their toll. Meat in the window, and men doing all the serving again. Eddy's wife and Mam did the accounts, though, in a little office at the back. Mam sent up for a cup of tea, and settled down for a gossip with Lizzie.

Mam enjoyed the office. She was much quicker at figuring than Father, and of course she had time now. Horry was old enough to run the errands after school and she still had Mrs Richards to clean the house. 'We women had to do the figures in the War,' she said. 'Haven't come stupid suddenly, just 'cause the men are home.' You wouldn't recognise Mam these days – talking about voting, next time, and, because she had Mrs Richards, inclined to give herself airs.

Lizzie sipped her tea. She didn't go upstairs. Seemed very empty up there, with so many of the family gone. Five of them were married, now. Gramps and Gan had gone, too, up to the cemetery on the hill, along with Elsie and Aunty Simmins, all victims of the Spanish Flu. Killed hundreds, even in Penzance. Lizzie sighed. She still missed Gan.

'Here, Mum, if Dad has sold those cows, can we have bought butter for tea?' that was five-year-old Lewis, tugging at her skirts. Funny name really, but Merran wanted it.

'We're going to Aunty Millie's for tea, see her new baby,' Lizzie replied. 'Daddy's coming, and I expect your other aunties will be

311

there too.' Daisy with five, Aggie with her two, Penny sporting her new-fangled 'engagement ring', and Dot and Alice in their 'flapper' dresses and cloche hats. Quite a houseful.

'Well, give her my love,' Mother said, and packed her off with a parcel of sausages. Lizzie had her own bacon and pork from the farm, but Treloweth's sausages were still a treat. She set off down the street with her sons.

'Miss Treloweth?' A voice behind her.

Lizzie turned. 'Mrs Jago these days.' She formed the words before she recognised him, and then she stammered, 'Ashton . . . Mr Masters, is it? I heard you were living in London.' With his mother, so the gossip ran. He had managed a desk-job in the new Air Force, and he wore the uniform. Sky-grey, she remembered. It suited him.

'In London, yes.' He was still beautiful, in spite of the scar that ran from eyebrow to chin, the brown eyes still hooded, the smile as mischievous as ever. 'Had to come back, you know, to pay my respects. You heard that Sir Gilbert had died? Such a pity, just before the wedding.' Lizzie must have looked baffled, for he went on, 'I'm sorry, I supposed you knew. Helena has qualified at last, and agreed to marry me, so I shall have a doctor for a wife . . .' He paused. 'Gulveylor is to be sold, you know. Aunt Winifred is moving to Fowey with Mater, and we're having the London flat.'

'And Tamsin? How is she?'

He laughed. 'Oh, very well. We don't see much of them. Uncle Gilbert bought them a place in Taunton and she's very busy playing Lady Bountiful and running the League of Nations Ladies' Guild. Silas bought up a lot of War surplus supplies, and is doing nicely out of selling them. Some things never change. Three children now.'

He seemed to be waiting for her to say something, but there was nothing to say.

He met her eyes intently, and then went on as if the words were wrung from him. 'I'm sorry Lizzie. It should have been different. I meant it to be.'

She nodded.

'My mother. I heard . . .' he stopped. 'I heard you had been to see me. I meant to have written to you.' His mother had prevented it, Lizzie guessed. It was just as well. Things might have been different else – and maybe worse for it.

'It doesn't signify,' she said. 'I wish you happy.'

'Are you happy, Lizzie?'

She smiled. 'I like farming. You know that.'

He wouldn't let it rest. 'I didn't mean that. You know what I mean. Oh, don't worry. Helena knows how I felt about you – feel about you.' He laughed ruefully. 'I never could keep anything from Helena.' He looked up the street. 'Will you stay and see her? She should be here any minute, she's gone to visit Mrs Rouncewell. Fading away, poor old soul, now the Hospital's gone, though she's as fierce as ever. And that bird too.'

Lizzie shook her head. She felt flustered. 'I should like to, but my sister is expecting us, and we shall miss our bus. Well, congratulations to you both.'

'Thank you, and to you. Fine children.' He nodded. 'Goodbye, Lizzie.'

It *was* goodbye. It was unlikely they would ever meet again. She felt a sharp, sweet twinge of regret. He had loved her once.

Lewis looked up at her as they hurried away. 'Who was that, Mummy?'

She smiled down at him. 'Nobody you know. Just an old friend.'

It was true, she realised. Ashton was a dream. A beautiful, hopeless, romantic dream. This was happiness: the boys, the animals, hard work and harvest, the cliffs and the sea. Merran.

She swooped up Lewis and took Mikey by the hand.

'Come on,' she said, 'let's go and see what Daddy's doing.'